John R. Maxim makes his home in Hilton Head Island,
South Carolina. *Mosaic* is his third novel for Piatkus,
following *Shadow Box* and *Haven*.

Praise for *Mosaic*:

"a suspense thriller with a fast, tangled plot" *The Times*

"seriously scary territory" *Birmingham Post*

Praise for *Shadow Box*:

"A page turner – readers may need blood pressure pills"
People

"A great read – fast-paced, original, and very frightening"
Michael Palmer, author of *Extreme Measures*

"terrific tension" *The Bookseller*

"fluid writing and well-drawn characters – [a] crackerjack
thriller" *Publishers Weekly*

Praise for *Haven*:

"Ingriguing tale – with a good plot" *The Bookseller*

"[a] high-octane thriller" *Publishers Weekly*

Also by John R. Maxim

Shadow Box
Haven

Mosaic

A Novel of Suspense

John R. Maxim

F/462423

PIATKUS

This is a work of fiction. Names, characters, places and incidents either
are the product of the author's imagaination or are used fictitiously. Any
resemblance to actual events, locales, organisations, or persons, living or
dead, is entirely coincidental and beyond the intent of either the author
or the publisher.

For more information on other books published by Piatkus
visit our website at www.piatkus.co.uk

First published  in 1999 by
Judy Piatkus (Publishers) Ltd of
5 Windmill Street, London W1P 1HF
email: info@piatkus.co.uk

This edition published 2000

The moral right of the author has been asserted

A catalogue record for this book is available from the British Library

ISBN 0 7499 3157 4

Set in Bembo by Action

Printed and bound in Great Britain by
Mackays of Chatham plc, Chatham, Kent

For Christine …
I can't begin to count the ways

Mosaic

Chapter One

Grayson knew that going back to the same place was foolish. It broke a cardinal rule of survival. Avoid routines; never follow a pattern. Assume that they're watching you, charting your movements, looking for their best chance to take you.

Major Grayson more than knew that; he'd taught it. But he needed to see that young woman again. She had seemed to be either the twin or the ghost of the woman he had probably murdered.

It had been three months since he'd last left the confines of a small Air Force base outside Washington. He'd been assigned quarters in a corner of the base that was sealed off by a series of checkpoints. He'd been given a small office that no one else used and whatever equipment he requested.

His superiors called it a cooling-off period, a time for his mind and body to heal. He would be out of the reach of those civilian authorities who would probably indict him if they knew how to find him. And safe from those who wanted to kill him.

He'd been given light-duty writing manuals, planning courses, but all human contact had been minimal. Not that he'd sought it. He kept to himself. His only visitors had been his debriefers. The debriefers, however, could hardly be called company because Grayson was never told any of their names. Debriefers were almost always anonymous. If one didn't know them, one couldn't name them if caught. They were, for the most part, dour and secretive men of the we'll-ask-the-questions variety.

The one exception was a Pentagon psychiatrist who at least seemed to see him as a human being and not as some sort of experiment gone wrong. But even the psychiatrist kept a distance between them. Grayson wasn't to know his name either.

He was certainly safe but grew increasingly restless until he could stand the isolation no longer. Grayson needed to get out, at least for a while, and be among people who knew nothing about him. So just after sunrise on a cool September morning, he had put on some shorts and an old hooded jersey and studied the effect in a mirror.

He could have been anyone; people said that was his gift. No two photos of his face ever seemed quite alike. His hair had returned to its natural dark brown. He had let it grow long since his last field assignment, for which it had been cropped and dyed blond. Even the color of his eyes seemed to vary. They were gray in some light, green in others. He could be almost handsome; he could be almost homely, depending on how he set his jaw and his brow. His face could be cold and cruel for one role; it could be stupid and slack for another.

But today, the look that he wanted was average. Uninteresting, unthreatening, don't stand out from the crowd. The look that he saw in his mirror seemed to do it, especially with the hood of his jersey in place. Satisfied, he sat and fastened his knee brace. That done, he went out and got into his car, and proceeded to drive off the base.

The sergeant at the main gate had known he was coming. The guards at the checkpoints had alerted him. The sergeant, clearly nervous, asked Grayson not to leave, or at least to wait for an escort. Grayson assured him that he wouldn't be long and would stay within sight of the perimeter. He was armed, he said, and had his cell phone and pager. He'd be back before anyone could miss him.

He wanted to run. Not run away, just run. But he had no intention of staying near the base. He wanted to drive the few miles into Washington and park near the Jefferson Memorial. From there, he would walk to the jogging path that circled the Tidal Basin. Few tourists, if any, would be out at that hour. There would be, at most, a few dozen runners spread over its two-mile length. They would all be civilians who lived normal lives. Unlike the personnel on the base, there wouldn't be anyone pointing him out and whispering stories they'd heard about him. The civilians would not drop their eyes as they passed him. The civilians would not be afraid of him.

For a time that first morning he felt wonderfully free. He had started with his hood up but it soon fell away. He had wanted to run the full two miles of the path but the knee that took the bullet wasn't up to it yet. He jogged part way and he walked part way. The knee, even so, began to swell inside its brace. He would ice it later; this was worth it.

He had almost made a full circle of the basin and was headed back to where he'd left his car. It was then that he first saw the two women running toward him. One of the two looked so much like Janice that he felt his stomach rise up into his chest.

The woman running with her, a light-skinned black woman, was wearing a Georgetown University sweatshirt. The one who looked like Janice wore a halter and shorts. Her body, like Janice's, was fit and tanned. Her proportions seemed exactly the same. She had the same dark blond hair, gathered loosely in the back and the same way of brushing errant strands from her face. She was about the same age, mid-twenties at most. The two women were chatting back and forth as they ran. They smiled and said 'Hi!' as they went by him.

It wasn't Janice, of course – Janice was dead. Up close he could see that her skin was clear where Janice's had been lightly freckled. The mouth was different in the way it formed a smile. But Grayson's stomach had not settled back because her greeting seemed more than a reflex civility. She'd made eye contact longer than was needed to say 'Hi.' He had nodded in response. He did not smile back. He lowered his head and kept going.

3

Grayson realized why her gaze had been more than fleeting. She had seen how intently he'd been staring at her. She was probably wondering whether they'd met and was simply trying to place him. Even so, he found himself starting to think that the resemblance was too much of a coincidence. He listened to the women's footsteps as they went on by, alert to any change in their cadence. He heard the scuffing sound of a sneaker turned sideways and he knew that one had halfturned to glance back at him. His left hand moved toward the pistol he carried in a speed rig under his jersey.

But the sneaker had resumed its soft slap against the pavement. The two women jogged on. Grayson felt like an ass. He had almost allowed himself to believe that a vengeful twin sister had appeared out of nowhere, having somehow been tipped that he was coming here. Or something. He was showing signs of cracking and he knew it.

He tried to put the woman out of his mind but she kept coming back all that day. When he slept, she appeared in his dreams. In the first of those dreams she began as the jogger, but the Tidal Basin background soon faded away until all that was left was her face, close to his. Grayson reached to touch it. He caressed her cheek. He saw that her hair was no longer tied back; it was brushing the back of his hand. She was no longer the jogger. She had turned into Janice. She no longer wore a halter; she wore one of his shirts and was sitting on the edge of a four-poster bed. She had thrown the shirt on to go down and get coffee. She was calling him lazybones. Time to get up.

He knew where they were. He recognized the four-poster. It was a country bed & breakfast in the West Virginia hills, just over the Maryland border. It was run by a pleasant older woman, Mrs. Clark, who, like him, had grown fond of Janice Novak.

Grayson knew that he should never have let Janice get close to him. She was an informant. He was there for her report. But she had come to his room in the middle of the night and asked him to please let her stay for a while. She said she was

4

frightened. She asked him to hold her. He did. He should not have. But that's how it started.

Some weeks later he was with her, same inn, same four-poster. They'd made love well into the morning. She snuggled against him, lightly tickling his chest. She said, 'You know what? It's such a beautiful day. I'm going to take you on a picnic.'

Grayson told her that a picnic was a lovely thought but a risk they did not have to take. Mrs. Clark was reliable, but if they ventured outside, the wrong person might see them together. Janice said she'd considered that and had the solution. She said that she knew a magical place where there was no chance of anyone seeing them.

It was a lake near Ice Mountain in the northern Shenandoahs. She said it was only a two-hour drive and yet hundreds of years back in time. She said her father used to take her there when she was a girl. It had trout that would practically jump into his net and deer so tame that they'd take food from her hand. In all the times that she'd been there, she said, she'd never seen so much as a footprint left by anyone but her father and herself. Nor had she ever shared it with anyone else. She told him to shower while she spoke to Mrs. Clark about fixing them a couple of box lunches.

She was right. It was a beautiful spot. She spread a blanket and had him lie back. She took his head in her lap. He lay there listening to the splashing of fish and the whisper of the wind in the trees. She had opened his jacket, put her hand on his chest.

She said, 'You know, there's something wrong with this picture. Did you have to bring a gun? The gun ruins it.'

It was in a holster under his arm. He tried to push it back out of view. She said, 'Uh-uh. Come on, Give it here. I'll cover it up with the blanket.'

Grayson drew the Beretta and laid it at his side. Janice folded the blanket on top of it. She bent and kissed his forehead, ran her fingers through his hair. Within seconds, Grayson had closed his eyes, feeling only the tender warmth of

5

her body and the gentle massaging of her fingers. Then at one point she lifted a hand and seemed to wave it. He felt the movement but he thought nothing of it. It felt as if she were shooing an insect or brushing a hair from her face.

But then he felt the muscles of her body go tight. He opened one eye and looked up at her. He saw that she appeared to be signaling someone. He tried to turn his head in the direction she was looking. He started to rise but she was holding him down. Her touch was no longer so gentle. His left hand, by reflex, groped for his Beretta, but she'd covered it with her knee and put her weight on it. As he struggled, she shouted, 'Get in here. Now, damn it!!'

Grayson wrenched himself out of her grip. He twisted and rolled until he was free. Now he saw two figures coming out of the trees. He recognized both; they were dangerous men. One carried a shotgun, one an automatic rifle. Both weapons were leveled at him. Even so, they held back, reluctant to close in until they were sure he'd been disarmed. Again, Grayson tried to locate the Beretta but Janice had beaten him to it. She snatched it from the blanket and flipped off the safety. She said, 'Roger, give it up. I don't want to have to shoot.'

'Don't talk to him; kill him,' called one of the men, now emboldened at seeing his gun in her hands. 'We can finish that psycho right here.'

'No,' shouted Janice. She had turned her head toward them. 'You were told to take him alive.'

At that instant, Grayson made a feint with one hand and slapped at the Beretta with the other. He remembered doing that. He was not quick enough. He remembered the muzzle blast from the pistol and hammer blow on his right knee. He remembered the ringing that began in both his ears and grew until it sounded like a siren.

He would remember almost nothing that had happened after that. He knew only that the screaming in his ears began to fade and he found himself standing, holding onto a tree limb. His Beretta, for some reason, was in his right hand. The two men were on the ground, not moving. One had crumpled backward, his legs folded under him. The other had fallen forward on his face. Grayson looked around him. He did not see Janice. For a moment he thought that she must have run away.

He tested his leg; he tried to take a step, but something kept the leg from moving forward. He looked down to see how badly he was hurt. He saw what was stopping it, Janice's body. She was lying face down, her long hair across his feet.

The back of her head was blown off.

Chapter Two

There really was no question that he had killed Janice. He had hoped that one of the others might have hit her with a shot that was intended for him. But the evidence, the pathologist's report, left no doubt. The one with the shotgun never got off a round. Although the one with the rifle had emptied half a clip, all the bullets that hit flesh had come from his weapon. And Janice was unarmed when he shot her.

Grayson had dreamt of that day many times but never about what had actually happened. The Pentagon shrink said his mind was protecting him. Grayson doubted that assessment because his dreams, while unreal, were in some ways worse than the truth. The dreams that tormented him the most were the ones that started gently on the morning of that day, of him and Janice in the four-poster bed. They would touch, they would whisper tender words to each other. But suddenly two men would burst through the door and he would know that she had betrayed him.

Strangely, however, he did not seem to mind. In those dreams, he seemed to feel nothing at all. All that mattered was that now he must kill those two men and then finish Janice as well. Lights would flash, guns would roar, and he'd wake up abruptly. More than once, he found himself sitting up in his bed, shooting a pistol that he wasn't holding, at people who weren't there. The imaginary gun was in his right hand again. In his dreams he was always right-handed.

This night's dream, too, was over but he still saw her face.

8

He had still never actually seen himself shoot her and his half-awake mind thought she might be alive. But he quickly realized that the face he saw was that of the woman he'd seen jogging. Grayson found himself wanting to see her again. He didn't know why; the wish made no sense. He would not, he decided, indulge it.

Even so, when dawn came, he drove back to the basin.

Grayson knew that the woman was not likely to be there just because he was hoping that she would. But there she was, coming toward him again, her friend, as before, keeping pace. Grayson's mouth went dry but when he got within range he managed a nod and a wave. The one who looked like Janice smiled again and said 'Oh … Hi.' She said it with a hint of pleasant surprise as if she had been thinking about him.

Grayson smiled back but his heart was in his throat. He continued on without speaking to her. That was it. Enough. He'd got it out of his system in time not to make a fool of himself. But, again, her face stayed in his mind all that day and, again, he went back the next morning.

That day, the third time he saw them approaching, he saw the black woman nudge the other with her elbow.

'Go ahead,' she mouthed.

'Will you stop that?' mouthed the other.

Grayson realized that the one who looked so much like Janice must have expressed an interest in him. Her friend had urged her to do something about it. But the blond one lost her nerve and kept going, just as he had the morning before.

They'd assumed, he supposed, that he was someone of interest because of the pager he wore on his belt. A young congressman, perhaps, or a presidential aide. They had looked at his hands and had seen no rings. They had looked at the brace that he wore on his knee and assumed … whatever … that perhaps he'd played football or had torn up his knee on a ski slope.

He was almost disappointed that they hadn't stopped. If they had, he might have taken a chance. He might have invited them for coffee. The black one, the matchmaker,

9

would have said yes. Then she, at some point, would have made herself scarce so that he could be alone with her friend. They'd have sat and talked and, maybe at the end, he'd have asked if she'd care to see a movie or something.

'Why didn't you, Major?' asked the Pentagon shrink.

'You're kidding, Doc, right?'

'What's the harm in a movie?'

Grayson shrugged. He wet his lips. 'For one thing, she would have asked what I do.'

'And?'

'Almost anything I'd tell her would have to be a lie.'

'Well … yes, but so what? If you told her the truth, she'd assume it was bullshit. This is Washington. Everything's bull-shit.'

Grayson almost smiled. He nodded.

'Let's have the real reason,' said the shrink.

'Doc, she's a ringer for Janice Novak. Don't you think that would be a little sick?'

'It … might raise an eyebrow. But there are other women who don't look like Novak. You don't try to meet any of them, either.'

'I'm bad luck for women. You know that.'

'I know that you've talked yourself into believing it. You're afraid of what, that you'd put them in danger? That those people would hurt them to get back at you?'

'Doc, they got to Mrs. Clark. They murdered her.'

'Mrs. Clark? Ah, yes. She owned that B&B. But why? She was not one of ours.'

'Her late husband was. Died of cancer, left her strapped. We looked for ways to use her place, help her out. All that did was get her killed in a terrible way. They hacked at her face with a bread knife.'

A sympathetic wince. 'And … you blame yourself for that.'

'Who else should I blame? My mistake got her killed.'

'What mistake was that?'

'I could have told Janice that she was discreet. Lots of B&B owners are discreet. But the word I used to describe her was

10

'reliable' and that's what gave her away. Mrs. Clark was probably packing up our box lunches while Janice was on the phone to her friends.'

'But you had no reason to think Janice was a plant.'

'I got suckered in a lot of ways, Doc.'

'Major Grayson ... Roger ... let me ask you a question. You're a nice-looking man ... you're only what, thirty-two? Is this how you plan to live the rest of your life?'

Grayson chewed on his lip. He did not have an answer.

'You used to have friends. You withdrew from them. Why?'

'It's the other way around. They withdrew from me.'

'You're under guard, Roger, but not incommunicado. You must have had calls ... invitations from some.'

'Doc, you don't kill three people and get asked to dinner parties. It makes one hard to seat, as my grandmother used to say.'

The Pentagon shrink had to smile.

'But I'm dealing with it, Doc. I'm doing my best.'

'No, you're not. All you've done is crawl into a hole that is more of your making than of ours. It's time you gave yourself a good kick in the ass. Get over it. Get back to work.'

Grayson thanked him for his sensitive words of encouragement. The shrink ignored the sarcasm.

'You still can't remember what happened that day?'

'Bits and pieces come in dreams. But even those are all wrong.'

'This blackout, then. This siren in your ears. That's never happened before?'

He looked away.

'Has it? You should tell me. Even if you're not sure.'

Grayson rocked a hand. 'Something like it, I guess, but only in sports. I've taken some hits and had my bell rung. But I didn't kill anyone I was playing against. If I had, the coach would have mentioned it.'

'Well, when you remember, and I think you will, I want you to call me and tell me.'

'Sure.'

11

'And I mean just me; it would stay between us. Don't let this thing fester by keeping it inside you. You've got to find a way to let it end.'

'Doc, I'm not the one who won't let it end. Those people have put a bounty on me.'

The psychiatrist sighed. 'I know, there is that. I assume, by the way, that you did change your route. There's no sense in asking for trouble.'

Grayson answered with a grunt. It avoided a lie. He'd gone back that way because ... and he knew this was dumb ... he needed to see someone smile at him.

They were there, same place, same time, and they were waiting. His sense was that they were waiting for him. They had stopped just past the new Roosevelt Memorial and were looking out over the Potomac River where a race of small catboats was in progress. The blonde one was sipping from an Evian bottle. She looked up, saw him coming, but had to look twice because Grayson was wearing a warm-up suit this time. As he drew near she said, 'Hi! Look at this.' She was pointing out toward a pair of catboats that had become tangled in each other's rigging. One was being pulled over on its side.

Grayson looked away. He jogged on.

Grayson, you putz, he muttered to himself.

He had done a rude and cruel thing and he knew it. He glanced back and saw that they had lowered their heads. The blonde one was probably kicking herself and her friend would be saying, 'Forget him. He's a jerk.'

Grayson answered in his mind, Yes, I am, and I'm sorry.

Let me tell you, he thought, just how big a jerk I am. I'm wearing this warm-up which is too hot to run in because it's easier to reach my gun if I need it. I wanted to see you, I wanted to meet you, but then all these voices started whispering in my head. What if I really am being stupid, and what if she's not what she seems? Maybe she's been trying to get my attention so her friend can stick a knife in my ribs from behind. Or more likely these two are exactly what they seem but perhaps someone else has been watching us. Maybe the price they'll pay for being friendly is getting in the way of a bullet.

So what did I do? Stay home? Change my route? No, what I did was come here to see you again, and behave like … you said it … a jerk.

The shrink, Grayson realized, had been right about one thing. He could not live the rest of his life in this way.

A message arrived — it did not come through channels — asking Grayson to meet with General Hoyt at the Pentagon to talk about a possible new assignment. It came while he was thinking about leaving the service.

'Leave the service? To do what?' asked the Pentagon shrink.

'I don't know. Do some traveling. Disappear for a while.'

'And then hope to resurface as a butterfly somewhere?'

'Doc … we've been through this. I'm not a bad man.'

'I know you're not. A poor joke. Forgive me.'

'I'm not a killer. I'm not even a hurter.'

'No, you're not. Not at heart. Tell me more about your plans.'

'No plans yet,' he answered. 'Just thoughts on what else I might do for a living.'

'Such as?'

'You'll laugh.'

'Not 'till after I've gone.'

'Well, I think I'd like to teach at a small college somewhere. Maybe do some drama coaching on the side.'

'Drama? Not sports? What qualifies you for drama?'

'What I've done, what I teach, is basically acting.'

The psychiatrist smiled. 'You know, you're quite right. I'd never thought of working undercover as acting but that's pretty much what it is.' He sat back. 'The groves of academe … I can see the appeal. But what in a standard curriculum would you teach? Your specialty has been rather narrow, don't you think?'

'Psychology isn't. I have two degrees. Psychology is what I know best.'

'Everyone's but your own. You really should give it time.'

'This assignment the general wants to talk to me about... is it something you recommended?'

'I merely suggested that he try to keep you busy; find you something more in line with your talents and interests than working on manuals that nobody reads. He said that he might have just the thing.'

'I'd be working with Prentice Teal. Do you know him?'

'I know him. He's ... an unusual man.'

'He does black-budget stuff. That's not my cup of tea.'

'You say you want to teach? Spend a month or two with Teal. You'll learn things that are not in any textbook I know of.'

Chapter Three

Grayson's posting, for most of the past four years, had been at Bolling Air Force Base outside Washington. Bolling, not strictly an Air Force facility, was the site of the Joint Military Intelligence College that officers from each of the services attended. Grayson had earned one of his two degrees at Bolling and had taught there when not on assignment.

The courses taught at Bolling had changed with the times. There was less emphasis on big power conflicts and more on the likelihood of brushfire wars and especially on the terrorist threat. A growing part of that threat was domestic and by terrorists other than Muslims. The Oklahoma City disaster spurred efforts to track some two hundred militias and certain religious cult groups. Sometimes working with the FBI but often not, the Pentagon's Defense Intelligence Agency would try to infiltrate those few that seemed the most prone to violence. Grayson taught the psychology of the terrorist mind and the art of penetrating such groups. He lectured, from experience, on both subjects.

General Harlan G. Hoyt was Grayson's ultimate boss. Grayson had never dealt with him directly but he liked what he'd heard about the general. Hoyt was said to be a shrewd, although honorable man and one of considerable intellect. A bachelor, he spent his evenings either studying or painting. He read Plutarch's Lives and Aeschylus in the original Greek. He was also an avid Chicago Cubs fan; he said it taught him humility and patience.

Grayson, in the days before his meeting with Hoyt, had also learned more about Prentice Teal. Except that Teal was unmarried as well, it was hard to imagine any two men who appeared to have less in common.

Teal, to begin with, was a civilian, not bound to any chain of command. He seemed to come and go as he pleased. He was employed in the deliberately vague role of consultant, attached to the Special Technologies Group at the Los Alamos National Laboratory. Los Alamos had, for the past sixty years, developed most of the country's new weaponry. But Teal didn't work with hardware and explosives. He worked with a section that explored the human mind for its uses as a weapon of war.

One such field was called 'psychotronics.' It referred to weapons that could be aimed by the mind and even aircraft controls that could be worked by the mind. This had nothing to do with mental telepathy or the use of telekinesis; circuits were literally wired into the brain, activated by the brain's own electrons. A related technology involved wiring the brain for purposes of interrogation. It effected a sort of electrical hypnosis that neutralized critical judgment. These were just two of about twenty such projects that he'd heard about from officers who'd been there.

A black-budget program, by definition, is one for which no accounting is given, not even to the congressional committee that approves the overall funding. Grayson understood the need for secrecy in matters of national security, but the black-budget system invited abuse. No one ever had to justify the cost of those programs, and some of that cost had been human. There were stories of volunteers whose brains had been fried and who needed to be institutionalized. There were others who'd suffered substantial memory loss or major personality changes. There were said to have been a number of suicides.

Grayson could not imagine results worth that price. Prentice Teal, he'd been told, was not burdened by such qualms.

*

16

'Well, this isn't psychotronics,' the general assured him. 'No weapons, no wiring, just human behavior.'

Their meeting was a private one, just the general and himself. The general had sent his own car for him. General Harlan Hoyt was important enough to rate a window office in the building's E-ring with a view of the Arlington National Cemetery. Hoyt himself was a rumpled old bear of a man, not one's image of a modern two-star general. He was one of those people who somehow defeated the efforts of the most skillful tailor. Behind rimless glasses, he had sad blue eyes. The eyes seemed more suited to a world-weary priest who had heard one confession too many. But those eyes missed little and his mind was quick. No one ever took him lightly more than once.

'And Teal's not so bad. Don't believe all you hear.' The general leafed through Grayson's file as he spoke. 'He might not be the sort you'd take home to meet the family but he's done some good work along the way. This new thing might be right up your alley.'

'Teal plays with people's heads. That's not what I do.'

Hoyt peered over his glasses. 'That's precisely what you do.'

'Sir ... I train people to work in deep cover. I teach them how to blend in and belong. I do not use people as lab rats.'

The general stared at Grayson's file for a beat. 'Your fitness report says that you have an open mind. Am I reading it correctly or ...'

Grayson let out a sigh. 'Please go on, sir.'

The general's manner softened. He opened his hands. 'Let me try easing in from a different direction. You've worked in deep cover yourself ... what, three times?'

It was all in his record. Grayson nodded.

'I suppose you'd have had to in order to teach it. You've done three penetrations of various hate groups who have threatened to target the United States government. Militias, white supremacists, that sort of thing. Those bozos didn't scare you?'

'Some did, I suppose.'

17

'Fact is, from what I've heard, they were more afraid of you.'

Grayson thought of the man who had called him a psycho, the one who wanted him killed then and there. 'Some... might have been afraid of who they *thought* I was, sir.'

'Well, see, that's the thing. That's what's very impressive. There you were, able to fit right in, pretending each time to be someone you're not. You've been ... let's see ...'

Hoyt scanned his file.

'A redneck racist who had burned down black churches and needed a place to hide out ... a self-ordained minister to whom God had revealed the coming destruction of the mud people. Mud people?'

'All nonwhites and all Jews, sir.'

'Ah, yes, the Jews. You've also been the grandson of a hanged SS colonel, now a rabid neo-Nazi yourself. That's quite a range. You do accents? You speak German?'

'Just enough. There were weeks of coaching and rehearsal.'

'Weeks of coaching, you say. That leads right to my question. How much better might you have pulled off such deceptions if you actually could have *been* those three people?'

'Um ... that's why I rehearsed. To help me live the part.'

'Take a minute to read something, Major.'

The general had handed him a thin report. It wasn't signed but Hoyt said it was from Teal. The report was stamped TOP SECRET on the cover. Grayson's clearance did not extend to top secret. He pointed that out to the general, who snorted.

'Don't worry about that. Remember Teal's from Los Alamos. You probably couldn't ask what they use to wipe their asses without someone telling you it's top secret.'

Grayson hesitated, but he opened the binder. His eyes fell on the title page. It read, 'The Uses of Multiple Personality Disorder.' Grayson scanned a few pages. He tried to hide his dismay. The report dealt with turning MPD, a crippling mental illness, into some sort of military asset.

'I am ... keeping an open mind, sir,' he said.

'You're not intrigued?'

18

All Grayson could manage was a shake of the head.

'Consider this, Roger, from your own perspective. Each of these people Teal is studying has as many as four distinct personalities. They're apparently able to call on them at will. What if you had four or five of your own when you were on these deep cover assignments? Imagine not just *pretending* to be someone else. Imagine *becoming* that person.'

'Um ... Teal's subjects ... this says that they're all mental patients.'

'All safely locked up in a Maryland asylum.'

'You're not thinking of actually using them, are you?'

'For what we do? Of course not. They're nuts.'

'Well, then why ...?'

'It's the *mechanism*, Roger, that we're trying to understand. We're trying to find out if it can be learned.'

'Um ... sir ...'

'Mightn't that come in handy in your line of work?'

'Sir, I've read some studies on the subject of multiples. That *mechanism* probably doesn't exist because the disorder itself is delusional. What you see is no more than subconscious role-playing by people who have come to believe that they're multiples.'

'Subconscious, maybe, but it isn't playing. Turn to page six. Read and learn.'

The general barely gave him time to find the page before deciding to summarize parts of it himself. 'Teal has one subject who is strictly right-handed and yet she has a left-handed alter. We're not talking about some awkward scribble, mind you. She writes and does everything else with her left hand as if she's been doing it all her life. How long would, say, you, have to practice to do that?'

'I'm already left-handed.'

'Don't play dumb with me, Major.'

Grayson nodded an apology. He flipped through the pages. 'These subjects of Teal's. This says they're all women.'

'They are. The disorder, as I'd think you would have known, is almost unheard of in men.' He waved the point

19

aside as unimportant. 'Another has an allergy to shellfish and peanuts. Eat either, her throat closes up; she can suffocate. But she has an alter who can eat them all day with no ill effect whatsoever.'

'The mind ... is an interesting place, sir.'

'Not the mind, Roger. That makes this too ethereal. We're talking about the physical brain. It changes ... it actually physically changes ... from one personality to the next.'

'Changes how?'

'I'll show you the PET scans. You'll see for yourself. But you know what I find most intriguing of all? Teal tells me that certain alters and hosts do not appear to share the same conscience. Some alters appear to be utterly untroubled by an act that would horrify the host.'

Grayson thought he could see where this was leading.

'That problem you had last time out,' asked the general, 'wouldn't you rather have emerged from it untroubled?'

'That would have been a lot to expect.'

The general filled a pipe. 'I see you're still limping. How's the knee shaping up?'

'Almost normal. Not much pain. Sir ... am I to be a subject in this study of Teal's?'

'A subject?'

'What you said about alters, no conscience, me untroubled. If you mean to have Teal experiment on me ...'

'Oh, no, no. Far from it.' Hoyt rushed to reassure him. 'You'd observe and evaluate what he's doing, nothing more.'

'Yes, sir.'

'You're here because you have the background I need. If your own mind has been in some interesting places, I'm inclined to regard that as a bonus.'

'I see, sir.'

'But there's another study. One not involving multiples. It's the one I had in mind when I used the word "untroubled".'

Grayson waited.

'You say you weren't frightened being out there alone?'

'I said some of them scared me. I could usually deal with it.'

20

'Usually, you say. What was different that last time?'

'That time, I wasn't playing a role. I didn't have to penetrate that group myself because we had … I thought … a reliable informant.'

The general nodded. 'That young woman who died.'

'She didn't just die, sir. I killed her.'

The general rubbed his chin. He returned to Grayson's file. He scanned a report by a board of inquiry.

'An interesting document. I've read it several times. This says that she shot you with your own service weapon. You, although crippled and probably in shock, were able to wrest it from her and shoot her. You then swung your weapon on two other men, both of whom had their weapons trained on you at the time. You dropped one with a head shot before he could fire and the other while he was shooting. Given that you're not greatly skilled with a sidearm, and given that you've never been shot at before, I'd call that a remarkable performance.'

Grayson said nothing. The general kept reading.

'Says here Novak claimed she had joined that group thinking all they did was go camping. A gun club. When she learned how they intended to use those guns … says here she was horrified, she went to the authorities, the authorities then called in your section. She volunteered to become an informant. Just like that, Major Grayson? Sounds too easy.'

'It was not just like that. She was patient and smart. She made us persuade her. It took several months. She pretended to agree if I'd be her sole contact.'

'Says here that you're what they wanted from the start. You put some of their people in Leavenworth?'

'Not theirs. Some people from an allied militia.'

'That Nazi bunch, right?'

'The Aryan Christian Republican Army.'

Hoyt mouthed the word *Christian*. He shook his head sadly. 'Their intention, this says, was to take you as a hostage, then trade you for some of their friends. Novak played you like a banjo, didn't she, Major? You've admitted that you became lovers.'

21

Grayson was silent. He lowered his eyes.

'Given that, you must have been all the more upset when you realized how Novak had deceived you.'

Still nothing.

Hoyt flipped a few pages. 'Ah, here it is. I have here your version of the event. It's somewhat at odds with official reports that came in from the local authorities. They seem to think it was more an execution than an act of pure self-defense.'

'Sir ... as I've said ...'

'I know. You don't remember. The psychiatrist says that your version of it was more a reconstruction of what must have happened. You insist that you remember nothing at all after that first bullet hit you. Is it possible that he conditioned you to block out such things?'

'He ... who? The psychiatrist?'

'As part of your training.'

'If we're talking about the psychiatrist I've been seeing, he was never more than ... I guess, an observer. He had no direct role in my training.'

That answer, or its vehemence, surprised General Hoyt. Frowning, he thumbed to the back of Grayson's file. He stared at some entry, then muttered, 'My mistake.'

'What did you just look up?' Grayson asked him.

'Just some notes by the psychiatrist. You were right. Never mind.'

'Who is he, by the way? Why can't I know his name?'

'You know the answer. Deniability. We've been known to bend the law here and there. Besides, he's not army; he's an outside consultant. We use them all the time. No big deal.'

He flicked a hand to show that the subject was closed. But he then drummed his fingers as if he'd had second thoughts.

'Um ... this man might try to grill you on what we've discussed. I know he has an interest in the subject of multiples. You're to tell him nothing, agreed?'

'As you wish, sir.'

'And as for you going blank after you took that bullet, I

22

don't doubt you. I've seen it in combat.'

'I … appreciate you saying that, sir.'

'But have you ever wondered,' the general asked slowly, 'whether there might be more than one of you, Major?'

Oh, Christ, thought Grayson. He said, 'I have not.'

'Well, these different roles you play …'

'I trained for them, sir.'

'Of course. Never mind. I shouldn't have asked. I've been hearing too much about multiples.' The general sat back. He closed Grayson's file. 'You're aware that those people put a bounty on you?'

Grayson gave a small shrug. He nodded.

'And it's not as if they're in Idaho, somewhere. West Virginia is just down the road.'

'I know, sir.'

'They know you live at Bolling because that's where you trained Novak. But as long as you stay on the base, they can't get at you.'

Grayson waited.

'And yet you jog around Washington, free as the breeze. Are you trying to get killed, Major Grayson?'

'No, I'm not, sir.'

'Those two joggers, Major, I've had them checked out. What if I told you that they're members of that group?'

'Sir … one of them was black. She would not be a member.'

The general grunted. 'A mud person. Good point. It is true, however, that I had them checked out. One's an art restorer at the National Gallery. The one who looks like Novak is a law clerk at Justice.'

'I … had assumed they were something like that.'

'Assume? You can't afford to assume. Those people say they'll skin you alive if you ever fall into their hands. One of them … he goes by the name of Nat Allen … has been faxing your photograph to some forty other groups. He's advertised the bounty on the Internet.'

'So I'm told.'

'Do you know this Nat Allen?'

'We've … bumped into each other.'

'Is the man really dangerous? Or is he all bluster?'

'He's their enforcer. He enjoys causing pain. He was probably the one who slashed Mrs. Clark. Yes, sir, I would say that he's dangerous.'

'Nat Allen, I assume, is not his real name.'

'I'm told he named himself for Nathan Hale and Ethan Allen. I guess he thinks that it sounds patriotic. We don't know his real name. Not even his group did. We believe that he is, or was, a policeman, but we haven't been able to find out any more.'

'You say you've bumped into him. Does that mean a confrontation?'

'Yes, sir.'

'Well, let's hear it.'

'He'd … been trying to pick a fight. He likes to intimidate. In this case, however, it might have been a test. I was supposed to be a vicious neo-Nazi myself. I thought I'd best react as if I were.'

Hoyt stared for a beat. 'How bad, Major Grayson?'

'I thought it best to be thorough.'

'Thorough means dead. How close did you come?'

'The others … stopped it when he couldn't continue. He'll have a few scars.' Grayson touched his own face. 'The man I was portraying would have marked him … humiliated him.'

'You're saying this happened in front of his own people. Were there women in the audience as well?'

'The audience was his choice, sir, not mine.'

Another long stare. 'And were you … quite yourself?'

Grayson darkened a shade. But he dropped his eyes. 'I remember it, if that's what you're asking.'

The general sucked on his still-unlit pipe. He studied Grayson for a moment before speaking. He said, 'I think you know why I asked about women.'

'I do, sir.'

'The word is that Mr. Allen would first like your woman. A

24

wife, if you have one, but a girlfriend will do. He wants to send you a Polaroid each day for a week, so you can see, step by step, what he's doing to her. He says it's in return for what you did to Novak, but I see that it's more personal than that.'

Grayson shrugged. The threat had no meaning.

'You are, in any case, unattached. Is that right?'

'That's correct, sir. There's no one.'

'And I gather that's why. If you had a lady friend, you would fear for her life.'

Grayson squirmed in his seat. 'Sir, where is this going?'

The general grimaced. He seemed equally ill at ease. He said, 'Forgive me, Roger, all this talk of fear and death. I am leading to something and I'm doing it poorly.'

'It has to do with this other study?'

'Yes, it does.' He leaned forward. 'What if fear could be controlled to such an extent that it would not affect one's performance?'

'Controlling fear … is the job of good training. Fear is not a bad thing in itself.'

'But panic is. And so is any judgment that is clouded by fear. Think beyond deep cover work for the moment. Think now of troops going into combat. Green troops, even veterans, they're all scared to death. Think of policemen and firemen in tough inner cities where they're sniped at from windows and rooftops. If there were a treatment that kept fear from being crippling, I think most would be eager to take it.'

'Is there such a treatment?'

'Teal is working on one. It's actually an outgrowth of the study of multiples. I'll want to know what you think.'

'I assume we're not talking about some kind of sedative.'

'Of course not. If anything, the opposite effect.'

'There are street drugs that have the opposite effect. Too many cops and military use that stuff already.'

'If this works, they won't need them. You think about that.'

Chapter Four

Grayson felt sure that he wanted no part of this, especially that MPD nonsense. He'd heard of other projects, some CIA, some Los Alamos, that were referred to as WTF projects. WTF stood for 'What the fuck.'

It essentially meant, 'What the fuck, let's try it. We have the money; we might as well spend it; now and then one of these ideas actually works.' One such was the CIA's recent study of people who claimed that they could leave their bodies and transport themselves to, for example, a meeting of Saddam Hussein's Privy Council. The CIA spent millions until the project was leaked. That agency was almost laughed out of existence.

The MPD project sounded every bit as dumb. He'd heard of several other black-budget studies in the field of behavior control, but was not aware of a single one that yielded a useful result. He had heard of one or two that seemed criminal, however, and he said as much to the general.

'Such as what? Pumping drugs into unwitting subjects? Teal's subjects will be carefully screened volunteers.'

'I would hope so.'

'And don't look for anything sinister here. These two projects, the multiples and the search for this "treatment" are two avenues for exploring the same end result. We're not trying to make it easy for anyone to kill. All we want are personnel who'll perform at their best, whatever their function or circumstance.'

Grayson wanted to believe that as well.

'No one enjoys killing. Well, except the odd psychopath. We have more than enough of those in the military. You of all people should understand that good men who have to kill are often ruined by the experience. My best friend was one. Did you know that?'

'No, sir.'

'Well, you wouldn't. He was Capt. Bradley Parker, West Point '65. Good athlete like you were, good-looking, good grades. Brad graduated tenth in his class and married a beautiful young lady, same day. She waited while he served two tours in Vietnam. Brad got back in one piece but he was never the same. Became a drug user. A lot of them did. They could buy drugs in Nam for the price of two beers. That's how thousands of our men wrecked their lives.'

Hoyt paused, drummed his fingers. He looked up at Grayson. 'I'm telling you this for a reason,' he said.

Grayson nodded. 'Yes sir. Please go on.'

'You know what scares combat soldiers the most? The fear that they might be cowards. You know why many veterans won't talk about the war? Even those who won a chest full of medals? They remember the times when they froze and did nothing while a buddy, for example, was screaming for help. Maybe no one else saw it; maybe no one else knows. But it eats at them as long as they live.'

Grayson knew that. He'd read several studies.

'Well, Brad never thought it could happen to him. He'd been gutsy all his life; nothing scared him. But in 'Nam, he was sent on night ambush patrols. There's nothing so scary as a jungle at night, full of bugs and snakes and VC. He did a lot of killing, never took any prisoners. The more killing he did, the more scared he got; he began to despise himself for it. Had a nervous breakdown the year he got back. The army tried to counsel him, get him off the booze and drugs, but in the end they retired him. Psychologically disabled. He tried different jobs. He kept getting fired. His wife stood by him as long as she could. She divorced him and I couldn't blame her. Would you?'

'Um …'

'Not a fair question. Forget it. Withdrawn. Anyway, the years passed and I had an idea. I invited him to come up to Washington for the opening of the Vietnam Memorial. I guess I thought it might give him... what's the word I want?'

'Closure?'

'Yeah, closure. It was closure all right. We spent several hours reading the names. He cried, but so did everyone else. I took him home with me. He seemed okay. The next morning I found him in my car in my garage. He'd sealed the doors and started the engine.'

Grayson started to speak, to offer his sympathy. The general cleared his throat and waved him off. 'For that and other reasons, this is personal with me. This treatment might have saved him. It can save others like him. It is not just some half-assed WTF. I assume that's what you've been thinking.'

'The ... multiple thing did strike me that way. Sir, this Maryland asylum ... it's government run?'

The general shook his head. 'The place is called Belfair; it's entirely private. It was founded by Dr. Norman Zales for the treatment of MPD patients. Zales has written a number of books on such illnesses. Perhaps you're familiar with some of them.'

'I've ... heard of Dr. Zales. I don't read his books.'

'You winced as you said that. Tell me why.'

Grayson couldn't think of a polite way to say it. 'He writes-... pop psychiatry. Whatever will sell. He seems to jump on every new fad that comes along and then makes the rounds of the talk shows. I would think you'd find it hard to take him seriously.'

'And his books, in your opinion ...?'

'Are crap, sir.'

The general shook his head. He seemed disappointed. His expression gave Grayson a flickering hope that his assessment of Zales had disqualified him. But the general reached back to the credenza behind him and picked up two books that had been lying on their side. He placed them on the desk in front of Grayson.

28

'One is *Hear the Child Weeping*. I think it was his first. The other is *Listening to Your Selves*. That's his last. Take them with you; try to keep that open mind.'

Grayson glanced at the covers, very glitzy, raised foil type. They did not have the look of a disciplined study. He turned one over to the author's photo. Zales was portly, almost fat, and had bushy gray hair; he was dressed in a dark suit and tie, wore horn-rimmed glasses. His facial expression seemed kindly and patient. At least, thought Grayson, he had the right look. A woman stood behind him; she was dressed in a lab coat. Her eyes were strikingly pale, almost colorless. In fact, everything about her seemed bleached.

'Who's the woman?'

'That's his wife. That's Leatrice Zales. You can read about her in *Hear the Child Weeping*. They met when she came to him as a patient. He cured her. She has since devoted her life to his work.'

'He ... married her? Why?'

'You're asking me why people marry?'

'I mean ... to marry a patient ... even one he thinks he's cured ...'

'Well, she seems not to share your opinion of Zales – she regards him as a giant in his field. There's also the fact that when her parents died, they left her a good deal of money. She used that money to buy Belfair for Zales.'

'The money ... is certainly a reason, I suppose.'

'She also brought in a few more rich patients and ... look, Major, forget about Leatrice. She's involved but she stays in the background. How much do you know about Congressman Andrew Carey?'

'I know he's on one of the Armed Services Committees.'

'Andrew Carey is chairman of the House Armed Services Research and Technology Committee. I don't like or trust the son of a bitch but that committee funds everything we do at Los Alamos. Zales went to Carey and pitched him on multiples. The committee wasn't much keener than you are but

29

Carey used his muscle to push through a grant. That done, I called Teal in as project director.'

'But why would Carey go out on a limb? What's his connection with Zales?'

The general hesitated, seemed reluctant to answer. 'The congressman ... has a daughter at Belfair. She's been under Zales's care for two years.'

'She's a multiple?'

'That might be the least of it. The girl is a mess. Rachel ... I know her ... was never a joy, not even when she was little. Never laughed, never cried, didn't like to be touched. She did, however, enjoy killing cats. She liked to set them on fire and watch them run. That should give you some idea about Rachel.'

Grayson didn't respond. There seemed nothing to say.

'In her teens, as you'd imagine, she only got worse. Into all kinds of drugs and promiscuous sex. Sex with women as well as with men. She's been in rehab twice, but was never sent to jail. The courts, as a favor to the congressman, no doubt, kept releasing her to still another therapist. Rachel's now twenty-two; her brain is pretty well fried, but Zales seems to think he can help her. Martha Carey, the girl's mother, doesn't have much faith in Zales but she hasn't had better luck elsewhere. I saw Rachel several weeks ago. She didn't know me. She doesn't seem to know poor Martha either.'

The general's voice had trailed off. He was staring into space. But abruptly, he recovered and sat up in his chair. He seemed to realize that Grayson had been staring as well.

'Martha Carey,' Hoyt said, as if reading Grayson's mind, 'is in no way responsible for what Rachel became. She's been a good mother; she's a good human being. She is far too good for ... never mind ... we're off the track here.'

Grayson shifted uncomfortably. He was not at all sure what to make of Hoyt's remarks, especially where the mother was concerned. There was sympathy, surely. Affection, perhaps. The words, 'too good for' seemed a reference to the daughter

30

but, given Hoyt's expressed dislike of the father, Grayson's hunch was that he probably meant Carey.

Hoyt looked at Zales's photo. He still seemed distracted.

'Zales claims to be the country's leading authority on Multiple Personality Disorder. Whatever you might think of his work, the man has made some powerful friends because he's helped some extremely rich people.'

'Helped them how?'

The general sat back. He looked away. 'By keeping their daughters out of their lives. By keeping them from being a bother.'

'That's their only interest? These rich people you mentioned?'

A dismissive gesture. 'Never mind them now.'

'Then, sir ... are you one of Zales's powerful friends?'

The general leaned toward him. His color had risen. 'Are you asking me if I'm in his pocket?'

'Um ... no, sir.'

'Then you're asking me what my interest is in this. Not a goddamned dime is the answer.'

'Sir ...' Now Grayson didn't know what to make of his anger. The question of money changing hands had never entered his mind.

'I've given my reasons. I'm not anyone's friend. Don't ever say that to me again.'

'Yes, sir.'

General Hoyt sat back. His color receded.

'That's twice you've tried to get me to send you back to Bolling. All you've done is made me glad that I've picked you.'

Grayson blinked.

'You're a decent, compassionate man and you're honest. You've got two degrees; you know all the terms. I'm sure that you'll recognize bullshit when you hear it, especially in the area of multiples.'

'Sir, if you're thinking that I might be a multiple ...'

'It crossed my mind. Might give you an insight. Either way,

31

I want to know what you think. If you come back and tell me that the whole thing is crap, I *will* pull the plug no matter who is involved.'

'Um … sir, why not just ask Teal?'

'I have. I want an objective opinion.'

'Sir … unless it's an order…'

'It is not, but do it. I'm asking you to give it two months.'

The general continued, 'Sure, some of this might sound crazy, especially the thing with the multiples. But imagine, just think, if it works. Think of an operative with 'functional' MPD. He or she has personalities that can be called on at will to suit any occasion that arises. And imagine if one is caught and questioned. She could defeat the most intensive interrogation just by switching to an alter who hasn't a clue what these people are asking them about.'

Grayson tried not to groan at this but he did. General Hoyt scowled; he tried to look stern. But the general's expression melted into a grin. He muttered, 'Well, who the hell knows?' He slid Teal's last report across the desk at Grayson. He reached into a drawer for another.

The second one, thicker, had a letter attached. The general had almost handed that one to Grayson when his eyes fell on part of the letter. He hesitated for a moment, then pulled the letter free. He dropped it back into the drawer.

'This report has to do with controlling fear. It'll tell you what's been learned, what's been tried, and what progress Teal says he's made with this … treatment. This project has by far the greater potential but in my view they're both worth a look.'

The report on the study of MPD patients was labeled 'The Chameleon Project.' Not much of a code name, too descriptive, thought Grayson. The project that studied the control of fear was called, for some reason, 'Project Richard.'

Grayson picked it up. 'Why Richard?' he asked.

The general grumbled. 'I don't name the damned things. The reference is to Richard the Lionheart.'

'I see.'

'Take them with you; read them; we'll talk more tomorrow.'

'Sir, I'm ... not at all sure that I can take on more work. I'm editing several manuals that are due ...'

'No one cares.'

'I've also been ordered to stick close to the base. You, yourself, said I shouldn't be running around ...'

'That order is rescinded. Any other objections?'

'Well, sir, I'm trying to get back some kind of a life ...'

'Your social life is zero. You're not trying at all. Use the time that you now spend avoiding young women. Read those, bring them back. You are not to make copies. Read Zales's books as well. Those you can keep.'

'I'm to read both Zales's books by tomorrow?'

'If they're crap, they'll be easy. Come at noon. I'll buy lunch.'

Chapter Five

Grayson had barely left the Pentagon Building when his cell phone chirped; it was the Pentagon shrink.

'You've had your meeting, Roger? How did it go?'

'Sorry, Doc. I'm not free to discuss it.'

'Well, I know it involves multiples. I can help you with that. I've done some research in that area.'

'Um … you told me you knew nothing about this assignment.'

'Yes, I did, and I lied,' the shrink answered cheerfully. 'You would have been negative about it from the start. I thought you should at least hear him out.'

'Hoyt thinks I'm a multiple. Did you tell him that?'

'I merely suggested that he look at your file. You're not, but you do have a similar talent. When will you be visiting Belfair?'

'Doc … you heard me. I've said all I can.'

'Then I'll tell you that you'll be wasting your time there. Zales has done some mildly interesting studies, but his patients are too damaged to be of much use. That's not where we're going to find the answer.'

'We?'

'I'm offering my help.'

'Sorry, Doc. You'd have to speak to General Hoyt about that.'

'You'll need me, Roger. You'll be out of your depth. General Hoyt, in this instance, is less than objective. Norman

Zales is … well, you'll see soon enough. Prentice Teal will run rings around the lot of you.'

'Then, as you said, I might learn a few things.'

A brief silence. A chill. 'Don't shut me out, Roger.'

'Look, Doc …'

'Very well, have it your way. But I'm going to ask a favor. There's one multiple in particular that I've been trying to locate. She has nothing to do with this assignment of yours, but I think Zales might know where I can find her.'

'Why not ask him?'

'I've tried that.'

'What's so special about her?'

'If what Zales claims is true, she's one in a million. She might be a genuine Mosaic.'

'Mosaic?'

'Never heard the term? I'm not surprised. Zales coined it. It refers to no more than a handful of women who seem to have been born as several people. Zales claims to have treated at least one such young woman, but he won't let anyone else near her.'

'You keep saying, `Zales claims.' Are you sure she exists?'

'She exists. I've confirmed it. I just don't know where. All I want is to locate her, do an interview, run some tests. She's important to some other work I'm doing.'

'So you're asking me … what? To be your mole up at Belfair?'

'Roger … one address. Is that such a big favor?'

'Doc, I probably won't even accept the assignment. Either way, this conversation is over.'

Grayson broke the connection. The call had annoyed him. The shrink had steered him to Hoyt for reasons of his own. So far everyone seemed to have his own agenda. Nor did he see himself as a babe in the woods who needed his hand held to go against Teal.

Grayson climbed into the general's waiting car for the forty-minute ride back to Bolling. He would use the time to browse through the materials Hoyt had given him.

He actually knew little about Zales or his work. His impressions were all second hand. He'd heard other shrinks snort whenever Zales's name was mentioned, but it was possible that some of them were jealous. Each book had a big yellow sunburst on the jacket that boasted a half million copies in print. Grayson, in fairness, would avoid a prejudgment. Zales might possibly have something worth saying. He began to scan through Zales's two books. By the time he reached Bolling, he realized he'd erred in giving Zales the benefit of the doubt. He'd made a few snorts of his own.

Hear the Child Weeping, published ten years before, had climbed on a bandwagon, then in vogue, that said if a woman had problems as an adult, she had probably been sexually molested as a child. If a patient insisted that no such thing had happened, she was presumed to be in denial.

Through Recovered Memory Therapy, however, she could be helped to relive the traumatic events that her mind had repressed while they were happening to her. She would soon remember being repeatedly raped and forced to perform oral sex. In most cases the rapist was her father. She would then understand why, ever since that time, she had suffered ... take your pick ... an eating disorder, a sexual dysfunction, depression, nightmares, or an inability to sustain a relationship. At the therapist's urging, she would then heal herself by confronting her thoroughly bewildered father and slapping him with a lawsuit.

RMT, which used drugs and hypnosis to restore repressed memories, had since been effectively discredited. Grayson had no doubt that many children were abused. Dreadful things are done to children all the time. Those children grow up; they might never mention it; they might try very hard to forget it. But there isn't any way that they can blot it out entirely. That isn't how memory works.

Yes, people do repress – and sometimes deny – memories that they find guilt-provoking or humiliating but they don't and can't obliterate them. The mind, Grayson knew, can block out details but not the whole context. Someone hurt in a car crash knows he's been in an accident even if he can't remember the impact. He doesn't think that he was home watching television at the time. It's the same with soldiers who are wounded in combat or boxers knocked out in the ring.

It's well known to police that adult rape victims often can't remember specific details, especially if they've been beaten. They are sometimes unable to describe the attacker but they know full well that they've been raped. It's tempting to believe that their minds had protected them from recalling the worst of the experience. The truth, as always, is simpler than that. The trauma had erased their short-term memories before they could be stored, long term, by the brain. It's known as traumatic amnesia.

Hypnosis has been shown to be totally unreliable as a means of recovering memories. A therapist, depending on his or her bias, can just as easily elicit memories of going to the guillotine with Marie Antoinette or of being abducted by aliens. One of Grayson's professors had described hypnosis as a state of believed-in imaginings.

Recovered Memory Therapy ran its course after thousands of lives had been shattered. Parents were divorced, bankrupted, ostracized by their neighbors and fired from their jobs after having been charged with imagined abuse. Quite a few had been sentenced to prison. Then, at last, a handful of responsible psychiatrists began to realize that something was wrong. Not one accusation based on recovered memory had ever been reliably corroborated in a courtroom. Not one. Not even by siblings who grew up in the same home. Not even by siblings who disliked the accused parent and were therefore unlikely to lie in his defense.

The RMT practitioners who had done all the damage began being sued for malpractice. Zales saw that it was time to get off that bandwagon and onto another that was just rolling by. The new one was Multiple Personality Disorder.

A patient would come in with this or that neurosis and the therapist would begin to dig for its source. The mind can't repress but it can certainly *create*, especially under hypnosis.

Certain therapists would ask, 'Well, if *you* can't remember any traumas in your childhood, is there someone else inside you who can?' As often as not, that someone else answered and, presto, an alternate personality emerged. Dig a little more, then another appeared. Keep digging as long as the insurance held out and as many as a hundred would turn up.

Nearly all, if not all, have been shown to be delusional, no more real than most of those memories of abuse that were only recalled through suggestion. No more real than memories of alien abduction or of having lived many past lives. The question is asked, 'Well, what caused these delusions?' There was, Grayson knew, a word for this phenomenon. The word was *iatrogenic*. It refered to an illness that is caused by the treatment, or one born of the therapist's bias. The therapist was looking for it, so the therapist found it. The patient, who had put her trust in the therapist, had little choice but to believe it.

If she had any doubts, they were soon put to rest upon meeting the therapist's other patients. They met the other patients in group therapy sessions. The other patients had had the same diagnosis and were utterly convinced that they were multiples. The delusions of each were reinforced by the others. They had locked themselves into a closed belief system where the possibility of error was never considered. They had come to accept a false reality as truth. And that, thought Grayson, was the essence of madness.

Zales had probably been burned by the RMT thing and decided not to let that happen again. He saw that therapists all over the country were discovering multiples by the thousands. He watched as MPD, in turn, was attacked as another iatrogenic disease. He said, 'That may be, but it's still a disease. These patients are stuck with all these alternate selves. I will help them put them back in the bottle.' He wrote *Listening to Your Selves* which made him the guru of repairing the damage other therapists had done. He was much in demand as an expert witness when all those other shrinks were being sued. The advantage of Zales being a repairer, thought Grayson, was that no one ever thought of suing him.

Some of these alters always seemed to be violent. That made them a danger to themselves and to others. They would, accordingly, need to be committed and that was where Belfair came in. The book says he took only the most difficult cases. Grayson had a hunch that these 'difficult cases' were those who either had excellent insurance or were the daughters of the rich men Hoyt had mentioned.

Hear the Child Weeping said that Leatrice Zales had been atrociously molested as a child. That had been Dr. Zales's diagnosis when she told him that she hated her body. He then helped her to remember years of sexual torture by parents who pretended to be pillars of society but who, in private, turned out to be monsters. Over time, Zales healed her aversion to sex and taught her to love what her body could do. She never got to confront her parents, never hauled them into court as Zales had urged her to do. The book said that both parents committed suicide, took strychnine, when they realized that she'd finally blown the whistle.

Strychnine, thought Grayson. Not an easy way to go. The spine goes into agonizing convulsions. The muscles of the neck and jaw contract. You die with a frozen grin on your face and with eyes bulging out of their sockets. Zales speculated that their guilt was such that it wasn't enough to pay with their lives; they needed to punish themselves.

That could be, thought Grayson. But there was another problem. We now had Leatrice, all better, all cured, having dealt with the memories she'd repressed. But when Zales later published *Listening to Your Selves*, he announced that nearly all such memories were false. One wonders how Zales explained this to his wife.

The only part of Zales's book that Grayson found at all interesting was the short chapter dealing with Mosaics. The term, as the Pentagon shrink had mentioned, referred to those multiples who'd been multiples since birth, or at least from very early childhood. There was a photo of the one Zales had treated, but the face in the photo was disguised. Her name, it seemed clear, was an alias as well. The text said, 'We'll call her Susannah.'

39

Susannah appeared to be quite a young woman, or she was when the picture was taken. She was said to be intelligent, unusually gifted, and more or less healthy emotionally. Zales took credit for the latter. He said she'd come to him for help.

Grayson found himself staring at the photo of 'Susannah.' It was a head and shoulders shot; it looked formally posed. He could not see her eyes; a black rectangle obscured them, but there was something oddly familiar about her. He wished that he could meet her, find out for himself if there was such a thing as a 'natural.' But he knew that he wouldn't. She was none of his business. As for meeting the others, the multiples at Belfair, he would duck that part of the assignment if he could.

Even Teal, in his report, did not seem very interested in finding that 'mechanism' Hoyt spoke of. Grayson sensed that Teal was only going through the motions, waiting for Zales's grant to expire. Teal was far more absorbed by the work on Project Richard. Although Grayson had doubts of his own about that project, it was certainly the more sound in terms of its science. Indeed, judging by Prentice Teal's latest report, it seemed on the road to success.

A background study bound into Teal's report cited previous work on Panic Disorder, an illness that affects some two million Americans. About a third of these are so paralyzed by fear that they're imprisoned within their own homes. The brain of a panic disorder patient is different. Stimulation studies using the drug yohimbine have revealed an abnormal firing rate in an area of the brain called the locus ceruleus, which is rich in cells that release the neurotransmitter, norepinephrine, the trigger for human fight-or-flight response. In panic patients, the trigger kicks in at too low a threshold. They're not cowards or neurotics; they're simply victims of their chemistry. That might have been what happened to Hoyt's friend, Captain Parker, who suffered a breakdown in Vietnam.

Taking Prozac helps. So does dopamine. They both alter the level of serotonin in the brain so that fight-or-flight kicks in normally. But those drugs take two to four weeks to take effect. Troops going into combat rarely have that much time, the Gulf War being an exception.

This same Dr. Zales, according to the report, had developed a cocktail of several drugs that took effect within an hour or two. He mixed a variety of antipsychotics, hypnotics, and other mood-altering drugs. He had tried the new compound on a number of his patients.

Zales saw that the patients were calmed but not dulled. They seemed more alert, more aware of their surroundings, than they had been since they were admitted. They wanted to *do* things, write letters, take walks. They took a new interest in personal appearance. Some had been drug addicts, some alcoholics, but they now showed no wish to use either, even when those substances were made accessible to them. Most seemed largely freed of those extremes of behavior that had put them in need of professional help. They showed less of a need to bring out their alters. That was good, said Zales, because as he'd feared, the alters seemed barely affected by the drugs.

His own MPD patients aside, Zales saw the compound's obvious potential to benefit the millions of others like them who were victims of their own inner demons. No adverse side effects had been noted thus far. He shared his findings with Prentice Teal who, impressed, passed them on to the general. Teal and Hoyt both saw an even broader potential, specifically its use to the military.

Grayson had to admit that he was intrigued. The most stunning evidence that something was working were the PET scans bound into the study. There were several. On each was the PET scan of one of Zales's patients and next to it the scan of a normal brain. The areas of neurological activity were shown by vivid colors. The two brains, sick and normal, were strikingly different. He had seen this in text books before, nothing new. Nor was Grayson especially impressed by the PET scans that the general had mentioned; those of a multiple versus one of her alters. They were radically different but that didn't surprise him. A brain experiencing hallucinations

41

would show pretty much the same difference. But a third set bound into Teal's Richard report showed the 'sick' brain after Zales had administered his compound. It resembled a normal brain in every respect. Hoyt was right. The brain had physically changed.

If true, this was a stupendous achievement. Grayson very much wanted to believe it. But given that Hoyt was suspicious of Teal, and given Teal's reputation, to say nothing of Zales's, he was troubled by all kinds of doubts. Not least was the question of what good it would do for him to stick his nose in these projects. If Teal was holding something back from the general, Teal would hardly share it with him. He'd discuss this with Hoyt when he saw him.

Chapter Six

At Duke University in North Carolina, a professor of psychology sat staring at his phone.

He was trying to decide whether he should make a call that might turn out to be needlessly upsetting. He knew that he tended to be overprotective, and reminded himself that she was not all that fragile. He punched out her number and waited.

As expected, he got her answering machine. He heard the recording of her soft Southern voice. It was a voice that always caused him to smile. At the tone, he said, 'Susannah, it's me. Professor Cohen. You can pick up, Susannah. It's me.'

He waited several seconds. He thought she must not be home. But then he heard the plastic clatter of a handset being lifted. A voice said, 'Uhh ... yeah ... hold on a minute.'

He knew that voice. It wasn't Susannah's. But it meant that she'd be on very soon. He heard a loud scraping sound and a couple of thuds accompanied by some grunts and labored breathing. There was silence and, again, the phone was picked up. A voice, much the same, except this time it was Susannah, said, 'Hi, there. Sorry to keep you.'

'Sounds like heavy work you're doing. Is this a bad time?'

'Oh, my dishwasher leaks. It's hard to get at the plumbing. He had to pull the whole thing out to get behind it.'

The professor knew who she meant by *he*. It was one of her alters. Her only male alter. 'You know, you really shouldn't let him answer the phone. His voice is lower than yours, but it's not a male voice. You don't want to have to explain him.'

'No, I don't, but we knew it was you.'

'All the same … well, you're right. Never mind.'

'Dr. Cohen, what is it? Has anything happened?'

'Oh, no. Just checking in. I was thinking about you.'

She was silent for a beat. 'Dr. Cohen … what's wrong?'

'Well … you know that you're a popular girl. There is always someone who's eager to study you and is willing to pay for the privilege. This time, however, they're raising the ante. I've been offered a great deal of money.'

'By whom? You don't mean Norman Zales.'

'God no, not Zales. He wouldn't dare call me. Um … need I assure you that I'd never …'

'No, you needn't.'

She had said it very warmly and with utter conviction. He was flattered and pleased that she trusted him so.

He said, 'I almost didn't call, but you should be aware that the competition's been heating up lately. They won't find you through me and there's no other way. All the same, there's no harm in asking you to be careful. Above all, be careful of what you let people see.'

'That's … not always so easy. You know what I do.'

'As long as they only see one at a time. In your case, even two is a crowd.'

Her voice dropped an octave. 'Yeah, well … back to work.'

'Susannah?'

'I'm just kidding. But I hear you, Professor.'

'How is everything otherwise? Seeing anyone special?'

Another brief silence. 'Not lately.'

'But you are getting out, meeting people, I hope. It's not good to stay too within yourself.'

'I meet lots of people. And I've made some nice friends.'

'You know what I mean.'

'Yes, I know. You mean a guy. He would have to be pretty darned special, Professor.'

'I wish I were younger.'

'I wish you were, too.'

'Well, I'm here if you need me. Any time you want to talk.'

'You're a dear. I'm fine, but my kitchen floor isn't. We do have to get back to work.'

'Take care, Susannah.'

'Stay well, Dr. Cohen.'

Chapter Seven

The general's idea of buying lunch was a sandwich from a Park Service vendor at the entrance to the national cemetery. Arlington was only a few minutes' walk from the general's Pentagon office. He told Grayson that he often went there to think. Grayson suspected that he also went there for meetings that he didn't want overheard. Hoyt pointed to a bench and asked Grayson to sit. Grayson opened his briefcase, and returned Teal's reports to the general.

'Any change,' asked Hoyt, 'in your opinion of Zales?'

'Since when did he become a biochemist?'

'You know shrinks; they like to dabble. This one got lucky.'

'You're saying that he really did find this compound.'

The general grimaced. 'As opposed to who else?'

'As opposed to Prentice Teal bringing it to him so that Zales could try it out on his patients.'

Hoyt threw up his hands. 'Will you stop with conspiracies? Teal knew nothing about it before Zales brought it up. Zales showed him the effect that it had on a number of his patients. Believe it; I know that to be true. Teal, however, has now taken over. He's set up a lab in the basement at Belfair. It's quite complete; you'll be impressed. Teal did bring technicians in from Los Alamos, but after this discovery, not before. There's a radiologist to run the PET scan and a number of full-time chemists. Zales's involvement at this point is strictly peripheral.'

46

'Yet this document seems to give Zales all the credit.'

'If it works, Major Grayson, who cares?'

The general had said this last through his teeth. Grayson thought it best not to press him.

Teal's report showed that further research had been done. Zales's original compound had already been tested on a group of volunteers from the military. The testing, it said, was not done at Belfair. Teal was using a research facility down at Langley, not the CIA's Langley, but the Air Force base in southernmost Virginia. Those first volunteers were placed in high-stress situations, including an escape-and-evasion course like the one that the pilots at Bolling were given. None of them reported ever feeling much fear beyond an ordinary level of excitement. Their PET scans seemed to bear that out. They felt sure that their judgment remained intact, but that was the problem, it didn't. During one exercise, they had stopped to relieve themselves in a minefield they were told was fully armed. It's one thing to be steady in the face of danger and another to be indifferent to it. Mines don't care whether or not you're afraid. They just want to blow both your legs off.

Grayson thought he understood why Zales was given credit. The flip side of credit is blame. The general was right about shrinks being dabblers. Psychiatrists are allowed to experiment with drugs in ways that no medical doctor would dare. Nor do they need informed consent once a patient has been legally committed. Zales was free to use the patients at Belfair. But Teal, when he needed a sane group of subjects, had to get each one to sign a statement that said they were under Zales's care. That way, Grayson realized, if anything went wrong, any fingers would point back to Zales. Except Zales was still covered. He could do as he wished. He could mix and match any damned drug he pleased. And now, for that matter, so could Teal.

'Those PET scans …' asked Grayson.

'Amazing, are they not?'

'You're satisfied that they've changed for the better?'

'Overwhelmingly better but not everything we'd like. The compound, remember, is still being refined.'

'As it is, how long do the changes last?'

'About a week if the drug is withdrawn. If continued, they seem to be indefinite.'

Grayson glanced at the report that he'd handed to the general. He remembered the letter that had been attached to it, the one that the general didn't want him to see.

He asked, 'Sir, that letter I saw you put back in your drawer. I assume that it was from Teal.'

'It was.'

'Then, I have to ask. What aren't you telling me?'

The general drummed his fingers. He took a long breath. 'That letter had to do with the congressman's wife.'

'Martha Carey?'

'She'd made a request regarding her daughter. I asked Teal what he thought. That letter was his answer. It doesn't concern you. It's personal.'

'But, if the daughter is involved in either of these projects ...'

'She is not. I have made that quite clear to Mr. Teal.'

Grayson rose to his feet. He looked at the sky. 'Sir, are you going to tell me what Carey's wife is to you?'

'As I've said, she is not your concern.'

Grayson grimaced. It was what he'd been afraid of. 'Sir, your private life is none of my business. For that reason, I'm going to decline.'

'We're not having an affair, God damn it.' snapped the general. 'Martha Carey used to be Mrs. Bradley Parker. Before that, she was Martha Hoyt.'

'Um ... your sister?'

'She divorced poor Brad. I told you I couldn't blame her. They had no kids; I got her a job. Legislative assistant on the Hill. That was where she met Carey. I didn't like him then; I don't like him now. You'll recall another remark I made yesterday when you asked why Zales married his patient.'

'"Who knows why some people marry?" I remember.'

'But she did and she stayed. She had two children by him.

It's now twenty-six years but I'm not any less fond of her. As for you thinking that I haven't been forthright ...'

'Sir, that's not what I ...'

'The question is not what I'm not telling you,' said the general. 'It's what Teal is not telling me.'

'General Hoyt, sir, I believe you. But why would he tell me?'

'He probably won't. But you'll be able to poke around as you please. You'll represent me. He can't stop you.'

Grayson hesitated. The general nudged him.

'Roger ... I'm asking you to do this for me. It might even do you some good.'

'Could I just take on Richard? Stay away from Chameleon?'

'No, you can't. They're interrelated.'

'Then I'd have free access? No restrictions? Full authority?'

'I'll take you up Belfair myself. Don't say no to me, Roger. Let's get started today.'

Hoyt was pleading, thought Grayson. Generals don't plead with majors. This particular general was too personally involved. Andrew Carey's sick daughter turns out to be his niece and now his sister, Carey's wife, is thrown into the mix. There's no way that Hoyt could be professionally detached. Grayson wanted to say no for that reason alone. But against his better judgment, he nodded.

Okay, he thought. He'd give it two months.

He might, indeed, learn something from Teal. He might, though he doubted it, learn something from Zales. And he knew what Hoyt meant about it doing him some good. He might even learn more of what he'd struggled to deny. That there might – just might – be a stranger within him who had calmly murdered three people.

Hoyt checked his watch. It was almost one o'clock.

'It's time you met Teal. He's waiting in my office. After that, we'll drive up to Belfair.'

'Teal's waiting? He already knows about me?'

'He does not. You're to be a surprise.'

49

Chapter Eight

The image of Teal that Grayson had in his mind was that of a ferretlike and bloodless little man who probably dragged a leg when he walked. The Teal who was waiting near the general's office looked more like one of those tanned, cheery salesmen who pitch time-shares at golfing resorts. He was tall and lean, curly hair, early forties. He wore a blue blazer, a golf shirt and slacks, and was flirting with an E-ring receptionist.

'If I might tear you away ...' said the general, approaching.

'My time is your time,' Teal answered with a smile.

If Prentice Teal was disturbed by Hoyt's news, it didn't show in the least. He nodded agreeably as General Hoyt cited Major Grayson's background in psychology. Hoyt told him that they'd be driving to Belfair, that a visit was long overdue.

'Objections, Mr. Teal?'

'Me? None whatever. Good to have you on board, Major Grayson.'

He offered his hand. Grayson took it.

'How's that knee, by the way? Back to normal, I hope?'

'Some surprise,' said Grayson as they walked to Hoyt's car.

'Don't let him fool you. He couldn't know yet.'

'General Hoyt, he even knows that I was shot in the knee.'

'That receptionist. What have you told her?'

'She ... saw the limp yesterday. She asked about it. All I told her was that I'd had surgery.'

'Then that's all Teal knows. He saw the limp, too.'

Grayson was doubtful. 'You're sure about that.'

50

'You said it yourself. He plays with people's heads. By now he's on the phone trying to get at your file. He won't learn much. I've had most of it sealed.'

'Won't he also call Zales? To let him know that we're coming?'

'Saves me the trouble. We'll be there in an hour.'

Grayson had also formed a picture of Belfair. Austere and clinical, resembling a prison, a white concrete building, small windows with bars. Once again, it was not what he expected.

They pulled up in front of the wrought-iron gate of what had once been a private estate on the Chesapeake. The property covered a parklike ten acres surrounded by an eight-foot wall of brown brick. Electrical wires ran along its top surface; they were almost invisible from the road. There was a two-story guardhouse just inside the gate but it did not seem to be occupied. A camera mounted on the nearest pillar took the place of the guards who'd once used it. Hoyt's driver showed his face to the camera. Motors whirred and the gate began rolling back.

'Teal called him, all right,' noted Grayson.

'Watch Zales pretend that he didn't.'

The main building was a good two hundred yards up the driveway. The old mansion was immense; Grayson guessed sixty rooms. Like the outside walls, it was built of brown brick, relieved by a pattern of Tudor half timbers. Grayson had only been right about the windows. Those on the third and fourth floors were small. He assumed that those rooms had once housed the servants. The windows were covered with decorative grillwork that served the same purpose as bars.

'His wife bought this for him?'

'Um ... what? Yes, she did.'

The general had been peering up at those windows. Grayson guessed that he was looking at one in particular, where Martha Carey's daughter was kept.

'How many other patients does he have?' Grayson asked.

'About thirty, total. Most of those are housed up on the top floor. The others, the ones taking part in Chameleon, are kept

51

separate; they're in rooms one floor down. The first two floors are Zales's residence and office. Some guards, staff, and orderlies live in the house; the rest live in what used to be the stables.'

'And Teal's lab?'

'Side door to the right; it's down in the basement. I'll introduce you, then we'll all take the tour.'

Dr. Zales stepped out through the front door to greet them. Grayson recognized Zales from his book jacket photos. Same bushy gray hair, same wire-rimmed glasses, perhaps even the same dark blue suit. Zales paused as if to gather himself. He wet his lips. He made himself smile.

'General Hoyt,' he called brightly. 'An unexpected honor. I was going to call you and invite you to visit.'

Hoyt threw a wry sidelong glance at the major. To Zales, he said, 'This is Maj. Roger Grayson. He'll be visiting from time to time as well.'

'Is that so? In what role?' He was looking at Grayson.

'As my eyes and ears, Dr. Zales.'

Hoyt declined an invitation from Zales to join him for tea in his study. He told Zales that he'd like to begin at the top, the fourth floor first, then work down.

'Why the fourth floor?' Zales asked. 'They're not part of Chameleon.'

'No, but they were part of Richard.'

'That is not strictly true. They were never your subjects. I'm sorry, but I really don't think ...'

'You were giving them that compound before Teal took over. I want to see how they're doing.'

'Well, you see ...'

'And I want to look in on Rachel Carey. Let's go.'

'Well, I do wish you'd called before coming,' Zales huffed. 'You see, this is nap time for most of those patients, while others are scheduled to bathe. Any change in their carefully planned routines ...'

'Are you telling me I can't see them?' Hoyt asked.

'Oh, certainly not. You're welcome, of course. I simply would ask for more notice in future.'

'We'll try not to peek at any bathers,' said Hoyt.

They entered a richly paneled front hall. Before them stood a graceful curved staircase. The hall furniture was massive and intricately carved, all antiques or expensive reproductions. The paintings were landscapes, all restful, pastoral. There were sprays of fresh flowers on every flat surface. Soft music played in the background. Grayson saw no staff, no reception area, no sign so far that any part of Belfair had been remodeled for use as a mental-health facility. Dr. Zales seemed to read Grayson's mind.

'It's the sort of home quite a few of them grew up in. It makes it easier on the parents. Committing them, I mean. And it's nicer should the parents come to visit.'

'*Should* come to visit? Are you saying they don't?'

'Well ... rarely. The experience can be so upsetting. One never knows when an alter might appear and some can be very unpleasant.'

'But I understood that your new medication ...'

'Most are off it now ... for a while, at least. Mr. Teal's chemists are refining the compound. All the same, some are doing quite well.'

'Rachel Carey?' asked Hoyt.

'We have very high hopes. She's made excellent progress. But why don't you judge for yourself?'

Zales led them past the staircase to a recessed wooden door that turned out to be the entrance to an elevator. He pressed a hidden button and the door slid open. Zales invited Grayson and the general to step in. He entered behind them and touched the button of a speaker.

'Leatrice? We have visitors. We're on our way up. It's General Hoyt and another young officer. Is everyone decent, my dear?'

A throaty voice answered, 'General Hoyt? Well, of course. Bring him up, Norman dear, by all means.'

Zales punched out several digits on a small electric panel. It seemed to Grayson that he did so in a way that prevented him from seeing the combination he used. The door slid closed and the elevator climbed. The door opened moments later; the three men stepped out. The floor was silent. There was no one in sight.

The fourth floor consisted of a single long corridor with a dozen or more rooms on each side. Each door had a window about eight inches square. Each of the windows had a built-in shade like those that are seen on airplanes. All of the shades had been drawn. Beneath each window was a list of names. At the top was the first and last name of the patient. Underneath were several other first names, not all female. Grayson thought he understood what the list of names meant. He had turned and was about to ask Zales when a door clicked open near the end of the corridor. Two women emerged, one in whites, and came toward them. He recognized Leatrice Zales from her photo. She was holding the hand of a much younger woman who was dressed in an oversized bathrobe.

'Rachel,' she cooed. 'Look who's come here to see you.'

The young woman seemed confused. She looked first at Grayson; her eyes remained blank. She next looked at Zales. Recognizing his face brought the start of a smile. Leatrice Zales whispered into her ear. All at once, her eyes seemed to fill with life. They darted about as if searching for someone. The general was standing not six feet away but it seemed that it took a cue from Leatrice before she was able to see him.

She said, 'Uncle Harlan? Is that you, Uncle Harlan?'

The general's lips moved, almost quivered.

Rachel took one halting step, then another. She reached out a hand to touch his cheek. She said, 'Oh, Uncle Harlan. I've done such bad things. How can you ever …'

She suddenly drew back. Her hands covered her face.

'I am so ashamed,' she whispered. 'And I must look so awful. Maybe after my bath … if I could just fix my hair …'

'I told him next time he should call,' added Zales.

The general ignored him. He took Rachel's hand. Gently he placed an arm on her shoulder and steered her away toward the day room. Grayson remembered that the general had told him that Rachel no longer knew who he was. But now she

54

certainly seemed to, thought Grayson. He held back, not wanting to intrude on their moment. Zales turned to him; he cleared his throat.

'Perhaps this would be a good time,' he said, 'to show you what's on the third floor.'

Grayson's sense was that he ought to wait for the general but he wanted to give him some privacy as well.

'On this floor,' he asked Zales, 'you said everyone's napping?'

'Until it's their turn for a bath.'

'And downstairs? Are they all asleep in their rooms?'

'Our chameleons are all quite alert. Come and see.'

Once again, he kept Grayson from seeing the code that activated the elevator controls. Zales pressed a button. They descended.

'Is this the only way up and down?' Grayson asked.

'There are fire stairs, of course. It's the old servants' stairway. But those need to be kept locked to keep the patients from wandering.'

'And if there's a fire?'

'The locks are electric. They'll open automatically at the first alarm. Never fear, Major Grayson. The patients are restricted, not entombed.'

The door, this time, opened onto a foyer. It was spacious, well furnished; there were more sprays of flowers. The rooms off the foyer were considerably larger than those on the floor just above. They had probably once been guest rooms, thought Grayson, or rooms that had housed senior staff.

It occurred to Grayson that he'd seen no staff other than Leatrice Zales. He asked why.

'Oh, they're on break during nap time,' Zales answered. 'On the whole, however, they try to be unobtrusive, much like the help in the homes our guests came from.'

Money ... rich parents again, thought Grayson.

'There are five women here. They're all quite remarkable. Have you noticed the lists of names on each door?'

'The names of the patients plus the names of their alters?'

'General Hoyt told you?'

'No, that was a guess.'

'Then a good one, Major Grayson. You're right.'

All of the doors on this floor were open. Grayson approached the one that was nearest. He saw a tiny young woman, aged twenty at most, half sitting, half kneeling on the floor. She was dressed in an Oriental robe, high collar. Her features seemed almost Oriental as well, but he could see that she'd achieved that effect with cosmetics. Her fingernails were at least an inch long.

She was wearing earphones, listening intently. Spread before her was a newspaper that was printed in Chinese. At her side was a blue three-ring binder and what looked to be a number of textbooks. She barely glanced up at Grayson. Zales touched Grayson's arm. They backed into the foyer. Zales gestured toward the name on the door.

'Her given name is Carita Camal. She is Mexican by birth but was raised in this country. At this time, however, her name is Shan Li.'

'An alter?'

'I think all you'll see today will be alters. Their hosts have been staying more and more in the background.'

'And the alter, called Shan Li ... she thinks she's Chinese?'

'She doesn't just think it; she's becoming Chinese. She is studying the Mandarin language and culture. But she's more than studying, she's remaking herself. Carita, by the way, is an hysterical mute. She's never spoken a word since she's been here. As Shan Li, however, she speaks perfectly well, but she doesn't like to speak English.'

'Does she ... think she was Chinese in some other lifetime?'

Zales almost chuckled. 'This is not Past Lives Therapy. We at Belfair give no credence to that nonsense, Major Grayson.'

At least not at the moment. Wrong bandwagon, thought Grayson. 'Well, then why Chinese in particular?'

'Carita, among her many psychoses, detests having Mexican blood in her veins. It has to do with an unfortunate childhood and an injury she suffered before coming here. She's produced

56

Shan Li. We don't quite know why. Perhaps because China is half a world away from whatever she wishes to escape.'

Zales steered him to the next room. Grayson looked in. It seemed empty at first until a bathroom door opened. A young woman stepped out and walked directly to a desk where she sat down in front of a computer. She was wearing shorts and a Rolling Stones T-shirt, and a baseball cap put on backward. She had what Grayson called surfer girl looks; golden hair, long legs, lacking only a tan, a body still naturally firm without effort.

'This case is even more remarkable in its way,' Zales whispered at Grayson's ear. 'The host's name is Amanda. You would not like Amanda. She's a liar, she's selfish, mean-spirited, and stupid. But the woman you are now looking at is Veronica. Veronica is a thoroughly engaging young lady and an absolute whiz with a computer.'

As if on cue, she looked up and smiled. Her face, more than pretty, seemed wonderfully open. Grayson guessed her to be even younger than Carita, eighteen or nineteen at the most. Her intelligent green eyes locked on Grayson's and stayed.

She asked Zales, 'Hi, who's your cute friend?'

She asked it with a softness and a warmth in her voice, not brazen at all, merely friendly.

'This is Major Roger Grayson. He is here with General Hoyt. How long have you been using a computer, Veronica?'

'Gee, I don't know. Almost always, I guess.'

Zales gestured toward a stack of disks near her keyboard. 'That's quite a collection. What's in it?'

'Files I've downloaded. Mostly technical manuals. It's amazing, the stuff you can get.'

'Does Amanda ever use your computer?'

'Amanda? I hope not. She'd probably crash it. But, now that you ask, let me look.'

She reached for a blue three-ring binder on her desk. Grayson saw that it was the same kind of binder that her neighbor, Carita, had kept at her side.

'Never mind,' Zales said quickly. 'It isn't important.'

57

Veronica had already opened the binder. 'Amanda's supposed to write down what she does.' Grayson watched as she flipped back through a number of sheets. It seemed to be some kind of log. 'She hasn't been out in, well ... more than a month. And no, there's no mention of her using the computer. I don't think she'd even know how to boot it up.'

'May I look at that?' Grayson asked her.

'It's nothing,' said Zales. 'Just a way of keeping track of who's in and who's out. We'd better get on with our tour.'

But Veronica had snapped open the rings of her binder. She handed him a stack of perhaps thirty sheets.

'You don't want to see the parts I kept,' she told him.

'They're private?'

'You just don't want to see them. That okay?'

'Fine with me.'

Grayson took the sheets from her and began glancing through them. They covered a period of roughly three months. He saw writing in several different hands.

'These are all you?' he asked Veronica.

'Well, once there were a bunch of us. We're now down to three. Actually, lately, we've been down to just me.'

She answered as if it were a normal occurrence, no hint that it troubled her in the least.

'That's me who writes with the big looping letters. The cramped little scribble with the curse words is Amanda's, and the entries that are printed, that's Henry.'

'Henry?'

She chuckled. 'I know. It's a stitch. He's a man and he can be a real horse's patoot but he seldom comes out anymore.'

'The reason he doesn't come out,' Zales explained, 'is that Veronica is gradually isolating herself. She is willing away her more troublesome alters so that ...'

'That's not why he stays in,' said Veronica, beaming. 'He forgets that he isn't really a man and he tries to hit on Shan Li and the others. He's had his butt kicked, but look who gets stuck with the damage.' She pulled her T-shirt up to her shoulder in order to show Grayson her ribs. She wore no bra

58

but was unabashed. Sure enough, he saw faded yellow bruises.

'We have to move on.' Zales tugged at Grayson's sleeve. Grayson handed the pages to Veronica.

She took them with a smile. 'Nice meeting you, Major.'

Grayson answered with a smile of his own. 'Call me Roger.'

'Will you come back and see me?'

'Yes, I will. Very soon.'

'You promise? I'd like that. I'd like it a lot.'

He and Zales left her room and returned to the foyer. Grayson stopped and asked. 'Why would she have a Henry?'

'A male alter, you mean? It's quite common.'

Zales explained that male alters are often found in women who've had cause to feel vulnerable and used. Some have lesbian alters for much the same reason. 'The male alter, you see, is better able to cope. He is usually more aggressive, often physically stronger, and better able to defend himself than ...'

'Doctor, I know that. Or rather, I've read it. But Henry seems to be none of those things.'

'Your point?'

'Why should that girl have a Henry?'

Zales started to explain, but in the vaguest of terms. The question seemed to make him ill at ease. Grayson sensed that he either had no idea or had a reason for not wanting to discuss it.

'Okay, forget Henry.' Grayson held up a hand. 'Let's talk about that girl in there, Veronica.'

'Your question?'

'Just so I'm clear ... I've been speaking to an alter who calls herself Veronica, but the host, your real patient, is named Amanda. Correct?'

'That's correct.'

'When you say that Veronica is isolating herself, what happens to Amanda, the real one?'

'Let me ask you a question. Did you like Veronica?'

'What I saw of her, yes. She's quite lovely.'

'Well, as I've told you, you would not like Amanda. Why

59

try to cure Amanda, when we've already got the sort of person whom Amanda would be if she could?'

'Um, you know that because ... she invented Veronica?'

'I invented Veronica, Major Grayson.'

'Excuse me?'

'Veronica said she's always used a computer. But she saw her first computer just three months ago. She did not exist before then.'

Zales tried to steer Grayson back to the elevator. But Grayson said he'd like to see more. He wanted to look in on the other three subjects and revisit the one who was studying Chinese.

'They all keep these logs? The blue binders?'

'Yes, but they contain some rather personal entries. I don't think it's right that you should read them.'

'Veronica let me. She handed them to me.'

'She handed you the parts that she didn't mind you seeing.'

'Fair enough. I'll ask their permission.'

Two others were nearly as pleasant as Veronica. They gave him their binders quite willingly, thought Grayson, as if having them looked at was a normal occurrence. The remaining two, one of whom was Shan Li, merely shrugged to show that they didn't care and went back to whatever they were doing. Grayson, to the clear annoyance of Zales, took the time to scan several pages in each.

If Grayson had never read about multiples, he would not have believed that the same person wrote them. The handwriting was different but that was the least of it. The alters in each were entirely distinct. Their mental states, their likes and dislikes, their views of themselves and of each other were all different.

He'd asked Zales whether any had left-handed alters. Zales pointed one out. He seemed glad to do so. The writing of that alter was, sure enough, just as fluid and practiced as that of her host. Another alter, Grayson noticed, spelled certain words correctly that her host got consistently wrong.

Zales directed his attention to a few other entries. At meals, another alter would eat only the vegetables and would flush all the meat down her toilet. Her host wrote her notes complaining about it, and asked that she put the meat aside so that it would be there when she came out again.

Grayson realized that Zales was trying to fill his head with minutia while avoiding a discussion of substance. Grayson didn't mind, for the moment. Some of the minutia was intriguing.

'These are not, I take it, what you call mosaics.'

'Mosaics? Oh. Then you've read my book.' Zales seemed more wary than flattered.

'I read about the patient you called Susannah. She was like some of these but your book says you cured her. Is there any way I could meet her?'

'She's changed her name. She's moved far away. She wishes to put that life behind her. I endorse and protect her decision.'

'Very well. No problem,' said Grayson.

Zales had managed to say no in four different ways. Grayson chose to let it pass. His mind was still on the binders. Even without Zales's attempts at misdirection, there was something about these logbooks that bothered him. He could not put his finger on what it was. Another thought that Grayson was surprised to be considering was that Zales might be doing some good.

'Let me see if I'm clear,' he said to Zales. 'You've got alters, Veronica and Shan Li, for example, who've become more real than their hosts. But the host is the patient who was sent here to be cured.'

'Your point is …?'

'When you send, say, Veronica back to her family, won't you be sending a stranger?'

'They … would not be going back in all cases, Major Grayson. I dare say that most wouldn't want to.'

'I understand that. But what if they did?'

'I am working on solving that problem, Major Grayson. You saw Rachel upstairs. I've been working with her. I hope to have a success very soon.'

61

Chapter Nine

The elevator opened before Zales could call it. The general was on it with Leatrice Zales. She was smiling that smile. The general seemed pensive. He said, 'If you're through here, we'll go down to the lab.'

Leatrice Zales excused herself. She remained with the women who were part of Chameleon. The three men descended to Belfair's main hall, walked out of the building and turned to their left. The laboratory was on the north side of the house, reached through what had once been a service entrance. The psychiatrist produced a coded card of the type that is used in place of hotel keys.

'There is no one here at the moment,' he said. 'Mr. Teal's technicians come and go as they please. I seldom come down here myself.'

He opened a door that was wood on the outside and plated with steel on the inside. Grayson entered a room roughly forty feet square but broken up by partitions. Off to his right, behind the partitions, it looked like a hospital emergency room. He saw three examining tables side by side, an X-ray machine, and a PET scan. In the center, the room was set up as an office. There were desks with nothing on them but darkened computers. He saw no safe, no locked filing cabinets. He assumed that all records were in the computers.

To his left, it was like any chemistry lab. Beakers and burners, a centrifuge, a sink, many jars containing various chemicals. The labels on the jars had numbers on them; their contents were not otherwise identified. Grayson asked Zales why the labels were coded.

'Security, clearly.'

'Do you know what's in them?'

'Not all, but I know some on sight, of course. Every mental health facility has them.'

He pointed his finger, ticking some of them off. Clozapine, chlorpromazine, and haloperidol, all antipsychotics. He named a few more with which Grayson was familiar, the generics for brand-name antidepressants such as Xanax, Mellaril, Wellbutrin.

'The more exotic drugs were brought in from Los Alamos. I don't really know what most of them are but Mr. Teal let me look at the literature on two of them. Have you ever heard of bromantan, Major Grayson? How about cyproterone acetate?'

Grayson shook his head. 'No, I haven't.'

'You wouldn't. They're drugs that the Russians developed. They give bromantan to certain of their troops, those stationed where the weather is severe. It's not only been shown to keep them more alert; it helps them to adapt to extremes of hot and cold. A logical addition to Richard, I would think.'

'It would seem so. What about side effects?'

'Ah, that was the rub. It caused sexual arousal. No woman was safe where those Russian troops were based. They behaved more like dogs in heat than like soldiers.' Zales pointed to a jar that contained a crystalline substance. 'So they gave them this other drug, cyproterone acetate. It reduces the sex drive, and it works very well without defeating the positive effects of bromantan.'

Zales paused for a moment. He smiled at Grayson. 'But that was not cyproterone's original purpose. Would you care to guess what it was used for?'

'No idea.'

'It was developed to inhibit growth in their gymnasts. That's why they're all four foot ten, ninety pounds, and sexless for all practical purposes. A wonderful art, pharmacology, no?'

This shrink does a lot more than dabble, thought Grayson.

He walked with the general back toward their car. The general had said very little. Grayson asked, 'Sir, how did it go with your niece?'

'My niece? Oh, Rachel. I don't think of her as my niece.'

'She ... seems to think of you as her uncle.'

'What, that 'Uncle Harlan,' you heard? She used to call me that long ago but she hasn't since she was a child.'

'Well, it took her a minute but she recognized you. Maybe she's really getting better.'

'I don't know. You saw her. All sweetness and light. Rachel was never all sweetness and light. It's almost too much of a change.'

Grayson thought of Zales's hope that he was near to a success. And he thought of Veronica who used to be Amanda. 'But as long as it's a positive change ...?'

'I don't know. I guess.' He waved off the subject. 'Tell me what else you've learned from this visit.'

'For openers? Never to call in advance.'

'Start at the top. What about the fourth floor?'

'Twenty-five patients don't fall fast asleep just because he tells them it's nap time. No baths running either. That whole floor was silent.'

'Conclusion?'

'He drugged them so we couldn't talk to them.'

'Not to them or to the guards, who always seem to be on break.'

'Teal's technicians work some pretty odd hours as well.'

'All except Rachel Carey. Why just her, do you think?'

'I *thought* to distract you. I could see you were shaken. But maybe she's really made progress.'

The general nodded slowly. 'One hopes.'

'As for the third floor, I spoke to all five. I have to say that I'm a little less skeptical. It's possible that he's actually giving new lives to women who were wrecks when they got here.'

'What does that do for us?'

'I was thinking of them.'

'Well, don't think of them. They were *your* distraction.

64

You're here to find out if it's something we can use in developing Chameleons of our own.'

'Um … Sir …'

'You're going to say what? That you can say no right now? Open mind, Major Grayson. Take your time.'

'Yes, sir.'

'That basement lab … notice anything there?'

'I thought I'd see a blackboard, a notebook or two. I did not see a single scrap of paper.'

'You won't. But perhaps now you see what you're up against.'

They were at the car. Hoyt's driver stood waiting. The general paused and reached into his pocket. He drew out an envelope and a small plastic card.

'In this envelope are all the authorizations you'll need to visit the Langley facility. You can also requisition any aircraft within reason so don't waste a lot of time driving. Take a chopper down to Langley, next couple of days. Teal's people are recruiting some new volunteers to test a different version of Richard.'

'Who are Teal's people? More technicians from Los Alamos?'

'They're from Los Alamos but they're regular army. A special unit that he's used in the past. They'll be polite, they may even seem cooperative, but never forget that they work for Prentice Teal. Look for a sergeant named Kristoff.'

Hoyt handed him the envelope. He held up the other item. Grayson saw that it was a key card like the one Zales had used to open the laboratory door.

'Put it in your pocket. It might come in handy. Zales's elevator code is 1446. I saw him block you from seeing what he punched. Don't use either unless you have to, however. They're both very easy to change.'

'Sir … why don't you just order them to give me free access?'

'Order who? You mean Zales?'

'And Teal and this Kristoff.'

'Because I don't know what free access is. They will all only show you what they want you to see.'

Hoyt climbed into his car. Grayson followed.

'Be a snoop, Roger. Be a pain in the butt. Question them, challenge them, go where you're not wanted. Except … well …'

'Rachel?'

'Leave that one alone. As you said, Zales might possibly be helping.'

Chapter Ten

On the lawn of an estate in Virginia's horse country, three men were taking turns pitching golf balls. All three of the men were in their early fifties. All three had daughters at Belfair.

One was dressed for golf; the others wore suits. They were aiming at a fountain in the garden below them. The hearts of the two men in suits were not in it, but their host had said that it would help them relax and take their minds off their concerns. They had met there to await Prentice Teal.

Their host, the one dressed for golf, was Charles Winston. His clothes, shoes, and bag were all white, as was his wide-brimmed straw hat. Winston also owned several white suits that he wore regardless of season. He was a large, fleshy man with the sort of complexion that turned a vivid pink in the sun.

The estate, called Oakmont, had been his home for ten years. For two of those years, since his daughter was committed, Winston had lived there alone. But the deed to Oakmont was held by a trust and the trust had decided to sell it.

Charles Winston was an officer – at least in name – of Winston Laboratories, Inc. Winston's grandfather had founded the company at the outset of the Second World War. A contract for supplying sulpha drugs and penicillin had helped it grow into a global corporation that controlled some forty subsidiaries. Grandfather Winston had groomed his son, Martin, to succeed him as chairman of the board. Martin Winston had no such ambition for Charles, a son whose conception he'd had cause to regret.

Charles, when only twelve, showed an interest in girls that his father, at first, thought was perfectly normal. However, it became clear that as Charles grew older, the objects of his interest did not. They remained, with one exception, under twelve years of age.

Family money managed to keep Charles out of jail. A fortune spent on counseling seemed to have good effect. All it actually did was make it clear to Charles that his urges were best kept to himself. His mother, however, let herself be persuaded that counseling had made a new man of him. She then found him a wife, not a strong one, but a wife, and that wife had given Charles a daughter. Charles now had a family, a solid foundation. As a Winston, as their son, he should be given a chance to earn a place in the family business.

She was, however, just enough of a realist to know that her son had his limits. She knew that he would never be given a position that involved any real responsibility. She had to find him something that seemed consequential but one in which he could do little harm. Her attention was drawn to a Winston Labs subsidiary on the outskirts of Warrenton, Virginia. It manufactured nothing; it developed nothing; all it did was warehouse and ship drug ingredients.

The family owned the nearby Oakmont Estate, although no one had summered there for years. But they still were members of the Warrenton Country Club as well as the Warrenton Hunt Club. Charles and family, therefore, would have a ready-made social life and an office to go to each morning. Martin Winston resisted but his wife wore him down. It might, he agreed, help keep Charles out of trouble. Better still, it might keep him away.

Several years went by, Charles's father passed away, and his mother succumbed some months later. A trust had been established to look after their affairs. Its auditors saw that Charles's small subsidiary had been hopelessly managed all that time. Tens of thousands of dollars worth of drugs had been contaminated by negligent storage and humidity control. Nor could they account for the whereabouts of many other costly chemicals that had been stored in that warehouse's vaults. The auditors suspected that they had been sold to cover Charles's growing expenses. Among these were the cost of hushing up certain rumors and the cost of his daughter's commitment.

Charles, if he had not been a Winston, would have been summarily fired. But his mother had seen to it that he was protected through certain stipulations in her will. The trust understood that her intentions were good even if they were sadly misplaced. The trust, therefore, would now ask the courts to allow it more freedom of action. It wanted to either close down the subsidiary or put competent management in place.

Charles's own legal firm was of the opinion that the trust would eventually prevail. They could delay the outcome for a year, perhaps two. After that, Charles's income would be drastically reduced. He would live on a modest allowance.

This news would have left Charles considerably depressed if the promise of redemption had not appeared in the persons of the two men hitting golf balls on his lawn and especially through that clever Prentice Teal.

The smaller of the other two, dark suit, garish cufflinks, was Luis Montoya-Camal. Camal, although a Mexican national, spoke English with almost no accent. He had lived in Washington for nearly two decades, representing the interests of his family. The family business was PharMex, S.A., a distributor of the low-cost prescription drugs that Americans crossed into Mexico to buy. A more lucrative aspect of the business was smuggling. It copied and smuggled certain foreign-made drugs whose sale had been banned in this country.

The third man was Congressman Andrew J. Carey. Carey came dressed in a dark suit as well, but had tossed his jacket onto a bench in order to better swing his club. The flesh of Carey's face had a heavy drinker's bloat and his abdomen bulged beneath his belt.

The three men had met through Norman Zales. They soon learned that they had interests in common. Beyond the fact that they had deeply troubled daughters who now were in

69

residence at Belfair, two of the men, Camal and Charles Winston, had an interest in amassing personal wealth independent of the wealth that their families controlled. Andrew Carey simply wanted the money.

Carey was about to take his swing when Teal's car turned onto the property. It was an older model Plymouth. Carey saw it coming. He rushed his shot, shanked the ball, and cursed.

'Andrew ... wiggle your shoulders,' said Charles Winston calmly. 'You can't play this game if you're tense.'

The Plymouth stopped. Prentice Teal climbed out. He approached them, head down, with long strides.

'Take Teal, for example. He's the picture of control, never flustered, always focused. He would probably play a fine game of golf.'

'He doesn't look so unflustered to me.'

Winston saw the dark scowl on Prentice Teal's face. 'You're right. He's unhappy. He doesn't like being summoned. Too bad. He should have kept us advised.'

'This is about Grayson?' Teal was clearly annoyed. 'I've taken three hours out of my day to drive down here to talk about Grayson?'

Teal stood, hands on hips, glaring at the three men.

'Mr. Camal heard about him from Leatrice,' said Winston. 'One would think we'd have heard it from you.'

'Heard what? That Hoyt's decided to pay more attention? Why is that a surprise? It's his job.'

'She mentioned,' said Carey, 'that he spent time with Rachel.'

'Yeah, and Leatrice fixed her up so he could. So what?'

'Last I heard, Rachel barely knew her own name. Now she's talking at length and to Hoyt of all people. Hoyt has hardly been a friend to me through the years.'

'Andrew ... what of it? She doesn't know dick.'

'My question ... why must she be talking at all? You know the sort of things she's said about me. I had hoped that it had ended for good.'

Teal understood. Carey didn't mean dead. He was simply more comfortable when Rachel was a turnip. Teal would try to remember to pass on his concern the next time he visited Belfair. He would also tell Leatrice that he'd have her white ass if she ever called these three again.

The Mexican stepped forward. 'What about this new man?'

'Grayson? What about him?' asked Teal.

'Well, he seems,' said Winston, 'to have rattled Dr. Zales.'

'Anyone who thinks Zales is full of shit rattles Zales. I rattle him every time I see him.'

'Leatrice thinks there's something queer about this Grayson. How much do you know about the man?'

'This is Leatrice, *our Leatrice*, calling someone else queer?'

'Even so, Teal, what can you tell us?'

'All Grayson is, is some army instructor who's taken a psych course or two. He'll look around a little and then he'll be gone.'

'But not before telling General Hoyt what he's learned.'

'What he'll learn,' snapped Teal, 'is what I want him to learn. In the end, he'll do a report on Chameleon. He'll see that it's crap and he'll say so.'

'And Richard?'

'Project Richard will impress him but he'll want to go slow. It won't matter. We'll already be in business.'

Camal stepped closer. 'You will handle this man?'

'Forget him. Leave Grayson to me.'

'Because, if you don't ...' Camal pulled back his jacket, showing Teal the Glock pistol that he wore on his belt. He half-turned so that the others could see it as well.

A weary grimace. Teal said, 'Louie ... be nice.' Even Winston was rolling his eyes.

Camal placed his golf club on the taller man's chest. 'I intend to protect my interests, Mr. Teal. You handle this man or I will.'

'Take the club away, Louie. Do that right now.'

'And, I have told you ... do not call me Louie. To you I am Mr. Camal.'

'Well, Mr. Camal, take that club off my chest or I'll shove it right up your ass.'

Fucking weenie, thought Teal as he returned to his car. He thinks flashing a gun makes him more of a man than the pile of shit that he is. The Glock, however, was at least an improvement. The gun Camal carried before this was a little Colt Mustang that he'd had silver plated and engraved. Teal had told Camal that his grandma had had a garter gun just like it. That was the end of the Mustang.

All the same, Teal supposed that he should have indulged him, not made him back down in front of the others. Weenie or not, he's a vicious little fuck who's hard enough to keep in line as it is. But his family and Winston, they had what Teal needed. He was stuck with them both, thanks to Zales.

What a foursome.

Three men who've been accused of porking their daughters and a bought-and-paid-for shrink who made the daughters go away.

Winston certainly was guilty. Teal knew because he had pulled his file. Winston collected child porn; he got it through the mail, and he thought the Feds didn't know it. In his teens, he was arrested for molestation twice but his parents bought off the victims' families both times. Both victims were in grade school. The oldest was ten. Winston thinks no one knows about those episodes either.

Winston's parents had told him to get married … or else … for at least the appearance of normality. They had bought him a wife who soon grew to loathe him, but she did provide Winston with a daughter and an heir. The wife stuck it out for about ten years. She must have known what he'd been doing to their daughter. She responded by climbing into a bottle and rarely leaving her room. In the end, she used a tumbler of vodka to wash down fifty Seconal pills.

He had started with his daughter before she was eight. It went on for nine years after that. But along the way, according to Zales, she became a semi-willing participant. The daughter, Amanda, was no bundle of joy. Zales said she grew into a nasty little bitch and probably would have regardless. She didn't seem to mind Winston having his fun as long as he made it worth her while. But Zales said Winston eventually lost interest. She was fully grown by then. Winston's tastes ran much younger. And what fun, after all, was a willing participant, especially one who liked to mock him while doing it. She told Zales that she was still almost a virgin because her father had the dick of a dwarf.

Winston finally decided that enough was enough. He canceled her credit cards and cut her allowance. She responded by picking up the phone and dialing the lawyers who managed Winston's trust. She told Winston that she thought she'd invite them down for a viewing of his child porn collection. An extra special treat would be the clips starring herself. All those photos and videos he'd made over the years.

Charles relented, but only to buy himself time and make certain arrangements with Zales. Amanda had bitten the hand that fed her, and that got her sent off to be reborn.

The Mexican, in his own way, was worse. He liked young girls and was a sexual sadist, but Zales said he never touched his daughter that way. Unlike Winston, who preferred the real thing, Camal used hookers dressed up as schoolgirls while he played the disciplinarian. Zales said that one night screams woke up his daughter; she got scared and ran to his room. Caught him at it. To try to convince her that such things were normal, that fucking dope tried to get her to join in.

She would not. She told him he was disgusting. He went to slap her; she kicked him in the nuts. At that, he beat her. He fractured her skull. He knew that any doctor would call the police if he saw the extent of her injuries. So he kept her locked away at his home and hoped that she'd heal by herself. She did, but she'd lost the ability to speak. The good news, to him, was that she'd also lost her memory. She had no recollection of what her father had done or even that he was her father. Camal knew about Zales because – surprise, surprise – Camal had a wife who was already at Belfair. She was one of

Zales's fourth-floor zombies. Stashing both his wife and daughter away was expensive, but Zales gave him a quantity discount.

This left Andrew Carey, who was probably innocent. He was a sleaze in other ways, his hand always out, but Teal doubted that he ever touched Rachel. By all accounts, he could barely stand the sight of her.

Teal had chosen not to risk upsetting these three by telling all he knew about Grayson. But Teal himself wasn't sure what to make of him. Grayson's file, the part that he'd been able to access, said that his specialty was deep cover penetrations of groups that are hostile to the government. An operative who did that had to play different roles and he had to be pretty damned convincing. But Belfair was hardly a terrorist hotbed, and Grayson was playing himself. How come?

The only real clue to explain his involvement was some stories Teal had heard on the grapevine. It seemed that last time out, Grayson blew away three people, but he claimed to have no memory of doing it. He took a bullet himself, which explained the gimpy knee. One of the three was some woman who had messed with his head. Before that, the word is, he stomped some Nazi half to death. They're not sure that he remembers that either.

Those incidents aside, Grayson didn't seem especially tough or especially interested in these projects. Teal could only guess that Hoyt dragooned him into this because Hoyt thought Grayson might be a multiple. But if Grayson had come to believe it himself, he was almost as screwed up as Rachel.

Speaking of whom, could she be getting better? Zales wasn't supposed to do anything with her except to keep her in her own little dream world. But he did say that Carey's wife had been pushing him to show some progress or let her go elsewhere. She'd found some new shrink at Duke University and was anxious to give him a try. Fat chance. Carey wants that girl right where she is.

He would try to remember to ask Zales about Rachel. He would definitely tell him to sit on his wife. As for Grayson, there wasn't much harm he could do as long as nobody did anything stupid.

Teal didn't care how much he poked around Belfair. Let him waste all the time he likes with Zales's loonies. But he didn't like Grayson popping in down at Langley, no notice, no warning, and whenever he pleased. Especially now, with that new group being tested.

He had thought of having Zales slip Grayson one of those drugs that apparently makes people see snakes in their soup. But Hoyt wouldn't be fooled; he'd see through it in a minute. The real trick would be to get something on Hoyt, but the guy was *so* damned straight that he was bulletproof.

The answer, Teal supposed, was just to be patient. The good news is that Grayson thinks these projects are bullshit. Maybe he'll only go through the motions, then go back shooting Nazis in his sleep, or whatever. Either way, we can't allow him to screw this thing up.

A hole in his knee? He has a hole in his head if he thinks he's going to mess with Project Richard.

Chapter Eleven

General Hoyt had asked Grayson to give it two months. He'd been at it for only two weeks. Those two weeks, in his opinion, were more than enough, at least where Zales and Belfair were concerned.

He had visited Belfair four times, unannounced, and had spent several days down at Langley. At Belfair, there was Leatrice, always hovering, always watching, until he finally had to tell her to find something else to do. She had flashed her teeth at him; it wasn't a smile. She went back to the elevator, closed the door and descended. He could hear her hyperventilating all the way down. That woman was not tightly wrapped.

At Langley, there was Teal's man, the sergeant named Kristoff. The sergeant, in most ways, was a welcome change. He seemed entirely professional, unfailingly courteous. But he answered, 'Sir, you'd have to ask Mr. Teal.' to almost every question Grayson asked him.

Grayson hadn't yet decided about Project Richard. There was one rather curious test that was in progress until Grayson asked Kristoff to put it on hold. Grayson told him that he wanted to discuss it with Teal. Teal, however, could not be reached. The sergeant pointed out that Teal ran several other projects and was often out of touch for days at a time. Grayson told him, 'I can wait. So can this test.'

He was willing to reserve judgment on Project Richard, but Chameleon was quite a different matter. He had seen all he had to of Zales and his work to know that the Pentagon shrink had been right – no useful answers would come out of Belfair. What Zales thought he'd proven was already well known: that suggestible people do remarkable things. Stage hypnotists demonstrated that all the time.

Zales did discover and encourage such talents but the process was totally random. Even with the lovely Veronica, all he'd done was keep asking, 'Who else is in there?' until an alter with a pleasing personality emerged. He then set out to try to isolate Veronica in the hope that the others would fade away in time.

Grayson would concede that, ethics aside, it was actually a fascinating premise. Some might even consider it a mental health breakthrough. If alters can be integrated into a host … but the host, at her best, is an unpleasant person … why not try to do it the other way around? Treat the host's personality as if it were an alter. Let the best of the alters be the host.

Grayson found himself hoping that Zales might be right, at least in Veronica's case. He had come to like her; he liked her very much. Even quacks have occasional successes.

But Zales had not, as he'd claimed, 'invented' Veronica. It was not as if he'd specifically asked for 'a nice girl who's good with computers.' He'd had no idea that she'd have that talent, or that two of the others would be linguists. As for Shan Li, Zales could do no more than guess why she was becoming Chinese. In no case, in fact, did he know at the outset what abilities he might find in an alter. That's what made Project Chameleon useless as far as the government was concerned; when the DOD needs of a particular skill, it searches, locates it, recruits it. It doesn't go and hypnotize a bunch of mental patients in search of a talented alter.

On a personal level, he was saddened by Veronica. It was more than pity for the childhood she'd had and for what her father had done to her. Those things, after all, had been done to Amanda and Amanda had pretty much vanished. He and Veronica had become, well … friends.

She was always thrilled to see him; he'd get that big smile and, the last time he saw her, a hug. He liked her so much for her warmth, her sense of humor, that at times he wanted to take her by the hand and walk her straight out of Belfair. But he'd had to remind himself that she wasn't real. Not only was Veronica, in essence, a delusion, but she'd started to have delusions of her own.

Veronica, who had otherwise seemed so rational, told him that she had a new little friend who came to visit her late at night. She would hear a dull knocking from inside the walls and suddenly her friend would slip into her room. Her friend, she told Grayson, was a child, a girl. Grayson thought that she meant a new alter had emerged, one that he hadn't yet heard about.

'From where? From me? That's pretty dumb, Roger. You think parts of me walk in through the door?'

'I guess I meant from some other patient, Veronica.'

'Well, she's not someone's alter. She's a real kid, this big.' She held out a hand, chest high.

'Okay, but where from? There are no kids at Belfair.'

'By the way, don't repeat this. I'm just telling you. How she gets through the walls is a secret.'

'I won't say a word. Cross my heart.'

Veronica frowned. 'You're giving me a look.'

'No, I'm not. What look?'

'Like you think I'm a fruitcake.'

'I do not. Lots of people have imaginary friends. I think it's great that you've ... made one.'

Her lips formed a pout. 'So this kid's in my mind.'

'Come on, Veronica. What was I supposed to think? The elevator's the only way up here and you're telling me she comes through the walls.'

'I don't think that's exactly what I said.'

'Okay, let's start over. I misunderstood. Tell me more about your new secret friend.'

'What if I told you she's really a ghost?'

'I would think that you're busting my chops now.'

'Ghosts or imaginary friends, what's the difference? They both can go anywhere they want.'

'Does your ghost have a name?'

'Sure, but now I won't tell you.'

'Well, why does she come to your room, in particular?'

'We talk. And I'm teaching her to use my computer. She's getting pretty good. She loves surfing the Net. We go everywhere on it because it's full of surprises. Can you guess what we found just last night?'

As she asked that question, she'd looked into his eyes. If it had special meaning, however, he missed it. He was thinking, sadly, of her need to invent someone from the outside who would visit her. No one else, beside himself, ever had.

'Listen, I have to go but I'll be back very soon. Is there anything you'd like me to bring you?'

'Sure, an access code for your file.'

'What file?'

'Your army file. Your DOD file. All I get is ACCESS DENIED.'

'You're saying you hacked into the DOD?'

A dismissive shrug. 'For what it was worth. It didn't tell me anything about you.'

'What it's worth, Veronica, is a few years in prison.'

She smiled. She gestured toward her present surroundings. 'Why would that frighten me, Roger?'

'Then, how's this? If they trace you, you'll lose your computer. Promise me you won't try that again.'

Another shrug. 'Okay. But the Net is still legal.'

He stared. 'You found … a surprise, you just said?'

'Last night we found you on the Internet, Roger.'

Grayson sucked in a breath. His eyes went to her computer.

'Unless I imagined it. Like I did my little friend.'

'Veronica … are we being serious now?'

'Yes, we are. We are even being sane at the moment. There are people on the Net who say you did something awful. But you wouldn't hurt a woman, would you, Roger?'

'Not on purpose.'

'An accident?'

'Not exactly.'

'What is in between those two?'

'Listen, Veronica ...'

'You don't remember, do you?'

Grayson drew in a breath. 'How would you know that?'

'Because *we* don't remember. It's why *we* write things down. Could it be that you're one of us, Roger Grayson? Is that why you spend so much time here?'

'No, it isn't.'

'If those people want to hurt you, you can stay here, you know. My new friend knows all the places to hide.'

'Veronica ... thank you. But I'll be okay.'

'I'm here. You can buzz me any time if I can help.'

'Buzz you? How would I buzz you?'

She pursed her lips; she gave him a look that said he was being dense. She tilted her head toward her monitor.

E-mail. Of course. Grayson hadn't been thinking. If she had access to the Net, she must have an address. He stepped to her table, picked up a pen and scribbled some numbers on a piece of scrap paper.

'Here's mine,' he told her. 'It's my personal laptop. It goes where I go, so I'm always within reach.'

She looked at the slip he had given her. 'That's a funny address. It looks more like a code.'

'It's different. It works off a satellite. Let's have yours.'

She wrote it down for him. 'Now give me a squeeze.'

She opened her arms; Grayson took her and held her. She had tears in her eyes when he released her.

He found it hard to leave Veronica there. She had to push him and say, 'It's all right. You can go.' He thanked her again for caring about him. Impossible though her offer of a hide-away might have been, he knew that it was made out of kindness and trust. All he wanted, more than ever, was to finish this job. And as soon as General Hoyt agreed to terminate Chameleon, he would get Veronica out of that place and into some competent treatment. He didn't know how, but he would do it.

He used his cell phone to alert Dr. Zales that he was ready

to leave, so that Zales could bring the elevator up. Grayson still thought it best to let Zales believe that he didn't know the elevator's code.

Zales asked him, 'Good visit?'

'Always interesting, Doctor.'

He would like to have asked who Veronica's father was, but he knew that Zales wouldn't tell him. All such information was off-limits to outsiders in order to protect family privacy. There had been no use in asking Veronica because she had no memory of any family.

'I know that I haven't spent much time with you, Major. It was not intentional. So busy, you know.'

'No problem. I'm happy to be on my own.'

It was just as well, thought Grayson, that he didn't know the father. He would have been tempted to drop in on him and discuss some new arrangement for his daughter. The father might have told him to mind his own business, and Grayson might have had another *episode*.

'But my schedule,' said Zales, 'has loosened up a bit. Tell you what … why don't you come back tomorrow? I'll set aside my whole afternoon.'

An invitation? That's a first, thought Grayson. 'Thank you, but I can't. I have another commitment.'

'You won't reconsider? Perhaps you can switch it.'

'I'll have to take a rain check. I'm sorry.'

Grayson thought he saw a look of relief, and wondered whether Zales, in his circuitous way, was simply making sure that he would not be dropping by. But sometimes a cigar is just a cigar.

He'd been in intelligence too long.

On the next day, a Friday, he went back down to Langley to monitor an experiment then in progress.

He'd been much more hopeful about Project Richard, even if Zales had been involved in it as well. Beyond what it might do for combat troops or the police, the effect the project was trying to achieve could change many millions of lives for the better. Assuming the right combination of drugs, and assuming that they could be shown to be safe, Grayson was able to imagine a day when therapists would have to find other work. The mildly troubled could stop searching for a cause that was probably unknowable to begin with.

But even that project now bothered him greatly. Grayson had dismissed the original volunteers within two days of accepting the assignment. They were the ones who'd become indifferent to danger. The drugs had left them free of measurable anxiety but the cost was their ability to recognize risk and to face it in a prudent manner. They might as well have been asked to smoke crack.

It had taken another week to recruit new volunteers, but when they arrived they were not what he had asked for. For one thing, they were only ten in number. He'd wanted at least twenty so that he'd have a control group. There was also something odd about the ten who arrived. They all seemed unusually impassive by nature. Even before the psychotropic drugs were administered, a number of experiments involving stress situations showed almost no change in their heart rates.

One of those experiments involved killing animals. The animals were laboratory guinea pigs that would have soon been dispatched in any case. The subjects, however, were told that they were tame and that the children on the base often played with them. None of the subjects showed the slightest reluctance to kill the small creatures, nor measurable stress at having done so.

Grayson didn't like it. Some should have protested. Some – especially because they were Army – should have asked to be told what objective it served.

Grayson asked Sergeant Kristoff for the full service records of this new group of volunteers. The sergeant stalled him; Grayson found them himself. He was surprised to find that several were not Army at all and had never even served in the military. Their histories seemed sketchy; some had unexplained gaps. He assumed that these gaps had been special assignments that were of a sensitive nature. If so, however, they were wrong for this research. The whole point of it was to test these drugs on the ordinary infantry soldier.

Grayson had told Kristoff to put the test on hold until he could discuss it with Teal. He had left Langley to do a few days' work back at Bolling and to make that last visit to Belfair. He'd left two messages on Prentice Teal's machine. Either Teal didn't get them, or he chose not to call back. On Grayson's return at the end of the week, he learned that not only had the test gone forward, but the protocols of the research had been changed.

In his absence, the subjects had been given small dogs. The dogs had been obtained from another research lab. The subjects were told that they would save these dogs' lives if they took them as pets and companions. Each one chose a dog and gave it a name. The dogs would stay with them in their private quarters. When the project was finished they'd be given a choice. They could keep their pets, or, if that were not feasible, they could give them to a child at an orphanage in Norfolk. They were even shown photos of the orphaned boys and girls and encouraged to choose the one whose life they would brighten by giving the child a pet.

But on the morning of the day when Grayson returned, the subjects had been told that their pets were 'a problem.' They were told that they could keep them and play with them through lunch but after that they were told to kill them. Only two of the ten subjects questioned the order and their questions concerned only method.

Grayson had arrived just in time.

'Who authorized this change?' he asked Sergeant Kristoff.

'Dr. Zales called it in, sir. It was after you left.'

'And you just went ahead without checking with me?'

'Sir, she said Mr. Teal had approved it.'

'Um ... what do you mean, *she*? Dr. Zales is not a *she*.'

'Dr. Leatrice Zales, sir. She ordered it.'

Grayson was outraged. 'She told you she's a doctor? That woman is not even a nurse.'

'I ... did not get that impression from her, sir.'

'What else did she say to you, Sergeant?'

'She said that she and Mr. Teal were discussing the design. They agreed that killing rodents was like stepping on bugs. She said that it didn't evoke a response.'

'It did with me. I'm shutting you down.'

'Sir, I'm not sure you have the authority ...'

'You're dismissed, Sergeant Kristoff. I'll take it from here.'

Grayson stayed until the volunteers had vacated the facility. He sat down to make several calls. The first and the angriest was to Norman Zales. Grayson now thought he knew why Zales had invited him to spend that day up at Belfair. Zales had hoped to keep him from Langley long enough for the experiment with the dogs to be completed.

Zales, however, did not come to the phone. A guard said that Zales was 'not available right now, but his wife is here if you want.'

Grayson did 'want.' He said, 'Put her on.'

He told Leatrice what he'd done and why and demanded to know what she thought she was doing. He did not even try to be polite. All he got from Zales's wife was her normal icy silence and a few strangled breaths that sounded like rage. He berated her until he heard a click in his ear. Leatrice had broken the connection.

Grayson thought about calling General Hoyt but decided that he'd rather hear from Prentice Teal first. He punched out the number of Prentice Teal's apartment, but Teal wasn't answering. Grayson said the same things to Teal's machine.

A call soon came in, but it wasn't from Teal. The laboratory that had supplied the dogs was calling to arrange their return. Grayson learned that the dogs had been scheduled to be blinded by a gas that the lab was then testing. Grayson told the caller he'd get back to him. Grayson next tried to find the name of the orphanage in order to donate the dogs as promised. There was no such orphanage. The photographs were all children of base personnel that the monitors had borrowed from the base day care center.

Grayson then found an animal shelter in Norfolk that

promised that most of the dogs would find homes. He borrowed a van and delivered them himself, all but one Pekingese that could not be found. He supposed that some married soldier had grabbed it for his kids before the lab could reclaim it.

On the matter of Leatrice Zales's interference, he would have that out with Teal when he saw him. On the matter of the study that he had aborted, one of two things had happened. The drugs, as before, sapped all critical judgment or else these subjects were near-psychopaths to begin with. Either way, it was exactly what the general didn't want.

Grayson had decided that he'd seen enough. He would fly back to Bolling, begin writing his report, wash his hands of both projects as quickly as he could.

He would not, however, walk away from Veronica. More than ever, he wanted her out of there.

Chapter Twelve

In truth, Zales had not tried to keep him from Langley. On the contrary, Zales had simply needed to be sure that Grayson would not show up at Belfair on that Friday. Zales had planned to be elsewhere himself.

If Grayson had dropped in, he would have seen that Zales was gone, but that would not have been the problem. Grayson also might have noticed that Rachel was missing. He would have asked questions. He might have ruined the surprise. Zales had created an entirely new Rachel, and she was about to get her first field test.

The field test, to be conducted in nearby Baltimore, was designed to determine how well Rachel would function in an unsupervised situation. Rachel Carey was to see the world outside Belfair for the first time in almost two years. It was to be a simple outing in the gentlest part of town. Four or five pleasant hours on an autumn afternoon.

'You mean ... by myself? No one with me?' Rachel had gasped.

'Only if you feel ready. Are you ready?' Zales had asked her.

'Oh, I am. And I'd love to. Oh, thank you so much.'

She was so excited that she couldn't sit still. She was flouncing about the room like a schoolgirl. The psychiatrist was suddenly concerned. Her dosage permitted enthusiasm, surely, but perhaps not this much animation. Nor had Rachel ever before made any expression of gratitude. Gently, he eased her back into her chair. He looked long and deeply into her eyes.

'I am … talking to Rachel, the new Rachel, am I not?'

'Absolutely,' she said, beaming. 'Oh, this is so great.'

'But this outing, understand, must be strictly for you. Don't bring any of your alters; they can wait for you here. Do you think you can make me that promise?'

'Of course, I can,' she said. 'And I will. I do things without them all the time now.'

Her eyes showed no guile, they were wide and unblinking. Zales decided that he could believe her. 'But what fun is an outing if you can't do some shopping?' He winked at her as he reached into his pocket. He produced an American Express card. 'This card belongs to Leatrice. I'm letting you use it. Feel free to buy whatever you please. The shopgirls will give you whatever help you need, but be sure to buy things that only Rachel would wear. Ask yourself, if in doubt, what things might please your mother. She has such impeccable taste, don't you think?'

Zales watched her eyes as he spoke of her mother. He saw no reaction. If anything, they had softened. Now they moistened at the thought of being able to buy clothing. She took the card and brought it to her lips. She kissed it and said, 'This is so really neat.'

'And here,' he reached into his pocket again, 'is a telephone calling card. On it I've written my number. When you're ready to come back, just call, I'll come get you.' The card was strictly to add to the illusion that she would be allowed to roam freely. In fact, she would be watched every step of the way.

'After shopping,' he suggested, 'pick a place to have lunch. See if real restaurant food is as good as you remember it. After that, take a walk, perhaps down toward the harbor. Fill your lungs with the smell of that healthy salt air. Sit on a bench and feel the sun on your face.'

That face was beaming, aglow with excitement. He had named all the things that she'd wanted most to do. All he asked was that she stay within an area he'd suggested, a strip along Baltimore's restored Inner Harbor.

'The people there,' he told her, 'are as nice as they can be. Are you able to promise that you'll be just as nice?'

'Can I buy some new shoes? I only have flats.'

'Buy whatever you wish. But first promise.'

'You'll be proud of me, Dr. Zales. Wait and see.'

Leatrice had disapproved of this field test and especially of its ultimate purpose. She felt that the risks far outweighed any benefit. She acknowledged that the compound had indeed worked wonders. But that was at Belfair, an unthreatening environment, not out on the streets of a city. In the end, however, she had to agree that that was the point of a field test. She asked only that Rachel bring a booster dose with her, to be taken should she feel herself losing control. Leatrice would prepare it and would give it to Rachel. She would feel so much better if she did so.

Rachel did go shopping on Holliday Street. Zales himself followed her at a distance, two orderlies kept watch from other vantage points. At first she did no more than look in store windows but she seemed to find delight in nearly every display. At one, she had her first real encounter in years with a person who was neither a patient nor staff. Another young woman had paused at the window of a dress shop that specialized in petites. The woman, midtwenties, was about Rachel's age. She was close to Rachel in size as well, although not so thin or so pale. The woman remarked, apparently favorably, about an outfit on one of the mannequins. Rachel seemed startled when the woman addressed her, but she did not freeze up or back away. She even returned the woman's smile.

The woman soon glanced at her watch and moved on, wishing Rachel a pleasant day. Rachel watched her go … a bit sadly, perhaps … as if she might have made a friend if only the woman had stayed with her longer. But she didn't call after her, she didn't pursue her. Instead, she entered the shop.

She looked at several outfits and had difficulty choosing, but this was considered entirely normal. In the end she opted for the outfit on the mannequin. This was somewhat surprising because the colors were bright and the skirt ended well above the knee. Rachel's taste had always leaned toward denims and plaids. But the woman she'd encountered had influenced her choice and the shopgirl offered further encouragement. The jacket was red, the short skirt was gold. The blouse was gold silk and it opened to the breast bone. It seemed rather daring for someone like Rachel who had always kept her body well covered in the past. Her mother, however, would very much approve.

When it came time to select the accessories she was seen to be grinning and chatting with the shopgirl as she tried several earrings with the aid of a mirror. She emerged a while later with a shopping bag in hand. The shopgirl stepped out on the sidewalk with her and seemed to be pointing toward a shoe store farther down. Rachel thanked the shopgirl, then turned and strolled on. She went into the shoe store where again she was helped to buy shoes that matched her outfit. She purchased two pairs; one of these had spiked heels. Zales had peeked through the window as she tried them on. He was somewhat surprised that she could wear them without effort after years of wearing nothing but slippers and flats; on the other hand it had always surprised him that any woman could walk in those things. Rachel left the shoe store and continued on her way, walking in the direction of the waterfront.

Once there, she paused at a busy seafood restaurant. She entered. This, too, was somewhat curious, because Rachel was not fond of fish. On the other hand, most of the fish that she was used to came steamed or poached and barely seasoned – few of the staff were very fond of it either. Rachel, in any case, studied the menu. So many items, so many dishes, for a woman unaccustomed to choices. But the menu didn't seem to intimidate her. She smiled at the waitress as she ordered. Dr. Zales decided to risk entering the restaurant to see what dish she had chosen. He would have been concerned if she had ordered a steak. One of her alters, the worst one, liked steak and would only eat it blood rare. He would have known in that instant that she was no longer Rachel. But all she had ordered was a large Caesar salad with strips of grilled chicken on top. He backed out unseen and waited while she finished it.

She paid her check with Leatrice's credit card, then opted for a leisurely walk along the harbor. She stopped at a place where seagulls had gathered and began to feed them with pieces of a roll that she had brought with her from the restaurant. A little girl and her father had stopped to watch the birds. Rachel offered half of her roll to the girl, first asking the father's permission. That she spoke to a man was remarkable in itself. The father then held the little girl aloft so that the hovering gulls could take pieces from her hand. Although the others watching Rachel could scarcely believe it, this was precisely what Zales had hoped for. Rachel showed no sign of fear for the child. She showed no loathing of a man who had his hands on her legs and whose lips were mere inches from the child's trusting face.

This part of the field test seemed a total success. But the girl and her father had been a chance encounter. And the girl had neither squirmed nor resisted when her father took her up in his arms. There was no telling what Rachel might have done if she had. A better indicator of Rachel's stability would come with the second phase of the test. Better and less risky because no children were involved. Next would come a series of staged confrontations that he had devised for her. In all, there were to be three.

The first would be an act of ordinary rudeness, a jostling without an apology. It would be the sort of thing that happened all the time and that most people learn to take in stride. Shortly afterward, the same thing would happen again but the jostler, this time, would pause to berate her. An angry response from Rachel would be perfectly acceptable as long as she then turned away and moved on or allowed the jostler to do so. After that, she would be left to stew for awhile. Her resentment would be given time to build, or more encouragingly, time to melt away. After that, a third man would attempt to pick her up.

The role-player chosen for the attempted seduction was an

90

orderly new to the hospital. He would seem to be a business-man about twice her age and he would have the smell of alcohol on his breath. He would wear a wedding ring on his finger, a sign that he was a betrayer of women. If she tried to ignore him, he would persist. He would do so in a lewd and leering manner. Zales had predicted that at worst she would rebuke him. But her observers would be standing nearby at the ready in case she should respond in an extravagant way.

They followed as she wandered over toward Light Street and its cluster of harborside shops and hotels. She paused at the entrance to the Hyatt Hotel. She had shown no particular intention of entering but then a family of four arrived by taxi. Another unplanned encounter ensued. The children, worse luck, were again little girls and the father seemed angry at one of them. The girls were aged perhaps eight and ten, and the older one must have been misbehaving because the father had reached to put a hand on her shoulder and he gave it a squeeze that had the look of a warning. The mother seemed about to interfere but the father spoke to her sharply. She drew back. Grim-faced, they entered the lobby. Rachel followed.

This was not good, thought Zales. A second unplanned encounter at this stage might invalidate the remainder of the test. He and an observer moved closer to the entrance where they might intervene if need be. But the father, apparently, had had a change of heart. Zales saw through the glass that they had stopped near the check-in. The father had lowered himself to one knee and was speaking softly to both of the girls. Whatever he was saying was making them giggle.

Rachel had seen this. She was keeping her distance. She had stopped at a rack on one side of the lobby and was pretending to browse through a selection of brochures. At length, the young family entered the elevator. The mother was joking with the father by then. Zales saw Rachel take a shuddering breath, perhaps in relief that it had ended well. He saw her reach into her purse for something. He assumed it was the booster that Leatrice had given her. But she changed her mind and snapped the purse shut. Zales was glad that she didn't feel the need for it yet. The first planned confrontation was still an hour away. That would give her state of mind time to settle.

Rachel had started to leave the hotel but then he saw her pause at a sign that pointed the way to the rest rooms. She turned down a corridor. Zales decided to follow. He needed to be sure that there was no other exit. There was none that he and the observer could see, only conference rooms and the rest rooms. They waited for her to reappear. She did not.

She was last seen at three in the afternoon. By midnight, she had murdered two men on a street half a mile away.

Chapter Thirteen

Dr. Zales had spent hours searching for Rachel. At length he returned to his office at Belfair to await some word from those still out looking. He jumped when the phone rang. He heard Rachel's voice. She had called, at last, with the card he had given her.

Her voice seemed entirely calm, untroubled. He asked where she was, whether she was all right, and scolded her for worrying him so. Rachel asked if she might speak to Leatrice. He told her that Leatrice was out trying to find her. Rachel seemed disappointed but then he thought he heard a smile. She asked that he come get her and to please come alone. She named a street intersection where she would be waiting. She said that she had something to show him.

She was waiting in shadows when he got to that corner. As he slowed to a crawl she stepped out of the darkness and into the glow of his headlights. She told him, using gestures, that he'd best dim the lights. He saw that she was wearing the new outfit she had purchased, and that it was mottled with stains. He saw to his horror that she had been beaten. Her lip was cut and had thickened grotesquely. Her left eye was swollen – almost shut – and blood still dripped from one ear. He saw blood on her hands and forearms as well.

'I think it will clean. Don't you think it will clean?' she asked as she opened the door and got in. She was talking about the stains on her clothing.

'But who ... what happened? Who did this to you?'

'Don't worry,' she told him. 'They've already been punished. Turn right at the next street. I'll show you.'

She was sure of the two. They would be where she had left them. There might have been others, but she didn't think so. She couldn't be certain where else she had gone after changing her clothing in that rest room. She could not recall how she got out of the hotel.

But if she was in pain, she gave no sign of feeling it. Her only concern was that her clothes might be ruined and that one of her earrings was missing. All in all, however, she seemed pleased with herself and could not understand why he seemed so upset. She had, after all, confronted her demons and that was the first step toward healing. He'd said so.

'Well ... yes, but whose demons? Which demons?'

'Mine, of course.'

'You say mine. But which mine? Am I talking to Rachel?'

'Oh, yes. This is Rachel. Can't you tell by my smile?'

It wasn't a smile. It was more of a sneer. She was certainly no longer the sweet and grateful creature whom he'd briefed at the start of the day. He saw that her eyes had an odd inner shine that he'd noticed in one of the others, named Emma.

'Yes, but was it Rachel who ... *confronted* these men?'

She squinted her good eye as if trying to remember.

He asked, 'What you're telling me you did to those men ... it seems more the sort of thing that Emma might have done.'

'I can tell you who should have. It's Teresa who should have.'

Teresa, thought Zales. She's the meek one, the timid one. Teresa would never have done this. 'I'll ask you again. I expect the truth. Am I speaking to Rachel or Emma?'

The shine in her eyes seemed to flicker, then fade. 'I'm not Emma,' she said quietly. 'Emma wouldn't have called you. Emma would be looking for more men to punish.'

Zales had contacted Leatrice by means of his car phone. She was waiting at the hospital when he brought Rachel back. She was gentle with Rachel. She said she'd attend to her. She, too, seemed dismayed at the sight of Rachel's clothing although not because the outfit had been ruined.

'You gave her … a credit card? What credit card was that?'

'One of yours, I'm afraid. I know. You needn't say it.'

'You gave her my credit card. Oh, that wasn't wise.'

'I thought that my own card might have raised eyebrows. What if the shopgirl or the waitress knew my books or had seen me on one of the talk shows?'

'There is cash, you see. She ought to have had cash. You were not wise at all in this instance, my dear.'

Leatrice was cool. She was seldom less than cool. Leatrice could discuss a multiple murder in the same tone of voice that one would expect if she noted that a cantaloupe in the market wasn't fresh. Even so, he would have thought that she'd have more on her mind than the use of a damned credit card. And as if Rachel's butchery were not enough for one day, he had learned that Major Grayson had aborted a test that Leatrice had designed for Project Richard. She had seemed more put out by that news, in point of fact, than by hearing what Rachel had done. But at least that kept Grayson in Virginia, not here. They'd have time to try to clean up this mess.

Zales knew, nonetheless, that Leatrice was right. He had made a serious misjudgment. And yet he'd been so sure that it was the new Rachel whom he'd set loose in Baltimore that afternoon. A gentler Rachel who fed birds and who played with children. A young woman who could chat with shopkeepers and waitresses. One who could see a man behaving harshly toward his daughter and do no more than sigh and walk on. She had seemed to be all that her mother had prayed for.

He had miscalculated, but what to do now? The episode certainly would have to be contained but the question was whether to tell Prentice Teal. If Teal learned that Rachel, of all people, was at large, he was bound to be considerably upset.

But he needn't know about it. Given time, for that matter, even Rachel needn't know. Given time, he could erase these events from her memory or so confuse them as to make them seem like fantasies. His hope had been to erase Rachel herself and replace her with a girl more like Teresa. Something had gone wrong. He didn't know what. Perhaps he had created some sort of a vacuum that Emma was able to step in and fill.

Zales was almost tempted to erase her altogether. An accident – an overdose perhaps – would be an act of mercy. It would put an end to the pain she had suffered, to say nothing of the pain she had caused. Her mother, however, might not share in that view; she would probably raise all sorts of hell. But perhaps General Hoyt would see it as a blessing. Her father, surely, would not be displeased if his daughter were no longer a problem. None of them would need to know what she had done.

The police, however, might. And that was the rub. The risk, he realized, in not telling Teal was that he might end up needing Teal's protection. Aside from the matter of that damned credit card, he could not be sure that she'd called no one else. Or punished no one else for that matter.

There was no way around it. Teal would have to be informed. Teal, unlike Grayson, would understand what was at stake here. He would not throw away all that had been achieved just because of a single mischance.

Chapter Fourteen

Prentice Teal was not pleased to hear Norman Zales's voice at four o'clock in the morning. He had only just drifted off to sleep in the Washington apartment that Los Alamos had provided. He was barely sober after being at a party given by a DOD contractor.

Contractors made a practice of entertaining those who might tip them as to whatever new technology was coming. Teal would sometimes give them a crumb or two in return for their generous hospitality. A young, quite attractive systems coder from that firm – no doubt with her employer's encouragement – had asked Teal to join her for a nightcap. The young coder was now snoring softly at his side.

'There's a problem with one of our patients,' Zales told him.

'Well, you see … that's why they're your patients,' yawned Teal. 'Tell you what … bounce this one off Grayson, for a change.'

'You won't want that *snoop* near this one,' hissed Zales. 'You'll want to come yourself and at once.'

The Grayson suggestion wasn't meant to be serious, and the sneered 'that *snoop*' seemed meant to infer that this problem should be kept from the General as well. Teal watched the rise and fall of the young coder's breasts. He was feeling a rise of his own.

'I'm lying here looking at my breakfast,' said Teal. 'You're sure this can't wait until morning?'

'No, it can't,' said Zales, his voice emphatic, almost shrill. 'The problem will be worse in the daylight.'

Teal muttered a heartfelt profanity. 'One hour, Doctor. You be waiting out front.'

Teal replaced the phone quietly and eased out of bed. He put on the clothes that had been strewn on the floor and added a hat and a raincoat. The hat was Irish tweed with a floppy brim that put half of his face in shadow. The choice of the hat was deliberate. Dressing and leaving took only five minutes. The drive to Belfair took fifty minutes more. The car he used was a five-year-old Plymouth, beige in color, few luxury amenities. Its redeeming virtue was that it didn't stand out and had plates that were virtually untraceable.

It was well before dawn when Teal drew near the gate, which had cameras mounted on each post. Teal had no intention of nearing those cameras. He turned his wheels into the curb cut, backed up, and flashed his high beams through the gate. The main house looked even larger at night, when it seemed to blend into the blackness around it.

He noticed that the third and fourth floors were dark. He had expected to see some activity there, some sign of the problem that had Zales so upset. Teal guessed that a patient had either escaped or had strung herself up in a bathroom. That patient would be the daughter of either Winston or Camal or perhaps Camal's former wife. He could not think who else would concern him so much.

His eye was caught by a movement on the grounds. Two guards dressed in hospital whites were approaching, with hands slipped under their frocks as if to show that they were carrying pistols. One of them held that menacing pose as the other unhooked a radio from his belt and used it to alert Dr. Zales. Teal doubted that either was actually armed with more than a Taser or Chemical Mace. Zales had told him that his guards did not need lethal weapons because they'd been trained in 'compassionate restraint.' It had taken some effort not to laugh in his face. Never mind that they couldn't carry guns if they wanted to – most of the orderlies and guards had been convicts.

Leatrice had done the research for one of Zales's early books by interviewing violent offenders in prison. Zales had gone there as a visiting counselor as well. They helped ten or so get early paroles by offering to hire them as unarmed guards and promising to continue their counseling. To keep their baser instincts in check, he'd been lacing their meals with libido depressants, especially that new Russian drug. Too many women lying around in pajamas, some of whom were still in their teens. They probably knew it but they didn't complain – Zales paid them fairly well and they did as they were told. They would soon be back in prison if they didn't.

Teal flashed his high beams on and off a few times until he saw the main door open. Zales stepped out quickly and closed it behind him, the headlights reflecting off his glasses. Zales took several breaths as if to settle his nerves. Teal could see the exhaust in the chill autumn air. One guard approached him, cocked his head toward Teal as if asking if he would be needed. Teal was about to tap his horn, saying no, when Zales waved the guard off himself. He was telling the guard, a bit frantically, thought Teal, that he wanted him back in the house. He then gave him a push in that direction.

Teal recognized that guard – Duane something or other. He was one of Zales's earliest parolees. Duane had once raped and murdered a woman acquaintance in a particularly innovative fashion. They were relaxing in a hot tub when Duane felt an urge. He seized her and entered her from behind while holding her head beneath the water. He described for Zales the transcendent thrill of injecting life in one end of the woman while it bubbled out through the other.

Belfair thought Teal, was no Sunnybrook Farm.

But Duane, he realized, should not have been at Belfair. Duane and a handful of Zales's other guards were supposed to be down in Virginia taking part in a Richard experiment. Teal assumed that something must have gone wrong there, and yet Zales said the problem was a patient.

He parked the Plymouth several yards up from the gate and across the street from the grounds. He pulled his hat farther down over his eyes, then got out and waited for Zales to walk down. The psychiatrist soon emerged through a narrow side gate that allowed the main gate to stay closed. A large man, he had to squeeze to get through. He paused before proceeding to look up and down the street. Zales's manner, Teal noted, was more furtive than his own. Zales gestured toward a park across the road that had been part of the estate before the road had been put in. Teal followed Zales's lead and joined him on a footpath that led to a row of stone benches at the shoreline. Zales stopped at a bench and sat heavily.

'There's a problem with Richard, I take it,' said Teal.

'Project Richard? That … too,' he said absently.

'Did I just see Duane?'

'Never mind that now. There's a much more immediate concern.'

Teal listened in silence and near disbelief as Zales recounted the series of events that had made this meeting a necessity.

'Where is Rachel now?' asked the project director, his expression one of disgust.

'She's with Leatrice. In the Quiet Room. Sedated.'

'And you're sure this really happened? It's not just in her mind?'

'I saw the two men, Mr. Teal. She showed me.'

It had been one in the morning when Zales drove her back there. Like Teal, he had hoped that she'd imagined it. The place was, by day, an industrial area. By night it was left to street-corner prostitutes and indifferently patrolled by the Baltimore police. At that hour no women stood offering their wares, no more lonely men cruised past in their cars in search of twenty-dollar oral sex. The two who had died there were still where she left them.

The first one, a man of fifty or so, looked as though he could have been napping in his car. He sat hunched behind the wheel, his body nearly upright. He seemed to be support-ing his chin with his hands. The car was a dirty and dented old Ford. Its trunk was fastened down with wire, the result of some earlier mishap. He had parked it near a loading dock, away from the street lights, hoping for a measure of privacy.

Zales had risked the use of a penlight. The man wore a baseball cap, knocked slightly askew. His eyes were partly open, not blinking. Blood, now almost dried, had oozed between his fingers. The man had not been supporting his chin after all – he had died trying to hold his throat together. Rachel had slashed it halfway to his spine. Zales shivered. He flicked off the light. He looked back at Rachel, who had waited in his car. She was busy rubbing spittle on one of her stains.

'You're a bit farther down,' she had told him.

'I'm ... what?'

'The other one, I mean. He's about two blocks down.'

She pointed him toward a darkened convenience store. The second man, more discreet than the first, had parked his car behind it. This one drove a late-model Mercedes and was dressed in a dark suit and tie. The car's engine, he heard, was still idling. Zales was surprised that a man of some affluence would want the sort of women who were reduced to working streets. But then Rachel must have seemed the cream of the crop, less obviously diseased or drug-addicted than the rest. No wig, no hot pants, no makeup, well scrubbed: She must have looked like a college girl out to earn some extra cash.

This one had not died so quietly. His body, a large one, was jammed between the bucket seats. It looked as if he'd been in the rear seat with Rachel and had tried to escape Rachel's knife – Rachel's or Emma's – whomever. His face, mouth agape, was turned in Zales's direction.

Zales used his penlight again. Something about the man seemed vaguely familiar. He was overweight, tanned, and wore horn-rimmed glasses; his hair was steel gray and worn long. But Zales felt sure he'd never seen him before and tried to push the thought from his mind. The beam of his light washed across the dead man's hand. It still formed a fist. His knuckles seemed swollen. Zales noticed a glint of gold between his fingers and assumed that it came from a ring. It was this one, apparently, who had managed to punch her.

The beam continued across the man's back. There were tufts of fabric all across the back and shoulders where a knife had been plunged many times. Reluctantly, Zales reached into his bag and extracted a pair of plastic gloves. He stepped from his own car to shut off the man's motor. His intent was to make the parked Mercedes less noticeable in case the police should come by. It was good that he had done so, because there in the back seat he spotted the shopping bag that Rachel had been carrying when he and the observers had last seen her. It contained the clothing she'd put on that morning and the receipts for the purchases she'd made. The name of the shop was printed on the bag. The police would have gotten her description from the shop girl. Worse, they would have gotten the credit card receipts. Leatrice was right. He'd been a damned fool. They would have been at his gate by midmorning.

'I don't need that stuff,' Rachel whispered at his shoulder.

Zales jumped at her voice. He hadn't heard her leave the car.

'But look for my earring. I want my new earring.'

Rachel leaned past him. She saw the man's hand, the one that had ripped it from her ear. She saw the same glint that Zales had noticed. Zales watched as Rachel picked up the man's hand and brought her face down to meet it. She was acting as if she was going to kiss it, but Zales realized with a start what she was actually doing. She was using her teeth to pry loose his thumb. The glint from his fist was indeed the lost earring.

She licked it clean and tried to put it back on, but she couldn't; the clasp had been lost. The fact that her ear lobe was ripped and bleeding didn't seem to bother her at all. Did she not feel pain? Could her mind so protect her? And how could she care about a damned earring and yet give no thought to the evidence contained in that bag? She had seemed so deliberate in all else that she did. It was then, as his mind formed the phrase 'so deliberate,' that her words came back to echo in his brain.

'You're a bit farther down,' is what she had said.

Zales stared at the dead man. Horn-rimmed glasses, gray

hair worn long, dark suit and tie, and driving a car much like his own. At a distance, or in darkness, that man could have been his twin. It was he, Norman Zales, whom Rachel thought she had punished. At least that's who it was in her mind.

Taking care to stay calm, he returned to his own car and opened his medical bag once more. He told Rachel that he wanted to give her an injection.

'Of what? No drool juice. You're not giving me drool juice.'

'No, no,' he assured her. 'It's not Thorazine. It's only some Benadryl to bring down that swelling. Why let anyone see that he was able to hurt you?'

She raised her fingers to her swollen cheek. It was as if she was only just discovering the injury. She thought for a moment, then nodded with a sigh. She turned her back toward him and bared her left shoulder.

Zales hadn't quite lied to her. He would have used Thorazine if he'd had some in his bag but the Demerol would be almost as good. He didn't bother to swab. He plunged a dosage of more than 400 milligrams into her soft muscle tissue. The dosage was three times what would have been sufficient. Within seconds she was purring like a kitten, half smiling.

If she had resisted he would have thrown himself at her and given the injection by force. Only then would he have searched her for the knife.

Chapter Fifteen

Teal understood why this could not have waited for daylight. That convenience store would likely open at six. Those bodies would soon be discovered.

'You're saying you even gave her a booster?'

The question jarred Zales back to the present. He moved to make room on the stone bench for Teal, but Teal did not wish to sit.

'Leatrice did. Rachel carried it with her. It should have calmed her in minutes.'

'Or numbed her, maybe. You say she couldn't feel pain?'

'One of her must have. It's not a narcotic. Which one of her felt it, I don't know yet. You see, with multiples, we often find …'

Teal raised a hand. 'Doc … don't even start. What about the knife? Did she have it?'

'She thinks she threw it away. She's not sure. Nor could she recall where she got it.'

'How about prints? Did you wipe those cars?'

'I wore gloves,' Zales answered. 'I left none of mine. As for Rachel, her records have been sealed by the courts. The police would have to find her to match them.'

Teal drew a weary breath. 'And you're sure you weren't seen.'

'It was late. No pedestrians, no traffic.'

Teal folded his arms. 'Well? Why did she do it? Was she able to give you a reason?'

'Not to me ... but Leatrice ... Leatrice thinks ... that she was probably avenging Teresa.'

Teal looked at him blankly. 'Teresa?'

'She's one of her alters. But more accurately, I think, it was probably Emma who did the actual ... avenging.'

Teal's expression became pained. 'And ... Emma ... that's the one who's a lesbian, right?'

'Well ... yes. But the role she was playing ...'

Teal raised both his hands to stop him; Zales was about to explain why a dyke would play a hooker and Teal could not have cared less.

'Teresa's a new one. Who is Teresa?'

'She's not new ... she's simply less assertive than Emma. You see ...'

'Dr. Zales ... in one sentence ... who the fuck is Teresa?'

Zales winced at the vulgarity, then looked at the sky. In a patient voice, he explained.

'As a child, Teresa was raped by two uncles. Not a one-time event. It went on for several years. The experience later turned her to drugs. Her need for drugs led to street prostitution. Nice young lady, however. Very sweet.'

Teal closed one eye. He waited.

'But then, as a prostitute, there were more men like those uncles and they were continuing to use her, you see.'

'Men like those two tonight.'

'Well ... the first one at least.'

Teal shook his head. He gritted his teeth. 'Except ... the thing is ... there is no Teresa. There were no two uncles, either. Am I right?'

'But you see, that's irrelevant. She believes that there were.'

'Um ... who does? Which one are we talking about?'

'They all do, I think. They can't talk to each other but they do keep a diary. As I say, however, I'd be surprised if Rachel did this. Up to now she's shown no great interest in Teresa. Emma's more capable but I can't think why Emma would care about avenging Teresa. Emma doesn't even like her. She thinks she's a weakling. She thinks that Teresa is ...'

105

Zales stopped when he saw Teal put his fingers to his temples. One hand came away and made circles in the air.

'You're ... talking as if you believe all this shit.'

Zales's jaw tightened. He answered, 'To them it's quite real. What they think is real *is* their reality.'

Teal closed both his eyes. The hand stayed aloft. He reversed its circle as if to suggest that they try a new avenue of discussion.

'Rachel's father,' he said quietly. 'Her congressman father. You do understand his importance to me.'

'I understand perfectly well.'

'And you do recall my specific instruction that his daughter was not to be a part of this project.'

'Which project? Chameleon? She isn't. You didn't want her to be one of the six but that doesn't mean she shouldn't have been treated. I've been working with her, reintegrating her, and of late she's responded very nicely.'

'Until ...'

'Until her field test. I don't know what went wrong. At the start, and throughout, you wouldn't have known her. By blending Teresa's superego into Rachel's, I'd created a new, a sweet-natured Rachel who ...'

'Who went out and sliced up a couple of johns.'

'Now you're going to complain that I shouldn't have tested her. But she was doing so well; even General Hoyt thought so. You can ask him. He thought it was actually Rachel. And her mother's been insisting that we let her go home to celebrate Thanksgiving with the family. She threatened to remove her if I didn't agree. I told her that I would consider a furlough if her daughter could show that she was stable.'

Teal blinked. He stared. He had known that Martha had asked. He had sent a letter to General Hoyt recommending very strongly against it.

'Does Carey know about this Thanksgiving visit?'

'Mrs. Carey ... said that she hoped to change his attitude toward Rachel. She wanted it to be a surprise.'

A *surprise*, thought Teal. He wanted to laugh. There were

106

two men tonight who'd been very much surprised. He reminded the psychiatrist of the last such surprise, when Rachel showed up at her older brother's wedding.

'That was three years ago,' Zales answered dismissively. 'Well before she came under my care.'

Teal settled for a smile and a shaking of his head. It was the 'care' of a half-dozen so-called therapists that had created the monster now locked in Zales's basement. Rachel had been under the care of her fourth or fifth therapist when she stood on that wedding's receiving line – just as dressed up and pretty as she knew how to be – handing envelopes to each guest who passed her. The envelopes contained a detailed description of a series of satanic-cult rituals in which babies were sacrificed and their hearts and livers eaten. It said her father and brother were high priests of the cult. She herself had been forced to bear several of the babies, impregnated by both her father and brother – dressed in robes – while her mother stood over them chanting.

The letter said that her brother's new bride had been chosen by none other than Satan himself. Satan had determined, according to Rachel, that the bride was uncommonly fertile. She was likely to bear twins, even triplets. She'd be chained to a bed for all her child-bearing years and impregnated on a regular basis by various members of the cult. At least one of those members, her letter revealed, was a current Supreme Court justice. The twins and triplets that she would bear in abundance would be grist for additional sacrifices.

Rachel had recovered the memory of these rituals with the aid of drugs and hypnosis. The therapist who had taken her down that road had been long convinced that such rituals existed and that memories elicited in this way must be real. They fit in with the therapist's personal belief in a worldwide satanic-cult network. How else to explain all the evil in the world? The therapist told Rachel that confronting her abusers was essential if she hoped to truly heal.

Rachel didn't need much persuading because she'd confronted her abuser before. Her first therapist – to whom she had

107

gone with a complaint no more serious than that no one seemed to like her – had announced that Rachel was almost surely a victim of sexual abuse in her childhood. Under hypnosis, Rachel soon remembered. Her father had forced her to perform oral sex starting at the age of four months. The evidence was all there, clear as a bell, for those not too dumb or anti-female to see it. One compelling piece of evidence was that she didn't like bananas and would sicken at the thought of eating yogurt. What else but a penis could bananas represent? What else but semen could yogurt represent? Another was the fact that she remembered fainting on the occasion of her first communion. What more proof could one need? Here was a man – one in robes, by the way – who was trying to make her take something in her mouth.

Either some of these therapists were crazier than Rachel or they knew a sweet scam when they saw one. At least two of them urged Rachel to threaten a lawsuit unless Carey confessed and apologized. But they probably realized that he'd do no such thing even if he happened to be guilty. A confession would end his political career, but so would a lawsuit, and therefore he'd pay. The therapists couldn't be charged with extortion because they never asked for money directly. What they would 'suggest' was intensive therapy that was likely to cost a small fortune. That last one, the satanic-conspiracy loon, was billing Carey for a minimum of five sessions a week whether Rachel showed up for them or not. Rachel, however, soon ruined a good thing by deciding to expose her father on her own. That was when she sat down to write her letter and ran off a few hundred copies.

It was General Hoyt, luckily, who first opened the envelope. He'd gone to grab a few puffs of his pipe out on the steps of the church. He opened the letter and read it. He rushed back inside and retrieved all the others including the stack she still had in her hand. He lifted her bodily from the receiving line and carried her, screaming, to a limousine at the curb. She was rushed to a private nuthouse, not Zales's, where, after several months of more hypnosis and drugs, Rachel's several personalities began to emerge. So now, after incest and satanic baby-eating, she had moved on to multiple personality disorder. Someone at the nuthouse had cut a deal with Zales, so Zales was called in to consult. Zales did his act for Carey and his wife. Rachel was soon committed to Belfair.

'Doctor,' Teal asked, 'who else knows about tonight?'

'Only Leatrice, I think,' Zales answered.

'Not the guards? Not Duane?'

'They know that we lost her, not what she did later. Some of them are still out looking for her.'

'What about Grayson? Would he know you'd planned this test?'

'Grayson? How could he?'

'That's what I'm asking you.'

'Can't you, by the way, do something about him? He shows up without calling, goes wherever he pleases, has long private talks with my third-floor Chameleons who are in a most delicate stage of their …'

'Doc, follow the bread crumbs. What could he know?'

'About Rachel? Nothing. She's not one of the six; he has no reason to go near her. I made sure, in addition, that he wouldn't be here yesterday. He does prowl around on the fourth floor, however. He reads their diaries and he has no right. Those patients are none of his business.'

'Doc …'

'But he seems to spend most of his time with Veronica. She's probably the prettiest of them all, you know. That should tell you something about Grayson, should it not? It speaks volumes about his professionalism.'

'I did not … drive up … to hear you bitch about Grayson.'

'Well, I wouldn't have to if you'd keep him in hand. I can't fathom why you tolerate his presence when he clearly has no grasp of what we're trying to achieve.'

'He grasps it all right. He just thinks you're a quack.'

'Then he's narrow and stupid. Get rid of him.'

'Let's … deal with one subject at a time, Dr. Zales.'

'I guess you're not aware of what happened down at

Langley. He dismissed that whole new group we were testing.'

Teal closed one eye. 'When was this?'

'Yesterday. Friday. He sent everyone packing, including my guards, but I don't think he knew who they were. What we're trying to accomplish is difficult enough without all this meddling. Nor will I tolerate his attitude toward Leatrice. He had the nerve to call her and berate her for making one little change in that study.'

'Don't start about Leatrice. What happened with that group?'

'The new compound was working. We are so very close. But that *boy* was unable to see that as well, and now we've lost more precious weeks. You say that Grayson's been some sort of instructor? I've given more lectures than he's probably attended. I've written more books than he probably has read. How dare he second-guess Leatrice and me. How dare he ...'

'I assure you, what he teaches, he's done, Dr. Zales. If you keep screwing up, you'll find out what that is.'

Zales blinked.

'Grayson's solved three problems this year alone. You don't want to be problem number four.'

Teal hadn't meant to say that. The words just came out. He had said it, he supposed, to get Zales to stop ranting and stick to the subject at hand. But he saw with satisfaction that Zales's eyes had glazed over, and he was seeing the young major in a very new light. Some sort of enforcer. One good enough to teach it. Except Grayson, in spite of once or twice when he lost it, was probably not a dangerous man. A dangerous man would not still be moping about killing some bitch who set him up.

Teal would ask the major why that group was dismissed and what had happened to make Zales so defensive about Leatrice. Maybe Grayson saw her turn into a bat and fly off to suck the blood of a villager. More troubling – if what Zales was saying was accurate – was that Grayson had interfered with that study. Grayson's job was simply to observe, nothing more. Teal would look into it, but it could wait.

110

He waved his finger and turned it toward the ground, bringing Norman Zales back to the present.

'Grayson thinks Project Chameleon is a crock. So do I, tonight more than ever.'

'You can say that after all we've accomplished?'

'Like what?'

'There's Shan Li, who speaks nearly fluent Chinese after only a few months of study. Another has learned both Hebrew and Arabic. You've seen what Veronica can do with a computer – she has mastered five different computer languages, including your Defense Department language, Cobol. She could probably hack into any system you could name. The other three subjects are equally gifted, with memories that are nearly photographic. Are you saying that you don't have a use for those talents?'

'We have lots of people who can do all those things.'

'None of whom, if captured, can become a different person at the flick of an internal switch.'

'All of whom, on the other hand, are more or less sane. We even let ours go home every night. While I think of it ... Veronica ... that's Winston's daughter, right?'

'Amanda is his daughter. Veronica is new.'

Teal grunted. 'Whatever. Deep-six that computer.'

'Take away her computer? Impossible. I can't. She might cease to exist if I took it.'

'She's a hacker, you said?'

'A bad choice of words. She's more of ... a hobbyist. An explorer.'

'Hacker, explorer, find her some other toy. You're teaching her a very bad habit.'

'Mr. Teal, just because you don't like computers ...'

'I don't like being argued with, either. Get rid of it.'

Teal was tired of even pretending to be interested in what tricks these creatures could do. Zales could see that. His feelings were hurt. He wet his lips before speaking.

'You wanted to know whether they'd kill. Well, now you have you answer. One did.'

Teal stared for a moment. 'Get on your feet, Doctor.'

'Get on my ...? What for?'

'Let's see if you're carrying a recorder.'

Teal searched him thoroughly, ignoring his protests. He checked the underside of the stone bench as well, mindful that the doctor had chosen that place. Taking Zales's penlight, he probed the shrubbery nearby.

'You wouldn't try to set me up, would you?' Teal murmured. 'You wouldn't try to suck me in as an accessory so that I'd have to bail you out of this mess.'

Teal checked one more bush as Zales stammered, tried to bluster. He searched until he was reasonably satisfied. He stood erect and turned to face the psychiatrist.

'No, of course you wouldn't. Because you don't want me mad at you. You won't like it very much if I get mad at you, Doctor.'

The psychiatrist demanded an apology. Teal ignored that as well. It was actually true that Teal had asked if they'd kill. But he'd asked it idly, nothing special in mind, an inquiry as to their limits. There had never been a question of so tasking Zales's multiples. That was where Project Richard came in, but only incidentally and only at the outset ... before they all saw its much greater potential. All except Grayson, who was not supposed to know. Why, therefore, did he cancel that study?

'In any case, Doctor, that was *not* what I wanted.' Teal smoothed Zales's coat and sat him down on the bench. 'Killing men for wanting blow jobs is even less what I wanted. That is hardly a practical use of these women.'

But Teal, as he spoke, saw something else in Zales. Perhaps it was the almost imperceptible shrug in response to what should have been an evident truth. Teal stared at him again.

'You intended this, didn't you?' he asked, very softly. 'You let her out knowing that she'd carve someone up if he tried to get into her pants.'

The psychiatrist was startled. 'That is utterly untrue.'

'If not you, then Leatrice. What was in that booster? Could Leatrice have slipped her some speed?'

'That's ridiculous.'

'It is? I know you slip speed to at least some of your patients. You do it whenever one's parents show up making noises like they want to take her home. A fast shot of meth and she's climbing the walls. Don't fucking tell me that's ridiculous.'

Zales tried to speak but no words would come. His eyes were staring through space. Teal guessed that Zales hadn't done it himself but was thinking that Leatrice might have after all. And now Zales was fidgeting. He could not look at Teal. Teal would have thought that a shrink, of all people, would have better control of his body language. It occurred to Teal, and not for the first time, that Zales was very much afraid of his wife.

'The question ...' said Zales. He had to pause to wet his lips. 'The question at hand is what to do now. This could possibly ... work to our advantage.'

'How so?'

'If her father should be less than fully cooperative ... this would make him ... think twice ... would it not?'

He was talking blackmail. Teal understood that. Zales's long-term concern was not the two murders or the need to cover them up. It was not even, really, his million-dollar grant that would soon be up for renewal. Aside from the royalties he might earn from Richard, Zales took in five times that amount every year from the families of his thirty or so patients. Each one of them paid twelve thousand a month to keep their daughters out of their lives ... except for Congressman Carey, of course, who had gotten a free ride in return for getting Zales his grant. What Zales cared about were the books he hoped to write and the lectures he would give on ... what does he call them? ... Reductive Mosaics. Whole new people created from several. It was what he'd tried to do with Carey's daughter.

Even there, it was not the money, but the fame. It was sweet revenge against all those psychiatrists who'd laughed him off the stage when he'd tried to present papers, and who'd written scathing reviews of his books. And Leatrice – to whom reality was even more of a stranger – had been talking in terms of a Nobel Prize for herself as well as for Zales. She thought Congressman Carey would sponsor them.

Not that Teal could ever allow that to happen. To go public or to even apply for a prize, Zales would have to produce all his records, and not just the records he'd let Grayson see. There was too much at stake to permit that to happen.

Teal's hopes had been modest when he first became involved, but now Richard's potential was beyond his wildest dreams. Rachel's father had seen it as well, but he knew that Zales's compounds would not have a prayer of ever getting an FDA approval. It would have to be made and distributed abroad, and that was where Winston and Camal came in. Those two realized that the money to be made from that compound could amount to billions of dollars. Two popular drug brands, Prozac and Xanax, already generated worldwide sales in excess of four billion by themselves. Richard's sales would dwarf them. Almost everyone would want it. In time, they'd more than want it; they'd need it.

Blackmail or not, Zales did have a point. How to turn tonight's disaster into an advantage had been the question in Teal's mind as well.

The problem with Carey … he was a crook but not a fool. Indeed, thought Teal, this might make him think twice. But the thing he was more likely to think twice about was letting Zales involve him in obstruction of justice. He might decide to cut his losses up front and call a press conference himself. He'd know that the public might not blame him for this. They might even pity him because it was true that Rachel wasn't his fault. Rachel, at her best, was a self-absorbed whiner, a sneak, and a liar from childhood. Shit happens, and so do bad kids.

'You'll say nothing to the congressman, or to Winston or Camal. Not you, not Leatrice, not a word.'

'Very well. Unless, of course …'

'There is no *unless*. Need I make this more clear? If you do, I will make a full report to General Hoyt. I will ask him to have Grayson finish it.'

114

Teal, this time, had said it on purpose and again it had an effect. He enjoyed seeing Zales's lower lip start to twitch, still not daring to ask what it meant.

'Well, what if ...' Zales struggled to get his thoughts back on track. 'What if the Baltimore police show up here?'

'More likely, they'll be looking for a hooker gone psycho. Have Leatrice call them from a public phone in town. Have her sound like a hooker, let them hear her chewing gum. Have her give them the description of a hooker in hot pants that she'd seen, all bloody, running near the scene and she thinks she saw a knife in her hand. Make the hooker a black one in a Tina Turner wig.'

'Why Leatrice?' asked Zales. 'Why not ... you, for example?'

'Because I wasn't here. I don't know about this. It's your mess; you clean it up.'

Teal had turned away to walk back to his car. He paused, closed one eye as another thought struck him. 'By the way, you said six. That's twice you said six.'

Zales didn't understand. 'Six of what?'

'You said Rachel's not one of the six under study. Last time I heard, there were five.'

Zales winced within himself. He hadn't realized the slip. 'We ... found one more. She has wonderful potential. We got her from a state institution.'

Teal almost kept going. He didn't much care. But Zales's reticence caused him to ask, 'How is she special?'

'Well, we think she's the real thing. A natural multiple.'

'Real as opposed to ...?'

'All the rest were the inventions of unstable women or creations of the therapists who treated them. This girl has never really undergone therapy. No history of emotional problems or abuse.'

'No recovered memories of incest with daddy? She's never been gang-raped by little green men?'

'In point of fact, she's a virgin,' Zales answered. 'She's surprisingly normal in every respect except that there seem to be several of her.'

115

Teal, again, saw something in his eyes. 'What aren't you telling me, Doctor?'

Zales took a breath. 'The thing is, she's twelve.'

'Twelve what? Are you saying there are twelve of this one?'

'No, Jennifer is twelve. Twelve years old.'

Chapter Sixteen

Jesus Christ, thought Teal. Now Zales is playing with children. Grayson could turn out to be dangerous after all. He'd want to wring Zales's neck if he knew. It was all the more reason to keep the major at a distance until this business with Rachel quieted down.

The new subject, Zales told him, had been abandoned at birth by a mother who believed her to be retarded. She wasn't.

A part of Jennifer's brain had not developed in the womb – possibly the result of fetal alcohol syndrome – but the rest of the brain eventually took over the functions of the part that had shown no activity. She spent her first five years in a state institution because her brain had taken that long to adapt. 'She's a pretty, if somber, little thing,' said Zales. 'She'd have long since been adopted were it not for her problem. She did, however, go to live in foster homes starting at about age seven. She was placed with several families. They all sent her back.'

'Could she learn? Read and write?'

'Oh, indeed. She's remarkably intelligent. She tests at least at an eleventh-grade level.'

'Then what was her problem in the foster homes?'

A shrug. 'I suppose they found her unnerving. She was docile on the whole but could become quite aggressive, especially if the other foster children tried to bully her. At times she would insist that her name was not Jennifer. She would talk to herself and write notes to herself. That's not so unusual in a child her age, but some of those notes were extremely unsettling in terms of both content and form.'

'The handwriting was different?'

'As I'm sure you would have guessed. Some notes seemed to have been written by a foul-mouthed male adult, but they'd seen that it was Jennifer who wrote them. The foster parents' first thought was demonic possession. They called the state institution. A social worker came to investigate and soon realized what she might have on her hands. The rarest of the rare, a true DID case. She brought her to me; I examined the child, and by the end of the day I'd committed her.'

'DID?' Teal asked.

'Dissociative Identity Disorder, my specialty. The literature doesn't call it MPD anymore although most of us still call them multiples. The new theory is that they're really not multiples but rather a ...'

Teal wasn't interested. 'Why'd she bring her to you?'

'She knew my reputation.'

Teal made a face. 'You also made it worth her while.'

'It was simply a referral,' Zales answered him evenly. 'I barely got to Jennifer in time. As you know, I have competitors in this field of study. One has made a standing offer of a hundred thousand dollars for a subject of Jennifer's quality.'

'Meaning one, unlike Rachel, who came by it honestly?'

'I would have said "naturally," but, yes.'

'And unlike the other five you've been working with, all of whom have been in therapy for an average of eight years. All of whom, by the way, are ten times more fucked up than when they first sat down with a therapist.'

'But, you see, that's the point. That's why Jennifer's such a find.'

Teal's pained expression returned. 'A find for what?'

'Think in terms of these "uses" you're so eager to explore. Who would ever suspect them in a twelve-year-old child?'

Teal had to turn away. He needed a minute to gather his thoughts and not least to control his temper. A twelve-year-old what? Another deep-cover spy? Why not an assassin while we're at it? We could have her skipping rope as a target walks by and garrote him before his bodyguards can react. We can dress her up in a Girl Scout uniform and have her knock on a target's door selling cookies laced with some of Leatrice's strychnine. We could stitch a bomb inside her Cabbage Patch doll and ...

Teal stopped himself. It was so *fucking* absurd. And yet Zales was perfectly serious.

'Let me ask you a question.' Teal finally sat. 'How many of these multiples are out there right now?' He gestured as if to take in the whole country.

'Diagnosed in the past fifteen years? Some ten thousand.'

'I mean real ones.'

'They're all real,' Zales answered. 'There are some who've tried to fake it but the rest are quite genuine.'

'Hold it.' Teal realized that he'd asked it incorrectly. 'You're going to say they're real because they think they're real. Put that bullshit aside for a second.'

'It's hardly bullsh ...'

'And forget about the past fifteen years,' said Teal. 'In all of medical history before that period, how many people have been diagnosed as multiples?'

'Well ... Freud thought he had two.'

'Okay, since Freud.'

'There was Eve, of course. *The Three Faces of Eve?* And Sybil was another whose case became a movie. Those are the two most publicized examples.'

'We're now up to four. Is that it?'

'By no means. The literature puts the figure at a hundred or so.'

'A hundred in what ... since psychiatry began?'

'Diagnosed, Mr. Teal. *Diagnosed.* There would have been more if doctors knew how to look for it.'

'And if we'd had tabloid TV back then. If we hadn't had Montel and that bunch dredging trailer parks for pathetic women who've concluded that since they wouldn't have fucked up their own lives, someone else inside them must be doing it.'

'The tabloids did not invent the disorder. They simply raised awareness of it.'

'They also raised awareness that we have angels among us. Do you consider that a public service as well? Angels and aliens, Dr. Zales. If people need to believe in them, does that, by your lights, make them real?'

Zales started to answer but Teal waved him off. It was useless, he'd learned, to try to argue with psychiatrists. They were all moving targets. Their theories changed as necessary to defend their positions.

'This Jennifer,' he asked, 'just how rare is she?'

'In this country? No more than a handful like her.'

'All children?'

Zales shook his head. 'The cases I know of are mostly adults. All women, of course. Men don't seem to ever ...'

'Are these women in treatment, running loose, or what?'

'They are ... living their lives. Doing various things.'

'Wait a minute. Are you saying you know who they are?'

'I detailed one case history in *Listening to Your Selves*. You haven't read it? I gave you a copy. Twelve weeks on the *New York Times* Best Seller List.'

Teal waved the boast aside. 'And this one, unlike Rachel and the others in this program, is not ... I don't know ... she's not damaged goods?'

Zales snorted. 'I'd hardly go that far.'

'Straight answer, Dr. Zales. Is she wacked out or not?'

'You want what? For me to tell you Susannah's perfectly normal? Well, she's obviously not. Read the book.'

'But this Susannah's living her life, as you put it. She's functioning.'

'More or less.'

'More than that bunch you have locked up inside. But what's the less part? Less than what?'

'Less than ... the normal integrated personality, I suppose. You're about to ask why I didn't recruit her. If I did it would have been on a voluntary basis. I would not have been able to commit her. That means she could walk out whenever she pleased and go straight to the press if she wished.'

'And say she's been studied? So what if she did?'

Zales muttered, 'Who knows what she'd say.'

Chapter Seventeen

The psychiatrist watched as Teal returned to his car, walking briskly, head shaking, no more civil in departing than he was when he arrived. The meeting had gone badly. So much had gone wrong.

Zales blamed himself for the turn it had taken. He of all people had lost his composure. He'd blurted out the existence of Jennifer in hopes that Teal would see her potential. But all he had accomplished by telling Teal about her was to open the subject of natural multiples. He had handled that discussion badly as well. He should have simply pointed out the obvious fact that there isn't any value in natural Mosaics. Why bother with multiples so rare as those naturals when we can *create* all we need?

But his mind had been distracted. He had not been prepared. He could have dealt with the insults, the snideness, the discourtesy, and even those threats which were something quite new. He had come to terms with having made a mistake in deciding to give Rachel that field test. What shook him, however, what caught him unaware, was Teal's suggestion that she was sent out to kill. Teal's question, 'If not by you, then Leatrice.' Teal's question, 'What was in that booster?'

The Quiet Rooms were in a part of the basement where the wine cellars had once been located. There had also been a kitchen and pantry until a modern kitchen had been put in upstairs. Zales had walled off and soundproofed that area of the basement. It was accessible only by elevator. The laboratory that Teal had installed was on the opposite side of the wall. Teal's chemists and technicians used an outside entrance that had once been used for deliveries. It annoyed him that they came and went as they pleased, never bothering to brief him on what progress they were making except when they had a new formula to test and needed a few fourth-floor patients.

But they didn't know that the Quiet Rooms existed on the other side of the wall. Teal knew they were there, but Hoyt and Grayson did not. How he disciplined patients was none of their business.

The five Quiet Rooms were additionally soundproofed by a lining of vinyl-coated padding. Each had a bed with constraints attached to it and a mask that was made of thick canvas. The masks only covered the lower part of the face. They had mouth holes that included a leather bit that kept patients from chewing their tongues off. The constraints were sometimes needed for patients who refused their medication or were otherwise unruly. More often, however, it was their alters, not themselves, who would need to be secured in this manner. Some, the more violent, were a danger to the staff – Rachel's Emma, for example, was no stranger to a Quiet Room.

Zales descended in the elevator that led to the basement. The code that he had kept Grayson from seeing was known only to Leatrice and himself and to a very few staffers. The door slid open, he stepped into a corridor and approached the glass-enclosed nursing station from which the five rooms were monitored. As he did so he sensed a presence behind him and heard a soft scurrying sound. His first thought was rats, his second was Emma. The thought that she might be loose caused his neck hairs to rise. He spun, arms up, as if to ward off attack.

'It's just the kid,' said the guard at the station.

The guard was Duane, who lived in the basement. He was subject to impulses, now under control, but Leatrice thought it best to keep him off the top floors in order to limit his access to the patients. Besides, the other guards all detested him.

Zales saw the child now near the entrance to the pantry. She was dressed in a bathrobe and fluffy pink slippers. She was holding what looked to be a small teddy bear. Little Jennifer was stroking it, speaking into its ear as if telling it not to be afraid, but her own large blue eyes were watchful and wary.

It had slipped Zales's mind that she was quartered there. Leatrice had decided to isolate her, as well, to keep her away from the adults. The girl had been seen wandering the third floor hallways and visiting several of the patients in their rooms. Leatrice had even caught her reading some of their diaries. The girl was given one of the Quiet Rooms which Leatrice had refurnished for her use. It had a TV and some children's books and a bed whose restraints had been removed. Her meals, like Duane's, were sent down by dumb-waiter. Leatrice felt sure that she'd be safe with Duane. His impulses had never involved children.

Norman Zales was about to move on when he saw that the teddy bear was wagging its tail.

'Duane,' he asked the guard, 'is that a real animal?'

'Yeah, it's a dog. It's a Pekingese puppy.'

Zales looked. It was. 'Where would Jennifer get a puppy?'

'I brought it back for her. Your missus said I could.'

'Brought it back? From where?'

'From that place in Virginia.' Duane lowered his voice because Jennifer was listening. 'They gave us all dogs to see if we'd kill them.'

Zales understood – that was Leatrice's idea. But young Grayson had stuck his nose in again and aborted what would have been an interesting experiment.

'I snuck that one out for the kid,' Duane whispered. 'I hear they were going to take it back to some lab where I think they would have blinded it and then cut it up. What do you call that when they cut them up alive?'

'Vivisection?'

'Yeah, right. I don't like when they do that.'

Zales shrugged to show that he had no objection. What surprised him, however, was Duane's act of kindness.

Thoughtfulness, compassion, were not normally qualities that one would associate with Duane. The drugs he'd been given – the ones for that test – were hardly intended to induce such behavior. Zales made a mental note to talk to the others and ask if they'd felt any similar urge; to send flowers to their mothers, or whatever.

He gestured toward the Quiet Room whose white door was closed. 'Is Leatrice still in there with Rachel?' he asked.

Duane nodded toward a video screen at his station. 'She's in there with one of her. I think it's the dyke. Your missus just gave her a sponge bath.'

Zales looked at the screen. There was no sound. He saw that Rachel had been stripped of her blood-spattered clothing. She was totally naked, partly covered by a sheet, and was straining against straps that held her ankles and wrists. A mask had been fitted under her chin and secured to the back of her cot. It allowed some head movement from side to side but it kept her head from rising and biting.

But she wasn't struggling in the violent sense. It was more a steady pressure against her restraints as if testing their ability to hold her. Her eyes seemed clear, remarkably so. The Demerol should have made her languid and indifferent. Zales felt sure that Duane was right – he knew that he was looking at Emma.

Leatrice was sitting at one side of the bed. She was running her hand along Emma's bare shoulder and now down one arm and over her chest. All the while she was talking, whispering softly, in a manner that seemed more seductive than calming. Emma seemed to be trying to ignore the stroking but it was having its effect nonetheless. The beginnings of a shudder. The wetting of her lips. And now Emma's eyes fell on Leatrice's hand. She made a gesture with her chin as if urging it to move, to move down, to go lower on her body.

Zales didn't like what he was watching one bit. It was one thing to empathize with a lesbian alter, quite another to become a participant. He flicked off the monitor and crossed to the door. He knocked and then inserted his key.

Leatrice, as Zales had expected, had her hands on her lap by the time the padded door opened. Rachel, or Emma, was not quite as quick. Her immediate reaction to his entrance was annoyance, but that was before she raised her eyes to his face. With recognition came a curious coldness. It was almost a look of contempt. But then came a rapid flutter of her eyelids. She would blink a few times and her expression would change. Now it was a meekness, a gentleness, that he saw. She looked up with eyes that were suddenly sad. She tried to speak; she couldn't quite form the words; but he sensed that she was trying to apologize. She blinked again, and again came a change. This last was a sleepily contented expression that he recognized as a Demerol haze. In a matter of seconds she fell fast asleep.

Amazing, thought Zales. It never failed to astound him. It was almost like watching a TV change channels. First Emma, then a flick to what was probably Teresa, then flick again to Rachel in her current drugged state. Some patients had so many that they seemed to be on cable. Only rarely, however, had he seen a patient whose alters could seem so totally impervious to a narcotic drug administered to the host in that dosage.

'Is she really sleeping?' Zales asked his wife. He reached for the joint of Rachel's toe and pressed his thumbnail into it. She showed no reaction whatever.

'She's asleep. She's resting. She's been through quite a lot.'

'Oh, she certainly has. And so have I.'

'Your talk with Mr. Teal was unpleasant, I take it.'

'You're to call the police. I've written down what you're to say.'

Her eyebrows arched as he handed her his notepad. The smile had faded but it quickly came back. 'I'm to play a black trollop? How inventive of you, Norman.'

'It was Teal's suggestion. I told him you'd do it.'

'How clever of him, then. I shall.' She tore off the sheet and tucked it into her lab coat. She reached to brush away a lock of damp hair that had fallen across Rachel's face.

'Leatrice ... he asked me if I sent her out to kill.'

126

She pursed her lips but said nothing.

'He then asked, if I didn't, did you?'

Still nothing.

'There's more to the question. There are two other parts. The second is Why Emma was glaring at me with a look of utter disdain? The third is why Emma would choose a victim who happened to look like me?'

'She is ... not fond of men, I'm afraid.'

'I dare say.'

Leatrice did not speak for another long moment. 'Don't you suppose,' she asked him at last, 'that it was better to know sooner than later what she'd do?'

'Oh, my God.' He felt the color drain from his face.

'Did you speak to Mr. Teal about Grayson?' she asked.

'Leatrice ... answer my question.'

Gently, Leatrice stroked Rachel's cheek. 'Emma gave you that look because she thinks you've been foolish. She knows full well what she'd do if she were furloughed.'

Zales frowned. 'She knows? Or you told her?'

She ignored the question. 'And as for that man, it was probably coincidence. But perhaps she decided to teach you a lesson. Perhaps she shared my disappointment with you when you acted against my advice.'

Zales felt lightheaded. He had to lean against her chair. He wanted to ask what was in the booster, but he knew that Teal had been at least partly right. It wouldn't have been anything so crude as a stimulant. It would have been ketamine, a hallucinogen, the same drug that Leatrice had given to Rachel when her mother showed up with that professor from Duke.

He wanted to ask, did she give Rachel the knife? Did she give her a map with a street marked on it where men who cruised in cars could be found? Instead he asked, 'Was that *ever* Rachel?'

'Here and there, perhaps. Yes.'

'Was she Rachel when I told her that she was to have an outing? When she seemed so excited and grateful?'

'If she wanted to please you, that was probably Teresa.'

Zales recalled thinking that she didn't sound like Rachel. Looking back, the only one who behaved like Rachel was the one who was annoyed that her clothing had been stained.

'Leatrice ... help me to understand why you did this.'

'What is it that you think I have done, dear?'

'You have sabotaged my field test, is what I think you've done. You have caused the deaths of two innocent men.'

'Innocent? Men who buy sex on the street? To the contrary, dear, I have saved several lives. She would probably have murdered her parents in their beds and anyone else who came for Thanksgiving. Consider where that would have left us.'

Zales started to speak. She raised a hand to his lips.

'The least of the harm it would have done is financial. Some thirty families pay us large sums of money to see that their daughters cause no further discomfort. But then all at once they would turn on the news and see what one of our charges has done. What effect might that have had on their peace of mind, dear? Might they not have considered transferring their daughters to a rather more conventional institution?'

'Yes, but, Leatrice ...'

'A greater harm would befall our patients. Other institutions would work to eradicate the alters that we have nurtured here at Belfair. All those talents lost forever – what a sin that would be.'

'Leatrice, even so ...'

'And you, Norman dear, would have lost the race to create the first Reductive Mosaic. You've been leading the field, but it is still nip and tuck. Close on your heels is that terrible man who very nearly beat you to Jennifer.'

'Leatrice ... please. Can we stick to one subject?'

'And a still greater harm would befall humankind if we had lost the man who has championed our compound. The congressman is well worth protecting, is he not?'

'You're saying ... those two died ... to save humankind?'

'No, dear. They just died. We will save humankind. In any case, all's well that ends well.'

Zales wanted to scream. 'It's ended? What has ended?'

He wanted to grab her by the shoulders and shake her. He wanted to point out that this could have destroyed him. That man who had fought Rachel – what if he had overpowered her? What if she'd been seen by a passing police car? What if Zales had failed to notice the shopping bag that Rachel left behind? But he said none of this because his wife had turned away. She had taken Rachel's hand. She was cooing in her ear.

'Leatrice … *would* she have murdered her parents?'

'I think so. Yes. More than likely.'

'But if you had told her not to …'

'Dear … you're so tired. Why not take a nice nap?'

'And she's not a toy, damn it. She is not your plaything. It sickens me to walk in and see …'

'Oh, Norman, for shame.'

'Shame on who? Shame on me?'

'My sexual proclivities are unaltered, I assure you. This is therapy, dear, nothing more.'

'And … the point of this therapy?'

'To dispose of our problem. Soon this whole episode won't have happened.'

Zales stared. 'You are … trying an erasure?'

'It is well on its way.'

'Leatrice … you don't have the skills to do this. Even I have not always succeeded.'

'Dear, do lie down. You've been under a strain. I will come to you later and – speaking of skills – I will ease you as only I can.'

Zales let out a breath. He looked at her hands. It was true that those hands could do wonderful things. Those hands … and her mouth … in the darkness. But tonight he did not think that he would feel all that eased. This was not the Leatrice who had flattered him, encouraged him. This was the Leatrice who started as his wife and assistant and now fancied herself a full partner. This was more like the Leatrice whom he thought he had cured. Perhaps he would sleep in his office.

'And see to Major Grayson; you'll do that, won't you, dear? We cannot have any more meddling.'

'I will … speak to Teal again. When I've collected my thoughts.'

'Or perhaps I should telephone Mr. Camal and ask his advice on this matter. His advice, you'll recall, has been sound in the past.'

'Teal has told you. You are not to call Camal.'

'I shan't have to if you will attend to it yourself.'

'I said I will talk to Teal, Leatrice.'

Zales had considered telling her what he'd learned. That Grayson might be something more than Hoyt's snoop. Grayson might be, if Teal was to be believed, some sort of fixer that General Hoyt used when matters got out of hand. He doubted it. Grayson didn't seem the type.

But Leatrice would have seized on that additional excuse. Leatrice would have said, 'Ah, then, you see? All the more reason to call Mr. Camal. There are times when one values the criminal mind.'

Indeed, one does. But within prudent limits.

Zales remembered the last time she sought Camal's advice. It concerned that therapist who had last treated Rachel, the one who'd convinced her she was the victim of a cult. She had been fired, but she wasn't about to go quietly because she saw Satan's hand everywhere, even in her dismissal. She took to showing up at Belfair, standing at the gate shouting, threatening to expose him as a willing tool of Satan unless Rachel was released into her custody.

Camal's advice had come in the form of a question. He asked, with a delicacy that was typical of the man, 'What good is having fucking mentals like Duane if you don't get your money's worth out of them?'

Zales, himself, had dismissed that advice, but Leatrice, he feared, might not have. All he knew for certain was that there soon came a time when Duane disappeared for two days. He came back, saying only that he'd gone for a walk. They never heard from that therapist again.

Zales had told himself that it was a coincidence and had tried to put it out of his mind. He had tried to tell himself that Leatrice was no murderess, that misfortune with her parents notwithstanding. But now, with those two men dead in their cars, denial was less of a comfort. One thing was clear. He would have to see to Grayson. He would have to get Grayson away from this project before another coincidence could happen.

Later, thought Zales. He would see to him later.

Until then, he just might lock his door.

Chapter Eighteen

Prentice Teal's young coder was still buried in her pillow when he returned to his Georgetown apartment. It was seven in the morning, a Saturday. The girl did not stir until he'd made a pot of coffee and had carried a mug to her bedside. She seemed barely to remember where she was at first, but she showed no sign of chagrin. Teal was less than surprised. She'd clearly done this before.

More important, the girl showed no hint of awareness that he had been gone for three hours. Teal thanked her for a most convivial evening. He assured her that he would tell her boss that she was an employee to be valued. He suggested that she dress while she sipped her coffee. He had already called her a taxi.

Alone, he took his own mug into the room that was meant to be his office away from Los Alamos. The office, now indifferently furnished, had once been equipped with a high-end computer and the latest communications devices. Teal had ordered all of it taken away and had bought his own telephone and answering machine at a local Radio Shack. He'd been assured that his phone line was secure, but he'd also purchased a tap detector that Radio Shack said was state of the art. He knew that nothing was state of the art very long, but it might make eavesdropping more difficult.

He'd specifically rejected the offer of a cell phone. Cell phones, to begin with, were impossibly unprivate. He thought the cell phone was at best an intrusion and, at worst, both a leash and a tracking device. He preferred it to be known that he could not be reached except when he wanted to be reached.

A bookcase stood against one wall under a framed Ray Ellis print of a Martha's Vineyard seascape. The bookcase's contents were reference works, largely. He kept nothing sensitive in that office. There were other assorted books he'd been given that he'd had no intention of reading. He found Zales's book where he had put it unopened.

Zales's name and degree blazed across the top, as befit a best-selling author. The title, less prominent, ran across the bottom. Over the title, *Listening to Your Selves*, the cover art showed, in silhouette, the head and shoulders of a woman. Around it, in the background, were several more silhouettes that were meant to represent the alters of the first. Each was clearly the same woman and yet each was different, a changed hairstyle here, an angled head there. Teal opened the book to note the inscription that Zales had scribbled in the fly leaf.

It read, 'To my good and valued friend, Prentice Teal.' Zales had added, 'Let us listen together.'

Teal curled his lip. He tore out the page.

Teal knew that he should have paid closer attention to what was going on with Chameleon. But it was only one of a half-dozen projects, each of which made demands on his time. Added to that, he'd never thought much of Chameleon. It was a bit like working with idiot savants. They were interesting, but so what? You'd have a patient who couldn't lace her shoes without help, but she'd have an alter who could learn Swahili or memorize phone books or some damned thing. That would be fine; it might even be useful if only other alters didn't keep popping out whenever one of them felt the urge. It had soon become clear that their only real use was as subjects for the testing of drugs.

It did seem a little Auschwitzy, perhaps. Even he had felt a few qualms at the start. He then learned, however, that it was done all the time by drug firms all over the globe. They tested many drugs in places like Belfair. He should have realized that because it made perfect sense. How else would one test a new psychoactive drug? Who in his right mind would take it?

Having his own mental hospital, therefore, seemed to Teal a most sensible idea. With the hospital came his own shrink, bought and paid for, who could do as he pleased with his patients. Shrinks can do things that would be indictable offenses in any other field but psychiatry.

Zales, for example, was trying to erase the personalities that his patients came in with. Not cure them, but erase them. Kill them off, basically. That was probably what their parents had hoped he would do. Certainly Winston, Camal, and Congressman Carey. They each would have been happy if their daughters became vegetables and remained in that state until they died. But Zales had his eye on that Nobel Prize. He decided on his own to give them new personalities. He thought he'd find a sane one if he dug deep enough. If successful, he would work on the 'popping up' problem. It wouldn't mean much to bring home a new Rachel if an Emma was in there awaiting the chance to get her hands on the kitchen cutlery.

Not that they'd ever be allowed to come home, even if they were actually reborn. Winston and Camal, those two human turds, would just pick up where they left off. And Leatrice understood, even if her husband didn't, the value of keeping them where they were. Having the daughters kept the fathers in line. Even more than the daughters, their diaries. Each one had had years to write down all the slime that their piece-of-shit fathers were into.

Teal was mindful of the diaries because he knew they might be useful, but he no longer needed Zales's patients. Project Richard was ready for much broader testing. The time had come for him to distance himself from Zales and that snake pit at Belfair. Seize all Zales's notes, either edit or destroy them, and also grab some of those diaries. Clean out that lab and move it back to Los Alamos. The trick would be to get General Hoyt's blessing without telling him more than was good for him. Teal would also need to keep Grayson at a distance until he'd had a chance to tidy up.

That thought brought him back to that other woman, the one named Susannah, whom Zales had declined to recruit. The reason Zales gave was, 'Who knows what she'd say?' In point of fact, Teal didn't really care, but that woman had given him an idea.

There were photographs scattered throughout the book. Several of these were of Zales himself, here addressing a conference of like-minded shrinks, there receiving an award that such shrinks give each other, and one with him holding the hand of a patient who was looking adoringly into his eyes. Leatrice appeared in that one as well. She was dressed in her whites and wore that same half smile that had seemed almost pleasant the first time he saw it. But eventually it began to send chills up his spine. One had the feeling that she'd have the same expression whether easing one's pain or inflicting it.

She wasn't wholly unattractive in the physical sense. Pale blonde hair, pale gray eyes, pale everything, in fact. Her figure was okay, not all one might ask for, but the parts were all there and more or less in proportion. Teal wondered if they screwed, she and Zales. With some women, screwing is hard to imagine. That smile. He'd be huffing and puffing, humping away, his teeth biting into the headboard. And there would be Leatrice staring off into space, blank eyes and still that damned smile. 'A bit higher, dear. That will do. You may proceed.'

Teal thumbed through the book to another group of photographs. He was looking for one in particular. The photos on that page were of three different women who were thought to be natural multiples. Two of these were old snapshots of nervous-looking women. The two, said the captions, had been classic cases that had long been studied and debated. One had lived in Canada, but was long deceased. The second, a Belgian, middle-aged in the photo, had dropped out of sight in the early sixties. She would be dead or very old by now as well.

The photo at the bottom was the one Teal had wanted. She was one who Zales claimed to have treated and taught how to live with her multiple selves. The photo of this one had been formally posed. She was young, an American, not very attractive. He could only see her forehead and jaw, but she struck him a rather mousy-looking girl for one who was supposed to be so interesting.

Teal guessed her age to have been about twenty at the time the picture was taken. Her name, according to the caption, was SUSANNAH. The quotation marks meant that it was probably false. Teal had a feeling that he'd seen that face before. He stared for a moment, wondering why she seemed familiar.

'Ah, yes,' he murmured. He turned back to the cover. It was this one's head and shoulders that had been used in silhouette. Teal opened the book once more to the index. He found the heading for MOSAICS and its subhead on SUSANNAH. He turned to the pages that applied to her case.

Teal was fascinated by a lot of what he read about Susannah, but unsure of how much he should believe. He had to keep in mind that Zales had written it with visions of best-seller lists in his head. Bizarre gets on talk shows. There was plenty of bizarre. There was even a smattering of sex.

Susannah, it said, had imaginary playmates for as long as she could remember. They were not invented to help her cope with abuse. Although Zales made it clear that he didn't believe her, she insisted that her parents were, if anything, distant. An only child, born late in their lives; the mother's pregnancy was apparently a surprise. She characterized her parents as distant but correct. She never felt neglected in any material sense. It was more that her parents were not quite sure of what to do with her but were willing to try to make the best of it.

Add to that, the book said, she was born in a place that was culturally and geographically isolated. A commune? An island? The book didn't say. It said only that there were few other children and, of those, most were not allowed to play with her.

Did this mean, Teal wondered, that she was weird from the outset? Or perhaps it was her parents who were the pariahs. Whatever the answer, it was easy to see why she'd look in her own mind for playmates.

But it hadn't yet occurred to Susannah that there was anything out of the ordinary in having imaginary friends. These playmates, she said, were like any real playmates in that some interests were shared and some weren't. One liked to sit and listen to music, another liked to take hikes and climb trees. One liked to read, another liked to draw, one liked little boys because they played better games, while another couldn't stand them, and so on.

During her first few years in elementary school she was a good though unexceptional student. But this, said Zales, was where it started to get interesting because her playmates had begun to develop lives of their own. Not separate, exactly. More like complementary. One, for example, was especially good at math. That alter would, of course, sit in math class with Susannah, because the alter was part of Susannah. One day, the teacher asked Susannah a question and she did not know the answer. But suddenly she heard herself answering correctly. The voice, however, was not quite her own.

This did not strike Susannah as odd because those voices had always been with her. Over time, she had realized that it simply made sense to let her friends do what they were best at. They attended certain classes pretty much by themselves. They took certain final exams. From the fifth grade onward, according to Zales, she never got less than an A.

Susannah liked to draw. She later took up painting. The one who liked music took up the guitar. While Susannah shared that interest to a certain extent, it was the alter, not she, to whom it came easily. And another of her friends, the one who liked little boys, eventually turned into a boy herself. It was not, evidently, a sexual thing, as it was with Veronica's Henry. He was just a boy who liked to take things apart and put them together again. He became a real Mr. Fixit, said Zales, who could build or repair almost anything. Susannah, Zales reminded us, gave this little thought. He said none of it caused her a problem in the slightest until her parents sent her off to a prep school.

Prep school, thought Teal. No trailer park here. Her alters —

137

though she didn't yet think of them as such – were growing increasingly distinct. Some would come out and then stay out for hours, especially those who were good at certain sports. Susannah herself played softball and tennis but had no great interest in track. The hiker, however, indulged that predilection by becoming a cross-country runner. Susannah tried to talk her into sticking with sprints so as not to be out quite so long. It was, after all, Susannah's legs that would ache for days after every cross-country event.

More troublesome, of course, were the blackouts. While the alters were out, Susannah was in. Hours, initially, and then days would go by, which to her were a total blank. She would realize with a start that it was suddenly Friday, when the last she remembered, it had been Tuesday. A friend or a classmate would suddenly seem cool to her. Another might be unusually friendly. She would not know why, or at least not exactly. But she'd know that these classmates must have had an encounter with an alter for better or for worse.

Her academic record and athletic ability won her a scholarship to Duke University. She took an eclectic array of courses befitting her multiple interests. Although her major was in the fine arts, Zales noted that she took two psychology courses. One was 'Personality and Psychopathology'; the other was 'Developmental Psychopathology.' The latter had to do with disorders in childhood. Zales saw this as an effort to learn more about herself, perhaps even the beginning of a realization that she needed professional help.

Zales's book didn't say what made her seek that help. But he noted that with multiples, there was often at least one alter who was sexually indiscriminate. He said that she got into some serious trouble during her second year in college. He hints that promiscuity was probably the cause. Eventually she developed a trusting relationship with one of her psychology professors. Zales said that their relationship 'may not have been sexual' thereby raising the suspicion that it probably was. In any case, they began months of sessions. Those sessions gradually brought results, but only after Zales was consulted.

The first breakthrough came in getting those alters to at least leave a note if they went out.

Leave a note?

Oh, like a diary. Same as Belfair.

Zales was quick to dismiss her professor's methods as an amateur's trial and error. The book gave him no credit whatsoever, not even the mention of his name. If the professor had consulted him sooner, Zales wrote, Susannah would have achieved integration much more quickly. The book made it clear that had it not been for Zales, there would have been no progress at all.

What exactly, Teal wondered, did *integration* mean? He checked the glossary in the back of the book. It said that a patient was said to be 'integrated' when all the alters merged into one. It said, 'See Multiple versus Dissociative.' According to the book, MPD is a misnomer because these aren't multiple personalities, really, but rather *incomplete* personalities. In the end, they add up to one, not several. Cure an ordinary patient of MPD and the alters are absorbed … integrated. What makes a Mosaic so special and rare is that the alters and their talents remain intact, but they're at the command of the host.

He put the book down and reached for his phone. He dialed Zales's number; it rang several times; a guard or an orderly finally answered. He said the doctor was napping, could not be disturbed.

'Who is this, by the way?' Teal asked. 'Is this Duane?'

'Naw, Duane's down the cellar. It's Leroy.'

Teal thought he knew that one. He'd seen him mopping floors.

Leroy said, 'He got your number? 'Cause if he got your number, that way he can maybe call you back.'

'Get him now, you moron. This is Teal.'

'What … what's happened?' Zales had groped for the phone. Teal guessed that he'd been dreaming about Rachel.

'I've been reading your book. Tell me more about Susannah.'

'My book? ... Wait a moment ... Susannah?'

'Come on, Dr. Zales. Clear your head. Up and at 'em.'

'You ... had Leroy wake me to talk about my book? And why ... why Susannah in particular?'

'You said read it. I did. Now I'd like to know more.'

'I cannot believe this. I'm going to hang up.'

'You never want to do that, Dr. Zales.'

'Then you'll have to be satisfied with what's in the book. Any more would violate the confidentiality of ...'

'Oh, stop it. Describe her. Tell me what she's like now.'

'You mean physically?'

'Okay. Start with that.'

'I've ... never actually seen her in person. The consultation was by telephone and fax.'

'Your book doesn't give that impression, Doctor. You certainly didn't give me that impression when I asked why you didn't recruit her.'

'She is ... jealous of her privacy. She would not have consented.'

'And yet she let you print her picture in this book?'

'She ... didn't. I acquired one. But as you see, I disguised it. In any event, I don't know where she is. Out West somewhere, last I heard.'

'She's not happy with you, is she? She's not happy with this book.'

He could almost see Zales baring his teeth. 'She would be far more trouble than she's worth,' Zales insisted. 'You'll just have to take my word for it.'

'As you wish,' Teal answered lightly. 'How's everything else going?'

Zales was silent. Teal could almost see him blinking, wondering why the subject had been so readily dropped. Zales finally exhaled, sounding relieved. 'It seems to be under control.'

'Your good wife, did she make that call I suggested?'

'She will. As it happens, she approved of your strategy.'

'Did she, really? I'm so very pleased.'

If Zales heard the sarcasm, he chose to ignore it. 'She asks, however, that you reassign Grayson. I support that request. I must, in fact, insist.'

'You know what? I agree. I'll take care of it.'

He could almost hear more blinks of surprise. 'I may ... tell my wife that we won't see him again?'

'You won't for a while; I've got another job for him. After that, however, if he needs to visit Belfair, he'll find everything in order, won't he, Doctor?'

Another long silence. 'Did you ... just threaten me again, Mr. Teal?'

'Did I? I don't think so. What did I say?'

'That reference to a ... *visit* from Grayson.'

'Just let's have no more problems, Dr. Zales.'

Teal was blinking himself as he broke the connection. Had he threatened Zales? He hadn't actually meant to. All he'd said was that Grayson might drop in.

Ah, yes, thought Teal. That must have been it. His earlier reference to what Grayson was good at had more of an effect than he'd realized.

Teal shrugged it off. He had phone calls to make. He needed to call his man at Langley to find out exactly what Grayson had done. After that, well ... he had made a decision. He would tell General Hoyt about Rachel's little field trip.

It would be a gamble but it was his best card. The bet would be how far Hoyt would go to protect Rachel's mother from knowing what her daughter had done. Teal wouldn't tell him everything. Hoyt might act if he knew everything. The idea would be to paralyze Hoyt, but he wouldn't stay paralyzed for long. Teal thought he could hope for two days, maybe three. Time to clean things up at Belfair, time to disengage from Zales, time for Winston and Camal to get things rolling.

He could get all this done without involving the general, all except keeping Grayson out of the picture. For that, he would need General Hoyt. He'd been wondering how to get rid of Grayson without Grayson getting overly suspicious. Thanks to Zales, he now had just the thing.

141

You think they're bad subjects, those women at Belfair? As it happens, the general and I now agree. So we'd like you to go and find us a good one. Go find and recruit this Susannah.

Chapter Nineteen

Major Grayson, on that Saturday morning, skipped breakfast and went to his small office at Bolling. He needed to use the office computer because that was where he'd filed his accumulated notes. Two hours later he'd completed a draft of the report that he would send to General Hoyt.

Grayson was reviewing it, making corrections, when he heard footsteps coming and a knock on the door. The door opened and a smiling Prentice Teal stepped in. He was dressed in a green golf jacket and cap, both embossed with the Burning Tree Country Club's emblem. He picked up a chair and sat in it by straddling it. He was carrying one of Zales's books in his hand.

'I just heard about the dogs. Good decision,' he said.

Grayson folded his arms. He leaned back. 'You're going to tell me you knew nothing about that?'

'What I'm telling you is I just heard of it this morning.'

'So Leatrice never cleared it with you. Is that what you want me to write in my report?'

'It happens to be true. But you write what you want.'

Grayson looked at him coldly. 'Those subjects ... where did they come from?' he asked.

'Here and there. Listen, Roger ... the reason I'm here ...'

'That's your whole answer? They came from here and there?'

'Here and there, in fact, is where volunteers come from. What's past is past. Let's move on.'

'What was it, Mr. Teal? What are you and Zales into? Was that some kind of school for assassins?'

Teal blinked in astonishment. He almost laughed. 'You think we start them with guinea pigs?'

'Mr. Teal …'

'Rodents, then puppies, is that what you think? If they're good at puppies, we let them kill a wino and eventually they work up to a woman. Is that how they started with you?'

Grayson leaned forward. He started to rise. Teal raised both hands but not in apology.

'I'm trying to make you see how stupid that sounds. But if you insist on making an ass of yourself, go ahead and put that in your report.'

'My report, Mr. Teal, is going to ask who they were.'

'You want the truth? They were psychos.'

'Um … what?'

'Psychopaths, sociopaths, assorted sick fucks. Some were Army, most weren't. I thought I'd check them out, see if one of the formulas turned them into nice people.'

Grayson couldn't believe that he was serious.

'I'll remind you, Major, that I'm project director. I can run any damned test I want.' He wheeled a finger and pointed it downward. 'Bad subjects is actually the reason I'm here. Your report … will it hammer Zales's multiples?'

Grayson, still stunned, gave a nod.

'Well, it should. They're useless. We'll probably end up dropping that project, but I'd like to see a multiple who isn't a mess. I've brought you a book I want you to read.'

'If that's *Listening to Your Selves*, I've read it.'

'Zales gave you a copy?'

'General Hoyt did. He thought it would help me understand how Zales thinks.'

'That changes with the wind – don't waste your time. Do you remember reading about a woman named Susannah?'

'She's supposed to be a multiple? Went to Duke University?'

'That's the one. I want you to find her and talk to her.'

'Why?'

'Because Zales doesn't want you to. How's that for a reason?'

'I don't much care what Dr. Zales wants.'

'You need another reason? Hoyt wants you to go. I've already cleared this with him.'

Grayson looked into his eyes. He could see no bluff. His eyes then fell on his telephone.

'Is this to keep me from submitting this report?'

'It's to help you complete it.' Teal slid the phone toward him. 'You want to hear it from him? Be my guest.'

Grayson reached general Hoyt at his bachelor apartment in Washington's Watergate complex. When Hoyt answered, his voice sounded distant, distracted. But he'd clearly been expecting the call.

The general said, 'Yeah, I just discussed this with Teal. I think it's a good idea. Find her.'

'Sir ...'

'Teal also explained what happened at Langley. Too many cooks, too little supervision. And I spread you too thin. My mistake.'

'Sir, even so, if you'll read my report ...'

'The Richard thing has gotten out of hand. It has also become, well ... more sensitive. I'm going to get involved in that one myself. I want you just to stick with Chameleon.'

'General Hoyt ... there's nothing there. Even Teal will tell you that.'

'And I hear that Zales is all bent out of shape. It wouldn't hurt to take a little break from each other. Go track down that girl for me, Roger. Go find me a genuine multiple.'

'Sir ...'

'Teal says she's supposed to be someplace out West. That doesn't narrow it down very much, but ...'

'General Hoyt, I would like this order in writing.'

'What order, Roger? I'm asking you to help me. Someday you might be glad that I owe you.'

Grayson chewed his lip. He wanted to refuse. Even more, he wanted to demand to know exactly what 'out of hand' meant. Did those subjects from Langley start murdering dogs the minute they were disbanded? Were they, come to think of it, the only such group or had Teal 'checked out,' as he called it, some others?

He wanted to know what Teal had told the general, why Teal's word was suddenly trusted by Hoyt. But the general had sidestepped every point he'd tried to raise. And majors don't make demands of generals.

'I will ... try to find the girl, sir.'

'Keep looking 'til you do.'

'Very well, I'll find her, but after that ...'

'You're a good man, Roger. I thank you.'

The line clicked in his ear and went dead.

Grayson hung up the phone. He turned back to his computer. He inserted a disk and hit several keys.

'What are you doing?' asked Teal with a sigh.

'I'm making a copy. You never know. This hard disk could crash while I'm away.'

'Ah. I see. It's a cover-up, right? First we get you out of town, then we wipe out your records. Isn't this where you go, climb into your car, and a bomb we rigged blows you to shit?'

Grayson ignored him. He was watching the backup as it copied his data.

Teal's smile had faded. He lowered his voice. 'I know you don't like me. So you won't believe this. But what's happening is not a bad thing.'

'I think ... we have different ideas of what's bad.'

'And I'll tell you something else.' Teal gestured toward the screen. 'If you think you're being set up, you're not. I don't care what you do with that report.'

Grayson retrieved his disk. He gathered other papers that were lying on his desk and dropped them into his briefcase.

'Hey, I'm trying to ease your mind,' Teal told him. 'I might screw you if I had to, but Hoyt's a straight-shooter. No one's looking to hurt you here, Major.'

Grayson glanced up at him. 'Will you answer a question?'

'Depends. Take a shot.'

146

'Why wasn't I simply relieved and reassigned? I mean, if all you want is me not interfering, why waste my time on some goose chase?'

'Because if anyone can be a chameleon, it's someone like her, not that bunch back at Belfair. If she can't, then we wrap up the project.'

Teal told Grayson about his conversation with Zales. Zales, he suspected, had had almost no role in whatever progress this 'Susannah' had made. Zales had never so much as laid eyes on the girl except for that photo in his book, and yet he had gone public with this girl's private life – almost certainly without her permission. Zales had even hinted that she was probably a nympho who may have been balling the professor who called him.

'Major ... not that I think you're that kind of guy, but if you want to stick it to Zales, here's your chance. If everything he wrote about Susannah is bullshit, that ought to be part of your report.'

Grayson tried not to show that the idea was tempting. He realized that Teal was trying to manipulate him. It's what Teal was good at, Grayson had to admire it.

'Say ... I find her. Why would she talk to me?'

'You're a nice-looking guy. What girl wouldn't?'

'I'm serious.'

'She might talk if you're straight with her. Try.'

'Well, yes, but how straight? You're not saying I should tell her about Project Chameleon?'

Teal had started to say that he shouldn't go that far. But he thought for a moment and then said, 'Why not?' She would know that there are probably dozens of studies underway, all trying to understand how MPD works. Just tell her we're interested in how alters learn languages. Say we're looking for ways to make our own people smarter.

'Again,' he said, 'it comes back to Zales. Ask her what she thinks of these breakthroughs he's claimed.'

Teal turned toward the door. He paused, then looked back.

'Are you any good at finding people, by the way?'

147

'I've never had to do it. I don't know.'

'Well … no great hurry. Take your time; do it right. Check in at the end of each day.'

Grayson sat for a while after Teal had left. It was true, he reflected, that he didn't trust Teal, but in some ways he almost enjoyed him. Teal was more than just devious; he was gleefully devious. He'd expected Teal to be ruthless, and he was. But in the time since he'd first met the man, he'd never known Teal to be mean. His mouth could be, but perhaps not his heart. Even now, here was Teal, clearly wanting him out of the way for a while, yet trying to be considerate of his feelings. But Teal had not been able to resist making sure that he had no experience as a tracer.

So be it, thought Grayson. Whatever the reason he was being sent away, in truth he was glad for the break.

He took another hour to reread about Susannah. After that, he left the office for his quarters, where he gathered what clothing he thought he would need. He would certainly not wear his uniform. He changed into a dark green blazer, tan slacks, and his only pair of brown loafers. He packed his laptop and cell phone into a briefcase. He used a key to open a lockbox that contained his pistol and holster. It brought Janice's face flooding back to his mind, but with effort he washed it away.

He thought about leaving the gun but that was foolish. He packed it, along with two extra clips. He called to arrange for a motor-pool car that had no government markings or stickers. He was on his way out of Washington by noon, driving south toward Durham, North Carolina, and the campus of Duke University.

He wasn't experienced, but he wasn't dumb either.

If 'Susannah' left a trail, that was where he'd pick it up.

148

Chapter Twenty

Grayson started with Duke's Psychology Department, which had its own building on campus. He had noted the courses that Susannah had taken, both dealing with abnormal psychology. He entered the building and asked a student receptionist if he might see a course catalog. It showed that the same man taught both of those courses and had for the past twenty years. That man, thought Grayson, could well be the professor who had worked with Susannah and consulted with Zales.

His name was Daniel Ezra Cohen, Ph.D., Psy.D. The receptionist checked Dr. Cohen's schedule. She said that he was probably having lunch at the moment, but was due back shortly for a faculty conference. Grayson thanked her and told her he'd wait.

Some twenty minutes later, a white-haired man approached, walking briskly across the quadrangle. Grayson looked at the receptionist. She nodded. Grayson guessed Dr. Cohen to be over seventy. He was dressed in a shapeless corduroy suit and wore wire-rimmed glasses set low on his nose. The receptionist greeted him and gestured toward Grayson. She said that this gentleman had asked to see him. Grayson gave his name and produced his ID. He asked if they might speak in private.

'Department of Defense? An intelligence officer?'

'Yes, sir. If you could spare a few minutes ...'

'What could you possibly want with me?'

'Sir, it's about a former student of yours. I think you know a woman called Susannah.'

A weary sigh confirmed that he did. 'Let's do this outside, if you don't mind.'

They returned to the quadrangle, both now walking slowly. Dr. Cohen paused and glanced at Grayson's leg.

'I see that you're limping. Do you need to sit down?'

'Just a little stiff from the drive, sir. I'm fine.'

'You drove here from Washington?'

'Yes, sir, I did.'

'Then I'm afraid that you've come a long way for nothing. I don't think I can help you, Major Grayson.'

'Sir, if you'll just let me explain …'

Grayson told him, in the most general terms, his purpose in wishing to interview Susannah. He said only that his agency was working with Zales on a highly classified project. Susannah, he said, had some knowledge of the subject and might be of valuable assistance.

The mention of Zales brought a grunt from Cohen. He peered over his glasses at Grayson. 'Does this … project … have to do with Rachel Carey, by chance?'

Grayson showed his surprise. 'You know about her?'

'I do. Is she part of this project?'

'No, she isn't.'

The psychologist sighed. He said, 'As you wish.'

Grayson leaned toward him; he opened his hands. 'Sir, I give you my word; I only know who she is. I promise you she's not involved.'

Cohen held his gaze. He seemed to believe him. 'But it does have to do with multiples, surely.'

Grayson nodded. 'Yes, sir, it does.'

'I wonder how you people live with yourselves, trying to find a use for someone else's misery.'

'Sir, I'm not "you people." I wish you'd believe that. The fact is I'm trying to kill this project. An interview with your patient could help me make the case that the project is an utter waste of time.'

Cohen seemed to waver. But he tossed a hand. 'To begin with,' he said, 'she was never my patient. She was simply a student I was trying to help. You saw where that got her. On the cover of a book. She's had a dozen talk show producers looking for her, to say nothing of all the legitimate researchers who were eager to run batteries of tests on her. I won't tell you where she is. She has a life. Let her live it.'

'A normal life, sir?'

'A private life, sir.'

'Would you tell me, at least, how you knew about Rachel?'

'I've seen her. I've been up to Belfair.'

Another surprise. 'Zales consulted with you?'

Cohen snorted. 'Not hardly. Her mother and I had spoken on the phone. She found me, I assume, much as you did. She finally came to see me, oh, two months ago and begged me to fly up and examine her daughter. I agreed to see Rachel, but I never saw Zales. He hid in his office while that ... woman ... brought her down.'

'Leatrice Zales?'

Another grunt. 'Yes, that one. In any event, the visit was dreadful. Rachel ignored her mother, or perhaps didn't know her. She hallucinated almost at once. She thought she saw snakes climbing out of my crotch and tried to attack them with her teeth.'

'I'm sorry.'

'I'll tell you something. She was waiting for those snakes. If I were not bound to keep such thoughts to myself, I would say she'd been conditioned to expect them.'

'Conditioned how?'

A shrug. He was unwilling to answer.

'That must have been terribly hard on her mother.'

He nodded. 'Mrs. Carey – who is not easily discouraged, by the way – then wanted to meet with Susannah. She was looking for some reason to hope, I think, that her Rachel might one day overcome her condition. But Rachel is nothing at all like Susannah.'

'Susannah, I take it, wouldn't see Mrs. Carey?'

'She saw her. I arranged it. They met on neutral ground at an airport halfway between them.'

'Could she help her?'

'Susannah listened, tried to comfort her, even cried with her, but no – she was unable to offer more than hope.'

'Could you? If you were able to get Rachel out of Belfair, I mean. If we got ... not just Rachel out of Belfair?'

'I've accepted, Major Grayson, that not everyone can be helped. But I'll tell you, I would do her less harm.'

Well, at least he'd learned something about Susannah, thought Grayson. It appeared that she wasn't a total recluse and he'd learned that she was probably good-hearted. He had also ruled out Zales's sneering little hint that her relationship with Cohen had been sexual. The difference in their ages was about fifty years.

Grayson walked from Cohen's building to the university library. He found a section that contained every yearbook dating back to when Duke was called Trinity College. He selected three, for the years around which Susannah would likely have graduated. He scanned each portrait of the graduating seniors, going page by page through each book. In less than an hour he had found the one whose silhouette matched that on Zales's book. He'd guessed correctly. This must have been where Zales found her picture.

Her full name was Susannah Card. That in itself was an agreeable surprise – 'Susannah' was no pseudonym after all.

Grayson's first reaction to her undisguised face was one of some disappointment. He'd been so impressed by all that she'd accomplished that he'd expected to see ... he didn't know ... at least some hint of vitality. Her expression was not just the vague, generic gaze that is common to many yearbook photos; Susannah's face seemed totally bland. She wore no makeup, her hair seemed unwashed. Her bone structure promised that she could be attractive but apparently she had made no attempt toward that end. One eye was squinting; she wore wire-rimmed glasses. It was the guarded sort of face that one often sees on people who are in therapy. Tight-lipped and withdrawn. A face that almost says, 'You wouldn't like me if you knew me.' She didn't look like a girl who ever did much of anything, let alone all the interests listed under her entry.

He turned to the pages that featured activities. He did not find Susannah in any group photographs because she'd failed to appear when they were taken. Her name was always listed with the note, 'Not shown.' The only exceptions were under the spreads for women's softball and tennis. She hadn't posed for those team pictures either, but each spread included a montage of snapshots taken during actual games. He recognized Susannah in two of them.

In the first, for tennis, she was shown serving. Her expression in that one was intense, determined. Her jaw was set and her tongue showed through her teeth. The shot gave him a full view of her body. It was lean, athletic, well proportioned. Grayson was pleasantly surprised.

The second, for softball, was another candid shot. She was standing to one side of the home plate backstop in a group with three other young women. They were cheering, shouting. jumping up and down at whatever was then happening on the field.

Grayson borrowed a magnifying glass from the desk and sat down to study those photos more closely. He wished they were in color but at least they were sharp. They were showing him an entirely different Susannah. This Susannah was pretty, but there was more to it than that. This was a face that seemed strikingly *alive*. The face in the yearbook photo she'd sat for bore little resemblance to these. That one suggested a limp, flaccid body that seemed not in the least athletic. The young woman standing next to her had grabbed Susannah's jersey in the excitement of whatever had happened. Another young woman's face was looking up into Susannah's as if to say, 'Isn't this great?' You only do these things, thought Grayson, with people you like. You don't do them with people who you think are strange or distant. You don't do them with people you're afraid of.

He went back to the posed photograph and then it hit him. He wasn't seeing two different people at all. He was seeing a

153

young woman who didn't like being photographed and who went to great lengths to avoid it. Both of these other photos were candid shots that she probably hadn't known were being taken. Grayson guessed that she could not avoid the posed photo so she did what he might have done; she disguised it. Messy hair, no makeup, that squint, a general sag.

Grayson smiled and the smile spread into a grin. Those glasses, wire-rimmed; they were like Dr. Cohen's. He would not be surprised if Cohen had suggested that she wear them as part of her disguise.

Grayson studied the Susannah of the softball photo. Her hair was dark blonde, or a very light brown and she wore it medium short. He couldn't tell the color of her eyes but he guessed they were probably blue. She had plastered her hair down for the formal photo but here it was light, clean, and stylish. It was a low-maintenance cut or the kind that is favored by women too busy to spend much time primping.

Busy was a word that certainly fit Susannah. She had graduated ... it would be five years next June ... with her primary major in art. With a course load as heavy as it was diverse, she still had time for team sports. This while studying guitar on the side and appearing in student productions. Not just performing, but building sets and helping to wire the lights.

Grayson wondered about that, the building and wiring. Zales had written about one of her alters who liked to tinker and hang out with boys, and eventually grew up to be a boy himself. Zales had pointed out that it was not uncommon for women to concoct male alters. Even normal women will indulge the fantasy of becoming a man for a while. Just long enough, usually, to kick someone's butt. But some multiples, apparently, will create a male alter just so *his* butt can be kicked. Grayson had never actually read of that happening, but Veronica's Henry seemed to be one example. In the case of this Susannah, however, he found himself not wanting to believe Zales's account. He did not want any part of this remarkable young woman to be even a little bit male.

Remarkable, yes. Accomplished, yes. But he reminded

154

himself that Susannah's range of interests did not necessarily suggest a multiple. A number of her classmates had explored as many interests according to the activities listed under their photographs. He knew that most young people try on many hats in the process of deciding who they are. In that sense, most people have been multiples at some point. Maybe the answer was as simple as that. Most of us grow out of it; a few never do.

Once he had her name, the rest was easy. It was only a matter of getting back to his laptop and entering a twelve-digit access code that got him into the FBI's databank.

It always amazed him how much information was accessible if you knew which keys to hit. His screen displayed her current address, all previous addresses, her credit and medical history. The latter showed treatment for a couple of injuries but nothing in the way of psychiatric treatment. Not when she was at Duke and not since. Her counseling at Duke must have been on the house.

Susannah was not 'living somewhere out West' as Zales had apparently told Teal. She was originally from a town in Virginia that Grayson had never heard of before. The town was Tangier. He checked his road atlas. He could find no mention of a place called Tangier but his atlas was not highly detailed. Still, not finding it struck Grayson as funny. To have an unlisted home phone was one thing, but to have an unlisted hometown?

In any case, she no longer lived there. Her current residence was in South Carolina. After graduating Duke, she had moved down the coast and settled on Hilton Head Island. Grayson's computer had produced her address and located it for him on a street map. He certainly had heard of Hilton Head Island – two or three years before, some Middle East terrorists had tried to destroy a good part of it. They saw it as a haven for the godless rich and a paradise they didn't deserve. Grayson doubted that they'd had Susannah in mind. She seemed well short of being rich.

Most homes on the island were in gated 'plantations' and

155

were, by most standards, luxurious. Susannah's was older and considerably more modest. The house she'd first rented, and later bought, was on a strip of land between two of the plantations, in a section called North Forest Beach. Modest, perhaps, but hardly deprived. All those houses were either on the ocean or mere yards from it. Susannah's had been built in the early fifties, well before the developers saw the island's potential. It had probably been a simple beach house.

The screen showed the number of rooms in the house, what she paid for it, and the amount of her mortgage. Grayson punched up a series of architects' blueprints. They showed the house as it was originally built and what remodeling had been done to it since. Susannah had improved it considerably and had done much of the work herself. Since buying it, she'd applied for several building permits and had named herself as the contractor. That handyman thing again, thought Grayson. The alter of Susannah's who grew up as a male. It still bothered Grayson, but he pushed it from his mind.

Another section showed what credit cards she had and what mail-order purchases she'd made the past year. Mostly art supplies, books, and building materials. It showed what magazines she subscribed to and even what catalogs she'd requested. Tool catalogs, home and garden catalogs, but also one from Victoria's Secret and others from elegant clothiers. Their variety suggested a whole house full of people, but Susannah Card lived alone.

One credit card charge was for an airplane ticket. She'd bought it only two weeks before. Round trip, same day, to Charlotte, North Carolina. That must have been where she met Rachel's mother. Her charges showed no other travel.

Grayson knew that he could enter another code and get a list of all the toll calls she'd made over the past sixty days. He wondered whether this very private young woman ever realized how much of her life was an open book to anyone who knew how to tap into it.

Susannah's parents were Randall and Helen Card. Her father, it showed, was deceased. It said he was a World War II

156

veteran; a sergeant. The mother was alive but in a nursing home in Richmond. The daughter certainly had come along late in life. Her parents had been in their fifties.

Grayson tapped a key and switched back to Susannah.

Her primary source of income was her work as an artist. She specialized in murals for banks, office buildings, and had sold a number of paintings. Another source was from a company that restored antique cars. My God, thought Grayson, she does that as well. A third was from a place called Cheryl's Cabaret. The IRS code for that source of income put it under *PERFORMING ARTS*. The amount was only a few thousand dollars. Grayson took that to mean that she played the guitar there, but not on a full-time basis.

He stared at all this data, not sure what he was feeling. Were alters doing all these things for Susannah, or was she simply a talented young woman who wasn't afraid of hard work?

Grayson closed his laptop. He looked at his watch. Hilton Head would be about a five-hour drive, which meant that he would get there after dark. He would locate her house, get the lay of the land, get himself a hotel room and some dinner. After that he'd drop into Cheryl's Cabaret and find out how often Susannah performed. It would seem to be the best place to watch her, to observe her, while sipping a beer at the bar.

Maybe talk to Cheryl. Ask Cheryl about her.

That is, thought Grayson, if there is a real Cheryl. That's if Cheryl and Susannah don't turn out to be …

Grayson … don't start, he said to himself. You're beginning to have alters on the brain.

Chapter Twenty-One

It was late in the day. The sun was almost gone. Prentice Teal took a taxi to the Watergate complex. General Hoyt had insisted on seeing him at once. The general, Teal realized, had recovered from the shock of being told what Rachel might have done.

Teal suggested the meeting place, a fountain nearby. Teal liked to meet at fountains, water splashing in the background. Like rainstorms, they defeated most recording devices.

Hoyt was waiting for him, pacing. He glared as Teal approached.

'That Baltimore business ... it's been on the news.'

'I've heard it,' said Teal. 'It's been on since this morning.'

'Then you know that Rachel did not kill those men. Why the hell would you tell me that it might have been her? If this was some ploy to get rid of Major Grayson ...'

'Grayson is the least of our problems, General Hoyt.'

'Well, I don't think Rachel is one of them either. The latest report says there was an eyewitness who saw the killer run from the scene. The person described had a knife in her hand. That person looked nothing like Rachel.'

'A black prostitute with a Tina Turner wig? General Hoyt, she doesn't exist.'

The general glared. He asked, 'How could you know that?'

Teal found a dry section on the rim of the fountain. He said, 'Please sit down and let's talk.'

Teal had considered telling Hoyt the whole truth. Yes,

Rachel did it, but she wasn't herself. She was Emma at the time, and occasionally Teresa. Teresa, you see, once had these two uncles ... Never mind; it'll give you a headache.

The problem with telling him the truth right up front was that Hoyt might feel honor-bound to call the police, especially since he wasn't involved yet. All he'd done so far was send Grayson on a snipe hunt to keep him from showing up at Belfair.

Another problem with telling the truth; it was hard to know where to stop. Yes, Rachel did the two actual slashings, but Leatrice Zales set them up. How? She doped her. Am I sure? Pretty much. Why would Leatrice do that, you ask? Well, aside from the fact that she's a fucking loon herself, she probably did it to keep Carey locked in. Why had Rachel been set loose? That was Martha Carey's fault — she'd wanted Rachel to come home for the holidays, and Zales thought he'd do a trial run. But we don't want to hurt Martha Carey, do we, General? We want to protect her if we can.

This last was Teal's hole card, but it wasn't an ace. Hoyt still might call in the police.

'We know,' Teal explained, 'that Rachel was in Baltimore. Zales took her on an outing. She got away somehow and was missing until well after midnight. When he found her, it was near where those two men were killed. Her face was cut and swollen like she'd been in a fight. She had blood on her hands and on her clothing.'

'So you claim.'

Teal darkened. 'I'm inventing this, right?'

'Well, what does she say? Is she able to talk yet?'

'Rachel doesn't even know who she is. Zales thinks she'll come out of it, maybe in hours, maybe in days. When she does, we can ask her what happened.'

Hoyt chewed his lip. 'And what if she did it?'

'We could turn her in but where would that get us? She would never go to trial; she's criminally insane. All it would do is put her back where she is; not Belfair but in some

159

state institution. Meanwhile, the press will be all over her father. They'll dig up some of Rachel's old charges, including the one that her parents are satanists. Do you want to see Martha's face in the tabloids? Have you thought about what this might do to her?'

The general grimaced. Teal thought he'd hit home. But the general stepped closer and spoke through his teeth.

'Mr. Teal ... don't insult me. Don't pretend that you care.'

'About who, the mother? Okay, then, I don't. I care about finishing what I started.'

'Project Richard.'

'If Rachel is even named as a suspect, the media will be all over Belfair as well. If they get a whiff of Chameleon and Richard, you know what Carey's committee will do. They will claim not to know what Carey was up to. They'll hang him – and you – out to dry.'

'Mr. Teal ...'

'We are so close with Richard. Let's not blow it now. Especially if Rachel turns out to be innocent.'

'What you don't want to blow is the money you'll make.'

Teal's expression didn't change. 'I don't care about that either.'

'Nor, I suppose do Carey, or Winston, or especially that criminal, Camal. Did you think that I wouldn't find out about them?'

'*They* are in this for the money. I am not.'

'Of course you're not.' The words dripped with contempt. 'A renowned humanitarian such as yourself would care only for the good that might come of it.'

Teal's eyes had turned hard. 'You don't know me at all.'

'Oh, I know you, Mr. Teal. You're a man who gets things done. You get things done by hook or by crook, and that is, of course, why we pay you.'

'Then let's talk about getting things done.'

Teal reminded Hoyt of how much the drug had helped nearly all of Zales's fourth-floor patients. Most of them with major psychoses, he said, that no shrink had been able to cure.

160

Even Rachel had started to come back to life. Not the old Rachel, a new one, a nice one. And the compound that had done the job was an early version. It had since been substantially improved.

It was time, Teal told him, to look forward, not backward. They were close to perfecting a miracle drug that could virtually eradicate many forms of mental illness. Depression, delusions, self-loathing, all gone. Think now, said Teal, of where Rachel might be if she'd had this drug when she was back in her teens. Back before she started seeing all those therapists.

'You want an incentive? I'll give you an incentive. This drug could put thousands of those quacks out of business. No one who takes Richard will need them.'

'So ... it isn't the money. It's a world free of therapists?'

'That's what Grayson would like, but it's only a start. What else do people do when they don't like themselves? They get drunk or they get stoned, am I right?'

'You will ... free the world of addictions as well.'

'It's not such a stretch. The world's free of smallpox. Who would have believed that was possible?'

Hoyt stared.

'You wanted this,' Teal told him, 'for soldiers and cops so they could perform at their best. What you also wanted was to help those poor stiffs whose heads are still back in Vietnam. You wish you could have done it for your brother-in-law. You want all these things. Comes to that, so do I. But you'd like it done legally, ethically, morally, and you know it can't happen that way.'

'I do?'

'Yes, General, you do. It's why you gave this to me. And don't fucking think I don't know it.'

Teal knew that he shouldn't have said that. But the general had broken the rules of the game by saying it first and out loud. Things do get done by hook or by crook. They get done, almost always, by people like himself, while the people who pay them are in church.

The general was pacing. He was struggling to control himself.

'When were you going to tell me about Winston and Camal?'

'Probably never. Long-term, they don't matter.'

'For the near term, however ...?'

'General Hoyt ... how much do you want me to say? I need them to make it happen. Without them, it won't. I'll spell that out for you if you insist, but I think you should leave them to me.'

The general, as he'd hoped, drew a breath and looked away. Teal had given him a way to back off and he took it.

Hoyt asked, very softly. 'How close are we with Richard?'

'Very close, but we need broader testing.'

'At Langley?'

'No. We're finished at Langley.'

'Then where?'

Now Teal looked away. His silence was a signal. It told Hoyt that he'd answer if the general asked again but that it would be best if he didn't. Hoyt's silence said that he understood.

He asked, 'What, by the way, was that last test about? The one that Grayson aborted.'

'We've been talking about who Richard could help. I didn't mention criminals ... sociopaths.'

'How does one ... go about recruiting criminals, Mr. Teal?'

'Zales had some on hand. His guards, the parolees. I added a few more from Langley's stockade. The drug seemed to make them ... I don't know ... more compliant. We'll try it on a larger sample later.'

'Zales's guards ... are now back at Belfair, I take it? Set loose among thirty-odd women?'

'Where Zales is observing them. They won't be a problem. As I said, if anything, they're calmer.'

The general stopped pacing. He was rubbing his chin. Teal knew that his mind wasn't on thirty women. It was back on Rachel Carey in particular.

'General, give me three days. If Rachel did it, we'll know it. After that you can follow your conscience.'

'Three days, you say.'

'She's locked up. It can't hurt.'

Hoyt looked into his eyes. 'What else do you need that time for, Mr. Teal?'

'To do what I do, General Hoyt.'

Teal left that meeting feeling reasonably sure that he'd get at least one of the three days he'd asked for. He had gotten Hoyt to agree to give him some slack without sucking that decent man in any deeper.

The problem, however, was just that. Hoyt was decent. Hoyt would sleep on it tonight. Toss and turn on it, more likely. By morning he might have a crisis of conscience. But Hoyt would not act on that crisis of conscience before calling to say what he'd decided. Teal was counting on that – it's what decent men do. It would give Teal tonight and perhaps Sunday morning to enact some decisions of his own.

Fucking Zales, thought Teal. All this extra trouble. All because he took Rachel for a walk without a leash.

As for Richard, the testing was going to be expanded, but no more would be done in this country. Winston had stockpiled the key chemical ingredients at the Winston Labs warehouse in Warrenton. He would ship them, unmixed, to Los Alamos. Los Alamos would add a few mystery ingredients and then transship them to PharMex. For the testing, Camal had said his people could deliver at least five thousand new subjects. Two units of the Mexican National Guard, a government hospital in Tampico, and a prison outside Cuernavaca. The Langley experiment that Grayson interfered with was a pilot for a larger one using Mexican convicts.

Testing in this country was never an option. Richard would never see the light of day if they tried to go the FDA route. So they'd do what all the big companies do. Test it and make it and sell it abroad. Spread the word that the stuff was better than cocaine, that every day would be like Christmas morning. Americans would flock overseas to get it. They'd be bringing it home by the case.

Until then, thought Teal, his immediate concern was to keep tight control of the supply. Hoyt was right about Camal, the man was a criminal, and Winston wasn't much better. Either one would go it alone if he could. But Winston would never have the whole formula; he'd think the Los Alamos additions were critical. Camal would get the finished mixture which he'd surely have analyzed, intending to then make it himself. But he'd never be able to be sure what was in it. The Los Alamos additions would change with each shipment. The mystery ingredients? They were vitamins.

Teal hadn't thought vitamins were much of a fail-safe when one of his chemists suggested their use. But then the chemist showed him the label on a bottle of multiple vitamin tablets. It came from a supermarket shelf.

'Never mind the actual vitamins,' he said. 'Just run down the forty or so chemical ingredients, all the chlorides and stearates and dioxides. It will utterly defeat any laboratory analysis. You can't even get the same reading twice on the contents of the bottle in your hand.'

So Los Alamos would control it. He, Teal, would control it. All he needed was the time to make it happen.

Chapter Twenty-Two

It was nearly eight o'clock when Grayson drove across the bridge that led onto Hilton Head Island. His first stop was at the Visitors' Center, where he picked up a map and a list of hotels. He saw that there was a Holiday Inn in the area called North Forest Beach. He called and booked a room from the center.

He continued on past several gated communities and was struck by the island's quiet elegance. No neon and none of the blaring signage common to most beach resorts. Even traffic signs were small with muted colors. That made destinations hard to find in the dark, but he did make his way to the Holiday Inn. He left his computer and his weapon in the trunk; he took his single bag and checked in.

In his room he found a Visitors' Guide that listed area nightlife. He opened it to an ad for Cheryl's Cabaret and saw that Cheryl's was a restaurant as well. The ad included a sampling from the menu. The cabaret was very nearby, and he decided that he might as well eat there. But Susannah's address was also nearby. He thought he'd first take a look. He left his bag unpacked and returned to his car.

Susannah's address was on Mallard Lane. It was one of several side streets, all named after birds, that ran from the one main road to the beach. There were no streetlamps in the residential sections. He knew that he wouldn't be able to see very much beyond what his headlights could take in. All the same, he was curious to see where she lived.

Her house was the second one in from the beach. Grayson drove slowly as if he were lost, then he pulled his car into her driveway. He'd expected some powerful floodlights to come on as he triggered her motion detectors. But her house had none. That surprised him somehow. A woman who wants to be left alone should have rigged every possible discouragement.

The house was quite pretty, painted blue with maroon trim; it stood among pines and live oak trees. The yard was small but well kept and well planted. He saw the addition that she'd built on herself, a combination workshop and studio. He felt a stirring of guilt. She had a nice life here. A part of him wanted to leave her alone. Another part wanted to know her.

He swung his car back out of her driveway and started toward Cheryl's Cabaret.

The cabaret was a nightclub and restaurant tucked back in a crazy warren of shops not far from Susannah's address. Judging from the plates on the cars parked outside, most of its clientele were tourists. A poster board hung in the window by the entrance with a picture frame glued to one corner. The frame was there to show who was performing in addition to the host-owner, Cheryl. The frame on this night held Susannah Card's photo, but Grayson would not have recognized her, had her name not been printed below. The shot was worthy of a fashion magazine. It showed only her head, back-lit, and in profile. Her lips were slightly parted, her chin and eyes were tilted downward; lustrous hair covered much of her jaw line. Grayson guessed that Cheryl had required a photo and this was as far as Susannah would go in allowing a true likeness to be shown.

That made sense, thought Grayson. It made perfect sense. Unless one asked why this private young woman would perform for the public in the first place.

He walked through the door; the bar was straight ahead. The room was fairly full, perhaps three dozen patrons. On the whole, they seemed middle aged or beyond. All the men wore sport shirts, no jackets. None glanced at him; they were all watching Cheryl. She was at a piano, to his left as he entered. Several people were seated around it. Grayson knew her at once from the poster outside. A striking woman, slender, vivacious. She was belting out a Cole Porter medley. She lifted one hand from the keyboard and waved at him. Startled, he smiled, then moved on toward the bar.

He chose a seat well back toward the rear. It gave him a view of nearly all that was happening. He ordered a beer from a very large bartender and said he'd like to look at a menu. When he looked up again, other people were entering. Cheryl waved a greeting at them as well without interrupting her playing. Grayson realized that she probably did that with everyone. But now he saw her looking back toward him again. Her eyes searched the bar until she located him, and then, for an instant, her smile disappeared. She pounded some keys just a little too hard. But just as quickly, she gathered herself and went on with the number she was singing.

Grayson told himself that the look had meant little. There was no way that she could know who he was. All she saw was a man perhaps twenty years younger than most of her other patrons. There was also the jacket, the green blazer that he wore. He knew that it made him stand out from the crowd. He knew that he should have given some thought to blending in better, but he hadn't. Grayson scanned the menu, and ordered a steak.

Cheryl finished her number. The crowd was applauding. She leaned into her mike and said, 'Glad you're all here.'

She said, 'I'm going to come out there and visit with you because I want to hear the gal who's comin' on next. You know who that is, so let's sing it.' At that, Cheryl sounded a chord and sang, 'Ohhhh ...' The crowd jumped in and picked up the 'Ohhhh ...' then burst into the song, 'Oh, Susannah.'

Grayson's head snapped up. He might have guessed that that song would be her signature intro. He was about to see her; he felt a thrill of excitement. He glanced around the room to see where she'd make her entrance. Most other eyes seemed to be looking toward him. He realized that she was

167

approaching behind him, on her way from a dressing room somewhere in the back. Grayson turned, too late. She'd already gone by.

She was wearing a white cowboy hat, smiling broadly. Her blouse was red silk, a bandanna at her throat. Her skirt looked like buckskin and she wore western boots. She was waving one hand at the crowd as she walked. The other hand held her guitar. Exchanging friendly greetings with the people she passed, she made her way to the small stage in front. This was Susannah, but a different Susannah. He never would have known her from her photographs.

She bantered with the crowd as she tuned her guitar. She seemed entirely at home there. Her accent surprised him. To his ear, it was Texan. Her tone was Texas loud, Texas friendly as well. Her first song was 'The Rose of San Antone.' She was good.

Grayson watched her, transfixed, as she did several numbers, all of them country and western. She was on for a forty-minute set. At its end, to applause, she stepped off the stage briefly. Grayson saw Cheryl walk over and hug her and whisper some words in her ear. Grayson guessed that she was passing on a request but he saw Susannah's mouth form the words, 'Are you sure?' Once again, he thought that Cheryl had glanced back toward him. Once again he put it out of his mind. He was only a face in the crowd.

Susannah, in any case, never looked up. She was fingering the strings of her guitar as if trying to recall a tune. She found it, she nodded, then returned to the mike. She did one more number as an encore.

Her set over, she walked back the way she had come. She made her way down the length of the bar, responding to flirtations with good-natured ease. Grayson would have liked a closer look at her face but decided that he'd best not show his own. Not quite yet. He thought that he'd better observe her for a while, then decide the best way to approach her. He turned his back to her, and not to seem rude, he pretended to be signaling the bartender. He could hear Susannah as she

168

drew near his bar stool but she seemed to be moving more slowly. He turned his head slightly to see what had delayed her. She was looking directly into his eyes.

She said softly, 'Good evening, Major Grayson.'

Three minutes later, he was waiting near his car for Susannah to change out of her costume. She had said that if he would meet her outside, perhaps they might reach an understanding.

Grayson was glad of the time alone. He needed it to compose himself and to realize how stupid he'd been. He should have realized that her professor might call her to warn her that a certain Major Grayson was looking for her. He'd have told her to watch for a man with a limp, last seen in a dark green blazer, tan slacks.

As he waited near his car he could still see inside through a curtain that was not fully drawn. A few minutes passed and Susannah appeared. All he could see of her was her head as she made her way through the crowd. He saw Cheryl rush across the room and move to intercept her. Cheryl raised one hand as if asking her to wait; with the other she was calling two bartenders over. Grayson saw that she was asking them to go with Susannah. Susannah shook her head. She did not want their help. She seemed to be saying she could handle it.

Grayson could not see much more of her than that until she stepped through the door. The Susannah who exited Cheryl's was stunning. She had brushed her long blondish hair back from her face and fastened it with a clip. She wore a dark pants suit, very tailored, very feminine, and a white silk blouse that was open at her throat. The suit made her look taller and leaner than she was. Texas was gone. This was New York. Maybe a model on her way to a shoot or a rich East Side deb going out on the town. But New York, to his mind, meant a few hard edges. He could see none, at least not on her face. She seemed very poised, unruffled, serene. When she spoke, her new voice very nearly matched the look, except for a slight, Southern drawl.

'You must be very good at what you do, Major Grayson. Would you mind telling me how you found me?'

'Miss Card, I was watching just now through the window. Believe me, I mean you no harm.'

'The harm, I'm afraid, has already been done.'

'What harm? That I've found you?'

'Will I have to move?'

'Not on my account, you won't. And no one else knows.'

She narrowed her eyes. 'Is that true?'

'On my word.'

'And you, I'm to believe, will keep it a secret? In return for what, Major Grayson?'

'Spend some time with me. Talk to me. No more than that.'

She took a step toward him. 'I would like to believe you.'

'The truth is,' he told her, 'no one else really cares whether I've found you or not. I'll explain why that's so if you'll talk to me.'

She looked into his eyes for what seemed a long time. She tilted her head sideways as if listening to his thoughts. Grayson never understood why some women did that. Stare back or drop your eyes, either way you looked guilty. It was Susannah, however, who broke off her gaze. She took a deep breath before speaking.

'You impressed Dr. Cohen as *perhaps* a decent man. Are you a decent man, Major Grayson?'

'I keep my word, if that's what you're asking.'

'Unless ordered to break it, I would think.'

'If I'm asked, did I find you, I won't lie. I'll say yes. But I will not tell anyone where you are living. I won't even tell them your name.'

'They don't know it?'

'Only Susannah, and they think that's an alias.'

She still seemed doubtful but somewhat relieved. 'Don't they bust you or something for refusing to answer?'

'I ... think I can persuade you that that's not a concern. Do you mind if we talk a little first?'

She chewed her lip. She held his gaze. 'You're saying the

170

right words but you seem very nervous. What am I to think, Major Grayson?'

'You're to think that I'm a lot less at ease than you are. I should not have been caught so off-guard.'

'Oh … I'm sorry, Major Grayson. I'm frightfully sorry. Here you've come all this way to intrude on my life and I've failed to put you at ease.'

'Would you please call me Roger? That might help things a bit.'

'You think a Roger is easier to trust than a major?'

'Rogers usually are. So are people named Fred. I don't know why that seems to be true, but it is.'

She was trying not to smile. She said, 'Let's walk for a bit.'

They wandered through the complex of shops. Grayson thought he might have seen two Susannahs already and he'd been with her less than five minutes. As they walked, he asked her how many there were and how she was able to control them.

'There isn't any *them*. There is me. Only me.'

'What about the Texas accent?'

'Can you imitate that accent?'

'Imitate, yes. Is that all you were doing?'

'Major Grayson …'

'Roger.'

'Roger, how would you like it if your every mood caused people to wonder which one of you was out?'

'I'd get sick of it, I guess. But then I'm not a multiple.'

'You're certain of that?'

The question startled Grayson. 'Why would you ask?'

'Because everyone is, to at least some degree. Dress a woman in jeans and she's one kind of woman. Dress her up in a sexy red sheath, she's another.'

Grayson felt a small wash of relief. He had feared, for an instant, that she'd seen on his face his real reason for wanting to meet her.

They walked on. She said, 'I assume you've read the book.'

'Zales's *Listening to Your Selves?* I had to.'

171

'As part of this project you and Zales are involved in? Some lunacy about trying to use multiples?'

'Not using. Understanding how it works.'

'Good luck.'

'Did ... Dr. Cohen tell you that I'm trying to kill it?'

'He told me you said so. He doubts that you can.'

'By myself? He'd be right. But the man I work for has the power to abort it. I work for Gen. Harlan G. Hoyt.'

Her expression was blank.

'You don't know that name?'

'I don't think so. Why would I?'

'I thought Martha Carey might have mentioned him to you. General Hoyt is her brother; he is Rachel Carey's uncle. I think you can trust him to do the right thing.'

A doubtful shrug.

'It was nice of you to meet with Martha Carey, by the way. I don't know how many people would have taken the trouble.'

'I couldn't do much. I mostly listened.'

'Even so ...'

'What I wish I'd done is told her to get far away from Zales. How could your General Hoyt not have known to do that? Why would he give Zales's theories any credence?'

'You detest Zales. Why? Just because of that book?'

'I detest him because ... well, okay, let's count the ways.'

And she did. Her litany went on for five minutes. At the top was that Zales was a liar and a fraud. His books were filled with anecdotal pap and not a single reproducible finding. Not able to show results of his own, he took credit for work that Dr. Cohen had done. He wouldn't know a true multiple if one dropped on his head. All he'd seen were the multiples other quacks had created and the ones he created up at Belfair. If Zales's inmates weren't multiples when they were first dumped there, they were before the first month was out.

'You say some weren't multiples. What else would they have been?'

'An annoyance to someone with money.'

'Some,' she agreed, 'might be victims of incest who needed to be kept from going public about it. But others are drunks, drug addicts, or tramps whose parents have social positions to protect. That's what asylums like Belfair are for. An addiction helps. It makes committing them easier. But it's getting them in and then *making* them crazy that keeps them locked up for the duration.'

She was silent for a minute.

'Is this news to you, Roger?'

'I'm ... not sure I believe it. How does Zales drive someone insane in a month?'

'He doesn't have to. He just makes them hallucinate. Did Dr. Cohen tell you of his visit with Rachel?'

Grayson nodded. 'The snakes. Yes, he told me.'

'Do you doubt that he drugged her just before that appointment?'

'Dr. Cohen was unwilling to say that.'

'I'm not.'

'Then I promise you this. I'll find out if it's true.'

'And then?'

'I will find a way to stop it, Susannah.'

She had changed again. She was serene again. She had paused at the window of a T-shirt store and was smiling at some of the more clever designs.

He asked, 'Would you answer a few questions?'

'Enough about Zales. It's too pretty a night.'

'I want to ask about you. I'm not sure where to begin.'

'You'd like to know if I'm really a nympho.'

'I ... saw that in the book. I never believed it.'

'Really? Why?'

'I considered the source.'

'You're weren't hoping just a little?'

'Never entered my mind.'

'I always thought it was every man's dream to meet a sharp-looking woman who fucks like a bunny. That's unless you think I'd be too much for you.'

'I ... did not think that at all.'

173

'Then you might be surprised. Will you be in town long, Major Grayson?'

Until then, he would have found it hard to imagine that Susannah ever used that kind of language. But she'd said it with humor, with a glint in her eye, and she'd thrown in some Texas again for effect. Grayson had to assume that she was pulling his leg ... trying to keep him off balance ... whatever.

The two walked on past other restaurants and shops. Grayson glanced at her face a few times. She was smiling at first. Even smirking, he thought. She seemed very sure of herself.

They walked a few more steps; he heard a sharp intake of breath. He glanced at her again and she was no longer smiling. This time her lips were drawn tight against her teeth. She was suddenly angry. She was muttering to herself.

'Is anything wrong?'

'No, I'm fine.'

'Did something just happen?'

'Roger, where are you staying?'

'At the Holiday Inn by the beach.'

'I live up that way. Farther down to the left.' She stopped and again she narrowed her eyes. 'But you already know where I live, don't you, Roger? Please tell me that you haven't been inside my house.'

'That's easy. I haven't. I only drove past.'

'To see if I was there?'

'To see how you live. Susannah, I'm just trying to know you.'

She seemed to understand. At least she didn't seem upset. Then she startled him by saying, 'You can come see it now.'

'You're ... sure you don't mind?'

'Plan on spending the night.'

Grayson tried not to stammer. 'Is ... this your surprise?'

She smiled. 'No, I'm not in my nympho mode, Roger. I want you where I can see you.'

'But ... why?'

'You've given your word and I think I believe you. But I

don't want to be lying alone in my bed, wondering whether you're on the phone to your general, telling him that you conned me into trusting you.'

'Are you saying ... you want me with you in your bed?'

'Get real, Major Grayson. In my guest room.'

Grayson still could not believe that she was serious, but was willing to play along for a while. He asked if he might stop off at his room to pick up a few things he would need. Susannah said, 'Sure, but I'll go with you.'

She wanted to keep him in sight, she said, because she'd seen this movie before. The government agent makes some excuse to be alone so he can get to some high-tech communications device. He contacts his control, says he's found the woman. In the next scene, carloads of specialists are dispatched, guys in vans with all kinds of electronic gear. They never seem to have anything better to do.

'My computer is about as high tech as I get. If you wish, you can even hold on to it.'

'You must have a cell phone. Care to throw that in, too?'

'Susannah, I promise, they won't care that I've found you. It's me they want out of the way.'

'How come?'

'There was this thing with dogs ... never mind, it's too dumb.'

'All the same, I think I'll stick close.'

They had taken his car and left hers parked at Cheryl's. They drove to the Holiday Inn. As they entered the lobby, the night manager looked up. He was young, Grayson's age, and he had a cropped beard. The face behind the beard looked startled, almost blushed, the instant he recognized Susannah. Grayson assumed that he had seen her perform.

She knew him as well. She said, 'How's it going, Eddie?'

He did not seem pleased to see Grayson with her. But he answered, 'Just fine. Hi, Susannah ... Mr. Scott.'

She glared at Grayson as they walked to the elevator. 'Which is it, Roger? Grayson or Scott? Or is your first name even Roger?'

'Susannah, I used a false name to check in. I paid up front and in cash.'

'I'm waiting.'

'If I used my real name it would be in their computer. If I paid with a credit card it would be in a computer. Anyone who wanted to would find me in an hour.'

'They would know you're on this island?'

'And they would guess why.'

'Then I'm sorry. I think.'

'Once I had your full name, that was how I found *you*.'

She thought for a moment. 'And who gave you my name?'

'No one. I got lucky. You left one small door open. If you're straight with me, when I leave here, I'll close it.'

That stare again. 'Let's get your stuff.'

She watched as he gathered his kit and some clothing. She asked, 'By the way, what did you do to your leg?'

With anyone else he might have said that he'd wrenched it. But this was Susannah, who understood blackouts. She understood because she'd had blackouts herself and had done what she would not have done otherwise.

'I got shot. Several months ago. Another assignment.'

She frowned. 'What kind of work do you do?'

'I investigate, mostly. Sometimes undercover. Like you, I play different roles.'

'Undercover, you say.' She was frowning.

'Something wrong?'

'I've seen that movie, too. You get close to people and then you betray them. Isn't that what undercover is about?'

'Not this time. Not with you. I am strictly myself.'

'But at other times, you become someone else. Am I about to be told that you're a multiple?'

'Not at all.'

'A while ago, I thought I saw a little tic when I asked if you're sure you're not a multiple.'

'You must have imagined it.'

'Look at me, Roger.'

'I am not a multiple.'

176

'I ... feel like I'm waiting for this great big *however*.'

'There were ... one or two incidents that caused me to wonder.'

'These incidents ... do you remember them clearly?'

'That's the problem. I don't remember them at all.'

'Blackouts?'

'Not long ones. A minute or so.'

'And I see you're left-handed.'

'What does that have to do with it?'

'Never mind. These blackouts ... had you been hurt? Was one of them after you got shot?'

'That one must have been shock.'

'Shock isn't a blackout. What happened after that?'

'I'd as soon not discuss it, if you don't mind, Susannah.'

'Yes, but you brought it up. You want to know what I think? It has *everything* to do with why you came to see me.'

'Not everything, Susannah.'

'Do I get to hear why else?'

'Could we ... lighten up just a little bit here? The "why else" is simply that I wanted to meet you. All you've done, who you are, what you've made of yourself. I want to know you ... for Pete's sake, who wouldn't? The other stuff almost doesn't matter.'

This time it was Susannah who could not look at Grayson.

Then she said, 'You still get the guest room.'

Twenty-Three

After leaving General Hoyt, Teal was suddenly hungry. He realized that he'd hardly eaten all day, nor had he gotten very much sleep. In the morning, he would need both his rest and his strength. He would dine and then go to bed early.

He walked from the Watergate to the Ritz-Carlton where the Jockey Club was located. He liked the Jockey Club, not so much for the food, but because many congressmen dined there. He cared not at all about mixing with them, but he'd noticed that they often had phones at their tables. Not cell phones, just everyday plug-in black phones. He supposed that they'd arranged to have the place swept to guard against taps or other listening devices. He made inquiries of his own. The answer amused him. The volume of bullshit coming out of those tables was so great that no agency had enough staff to parse it. For that reason, no agency bothered.

Content in that knowledge, Teal asked for a booth and had a phone brought to his table. The first call he made as he scanned the menu was to the machine in his apartment. He checked it for messages. It announced that there were none. He glanced at his watch. It was a quarter past eight. All was calm, he assumed, with Dr. Zales up at Belfair. Nor was there any word from Major Grayson.

He had asked Major Grayson to call in each day, but only so he'd know where Grayson was. Teal was satisfied, however, that Grayson was gone. He had learned that the major had logged out of Bolling and had gassed up a motor-pool car. He imagined that Grayson had headed for Durham, because Duke would be the sensible place to start. He would look for the professor who treated this Susannah. If Martha Carey found him, so, surely, would Grayson, but probably not on a weekend. It would probably be Monday before Grayson located him and was told by that professor to buzz off.

Monday, thought Teal. Grayson will be gone through Monday, at least. And he probably won't call before then.

Teal drew an address book out of his pocket and made a number of very brief calls to the technicians who'd been working at Belfair. He told them they were not to return there. He told all but one to get back to Los Alamos where they would continue their work. The technician who remained would visit Belfair one more time and help him to clean out that lab. That technician would be able to tell him what, if anything, was missing. He would know if the laboratory's computers had been breached. He would know which of Zales's own files they should seize. Teal, meanwhile, would gather the blue binders that were kept by the daughters of his three associates.

Zales, of course, would be outraged. He would realize at once that he had been snookered and so, in short order, would Hoyt. Zales wouldn't have the balls to put up much of a fight, but Leatrice would surely try to stop it. She'd be on the phone to Carey, even Hoyt, in five minutes. She'd offer them the choice of either stopping this piracy or seeing sweet Rachel in a Baltimore jail. In the meantime she'd probably order her guards to stand at the laboratory door with their Tasers, zapping anyone who tried to get past them.

We can't have that, thought Teal. It would be very untidy. So the next call he made was to Langley, Virginia. He told Sergeant Kristoff what he'd need. Kristoff was to pick four men from his unit and arm and equip them for night work. He would next requisition two stout army trucks. One truck should be big enough to hold the lab's contents, including the PET-scan equipment. The other would serve as a crash truck or decoy, depending on what problems might arise. Kristoff wouldn't have much time to put this together. He'd have to be on the road, heading north, by midnight. By 5:00 A.M. latest, he'd reach the nation's capital, where Teal and his one technician would meet them. They'd then proceed to Belfair, arriving well before dawn. With luck, thought Teal, they'd be out by first light. After that, it wouldn't matter who Zales called.

Teal considered putting someone inside the walls early – someone to make sure that the front gate would open and perhaps to cut all the phone lines. But a truck should make short work of the gate, and cutting phone lines didn't do much good anymore, with all those damned cell phones. Everyone seemed to have them.

On the matter of Zales's goons, he knew that Kristoff's men could handle them. Lock them up somewhere under guard. But a better idea might be to keep them too busy to worry about what else was happening.

Freeing some of Zales's patients might be just the ticket. Teal smiled at the thought. Zales likes to give field trips? We'll show him field trips.

We might furlough his entire fourth floor.

Chapter Twenty-Four

Jennifer had been waiting for Duane to go to sleep so that she could sneak up and see Veronica. Most nights she would hear him go into his room and turn on his TV about nine. She would hear the squeaks when he got into his bed. Most nights she would soon hear him snoring.

But this night it wasn't his own bed that was squeaking. He'd gone into the Quiet Room where Emma was strapped down. Jennifer could hear because he hadn't closed the door. She was afraid that he had climbed into Emma's bed and was going to try to have sex with her. In the foster homes, sometimes, that's what squeaking beds meant.

Very quietly, she went to the door and looked in. They were not having sex. Duane was not in the bed with her. He was sitting at its side and he was torturing her.

She saw that Duane had cranked up her bed so that Emma was halfway to a sitting position. He had pulled up a chair and had a pen in his hand. He was sticking the blunt end into her ribs and sometimes into her ear. It was making poor Emma buck like a horse and making her gasp and try to scream at him. Her wrists and her ankles were raw from the straps but she never stopped trying to pull loose. In between pokes, Duane was whispering things. Jennifer couldn't hear much of what he was saying but she knew that he was taunting her by the way Emma acted. The one bad word that she did hear was 'dyke.' Duane didn't like women who liked women.

Emma made noises like only cats make. She'd hiss and she'd

181

snarl and try to spit. She couldn't make noises much louder than that because she still had that leather mask on her face. You could see that she wanted to rip Duane's eyes out, but that didn't bother Duane. He'd just keep on talking – very quiet, almost nice – and poking her with that pen.

Jennifer blurted, 'Duane, stop it.' And he did.

He got up, sort of smiling, and came to the door. He said, 'I'm not hurting her. Go back to your room.'

'Duane, you're sticking a pen in her ear. How can you say you're not hurting her?'

'I'm not hurting her much. It's for her own good. I'm supposed to keep her from falling asleep until the drugs work out of her system.'

'Why can't you let her sleep? Can't she sleep the drugs off?'

'Yeah, but what if she vomits? That's the problem we got here. She could drown if she vomits in her sleep.'

'So, why don't you take off her mask?'

'What, you kidding?'

'Then at least turn her over. Lie her flat and turn her over.'

'Look, Jennifer … you have to go back to your room. This isn't none of your business.'

'I could help you turn her. That way she won't choke.'

'No one touches her straps as long as she's Emma. That's also why I got to hurt her a little. I got to make her want to stop being Emma.'

'Duane, that's dumb. She won't stop for that reason.'

'Hey! No calling names. That's enough.'

He raised a hand as if in warning that he'd smack her if he had to. 'You get back to your room and go to bed.'

She wanted to ask, '*Why don't you?*' but she didn't. Duane had never hit her, but he might. She yawned, rubbed her eyes, and nodded instead so Duane would think she was sleepy. She went back to her room. Duane watched her go. Then he shut the door so she couldn't hear.

Jennifer didn't know what to think about Duane. When she first saw him she thought he was scary. He would stare at her with his head tilted down and his eyes turned way up in his

182

head. But that was before he went away on his trip and came back with Chewey under his coat. Chewey was the name that she gave her new puppy, because he looked like Chewey from *Star Wars*. Duane smiled at her, almost. He almost was nice. Except that's the way he just was with Emma, even while he was wiggling that pen in her ear.

The other thing that happened after supper that evening was that Dr. and Mrs. Zales had a fight. She wasn't mad or yelling; she always spoke real calm, but the doctor was very upset. What got him so upset was that Emma was still Emma, and they couldn't find the two others. He told Leatrice that he'd warned her not to try to erase Rachel because now they couldn't find Teresa either. He said Leatrice didn't know what she was doing.

Maybe not, thought Jennifer, but she'd bet Emma did. Those other two weren't going to get out until Emma was good and ready.

Jennifer wasn't letting her own friends out either. Dr. Zales kept asking; he said he wanted to meet them, he said it would make him very happy. He kept trying to make her lie back, close her eyes, and pretend she was floating on a soft pink cloud that felt all cozy and warm. She didn't know why psychiatrists always seemed to think that all girls would like to ride on pink clouds.

Last time, he asked if she wasn't being selfish, keeping Chewey all to herself. He said he thought she should let her friends out at least long enough to pet him. Well, maybe she was being just a little bit selfish. She knew that they would love to play with Chewey. What they wouldn't love is being kept in a basement. Anyway, she shared Chewey with Veronica.

Dr. Zales hadn't talked to her for two whole days. Yesterday he had never even come down; Duane said he'd had to go to Baltimore. When he came down last night, it was real late, real dark. That was when he and Leatrice first brought Emma down and strapped her onto that bed. They brought her down in the elevator, out cold, and they had to drag her to the room where they put her. The first thing that

183

Jennifer saw about Emma was that she wasn't dressed like a patient. She was wearing street clothes and they looked crisp and new. The second thing she saw when they dragged Emma by was that her clothes were all splattered with blood.

Dr. Zales went back up, then came down a while later when the sky was just starting to get light. Jennifer only knew when the sun was coming up by the light that came through Duane's window. It was a tiny little window up high on his wall and the only one in the basement. Duane, a few times, had let her stand on his dresser and look out at the trees and the lawn. In fact, she had just got down from looking out when Dr. Zales saw her walking back to her room. That was when he saw her holding Chewey and thought Chewey was a toy. That was also when he caught his wife doing something with Emma and said Emma was not a toy either. Leatrice changed the subject; she kind of always did. She told Dr. Zales to lie down and take a nap and she said some other stuff about sex. She also asked him what he was doing about that soldier, Major Grayson, the one who Veronica likes.

She told him that she might ask Mr. Camal about how to get rid of the major. Dr. Zales got upset again. He said don't you dare. He said he'd speak to someone named Teal. Jennifer didn't know who that Teal person was, but she knew that Camal used to be Shan Li's name before she became Chinese. It still said so on the plate outside her door.

After Dr. Zales left, it was quiet again. Leatrice stayed for another half hour. Jennifer peeked in once to see what she was doing that her husband didn't want her to do. She wasn't doing much, just sitting there writing, with Emma's blue binder on her lap. Then Jennifer saw her rip a page from the binder and replace it with the one she had written.

She was changing Emma's diary and she wasn't supposed to. Only patients and their alters were supposed to write in diaries, but Jennifer had seen Leatrice doing this before. She had seen her do it, late at night or during nap time, when she didn't think anyone was watching. She did it, mostly, up on the fourth floor, but she'd also done it on the third floor a couple of times. One time, she left and Jennifer snuck in to try to see what she had written. But Leatrice caught her and grabbed her by the ear. That was when she moved her to the basement.

Jennifer had turned off the light in her room and pretended that she'd gone to sleep. But she'd left her door open a crack in order to hear Duane's movements. Some twenty minutes later, he finally came out, but he still wasn't going to bed. She saw him cross the hall to his bathroom. He went inside but he came right out again. She saw him look through some magazines at his station. He picked one and went back into the bathroom.

The magazine meant that he was going to take a dump. It meant he thought that the dump would be a long one. Jennifer decided to look in on Emma. She crept to Emma's room, stuck her head in the door and asked Emma whether she was okay.

Emma stared for a long time, then she slowly shook her head. She couldn't move it much; it was tied down. Jennifer asked if there was anything she could do. Emma nodded. She tilted her head toward her wrists.

'I can't let you up. We would both get in trouble.'

Emma tried to say words. Her eyes were all shiny. She kept pointing her chin toward her straps.

'They're cutting you, I know. I'm real sorry.'

Emma started to sniff. She was crying.

'Tell you what. I can loosen them a little. That's the best I can do.'

Emma's eyes went all pleading and grateful.

Jennifer eased one wrist strap very slowly and carefully. She was waiting for Emma to struggle. Emma didn't. If she had, Jennifer would have stopped. It was the same with the other three straps.

'They still aren't loose but they're not too tight either. Does that feel a little bit better?'

'Mm-hmm.'

185

'Would you like a drink of water? I can give you some water.'

'Mm-mm-hmm.' Her eyes got excited.

Jennifer filled a plastic glass and looked for a straw. She found one in a stand across the room. Emma gave a loud grunt and shook her head to say no. Jennifer understood; she did not want the straw; what she wanted was her mask taken off.

'I can't do that either. Do you still want the water?'

Emma's eyes flashed, but she nodded. She took the straw and she sucked on it thirstily. She drained a second glass after that one.

The stand across the room had a bed pan underneath it. She picked it up. It was clean. She asked, 'Do you need to use this?'

Emma shook her head, no.

'Well, you will. I'm going to leave it here on your bed. That way it will remind Duane to let you use it.'

She nodded.

'Can I get you a blanket? You'll catch cold with just a sheet.'

A grunt. It meant yes. Jennifer went and got a blanket. She draped it across Emma's body. She tucked it in around her feet and then her shoulders. Emma grunted again, this time softly. Jennifer looked into her eyes and thought she saw that Emma was trying to say thank you.

Jennifer stepped back to the door and listened for sounds from Duane's bathroom. She heard nothing. Her eye fell on Emma's blue binder.

She asked Emma, 'Do you mind if I look?'

Emma shrugged. She didn't care.

Jennifer found the page that Leatrice had written. It was the last one in the binder, small and scribbly. On the top line, it said, 'This is Rachel.' Except Rachel didn't write it. Leatrice did. Leatrice was pretending to be Rachel.

Jennifer read the page. It was all about an outing that Rachel had been on. It was yesterday afternoon. It was to Baltimore. It must have been the one that Duane had referred to when he said that Dr. Zales had gone to Baltimore. For an outing, it was mostly boring stuff. It said she went shopping and then went to lunch and then she took a walk by the harbor. She got back here for supper, had ice cream and cake, and after that she played checkers with Leatrice. The shopping must have been to buy those new clothes but it didn't say how they got so bloody. And it didn't say a thing about Emma.

Jennifer wanted to ask Emma about it. She could ask her with yes or no questions. But right then she heard Duane rolling off some toilet paper. She hurried back to her room.

She sat in the dark. Duane wouldn't go to bed. He was still in there pestering Emma. It was almost ten o'clock and Veronica would be wondering why she hadn't come upstairs to see her. She decided not to wait any longer.

She fixed up her bed so it looked like she was in it. Duane hardly ever looked in her room after she'd turned out the light. She took Chewey and, quietly, she slipped into the hallway. The door to Emma's room was closed again. She tiptoed past it and hurried down the hall to the end where the dumbwaiter was. The dumbwaiter was used to move meals, trash, and laundry. It wasn't used for anything at night. She put Chewey in first and then climbed in herself and pulled the wooden door shut behind her. The dumbwaiter ropes weren't very hard to pull but she'd learned to go slow or it would clunk against the sides. Veronica had told her to try not to clunk because Leatrice or someone might hear.

It only took a few minutes to reach the third floor. But then she had to sit and listen for a while to make sure she couldn't hear any guards. After that, she climbed out and snuck up on Veronica. She had to tiptoe over and peek in the door because Veronica had told her it was a good idea to make sure that Veronica was Veronica.

She was. Veronica saw her. She whispered, 'Hi, Jennifer.' She jumped up from her computer and came to the door. She pulled her in and closed it behind her. Veronica took Chewey and gave him a kiss. Chewey liked her, too. He got all squirmy.

Veronica got up and put some paper down for him. Jennifer walked over to look at the computer. She saw that Veronica was at that web site again, that group called the ACRA. It stood for the Aryan Christian Republican Army. She'd had to ask Veronica what an Aryan was. An Aryan is someone who hates coloreds and Jews and almost everyone else except Baptists. These were also the people who hated Major Grayson and would even hurt his girlfriend if they couldn't get him. But the major had told Veronica that he didn't have a girlfriend. Veronica was glad. She said she would be his girlfriend and he wouldn't have to worry. Those dumb militia people could never get her. They could never get past all the guards.

'Veronica? Did they find him? Is that why he hasn't come?'

She smiled and shook her head. 'They won't find him.'

'How can you be so sure?'

'Because this morning, I had an idea. I decided to tell them where to look.' She slid her chair back to show Jennifer her screen and the E-mail that she'd sent earlier. She had signed it, MOLLY PITCHER, AN AMERICAN. 'Up to now, they think he's on some Air Force base. But I told them where else he likes to hang out and I said that's where they should look.'

'You're telling them real places?'

'No, I'm making them up.'

Jennifer squinted to read the last message she'd sent. 'He's in Warrenton, Virginia? Where's that?'

'Just a town. A place. I invented it. I think.'

'You think? How could you only think?'

'Don't names ever just pop into your head? This one popped into my head.'

'Then where's Oakmont?'

'That's a place in that town. It might be a hotel. It's big and it has a fountain in front.'

'But the major isn't there?'

'He'd better not be.'

'And you've never been there?'

'I don't think so. No,' said Veronica absently. She had switched off her E-mail and was surfing other sites.

'Veronica …'

'Mmm?'

'You don't sound very sure. How do you know that the major doesn't go there? Maybe he told you that's where he grew up and that's why it popped into your head now.'

'No, I'd remember that. He never mentioned those places.'

'Then maybe Amanda or Henry have been there.'

'Maybe. I doubt it.'

'Can't you ask them?'

'I can but I'd have to go to sleep to do that and then see what they wrote in my diary. Even then I can never be sure. Amanda tells lies and she hates everybody. Henry's a creep; he never gives a straight answer and all he cares about is … you know … having sex.'

'Hey, that reminds me. What are sexual proclivities?'

'Proclivities? Could you mean cavities?'

'No, it's proclivities. They're what Leatrice has. I heard her tell Dr. Zales.'

'Never heard of them.'

'How about just sex? Do you like having sex?'

'I don't think I ever have. I wouldn't know.'

'Then how come Amanda wrote down that you did? She says you had sex with her father a lot.'

'Well, I didn't. I've never even seen him.'

'Did you mind me asking?'

'I think I'd like to change the subject.'

'Do you ever think about sex with Major Grayson?'

'Jennifer …' Her cheeks reddened. 'You shouldn't ask me that.'

'I thought so. You do.'

'I … think about us cuddling. But I start to get scared. I mean, I'm thinking about him but his face begins to change and suddenly he's this big pink-faced fat man.'

'Who's that?'

'I don't know. Some man. He's all dressed in white.'

'An angel?'

'No way.'

189

'Well, what does he do?'

'I don't know. I can never remember.'

Jennifer's eye found Veronica's blue binder. She was hearing a small distant voice in her head.

'Would you mind if I looked at your diary again?'

'I'd rather you didn't. There's some nasty stuff in it.'

'Just a quick peek. Two minutes. I've been wondering about something.'

'Okay. Just don't read it aloud.'

She took the blue binder from Veronica's table and opened it up on her lap. She had to go back about thirty pages before she found some old entries by Amanda. She read a few. More than bad, they were gross. They were all about her father, how disgusting he was. But the voice had been right. Or at least, so it seemed. They were written with the same tiny letters, all scribbly, that she'd seen Leatrice write in Rachel's diary.

'Veronica, look at this. Look at this writing.'

Veronica glanced over, saw the page she was on. She answered, 'I don't read that garbage, Jennifer.'

'Yeah, but this …'

'I don't read it,' she said firmly. 'All that stuff … it's not me.'

'I know. That's what I'm saying. It's …'

'Don't you read it either. You're too young. Put it down.'

'Yes, but …'

'Jennifer, I don't want to hear it.'

'Okay.'

'I'm … sorry. I didn't mean to snap.'

'You had a right to,' Jennifer told her. 'You know what I'd do with this stuff if I were you?'

'What?'

'Flush it down the toilet. All the parts you don't like.'

'We're not allowed to do that.'

'Then I will. Okay?'

She bit her lip. 'Sure. Go ahead.'

Chewey had done his business on the paper. Jennifer picked that up and flushed it as well. She washed her hands and dried them on her robe. She had a look of distaste on her face.

190

'You know something, Veronica?'

'Hmm?'

'I don't think I'd like sex.'

'You haven't ever had it?'

'Hey, I'm only twelve.'

'You know what I mean. Has anyone … touched you?'

'Uh-uh. No one wants to. They might if I ever have a body like yours but no one wants to touch skinny kids.'

'That's not what I've heard. Lots of girls here were touched. When it started they were littler and skinnier than you.'

'Maybe so. But I wasn't.'

'How can you be so sure?'

'I'd have to have been there, Veronica. I'd remember.'

'You might not if it happened to one of your alters.'

'They're not alters, Veronica. They're just my friends. Why does nobody understand that?'

'I'm sorry.'

'And I'm not crazy either. Not the way they are here.'

Veronica looked away. She was suddenly sad again.

'Veronica, I didn't say you. I said they.'

'It's all right.'

'Did I hurt your feelings? I'm sorry, Veronica. Some of them might be nuts, but you're not.'

'Oh, it's not about that. I just wish mine were my friends. I get very lonesome sometimes.'

'Isn't Shan Li your friend? Or those other three up here?'

'Shan Li doesn't even speak English anymore. All the others ever want to do is study.'

Jennifer reached out. She gave her a hug. 'Well, I'm your friend. Maybe not like Major Grayson. I'm just a kid, but I'm your friend.'

'I know. Thanks.'

Jennifer hated to see her so sad. She hated to think how sad she would be if her major couldn't come anymore. And that might happen. Even if those people on the web site didn't get him, Mrs. Zales told the doctor to get rid of him.

She said, 'You really like him, don't you, Veronica.'

191

'Uh-huh.'

'I bet I'd like him, too.'

'Hey, I've got an idea.' Just as suddenly, she brightened. 'Why don't both of us send him an E-mail?'

'You know where he is?'

'He's wherever his machine is.'

'Yeah, but you send the E-mail. I don't even know him.'

'No, we both should because he thinks you're not real. It's my fault for telling him you come through the walls. He thinks I made you up because I never have visitors.'

'But how is an E-mail going to make him think I'm real? He can't see who's sitting here typing it.'

'Then we'll have all the more fun when he finally meets you. He's even going to think I made up your dog.'

Jennifer wasn't sure that this was such a good idea. People don't like you better when they think you're acting strangely. Most times, they just want to get away from you. But maybe, she thought, Major Grayson wasn't like that. Maybe a good E-mail would make him want to come back. At the least, it would cheer up Veronica.

'Okay, you go first.' She made room for Veronica. 'Let me think for a minute what to say.'

Chapter Twenty-Five

Grayson turned his car into Susannah Card's driveway. Stepping out, he popped the trunk and recovered his laptop. He paused to glance at the neighboring homes as Susannah searched her purse for her house key. She raised her head. A little half smile.

'Are you worried about what the neighbors might think?'

'Well ... yes, when they see a strange car here.'

'You're assuming that they're not used to it, Roger. How do you know I don't do this all the time?'

'I'm sure that you have many admirers.'

She dropped her eyes. The smile had faded. She turned and walked to her door.

Actually, he had made no such assumption. All he'd thought was that maybe he should have backed in so that his license plate wouldn't show. But Susannah had just made one more oblique reference to her sexual activity or the lack of it. He supposed that he should have been more gallant and responded with greater conviction. His answer seemed to have annoyed her. Or hurt her.

They entered through a door that led directly to her kitchen. She said that she was going to brew up some coffee and asked him if he'd care for a cup. He said, 'Please.'

'You're welcome to look around if you'd like. Just leave your computer and your phone on the counter.'

Grayson wandered into her living room. He already knew how the house was laid out from the records his computer had retrieved. Her studio had once been a porch. Susannah had done the remodeling herself. The interior, in general, surprised him a little. He'd known other artists; they tended to be slobs; or at least they spent very little time keeping house. That was time that they could have used painting.

But Susannah's house was entirely neat. Not painfully neat in the compulsive sense. It was more that she probably found comfort in order, considering how chaotic her life had once been. On the other hand, thought Grayson, that was probably crap. He had taken too many psych courses.

Much of her wooden furniture was old. Not antique perhaps, but of very good quality. Her use of color was imaginative, not quirky. He spotted a number of those little delights that only seem to be found in flea markets. Overall, this was a house that was meant to be lived in, not a house that was meant to make a personal statement. In fact, Grayson realized, it made very few statements. What he looked for, but didn't see, were books. He knew from his computer that she'd bought quite a few on subjects that were widely diverse. He felt sure that there were many books in the house, probably stacked on closet shelves somewhere. Susannah would know that bookshelves can talk. Someone scanning the titles would know more of her in minutes than an hour in her presence would reveal.

'Coffee's ready,' she said. She came in with a tray.

He watched Susannah as she set the tray down. She had taken off her jacket and now wore her blouse loosely, no longer tucked into her slacks. As she leaned over, he could not help but notice that she wore no garment underneath. Grayson would have admired what he was seeing if this were any woman but Susannah. Well, he did admire it, but it also surprised him. He would have guessed that a Susannah would stay buttoned up tight. But there on her face was that smile again – Susannah looked good and she knew it.

'Am I making you uncomfortable? I could throw on a raincoat.'

He said, 'It's no problem. I've had myself neutered.'

194

'Oh, really?'

'A lot of us have. It's so women can't vamp us.'

'*Vamp* you, Roger? Do women still vamp?'

'Sure they do, but it's useless. You could sit there buck naked for all that I ...'

'Grayson ... shut up and drink your coffee.'

Grayson still wasn't sure what game they were playing. He had already told her that he thought she was beautiful, and the way he'd looked at her had said even more. He would not have thought that such a good-looking woman would need reassurance from him.

'Can I ask you some questions?'

'That's the deal. Go ahead.'

'How much of Zales's book was right about you?'

'Right, how? His conclusions or his facts?'

'Start with facts.'

'They were all pretty accurate because they came from Dr. Cohen. I was never abused in any way.'

'You're sure.'

'I was never even yelled at. Don't waste your time there.'

'But I gather you were lonely. You invented some friends. Where, by the way, is this town you grew up in?'

'Tangier is an island off northern Virginia.'

'I couldn't find it on my map. Another island, you say?'

'A small one. Remote. Mostly fishermen live there. Ask me how remote the place is.'

'I'll bite.'

'So remote that they still speak Elizabethan English. This is true, no joke; they really do. Captain John Smith founded it in 1608. The same families have lived there almost four hundred years.'

'Yours among them?'

'No. They moved there after World War II ended. My father was an American soldier from Ohio. He met my mother in Europe. She was Dutch, a war orphan. They decided that they'd seen enough of the world. They never even bought a TV.'

195

'You were totally isolated?'

'I never thought so at the time. We traveled through books. We read a great deal.'

'But they must have made friends on the island.'

'A few. Not many. They were seen as outsiders. It's true, by the way, that I did invent friends. But I don't remember being all that lonely.'

'You invented them? Or they simply appeared.'

'Roger ... none of them simply appear. Somebody has to create them. In my case, I invented the sort of friends that a lot of little girls would like to have. Some were like kids I'd only read about in books. You know ... like Nancy Drew, Girl Detective. I had a Heidi for a while but she was too goody-goody. I replaced her with a Huckleberry Finn type.'

'A boy.'

'He wasn't real bright but he was nervy.'

'But you ... realized at the time that these friends weren't real.'

'I'm sure I did, but I didn't think about it. Little girls don't sit around searching for truth. Little girls sit around pretend-ing.'

'But they did become real as time went by?'

'Some grew as I grew. They developed.'

'And began to take over?'

'They never did that. It was more that a situation would arise that one of them was better equipped for. But sometimes they'd stay out a little too long. Sometimes they'd do things that I wouldn't do, but that's what alters are for.'

'To misbehave?'

'Roger, think of an alter as a fantasy figure. If you're timid you'll fantasize being tough. If you're not so good at sports you'll have a sports-hero fantasy. If you're sexually inhibited you'll invent some tigress who always has men at her feet. It's a very small step from having this kind of fantasy to having it affect your real life.'

'But you're talking about an alter you invented, as opposed to one that some therapist dug up.'

'I'm not sure there's all that much difference.'

'How so?'

She turned her head. 'Did you hear a beeping?'

'It's my laptop. Don't mind it.'

'Are the batteries running down?'

'It's signaling a message. Never mind. This is interesting.'

'A secret message, or might you let me see it? I mean, now that we're being so trusting and all ...'

'Whatever it is, you're welcome to read it. Right now, I'd like you to finish your thought.'

'Where were we?'

'Natural alters versus therapy alters.'

'Oh. Therapy alters are fantasies as well, except that they show up full-blown.'

'But from where? How could patients produce them on the spot?'

'It's not on the spot. They learn how over time. Women who've been diagnosed with MPD have been seeing a therapist for seven years on average. Meanwhile, they've been reading just about every book that every self-appointed expert gets published. They know about multiples; they've read all about them; they've heard them described on TV. That's why you can see the same alter popping up in a hundred or more different patients.'

Grayson knew that. He'd seen it at Belfair. Several of the diaries kept by Zales's patients seemed to have very similar alters. But something about them had nagged at him from the time he began reading through them.

He narrowed his eyes. 'The *exact* same alter?'

'I meant to say the same general type.'

'But not exact.'

'You look troubled about something. What is it?'

'The handwriting in some of them. I think it's the same. Can several of them have the same handwriting?'

'No.'

'But say they do. How would you explain that?'

'We're talking about entries in diaries at Belfair?'

197

'Yes.'

'Easy. Someone else made up the entry.'

'But, why?'

She shrugged. 'One reason, a benign one, would be to prime the pump. You invent an alter, one you think you can work with, and you write in some entries by that alter. Next you show the patient that this alter has been out. She believes it and from then on that alter exists. It saves a lot of hit or miss digging.'

'And a less benign reason?'

'To keep her at Belfair. All you'd do is invent a new and dangerous alter and show those new entries to the parents or a judge. Have that alter write some awful things about her parents; things that they wouldn't want some new therapist to hear. They'll be happy to keep her on ice.'

'That's extortion.'

'No kidding. Now let's hear about you.'

'No, wait. I have a ton of other questions.'

'They'll keep.'

'You never told me how you got control. I mean, how did you put yours back in the box so they wouldn't come out on their own?'

'Too late. It's your turn. Who'd you shoot?'

'I didn't say I shot anyone. I said I got shot.'

'Are you carrying a gun right now, by the way?'

'It's in my trunk.'

'That's a good place for it. Now tell me, Roger, you said you blacked out. What's the next thing you knew after that?'

Grayson was not about to sit in her living room and tell her about Janice's brains on his shoes. 'It's not important,' he answered.

'It isn't? Since when? A half hour ago you as much as admitted that you think an alter took over.'

'No, I didn't. However ... for the sake of argument ...'

'Roger, just tell me. What did you do?'

'Not now, okay?'

'But you'll tell me?'

'I'll try to. But first let me ask … a while ago, you said we're all multiples. How would that be true in my case?'

'How would I know?'

'That's it? How would I know? That's all you can offer?'

'Roger … you want answers that nobody has. I've read all the theories. I don't know what applies. Except maybe the one about left-handers.'

He recalled that she'd noted that he was left-handed. He asked, 'What theory is that?'

'There are actually two that try to explain it. Start with the fact … or I'm told it's a fact … that every human conception is a multiple conception. That means several eggs get fertilized at once. The extra eggs, in most cases, don't survive. They are neither expelled nor absorbed by the body. They're absorbed by the healthiest egg. If that egg absorbs the tissue of the others, it also absorbs their genes. So right off, you have an egg that's maybe six different people, but just one of those people is dominant.'

'This applies … to which one of us? Is that me or you?'

'Assuming it's true, then it's everyone, I guess. It's what makes us complex human beings.'

'What about the left-handers? What's the theory there?'

'That one applies to the conception of twins. Far more twins are conceived than ever develop. One, most often, is absorbed by the other before the mother even knows that she's pregnant. Because twins are one cell that has split into two, one is the mirror image of the other. Therefore, one is right-handed, its opposite is not. The theory is that all left-handers are survivors of what would have been twins.'

'But the other twin … you believe he's still there.'

'I didn't say I believe it. I said it's a theory.'

Grayson's stomach had tightened. He remembered coming to. He remembered holding onto that tree limb for balance. He remembered his Beretta being in his right hand. But perhaps he had shifted it when the shooting was over. Perhaps he had needed to free his left hand because it was nearest the limb.

'Well, does it have any basis?' he asked. 'Do you know of any research that's been done?'

She glanced toward the kitchen. 'Your laptop just beeped again.'

'Never mind the damned thing. Can you answer my question?'

'Roger, why are you getting upset?'

'Because like you, I get tired of crackpot ideas from every shrink who wants to get published.'

'I'm sorry I mentioned it.'

He took a breath. 'No, I'm sorry. It's me. I guess that touched a nerve.'

'Drinking coffee's no good if you're starting to feel wired. How about if I get you a beer?'

'I'm okay.'

'You like Scotch? Someone gave me a good single malt.'

'Nothing, thanks. This theory … do you recall where you read it?'

She answered that she hadn't, but Dr. Cohen had. It was a paper that he'd picked up at a symposium. He told her about it during one of their sessions. No relevance to her case, just shooting the breeze.

The gist of it was that surviving twins – those who *knew* that they were surviving twins – always seemed to feel a sense of incompleteness. No surprise. But surviving twins who *didn't* know, reported identical feelings. These were people who tended to try many things – jobs, hobbies, relocations, whatever – and always seemed to be searching for something without ever understanding what it was. They tended to try to reinvent themselves far more often than other people did.

Even this, said Susannah, was fairly understandable given the fact that they'd lost a twin. But then some other researcher noticed that left-handed people had the same characteristics. That eventually led to the postulation that left-handers might be surviving twins. If so, they had absorbed the dead twins' genes and therefore had absorbed all their predispositions. These predispositions – and genetic

200

compulsions – were often not shared by the surviving twin, but they nagged at him throughout his life, all the same. It was sort of a genetic haunting.

'Does any of this touch that nerve?' she asked.

'Not really. My ... episodes were not a frequent occurrence.'

'But this work you do. You said you play many roles. That does sound a little like searching.'

'Susannah ...'

'On the other hand, maybe you just popped your cork. You did something terrible, didn't you?'

'I ... might have.'

'Was a woman involved?'

Grayson blinked. 'What made you ask that?'

'Men aren't quite as bothered when they shoot other men. I know you shot someone. Was that someone a woman?'

Grayson stared for a moment. Then he nodded.

'A woman you felt something for, am I right?'

He didn't respond.

'I see. You were lovers.'

'You ... might say that.'

'Don't dance around, Roger. You've gone this far.'

'Look, Susannah ... I've been through this with a Pentagon shrink. The only reason I've gone into it with you ...'

'You thought I'd have an answer. Why would I?'

'Because the shrink I dealt with has never blacked out. He never became someone he didn't know. You, however, have done both these things and you've also gotten into some trouble. I just thought that you might ...'

'What trouble was that?'

'Zales's book. It says ... well, I'm sure you had lovers, too.'

'And one of my hundred or so knocked me up. Is that the kind of trouble you think I was in?'

'Well, I ...'

'You see that, Roger? You believed that damned book. Do you see why I keep to myself?'

'Susannah ... I'm sorry. What trouble were you in?'

'They thought I had cheated on my midterms.'

'Cheating? That's all?'

'Well, it might not be up there with homicide, Roger, but in college they take a dim view.'

He said, 'Look, Susannah … I have an idea. Why don't I apologize now, in advance, for every dumb thing that I'm going to say while I'm trying to figure both of us out?'

'It was my handwriting.'

'In what? In a diary?'

'No diary. Two exams. I took both courses and I took both exams, but the writing in each was very different.'

'Yours and an alter's?'

'Mine were friends; they weren't alters.'

'Sorry. I forgot.'

'There's a big difference, Roger.'

'I understand. So, what happened?'

'The school first thought that I'd sent in a ringer to take one or both of those exams. Duke would have expelled me but Dr. Cohen wouldn't let them. He'd seen me in both of those exam rooms.'

'So he knew you were a multiple.'

'He suspected that I was.'

'And he offered to help you.'

'He helped me a lot.'

'He did what? Taught you how to integrate your various friends? Make you into what Zales calls a Mosaic?'

'Pretty much.'

'So now all you are is just plain Susannah Card. No more blackouts, no more problems. Dr. Cohen did all that?'

'Yes, he did.'

'Before Zales was in the picture?'

'Zales contributed zip.'

'Then why would he have needed to consult with Norman Zales?'

'It wasn't just Zales – Zales was far down the list. Dr. Cohen consulted with anyone who might have treated a Natural. Naturals don't turn up every day.'

202

'Susannah ... I think you can see what I'm asking. Why do all that consulting if he'd already cured you?'

'I'm better. It's over. That's all you have to know. I'm ... going to go make up your bed.'

She went to a closet for fresh linens and a blanket. A voice in her head said, '*He's not fooled, Susannah.*' The voice had a loud Texas accent.

She answered, '*I know.*'

'*Is he going to be a problem?*'

'*He's got problems of his own.*'

She stepped into the guest room and stripped the old sheets.

'So, why'd you bring him back here? You're hot to get laid?'

'That's not going to happen. Don't start.'

'Why not? He's a hunk and you're way overdue.'

'And quit popping in while I'm talking to someone. Especially don't pop in and tease him.'

'Who teased?'

'That nympho-who-fucks-like-a-bunny thing you said. And calling me a great-looking woman.'

'I didn't say great-looking. What I said was sharp-looking. What I could have said was sensational, Susannah. You really do look good tonight.'

'So did you, but it's tacky to say so yourself.'

'We're ... talking modesty here, is that right?'

'We're talking about being a lady.'

'That's a hoot. You brought him coffee with your tits hanging out. I was right; you're looking to get laid.'

'Susannah?' Grayson's voice. 'Can I be of any help?'

'*You think you're never going to see this guy again. So you say, why not, what's the harm?*'

'I'm fine. Be right out. *That is not what I think.*'

'*Because this one might not go away, Susannah. That thing about vamping? He's vamped.*'

'*I'll be back in a sec. We need to have a little talk.*'

203

Chapter Twenty-Six

Charles Winston had an early teetime on Sunday and had decided to go to bed early. He took two sleeping tablets washed down with vodka and was under the covers by ten.

He had just drifted off when his telephone woke him. He squinted at the clock on his bedside table. It was only twenty minutes after ten. As the telephone kept ringing, he became aware of a blue light strobing outside. Police? He snatched the phone to his ear.

'What ... what is it?'

'Mr. Winston, sir, it's the Sheriff's Department. Are you okay, Mr. Winston?'

Winston barely understood the accent at first. What he said sounded more like 'chef's parment.' Winston rolled out of bed; he was naked. He picked up a robe to partly cover himself and carried the phone to his window. He looked down at his driveway, saw the deputy and his car. The deputy was wearing a trooper-style hat. Winston couldn't see much of his face. To one side, he saw a second man in a gray uniform. The second one was scanning other windows with his flashlight and he had one hand on his pistol.

'Okay? Yes, I think so. What's happening down there?'

'Are you alone in the house, sir?'

'Am I ... what?'

'Are you alone, sir?'

He had to think before answering. He had to clear his head, which was fogged with old pictures of police, years ago, crashing in and putting him in handcuffs. He stepped to a lamp and turned it on.

'Mr. Winston?'

'Just a minute.'

He looked around his bedroom. There was no one, of course. It was only the pills and the vodka. He never brought his little friends home anymore. It was better, by far, to take them elsewhere.

'Yes, yes, I'm alone. What's the matter?'

'Sir, don't be alarmed but we're after a prowler. He was spotted trying to open some of your windows. Sir, do you have a weapon? Any weapons in the house?'

'A gun? No, I don't. Am I in danger?'

'No, sir. I just don't want you shooting us while we're checking the perimeter. Okay, sir?'

'Yes, yes. By all means.' Winston put on his robe.

'But you stay on the phone, keep in contact. Will you do that?'

'Shall I turn on some lights?'

'No, I don't think we … what?'

Winston saw the trooper turn toward his companion. He listened, then nodded, then looked up again.

'Mr. Winston, you'd better let us come in. The door to your kitchen's been jimmied.'

'Oh, my God.'

'Leave your phone off the hook so I can hear any sounds. Get down here real quick, switch off your alarm, let me and my partner find who's in there.'

Charles Winston felt a flush of relief as he opened the door for the trooper. He saw that the deputy had turned off his blue light. He saw the car, green and white, an older model Chevrolet. It seemed unlike those of the local police or those of the Highway Patrol. The deputy, moreover, had the sort of battered face that one would expect of a prizefighter. Scars around both eyes, a nose mashed and bent, and a permanent bruise at his jaw line. His hands, Winston noticed, were misshapen as well. They looked as if they'd been caught in a mangle and had never properly healed.

'Did you say that you're from the Sheriff's Department?'

'You're wondering about the car? Special burglary unit. Are you sure you're alone in the house?'

'Well, I hope so. I ...'

'You didn't seem sure when I asked you before. No maid, no butler, none of those?'

'The help works by day. They don't stay here at night.'

'Let me ask another way. Where is Grayson?'

'Um ... who?'

'You heard me. Where's Grayson?'

Winston didn't understand. 'Could you ... mean *Major* Grayson, by chance?'

'Yeah, I do. Do you know him or not?'

'Well, no. I mean ... I know who he is. Why on earth would you think that he's here?'

'We'll take a look. Turn around, Mr. Winston.'

'Turn around? What for?' But Winston obeyed.

'So I can whack you in the head, you dumb shit.'

Winston came to gradually, as if emerging from a fog. He felt a searing pain at his temple. The next thing he felt was the hard floor beneath him. He was rocking. He was on his bare stomach. He realized, to his horror, that he'd been tied up. He could feel that they had used the sash of his bathrobe to bind his hands and his feet together and draw them up tightly behind him.

He heard a man's voice say, 'There's no one else here. I can't see that anyone else even stays here.'

'You checked all closets? Under the beds?'

'There's no one hiding. There's no one else's clothes. All the clothes are his size and mostly white.'

'You looked in the bathrooms?'

'Not even a toothbrush. There's nothing that doesn't belong to this porker. It looks like we got a bad tip.'

'Yeah, but you heard him. He knows who Grayson is. He's got to know more than he's saying.'

'Hey, you want to see something? Go look in his basement.'

'What's there?'

'This guy's into kiddie-porn. I mean, really sick shit. He's got maybe fifty video cassettes and a big stack of dirty magazines. There's also pictures of him with little girls. There's this one where he's …'

'You watch him. I'll go take a look.'

The first man, the one with the battered face, was gone. Winston tried to feign unconsciousness but he couldn't keep from gasping for breath. His shoulders and his thighs felt on fire from the strain of being trussed up like a hog.

He whispered, 'Please. Can't you loosen this? I won't run. I won't move.'

'I know you won't, friend. Where is Grayson?'

'I swear to you … I've never … I've never set eyes on him. All I know is that he is some sort of snoop. I wouldn't know Grayson if he walked in the door.'

He heard heavy boots climbing up from the basement. He heard the man mutter, 'Oh, sweet Lord above.'

The one standing over him asked, 'Did I tell you?'

'I think I want to puke.'

The man approached and aimed a kick at his ribs. Winston gagged, tried to scream. He could not. The man lowered himself into a squat and produced a thin knife from his boot.

'He still says he doesn't know Grayson,' said the other.

The first man began pricking Winston with his knife. Winston squealed, tried to wriggle away. In the effort, he rolled on his side.

'Looky there,' said the man. 'I see your dick's hanging out. Hard to find it under all of that flab.'

Winston tried to roll further. He could not.

'Two things,' the man told him, 'you should try to keep in mind. The first is, back home, I had two little sisters. I was their big brother and I loved them to pieces. Now I come to your house; I go down to your basement; I see other little girls just like them.' He stuck him. 'Do you begin to sense that I don't like you, Mr. Winston?'

Winston burst into tears. 'I … I never …'

207

'Second thing is why you should not protect Grayson. Three friends of mine are dead. Grayson killed them, all three. One of the three was a beautiful woman. This woman, name was Janice, never hurt a living soul who didn't purely deserve it. But while she was helpless, on her knees looking up at him, Grayson put a hole right between her eyes. She's with Jesus; that's my only comfort.'

'Then for Jesus sake, listen. I don't know ...'

The man stuck him.

'So all this considered, you should probably figure that I won't be real gentle when I ask you. You'll tell me where he is, where he goes, who he's with. You're truly going to tell me, Mr. Winston.'

'But, I swear ...'

'If you do, there's a chance ... not a big one, but a chance ... that you'll still have your little wee-wee when we leave here.'

Chapter Twenty-Seven

Susannah told Grayson that his room was ready. But she added, 'Look, Roger ... you don't have to stay.'

He seemed disappointed. 'What changed your mind?'

'I know you're not here to ... cause me any problems.'

'Would it matter if I say that I like being with you? We don't have to talk about this stuff anymore. Maybe you could show me your studio.'

'It's getting pretty late. I really ought to get to bed.'

'Susannah!!'

'All right!!!'

'But, sure, if you'd like to, you're welcome to stay. Um ... wait here a minute; I need to go freshen up.'

She flushed her toilet and ran water in the sink because sometimes she answered out loud. The voice in her head said, 'You see, Sooz? He likes you.'

'Let's leave that alone.'

'Lots of guys would be real happy to be where he is.'

'You don't see them lining up at the door.'

'Because you scare them off.'

'And I think we know why.'

'What? That one time with Eddie? Come on, that was different.'

A snort. 'Eddie certainly thought it was different.'

'I still don't know how you can blame me for that. You took the wrong guy to bed for all the wrong reasons and then

209

suddenly you say, "What the heck am I doing? Why am I here with this turkey?"'

'Eddie isn't a turkey. He's perfectly nice.'

'And what, it was his birthday or something?'

'He was just … sad and lonely and I guess so was I.'

'Mercy-fucking, Susannah. That's what it was. Gorgeous women do not mercy-fuck.'

'Oh, really. Then explain to me why …'

'Why I did? I had to. You were getting cold feet. Who knew that an orgasmic aria or two would end up scaring him shitless?'

'Yeah, but it's me who has to see him when he comes into Cheryl's, or like tonight at the Holiday Inn.'

'I saw that. He ain't mad. Fact is, he's still stuck on you.'

'All the same, stop doing me favors. Next time wait to be asked.'

'I will. Next time. Now what about Grayson? If you're sure you don't want him, can I have him?'

'No.'

'He's a killer, Susannah. Doesn't that turn you on?'

'That man is a killer like I was a cheat. If it happened, it was not him who did it.'

'Then who? His dead twin?'

'He … how would I know?'

'Take him in, screw his brains out, bring his blood to a boil. Maybe the dead twin will surface.'

'Sally … could you try to show a little more class?'

'The class act is you. I'm the trash-talking tramp. Do you think there's really a twin?'

'I don't know. My guess is traumatic amnesia.'

'Or an out-of-body thing. You know, like you have?'

'Mine are different these days. I still know what's happening.'

Susannah raised her hand. She heard footsteps approaching.

'He's coming. He probably thinks you fell in.'

Susannah turned off the faucet. She opened the door. She saw Grayson with a haunted look on his face. For a moment, she thought that he'd heard.

210

'Could you … come out to the kitchen for a minute?'

'Um … is there a problem.'

'I went ahead and checked my machine. There's some E-mail from Belfair that I'd like you to see.'

Chapter Twenty-Eight

Hoyt's crisis of conscience would not wait until morning.

He was pacing his apartment, in no mood for sleep. He was furious with himself; he was blaming himself. But for him, none of this would be happening.

Even after Carey had pushed through that grant, Hoyt could have blocked his access to black-budget funds. But Martha had said, 'Please, I know you don't think much of Andrew, but this is for Rachel, it could help her.'

He'd listened as she outlined the work Zales was doing. He'd said, 'Very well, I won't stand in your way.'

She answered, 'No, Harlan, that's not what I'm asking. What I'm asking is for you to keep an eye on it.'

Well, he did and he didn't. He tried to stay at arm's length. But then along came Zales's compounds and Chameleon expanded and soon it split off into Richard. He began to believe that Project Richard might work; or rather, he needed to believe it. But could the work be done legally, ethically, morally? No, of course it could not. He'd known that from the start. As Teal said, 'That was why you brought me in on this. And don't fucking think I don't know it.'

Teal was right. He'd used Teal, but that's what Teal was for. He had also, however, used young Major Grayson to further distance himself. And now to cap it off, he'd sent Grayson away, and had lied to him about the reason.

We always, he reflected, send the Graysons away. We want them because they are honorable men, but in the end, that's why we get rid of them. And who do we keep? We keep the Winstons and the Camals because we need the sort of men who know their way through a sewer. We elect the venal Andrew Careys to office because we need to have that office in our pockets. We buy the books of a Norman Zales because he tells us that nothing is our fault. We hire buccaneers like Prentice Teal because we know they'll ride roughshod over law and procedure while allowing us to pretend we didn't know.

And now we're pretending that we're not at all sure that Rachel has murdered two men. Well, enough is enough. He would ask Zales himself. He tapped out Zales's number at Belfair.

'Oh, good evening, General Hoyt.'

It was Leatrice who answered in that odd, detached voice. She said, 'It is always a pleasure, even at this late hour. How might I be of assistance?'

'You can put your husband on. I want to speak to him.'

'I'm afraid that Norman is already asleep. He's had a rather exhausting day.'

'Please wake him.'

'But he's taken some medication, you see. He would not be terribly lucid.'

'Very well, I'll ask you. I want a yes or no answer. Was Rachel in Baltimore yesterday?'

'You've heard,' she answered brightly. 'Then you must be so pleased.'

'I must? Why is that?'

'Oh, look what I've done; I've spoiled the surprise. She wanted to tell you herself. She wanted to tell both you and her mother what a wonderful triumph it was.'

'Leatrice ... two men were murdered last night.'

'Two men? What two men?'

'It's all over the news. The two who were found in their cars.'

'Oh, those. Yes, I do recall hearing the report. But what could they possibly have to do with your niece?'

'Are you telling me that she wasn't involved?'

213

'Involved? She was here. How could she be involved?'

'When did she return there, exactly?'

'She was back in time for supper. Weren't those two men murdered much later at night?'

'That's what I'm told.'

'General Hoyt, I'm afraid you have me at a loss. Your niece spent a wonderful afternoon in the city. She shopped, she had lunch, she fed seagulls at the pier. She was never unobserved for a moment.'

'Not at all?'

'Well, we didn't follow her into rest rooms, of course. I trust there are no murdered attendants.'

'She was back before dark?'

'And we had a little party. She consumed two helpings of ice cream and cake. I suppose we were all a little giddy as well but, you see, we were just so delighted.'

'Was Mr. Teal there?'

'At the party? Heavens, no. Can you picture Mr. Teal eating ice cream?'

'Leatrice … listen. Never mind about the party. I am asking how Teal could have gotten the idea that Rachel might have killed those two men.'

'Ah, that she *might* have. Is that what he said?'

'Please answer my question.'

'I'm sure I don't know.'

'What about Rachel? Is she still awake?'

'I'm sure she's sleeping soundly, but I'll look in once more. I was just about to do that when you called.'

'Very well. I'll speak to Teal. I may have misunderstood.'

'It's all in her diary. Her whole day, you know. You're certainly welcome to read it.'

'Perhaps … another time.'

'We won't be seeing you, then?'

'No, not for a while; I'm going to be tied up. Leatrice, I am sorry I alarmed you.'

'Your Mr. Teal is a trickster, I think.'

'That has been said of him, yes.'

'Well, please tell him for me that, whatever his scheme, he has been rather reckless in this instance. Please impress upon him that young Rachel, your niece, has an incontrovertible alibi.'

'I expect I'll take that up with him, Leatrice.'

Hoyt tried Teal's home number. He got his machine. He left a message that said only, 'Call me.' He had no other means of contacting Teal. Teal never used cell phones or pagers.

What the hell was going on here? Who was lying and why? If it was Teal, it was an incredibly stupid lie, very easily found to be false. Prentice Teal, however, was anything but stupid. If he lied, it was part of a much larger weave. Prentice Teal always had a scheme.

If it was Leatrice, same question. How could she have hoped to make it stick? Rachel was at Belfair eating ice cream or she wasn't. Leatrice could probably make her think that she was. She could probably even make *herself* think she was. But the proof, in the end, would be on Rachel's face. Her face would show signs of a beating or it wouldn't. He was damned well going to find out.

He dialed one more number. It rang several times before his sister picked up her phone.

'Martha, it's Harlan. I know it's late to be calling.'

'I'm still up. I was watching the news.'

'The news?'

'Uh-huh.'

'Any story in particular?'

A brief pause. 'Why would you ask?'

That was clumsy, he thought. 'Oh, no reason at all.'

'Harlan ... talk to me. What's this about?'

'Nothing in particular. I just thought I'd ask you ...'

'Harlan, is it Andrew? Is he in some trouble?'

'Your husband? No, not to my knowledge.'

'He's not here – he's at a meeting. Is he really at a meeting?'

'Martha, slow down. I know nothing about Andrew. I don't know or care where he is.'

'I'm sorry.'

215

'I've been talking to Leatrice Zales up at Belfair. She tells me that Rachel has ... not been herself. I thought I'd drive up there first thing in the morning, drop in unannounced for a change.'

'What would ... *not herself* mean in her context, Harlan?'

'That's what I'd like to see. I'd like you to go with me.'

'I think that I'd better. Name the time.'

'Would 6 A.M. be too early? I'll swing by with my driver.'

'Six will be fine. Now tell me the truth. What is really going on here? What have you learned?'

'Oh, for heaven's sake, Martha ...'

'Harlan, I know you.'

'We'll talk when we've looked in on Rachel.'

He supposed he should have told her to say nothing to her husband. If he had, however, she'd smell more of a rat than the one she was smelling already. Martha was nobody's fool.

He wasn't at all sure that he'd done the right thing by involving her at this point. All he knew was that he had to find out for himself why Teal would have told him such a story. No matter who had lied, whether Leatrice or Teal, he had made up his mind about Rachel. No matter whether Rachel was better or worse, he was going to take her out of Belfair. No matter whether Rachel killed two men or ate ice cream, he was going to take her and put her in a place where her welfare was the only concern. There must be such a place somewhere.

It was what he should have done a long time ago. It would have removed any conflict of interest and made this whole enterprise more impersonal. Come to that, if Rachel had been out of the picture, so would he. He might never have touched either of these projects.

He had not thought out where he would take her, where he'd put her. That decision, in any case, would be Martha's, not his. And it damned well would not be her husband's this time.

216

Chapter Twenty-Nine

The first E-mail read:

Hi, Roger the Dodger!!!

You're not at a place called Oakmont, are you? The men who want to get you might be looking for you there. I told them on the Net that it's where you're hiding out and I'm pretty sure I made the place up but Jennifer is afraid that it was something you said. You didn't, did you? Tell me you're not there.

Who's Jennifer, right? Well, I tried to tell you. She's my little friend who comes through the walls, the one that you wouldn't believe in. Jennifer's a natural, not like most of us here. She's only twelve years old, but she's special, really bright. Zales brought her to Belfair about ... wait ... two weeks ago. I said wait just now because I had to ask her. Two weeks. She said it's two weeks.

You'll like each other, Roger. We've already decided. But I'll have to sneak her up here next time you visit because Zales keeps her down in the basement. Jennifer ... wait ... oh, she's reminding me to tell you that she doesn't really walk through the walls. That was something that you thought I said but I didn't. It was you who just heard it that way. She comes up by the dumbwaiter. Now don't you feel dumb? She comes up by the dumbwaiter, dummy.

Just kidding. E-mail me. Let me know you're okay.

I love you, Roger.

Veronica. 'Zales has patients with computers and modems?' asked Susannah.

'Just this one. It's part of an experiment.'

'What's Oakmont? Is it anything like Belfair?'

'Never heard of it before. No idea.'

'She says some men want to *get* you. Is it true?'

'Talk is cheap. It's posturing. Don't give it a thought.'

'Is that "get" as in "get even" for that shooting you were in?'

'Susannah, it's this Jennifer that bothers me now. Damned Zales. She's only a child.'

'If she's real.'

'I didn't think she was either. But look.'

Grayson clicked his mouse on the second E-mail message. It winked on and filled the small screen.

It read:

Hi, Roger the Dodger the Codger the Lodger:

Just kidding. I'm silly. I'm not sure what to say. Except Veronica wasn't kidding. I'm here and I'm real. I live down where the Quiet Rooms are. My new puppy, named Chewey, lives down there with me. At night we go all through the building and visit but mostly we stay with Veronica. You saw where Veronica said she loves you? Well, she does. She wasn't going to say it but I said, go ahead, and you should see how she's blushing right now …

Wait …

Veronica doesn't want me to talk about that. She's afraid I'll tell you that she thinks about having sex with …

Okay. She says stop or she'll hit the Reset button.

Next time you come, come at night after ten. That's when it's easiest for me to get up here because Duane is almost always asleep. Duane is the guard who lives down in the Quiet Rooms. He's pretty creepy most of the time. Like tonight with Emma. You know Emma, I think. They brought her down last night with her new clothes all bloody. Duane likes to tease her and she tries to bite him but she can't because she's strapped to a bed and has a mask.

Never mind. That's too yucky. Veronica just said so. Speaking of biting, she's playing with Chewey and he's trying to stretch out and bite her nose. Oh, I started to say that Duane can be creepy. That wasn't fair because sometimes he's nice. It was him who just brought me my Pekingese puppy from a place where they were going to put him to sleep.

Wait …

Uh-oh.

Our toilet's overflowing. Just paper, no poop, but we gotta go.

Come see us, okay?

Love, Jennifer.

Quiet Rooms, thought Grayson. Once called padded cells. He'd never been shown that part of the basement, but he knew he should have realized that Belfair would have some. Any mental health facility would. He was now also sure that this Jennifer was real and he knew that her pet was a real one as well. He realized, with a start, where that Pekingese had come from, barring an unlikely coincidence. One Langley dog had been missing, a Pekingese pup. He was trying to envision which of Teal's 'sick fuck' subjects must have been the creepy guard named Duane.

Susannah was silent. She was staring at the screen. Grayson asked, 'What are you thinking?'

She wet her lips. She dropped her eyes. 'Please tell me that you haven't had sex with Veronica.'

'Um … what?'

'I think you heard.'

'Me with one of Zales's patients? Where did that question come from?'

'Roger … there's a level of affection that's clear.'

'There's a level of affection in what Jennifer wrote, too. Do you think I've had sex with a twelve-year-old?'

She hesitated. She bit her lower lip. 'You could have if Jennifer is Veronica's alter.'

'Susannah!!!'

'Not now.'

219

'You are being such a jerk.'

She stood up abruptly and crossed her arms. She stood that way, hugging herself for a moment. 'Roger,' she said, 'she …' And at that she stopped herself. She brought a hand to her mouth. 'Roger … *I* am sorry. I am terribly sorry that I said that.'

Grayson was blinking. The emphasis confused him. But he shrugged. 'It's okay. I understand.'

'I know that you wouldn't have shown me these E-mails if anything like that had happened. I'm sorry.'

'And I know that things happen in snake pits like Belfair. I don't blame you for fearing for those patients.'

'Give me a second. I think I need to get a grip.'

'You're trembling.'

'I'm embarrassed. I've been … well …'

'A jerk.'

Grayson wanted to reach out, to touch her, to hold her, but he didn't want his hand slapped away. 'This would … not be the time to put an arm around you, would it?'

'No, but thank you for the thought.'

'Yeah, it would, Suz. It would.'

'Beg pardon?'

'Well … maybe,' she told him. 'Maybe it would.'

Grayson reached for her, slowly, one arm and then the other. She did not respond, nor did she resist. He took one step closer; he embraced her.

'What was all that, Susannah?'

'Just leave it alone.'

'You want to know what I think?'

'No.'

'You thought this guy was showing you his E-mails just to rub it in that somebody loves him.'

'That's what you think? You think I'm that brittle?'

'If it's not that, then it's something real close. When will you get it through your thick head that you are one hell of a woman?'

'Sally, look … we both know what I am.'

'Yeah, we do. But you think every guy will run out the door

screaming the second you act a little nuts. Well, I have a flash for you.
All women are nuts. And don't say this is different. It isn't.'

'Listen ... Sally ...'

'He's holding you, Sooz. Hold him back, for God's sake. What
are you waiting for, music?'

'Susannah?' Grayson's lips were close to her ear.

'Quick. This is where he looks into your eyes. Don't let him.
Squeeze back. Push your face into his chest. Let him feel that little
thump you get in your belly when your juices are starting to flow.'

'Thank you, Roger. I'm fine. I guess I'm just tired.'

'Jeez, Susannah. You had him!!'

Susannah ignored her. She raised one hand so that it
touched Grayson's shoulder. She gave it a self-conscious
squeeze, then stepped back. She touched him again, this time
on his chest, and cocked her head toward his machine. The
gesture was meant to say, *Thank you, but wait. I'd like another*
look at those E-mails.

She sat down again and typed a command. She brought up
the two E-mails together by tiling them. Grayson's mind, for
that moment, was not yet back on Belfair. He was still feeling
the warmth of her body and remembering the soft, clean scent
of her hair. She had, perhaps, broken off just in time. His own
body had begun to respond.

Susannah squinted at the screen. 'The little girl is a natural?'

'A natural? Like you were? I don't know.'

'I've never heard of this one. How and where did Zales find
her?'

'Susannah ... I don't much care what she is. What I care
about is that she's a child.'

'I'm glad to hear you say that. Tell me more about
Veronica. She's one of the multiples you're studying?'

'Um ... no. Not exactly. Veronica's an alter.'

'One who's out all the time? Who's the host?'

'A young woman named Amanda. I've never met her.
Amanda, I'm told, is severely disturbed. Zales claims that he
invented Veronica as a ... well ... as a much more attractive
alternative.'

221

'And she is?'

'She's a sweetheart, as far as I've seen.'

'Zales didn't invent her. What he's doing is harvesting. That alone should cost him his license.'

'Harvesting?'

'Choosing one preferred alter and suppressing the others. Isn't that what you're doing in this project of yours?'

'Nothing like it, Susannah.'

'And you've never heard that term?'

'I have not, but you sound as if others have tried it.'

'Tried it? Oh, sure. You can't think that Norman Zales thought of this by himself.'

'Who else, then? Has anything been published?'

'Not likely. The whole thing's an ethical minefield. Turning one of life's losers into someone much better would seem to make all the sense in the world. The big question is: who decides what you'll keep? Did Amanda agree to become your Veronica? If someone else made that decision for her, how does that differ from killing her?'

'But you ... I take it ... think it can be done.'

'Did I tell you? He's on to you, Susannah.'

'Be still.'

Susannah touched a finger to the screen. 'Who is Emma?'

'I don't know.'

'Jennifer says you do.'

'If I do, it's by some other name. Let me ask her.'

He retrieved the slip of paper that he'd put in his wallet, and from it typed Veronica's E-mail address. He hesitated before typing his message, aware that Susannah was watching.

'Is it ... okay to be friendly?' he asked. 'I mean, I can avoid any use of endearments if that will make you more ...'

She swatted at his arm. 'Just write the damned note.'

His E-mail asked Veronica who else Emma was, how she was injured and how seriously. It said that he was well and knew nothing about Oakmont. He added that he was pleased to have heard from young Jennifer and very much looked forward to meeting her. He signed it, 'Affectionately, the Dodger.'

They waited for an hour. There was no reply. Grayson wasn't surprised; it was almost midnight. Victoria had probably shut down her machine and Jennifer had gone back to the basement.

'I ought to get to bed myself,' said Susannah.

'Me, too. It's been quite a day.'

'Now ... Roger ... I should tell you ... that I sleepwalk sometimes. I've, um ... found myself walking around ... not always dressed. If I should do anything that might seem a little strange ...'

'I should ... wake you?'

'Just ... don't take advantage, okay, Roger?'

'On my word.'

Unless, of course, she starts calling you Cowboy. In that case, big fella, it's me, so hop aboard.

'Oh, shit.'

'Susannah?'

'Listen, Roger ... you'd better not stay.'

'Well ... sure, if you say so, but ...'

'Roger ... if I should show up at your hotel room ...'

Grayson blinked.

'Just pay no attention. Do not let me in.'

'Um ... because you'd be sleepwalking, right?'

'Oh, shit. Roger, go.'

'I ... think we should talk.'

'I know how this sounds. I know you don't understand ...'

'Susannah, what if we *both* go and walk out the door.'

'We both? What for? I don't get you.'

'Are we able to do that? Just us? You and me?'

She stared at him. 'What are you saying?'

'Out the door and to the right is a beach I haven't seen. I would like you to take me for a walk on that beach. You don't have to tell me a thing if you don't want to, but I wish that you would try to trust me.'

She seemed torn. She wet her lips.

'Let's do it, Susannah. Just us. Can we do that?'

She looked into his eyes. She nodded. 'I think so.'

'Then say goodnight to your friend.'

Chapter Thirty

Leatrice had been troubled by that call from General Hoyt. She could not imagine why Teal would have told him that Rachel might have killed those two men. Had he not told her husband to say nothing?

'Norman, dear.' She tried the knob on his door. He had locked it again, so she knocked.

'Norman, you are being a child, you know. You can't be locking yourself in your room over every least little thing.'

She heard him stir. He said, 'I'm trying to sleep.'

'Norman, I've just had a call from General Hoyt.'

A loud bang. He had knocked something over.

'What about?'

'Norman, for pity's sake, open the door. You will force me to raise my voice, don't you see.'

She heard shuffling feet and what sounded like lurching. He was making his unsteady way to the door. The lock clicked and he opened it partway.

He was a sight. He stood in his shirtsleeves; no tie and no shoes, and his hair was in total disarray. Worse, he had been at his vodka again. His breath was more vapor than air.

'I see that you've chosen strong drink over me. You'll recall that I'd promised to ease you.'

He said nothing to that. He only rocked on his heels. His eyes showed a drunken defiance. Very well, thought Leatrice. It was hardly her loss. The next time he finds himself in need of release, let him look at Mr. Winston's dirty pictures.

'You said General Hoyt called? Why? What did he want?'

'Mr. Teal had told him that we might have a problem. Did he not advise you to say nothing of Rachel?'

'He said ... don't tell her father. He made threats if I did.'

'What sort of threats? Against your person, you mean?'

Zales raised a hand to his temple. He rubbed it as if trying to make his brain work. 'He said ... don't tell Carey or Winston or Camal. He said, if I did, he would tell General Hoyt. And then Hoyt would send Grayson to finish it.'

'Finish it? Finish what?'

'Grayson seems to be more than ... I don't know. Never mind.'

'More than what, dear? Specifically, please.'

'An assassin. A fixer. But that may have been a bluff. You know Teal. He does that. Forget it.'

'An assassin. Oh, my.' She put a hand to her chest. 'One ought certainly to bear that in mind.'

'But do nothing.'

'You did, in any case, say nothing to those three?'

'To my partners? No.'

'To *our* partners, dear Norman.'

'Leatrice ... our partners, your partners, take your pick. Tell me what you said to General Hoyt.'

'I reassured him, of course.'

'You denied it? He believed you?'

'He believed me because it never happened, dear Norman. She wasn't there; she was here with us. She'll believe it herself, by and by.'

She could see that he still disapproved of what she'd done, but that was neither here nor there at the moment.

'As to Mr. Teal dropping his hint to General Hoyt, he's clearly protecting himself – don't you think? – in the event that there are further complications. Oh, if only you hadn't summoned Mr. Teal. If only you'd discussed it with me first.'

'Will there be ... complications?'

'Rest assured, there will not.'

'Is Rachel still Emma?'

'Dear, look at your hair.' She reached up to rearrange it.

He pushed her hand away. 'Never mind my damned hair. I asked you if Rachel is still Emma.'

'For the moment.'

'We need Teresa. We need only Teresa. What if someone comes here and wants to see her?'

'Then they'll see Teresa.'

'You're quite sure of that?'

'Teresa or no one, dear Norman.'

It had been a long day for Leatrice as well. But before she retired she would make one more attempt to get Emma to listen to reason.

She left Norman to himself and walked back down the hallway where she pressed the call button of the elevator. It did not respond. She heard a whirring sound. She recognized the sound that an elevator door makes when something is preventing it from closing. She knew that an orderly must have left it propped open. She rapped sharply on the panel. A muffled voice answered. He said, 'Sorry. I'll be down in one minute.'

She knew the voice. It was the orderly named Leroy. She heard the wheels of his janitor's cart clacking onto the elevator's floor.

Very well. She would wait. While she did, she would make up her mind about Emma.

Emma, she reflected, must be made to understand that she had little choice in the matter. She must let Teresa come out and that was that. If she insisted on being stubborn she would stay strapped to that bed. She would be medicated in ways that she would find most unpleasant. But if she should cooperate, she'd be guaranteed that Teresa would be out for a few days at most. She would have the solemn promise of her friend and protector that no one would try to erase her.

But Emma, she feared, would take some convincing. Emma knew that a similar promise had been made to Rachel. And now Rachel was gone. Or very nearly gone. Only the odd flicker remained.

Emma had never objected to that. She had never liked

226

Rachel very much. What she did object to was that Teresa remained. Emma loathed women who'd been victimized by men and who then whined about it to therapists. The abusers, she pointed out, all have to sleep sometime. That presented an opportunity to do corrective surgery on any and all offending organs. If the delicate Teresa couldn't bear the sight of blood, there was always gasoline and a match. If Teresa didn't have the guts to do either, she deserved everything that was done to her.

Leatrice, of course, had agreed, but to a point. It was certainly a view that she'd embraced in the past in her dealings with her own parents. The problem she'd had was making Emma understand that Teresa's abusers didn't exist, because Teresa had not existed either. Emma had difficulty grasping that concept. It implied, a priori, that she didn't exist either, yet there she was, big as life. And if Teresa, in fact, had not been abused, abuse in the future would surely occur because men lie in wait for trusting women. Emma, in short, did not have an open mind where the appetites of men were concerned.

The elevator came. The door slid open. Leroy stood in it with his cart and equipment.

'Sorry, ma'am. We had a mess up on three. Toilet backed up and went over.'

'This old plumbing has seen better days, I'm afraid.' She stepped aside to let him wheel out his bucket.

'It weren't the pipes. It was what got flushed down them. You can't flush loose-leaf paper or newspaper, neither. They get wet and they get like a plug.'

'Whose room, do you say?'

'Winston girl. Said she's sorry.'

'I'll have a word with her all the same, Leroy. Thank you for your excellent work.' She stepped into the elevator and punched out the code that permitted it to descend.

Loose-leaf paper, wondered Leatrice. Why would that have been flushed? She now wished she'd thought to ask if it had handwriting on it. But the incident had happened in Veronica's room. Veronica would not have taken pages from her diary. Veronica had always behaved. If only Emma were more like Veronica. No trouble, obedient, always pleasant.

But Emma was Emma. There was no help for that. Leatrice had made up her mind. She would make one attempt at soft-spoken persuasion.

After that, she would try another tack.

The basement door opened. She could hear Emma struggling and snarling. She had instructed Duane to keep Emma awake and Duane, she had no doubt, had approached his task zealously. But she'd hoped he'd have the sense to keep the soundproofed doors closed so as not to upset little Jennifer.

She took keys from her pocket and walked to Duane's station. She used one key to open a locked cabinet near his desk. From its contents she selected the items she would need; a jar of jam and a butter knife and a crystalline powder that came in a calibrated vial. The jam was for mixing with a bit of the powder. The butter knife was for troweling it through the holes in Emma's mask. The powder was strychnine, about half a gram, enough for four or five fatal doses.

It was not her intention to give Emma such a dose. A small fraction of that much, about thirty milligrams, should be more than enough to persuade the poor creature that she'd rather not have any more. Her spine would feel as if it was snapping in two. The pain would be so great, she'd be unable to scream; she would barely be able to breathe.

Oh, Emma, thought Leatrice, you won't like this at all.

Wouldn't you rather have it felt by Teresa?

Be a good girl and give me Teresa.

228

Chapter Thirty-One

Jennifer had been hiding in Shan Li's room while Leroy mopped Veronica's bathroom. She had quietly snuck in, trying not to wake Shan Li, but Chewey had sneezed and that woke her.

Shan Li whispered two words in Chinese that probably meant, 'Who's there?' Jennifer stepped closer to her bed so she could see. She said, 'Shhh' with her finger to her lips. Shan Li stared for a moment but then she said 'Ah.' She nodded and said some more Chinese words. She was pointing next door as she said them.

'Yes, that's right. I'm Veronica's friend. Can I stay here for just a few minutes?'

'Xien-fu *ma*?'

'Shan Li, I don't get you. I don't speak Chinese.'

'*Wo* ... Shan Li,' she said slowly. She was pointing to herself. '*Ni* ... Xien-fu.' She then pointed to Jennifer.

'What's my name? My name's Jennifer.'

She nodded. 'Xien-fu.'

'Oh, I get it. Jen-foo. I guess that's close enough.'

Shan Li grinned and clapped her hands, but then her eyes went very wide. She had just noticed Chewey under Jennifer's arm. She whispered, 'Ooooh, *gou*. *Xiao gou*.' and reached to touch his paw. She was more than pleased to see him; she was very excited. She jumped up from her bed and turned on a light. She rummaged through a pile of books on her table and opened one to some illustrations. One old photo showed a family wearing rich Chinese robes. The children held dogs that looked like Chewey. She held it up for Jennifer to see.

She said, 'Kanjian ma? Peking gou.'

Jennifer understood her. A gou must be a dog. So Xiao had to mean either little or cute. She said, 'Yes, xiao gou Pekingese.'

Shan Li clapped in delight. She put down the book and held out her hands. She was asking if she could hold Chewey.

Jennifer pointed to her fingers and their inch-long nails. 'Okay, but watch your nails. You could poke out his eye with those things.'

Shan Li seemed to understand. She opened both hands. She arched them like cats do when they're stretching. She was saying that she'd be extra careful.

While Shan Li played with Chewey, Jennifer glanced through her book and looked up a few words in Shan Li's dictionary. The word ma only meant that what was said was a question. Kanjian just meant see. Wo and Ni was me and you, but she'd guessed that. She considered calling on one of her friends who had a much better memory than she did. But that friend would want to stay there all night once she saw that there was something new to learn.

Jennifer couldn't stay either. She'd just heard Leroy. He had called out to someone, saying he'd be right down. After that, she heard the sound of his wheels as he pulled his cart into the elevator.

'Shan Li, we have to leave.' She said this using gestures.

'Oooh, qing.' Shan Li said, her eyes going sad. She hugged Chewey closer to her chest.

Jennifer realized that qing must mean please. She brought her thumb and forefinger together in a gesture that meant, Okay, but just for a while. Shan Li understood. A big smile lit her face. She made the same gesture back to Jennifer.

Veronica's room smelled of Lysol and lemon. The fumes were enough to make Jennifer's eyes water but Veronica seemed not to notice. She was bent, chin in hands, in front of her monitor. She was reading a message on her screen.

'Come look at this.'

'From Roger?'

'Uh-uh. This is weird.'

The message was addressed: *Molly Pitcher, An American*, followed by her numerical E-mail address. It read:

Good lead, Molly Pitcher, we followed it up, but our soldier boy wasn't there. Man who lives there claims he's never met soldier boy, but he knows who he is, told us one more place where he goes. Man who lives there was a pervert but he isn't one now. We left a little message for the major. As for you, stay in touch. You'll still get at least a share of the bounty if your info leads to justice being done.

Nat Allen

Sergeant-at-Arms ACRA

'Weird is right,' exclaimed Jennifer. 'You told me you made that up.'

'No, I didn't. I said it popped into my head.'

'Who's Nat Allen and who is the pervert?'

'I never heard of either one before this. Hey, where's Chewey?'

'Shan Li wants to play with him,' said Jennifer.

'And you let her? That's nice.'

'Will he be okay? How nuts is Shan Li?'

A shrug. 'I'm not sure that she is.'

'She's like ... Mexican, isn't she?'

'She used to be, yes.'

'You don't think it's nuts to believe she's Chinese?'

'No. At least, not for her.'

'How come?'

'Because being Chinese might be where she's not crazy. Maybe she's only crazy when she's Mexican.'

Jennifer thought about that. She said, 'I guess that makes sense.'

'Never mind. Let's send your answer to Roger.'

'What answer?'

'He wanted to know who Emma is and what's going on in the basement.'

'Oh, that's right.'

'He also said he's never heard of Oakmont, but someone at Oakmont knows him. We'd better tell him.'

'Okay. Move over. Give me room.'

Jennifer sat. She started to type. She filled the little box with all that she'd seen and some of what she'd overheard. That done, she asked Grayson if he knew a pervert who lived at a place called Oakmont.

'Can I forward that E-mail that Nat Allen sent?'

'I'll show you how when you're finished. It's easy.'

As she wrote, she asked Veronica, 'Have you ever met Emma?'

'Only when she was Rachel.'

'Did you like her?'

'Who, Rachel? No, she's too much like Amanda.'

'And Emma?'

'From what I hear, she's about ten times worse.'

'Even so ...'

'Don't tell me "even so" Don't you ever go near her.'

'I just did. She wasn't so bad.'

'When was this?'

'Just before. I gave her water and I got her a blanket. They had her all strapped to a bed, really tight. I loosened the straps just a little.'

'How little?'

'Enough not to cut her. They were hurting her, Veronica.'

'Well ... just watch that she doesn't hurt you. Send the E-mail.'

Jennifer's finger had reached for the button when she suddenly stopped and cocked an ear. 'Did you just hear screaming?'

Veronica listened. 'Far away. But not now.'

She slid from her chair and went to the door. She opened it a crack and listened. She slipped through the door and went to the panel that covered the dumbwaiter shaft. She was sure that was where the sound came from. She listened. There was nothing. She returned to Veronica.

'Someone screamed and then a thunk. I bet that was Emma.'

'It could have been anyone, Jennifer. A nightmare. The thunk was someone falling out of bed.'

'Not that sound. I know it. It's a Quiet Room door. I bet it's Duane hurting Emma again. I think I should go back down and stop him.'

'You can't. If he sees you climbing out of the shaft ...'

'He won't. He'll be busy. I'll just say he woke me up.'

'Jennifer, don't risk it. We'll tell Roger about it.'

'He's not here. We are. Come on, lower me down quiet.'

'But why do this for Emma? I told you; she's horrible.'

'Because we're not like Emma. Let's get moving.'

Chapter Thirty-Two

'I'm not a slut, Roger.'

'I am sure of that, Susannah.'

They were on the beach, near the shallow, lapping waves. They'd been walking in silence for some minutes.

'Would you like to know what my sex life is like?'

'The ... gentlemanly answer would be no.'

'What Zales wrote in his book was not entirely wrong. It's true that ... a part of me ... was more active at one time. These days, it's not even an annual event.'

'Susannah, you don't owe me ...'

'I did give some thought to letting you sleep with me. I mean, if you were interested. I do not do that often. I would not have done it well.'

'I believe you.'

'Which part?'

'The part where you're not very sure of yourself. You didn't strike me as having it down pat.'

She walked on a bit. She threw up her hands. She said, 'Roger ... cards on the table, okay? What is it that you think is going on here?'

'I think I've met two of you. If I have, I like you both.'

She stopped. 'You don't mean that.'

He answered, 'Okay, let me say it again.'

He liked her, he told her, before he had ever set eyes on her. He liked her for her energy, her talent, her kindness. Add to that, upon meeting her, her intelligence, her wit, her extraordinary grace and femininity. He also happened to like country music.

She was silent for a moment. 'Now let's hear the "if only." '

'There is no "if only." '

'You don't wish there could be ... perhaps fewer surprises?'

'I don't know. I'm not sure that I've been all that surprised. Correction. The raunchiness came as a surprise.'

'That wasn't me.'

'I didn't think so.'

She turned away.

'Susannah ... is she here? Is she with us right now?'

She paused and cocked her head as if to listen. 'She's asleep.'

'You can do that? You can make her go to sleep?'

'I can ask her.'

'And she'll do it? Every time?'

'If she thinks I'm okay.'

'Then she sounds like a very good friend. What's her name?'

'... It's Sally.'

Grayson mouthed the name. She had sounded like a Sally. He said to Susannah, 'Tell me if I've got this right. I heard her sing at Cheryl's, and I've spoken to her since. When the nympho thing came up, that was Sally, correct? That was Sally who was teasing me about it.'

'I guess.'

'You only guess?'

'There are times when Sally says out loud what I'm thinking.'

'And she does things that you might think twice about doing?'

'Hey, Grayson.' She bridled. 'Sally's not a slut either.'

'I'm ... sure that she isn't.'

'Don't say you're sure. You don't know a damned thing. And why are you taking this so calmly?'

He thought for a moment. 'You're right. I guess I am.'

'That's another surprise?'

'That's the point; it isn't; I guess I'm used to it now. I suppose, a few months ago, I might have been uneasy ...'

235

'Oh, I see. You're now an old hand with multiples.'

He groaned.

'Susannah, let's sit for a minute.'

Grayson took off his jacket, spread it out on dry sand. She sat on it, hugging her knees to her chest. He lowered himself next to her, taking care not to touch her. They looked out toward the glow of the moon on the water.

He said, 'I'd like to try a little game.'

'What sort of game?'

'A pretend game. Let's see where it leads.'

He would pretend, he told her, that this was not their first meeting. They'd gone out maybe five or six times. They'd had lunch and dinner, seen a movie or two. They'd gone for a swim; they'd played tennis. They'd kissed a few times, danced close a few times, but they hadn't rushed into sex.

'And you know about Sally?'

'You were very up-front. You told me about her on our very first date. That's this one, incidentally. I hope.'

'We'll ... pretend that it is. What did you think?'

'You mean since? I haven't. Since then, you see, I've been too busy being dazzled by this utterly spectacular woman I've met. She's more intriguing, more lovely, more everything else than any woman I've dreamed of ever meeting. Let's imagine that I've even come to terms with the fact that she's so much more talented than I am. Let's imagine that she ... well, she likes me a little. She probably knows that she could do a lot better but I'll do until somebody else comes along.'

'I ... think she might like you a bit more than that.'

'Oh, okay. That makes it better. Good input.'

She smiled.

'But we're talking about me, and what's in my head. Where were we? Sixth date?'

'And no sex yet.'

'Well, in that case, what happens is I daydream about it. I begin to imagine what it would be like to wake up with her in the morning. I dream of lazy evenings on a beach just like this

236

one. We're sitting together; we're watching a sunset; we're sharing a bottle of wine.'

She said nothing. Just a sigh.

'It won't happen, of course.'

She straightened. 'Why won't it?'

'Because she can't seem to get it through her self-doubting head that I like her just as she is.'

'Look, Roger …'

'And that her friends are my friends. Wait … how many are there?'

'Just Sally. Pretty much.'

'Pretty much?'

'Just Sally.'

'Whom I like. So I'm asking, where's the problem?'

She was quiet for a while. Then she nudged him.

'Are you this good with women? Other women?' she asked.

'Other women? What, you think this is a line?'

A small shrug.

'You think what, that I've fine-tuned it in singles' bars somewhere?'

'Maybe multiple bars.'

'Are there … multiple bars?' Oh, dear God, thought Grayson. He had actually asked that. She had turned her face away so that he would not see her laughing. But she couldn't stop her shoulders from shaking.

Grayson had to smile. He said, 'I'll get you for that.'

They were following their footprints, walking back toward her house.

She said, 'You're a nice person, Roger.'

He had taken her hand. He squeezed it.

'Well, what now?' she asked. She was looking toward the sea.

'Do I get a vote? I'd like my dream to come true. I'd like to wake up with you tomorrow.'

'I mean after tomorrow. Will I see you again?'

'You will if you want to. And I'll want to see you. Don't doubt that for a second, Susannah.'

'How long will you be here?'

'I'm not sure. A few days. But I hope you'll ask me back.'

She returned his squeeze. 'If we were to make love ...'

'Susannah, there's no hurry. I won't push it.'

'Yes, but if it should happen ...'

'We would go by your rules.'

'You think I have rules?'

'I mean, any way that would make you more comfortable. You were pretty tense back at the house.'

'That was just about Sally. I don't think she'll ... intrude.'

'But she would have before? Why then and not now?'

'If ... she knew that I wanted to, but didn't, she'd come. She's a bit more aggressive than I am.'

'I see.'

'If she were to see me in bed with a guy ... but she knew I thought I'd made a mistake ... not that this has ever happened, I'm just giving an example. Well, she'd come then, too, and take over.'

Grayson smiled.

'What's funny?'

'Oh, nothing. Nothing, really.'

'Are you laughing at me?'

'I'm enjoying you, Susannah. Big difference.'

Susannah felt good about this man, Roger Grayson. His pretend game had helped. It had put her at ease. She could see why his Veronica was so fond of him.

Sally would say, *'Well, it took you long enough.'* She was sleeping, but that's what she'd say.

She'd say, *'Here's a guy who can handle it, Susannah. Here's a guy who won't be scared off.'*

Her answer would be, *'There are still a few surprises.'*

'Yeah, but later. This is now. Are you gonna go for it?'

'I don't know. You heard him. He said he won't push it.'

'Then the ball's in your court.'

'I won't push it either.'

'Okay, but if it happens, let it happen.'

She'd already imagined how it might go. They'd go home;

she'd say that they'd better turn in. She would tell him that she'd see him at breakfast. She would then go into her room and undress. She would put on a nightgown from Victoria's Secret. Not a short one, the white one that was almost full length. She would undo and brush out her hair. She would wait until she heard him finish brushing his teeth. She would open her door and say goodnight to him.

He'd see the white nightgown, her bare shoulders and arms. He'd move closer, and he'd smile, and he'd say goodnight back. She'd look into his eyes and count to ten in her head. He would either move to kiss her or he wouldn't.

Say he did.

The kiss would be a light one. He would touch her cheek first. He still wouldn't be sure of what to do. She would close her eyes and lean her face against his chest. She would slip both her arms around his waist and squeeze gently. Just enough so he'd know he didn't have to break off. Just enough so he'd know that she might not refuse him if he'd like to come into her bedroom.

She'd tremble a little. She wouldn't have to fake it. He'd feel it and he'd hold her because he'd know that she's scared. He'd probably hold her for a minute or two. He'd move one hand over her back and bare shoulders. He'd brush one of them lightly with his lips.

'Why don't you write all this down for the guy? That way you can be sure he knows his moves.'

'Shut up, Sally.'

He'd turn her, very gently, into her room. He would probably turn off the light. He'd lead her to her bed, he'd kiss her again. She'd start to unbutton his shirt. As she did, he'd reach his hands to her hips. He'd feel his way over the contours of her body, first her waist, then her thighs and then the tightness of her buns. He'd raise his hands to her ribs where they'd barely touch her breasts. One thumb might stray and drift over her nipple to see if it'd begun to get hard.

He'd be slow, oh, so slow; every touch would be so light that she'd probably shudder and gasp. His shirt would be

239

open, pulled loose at the waist. She'd put her hands to his chest and slide them up and to the sides. His shirt would fall to the floor. He would probably kiss her bare shoulder again before reaching to gather the fabric of her gown. He'd lift it up over her head.

One way or another all the rest of their clothing would end up all mixed on the floor. He'd hold her and feel her, then he'd pull back the covers and ease her into her bed. He'd snuggle up close but not so close that she couldn't move. He'd kiss her lightly all over her face as he told her how beautiful, how wonderful she was.

She'd probably have to tell him when it was time to come inside her. Good lovers are never in a hurry. When he did, and when she helped him, he would gently turn her sideways. He'd say, 'Let's just lie this way for a while.' He'd say soft purring words. He'd even make little jokes. Good lovers know to do that. Considerate lovers do that. It helps a woman know that she's a person to them and not just someone to have sex with. They want to have sex; they love having sex, but it's being there with her that means the most to them.

Before long, they'd make love. Oh, boy, would they! After, they'd both be exhausted. They'd fall asleep all twined together. They'd wake up a little later and they'd do it again. This time a little wilder. The shyness would be gone. She'd sit on him and ride him, maybe not like Sally would, but the way women do when they think sex should be fun. She'd have to make sure that he knows she's not Sally. Better yet, she might ask him if he'd like her to show him what Sally might do if she were there.

'Small doses, Susannah.'

'I know. Better not.'

That could wait until some other time.

But there wasn't another time. There wasn't even a this time.

They got back to the house; he was holding her hand; her stomach had already started to thump. She got as far as leaning her head against his shoulder when they both heard his laptop beeping again.

She asked, 'Can't that keep?'

He said, 'Just let me take a look.'

She said, 'Go ahead. I'll get ready for bed.'

About two minutes later, he called her name from the kitchen.

He said, 'I'll have to leave. There's something ugly going on. Rachel Carey seems to be in big trouble.'

He let her read the E-mails. There were two.

The first was from Jennifer. That one came in two parts. She had started it and later came back to it. The first part was in answer to his questions. She had written:

Hi, Dodger:

You asked about Emma. She's an alter of Rachel's. But Veronica says Emma is ten times as mean. She's a lesbian who hates men but that's not saying much because she hates almost everyone else, too.

I don't know how she got bloody but she got her new clothes when Dr. Zales took her to Baltimore. That, at least, is what it says in her diary, but she didn't write it. I saw Leatrice write it. I've seen Leatrice's writing in Veronica's diary too. I think she writes in a lot of them.

We're forwarding an E-mail that came from this man who Veronica sent to Oakmont, remember? She still doesn't know why she sent him there but, you'll see, he found a guy there who knows you.

Veronica's asking, are you still okay?

Can't wait to meet you.

Roger? there's more. I've just been downstairs. I don't want to upset you when you're far away but Leatrice and Duane are torturing Emma. I would have tried to stop it if it was just Duane but Leatrice – what she was doing – gave me the shakes. Veronica says it is good that I came back up and she says it might not be so bad. She says they do that sometimes. She says they do it when an alter stays out and they want to make her let someone else out.

I don't care. It's still bad. We both wish you were here.

Jennifer Grayson touched a key and brought up the second

241

message. It was an E-mail she forwarded from the man called
'Nat Allen.' Susannah saw that Grayson's face was flushed red.
She read it. She frowned and sat back.

'What's happening, Roger? What's the ACRA?'

'A militia group. Neo-Nazis. Never mind them.'

'Are you the soldier boy? The major?'

He didn't answer.

'And you know this Nat Allen?'

His jaw tightened. 'Not really.'

'I'm going to try one more time. Who's the pervert?'

'Susannah ... truly. I don't have a clue.'

'Well, Veronica does and it sounds like they've killed him.
It also sounds like she set it up.'

'No way. I know her. She wouldn't do that.'

'Roger ... she's a multiple. You only know one of her.
Even she might not know why she does things.'

Grayson waved off the subject. He didn't much care who
the pervert might have been. He knew that he wouldn't get
much more from Veronica; he felt sure that she simply didn't
know. He touched another key. It brought back the E-mail
from Jennifer.

'She says Emma's being tortured by Leatrice Zales.'

'And she's also a twelve-year-old kid.'

'Meaning what? That she's imagining?'

'Shock treatments ... or restraint ... might be torture in her
eyes.'

'You're not saying that I should ignore this.'

'No, Roger, I'm saying you should pick up your phone.
Get someone to go in and see.'

He knew that she was right. The question was who. He was
beginning to realize that he'd been sent away to keep him
from Belfair, not Langley. If so, calling Teal would be a waste
of time. He certainly couldn't call Zales. He could call
General Hoyt, but it was Hoyt whom Teal had enlisted to
send him away. Even so, he decided, he would have to try. He
punched out Hoyt's number. A sleepy voice answered.

'Major Grayson? What time is it?'

'Sir, I know it's late, but …'

He told the general, briefly, about his concern that Rachel was in serious trouble. He told him of a possible ACRA murder of a man who they thought had been shielding him. He told him that the killer seemed to be Nat Allen. He expected General Hoyt to react to this last fact, especially since he knew about Allen. But the general ignored it. It was as if he hadn't heard.

'What trouble with Rachel?' he asked, his voice cold.

'She … had blood on her clothing. Street clothing.'

A pause. A swallow. 'What else have you heard?'

'They have her strapped to a bed in the basement, possibly being given shock treatments. Beyond that, I don't know very much.'

'You … mentioned a dead man. Who would that be?'

'I don't know. All I do know, assuming it's true, is that he might live in Warrenton, Virginia.'

'Major Grayson … where are you?' Now his voice sounded strained.

'Sir, I'm … just north of Georgia at the moment.'

Susannah touched his arm. She mouthed, *'Thank you.'*

'And how has this intelligence reached you, Major Grayson?'

'Sir, I'm not at liberty to say.'

'Never mind. I can guess. I'm sure it's one of Zales's guards. You haven't learned your lesson, have you, Major?'

'My lesson?'

'I would have thought that your debacle with the Novak woman would have taught you how to better choose informants.'

'Sir …'

'You were given a mission. Complete it.'

'Sir, I think I should get back to Belfair at once.'

'You needn't. I'll look into this myself.'

'Sir, I know she's your niece …'

'Try to keep that in mind. You just find that woman … what was her name?'

243

'Zales ... only said that her name is Susannah.'

'Don't show up at Belfair without her in tow. That's an order, Major Grayson. Good night.'

'Sorta broke the spell, didn't it?'

'That's not important now.'

She had listened as he told her what his general had said, and the order that the general had given him. She had watched as he sent one more message to Jennifer, telling her to lie low, turn off her lights, stay with Veronica, not to go back to the basement. Let him know if anything else happened.

Having sent it, he paced her kitchen floor. He told Susannah that she might as well get some sleep. He said he needed to sort some things out. He was angry and he seemed terribly confused. The anger, the frustration, had no place to go. He said he was tempted to get in his car and begin driving straight through to Belfair. But Belfair was a good ten hours away. Besides, Hoyt had ordered him not to.

'Speaking of frustration ...'

'That's not important either.'

'That dream you were having ... with you and him in bed ...'

'Don't you dare make fun of me for that.'

'I'm not, Sooz. I wouldn't.'

'Then what about it?'

'If you ask me, I think it was more than a dream. I think that's the way it would be with him.'

'Thank you.'

'The question is, will he live long enough? I'm not getting a good feeling about this.'

'Me neither.'

'If it wasn't enough that some Nazi wants to kill him, his own people are letting him dangle.'

'He protected me. Did you hear him on the phone?'

'I did. He kept his word. I thought he might.'

'So, what now, do you think?'

'You could try to keep him here.'

'He won't stay. Not long. He'll go back to Belfair. His general told him not to, but he will.'

'For Jennifer?'

'And Veronica and for God knows who else. He won't walk away. It's not in him.'

'Then go with him.'

'You think so?'

'You ... ought to stick by him.'

'I thought so. You want to go yourself, am I right?'

'It ... might be exciting. We could use a little fun. We might even get to punch out Norman Zales.'

'Sally, we're trying to live quietly, remember? Anyway, forget it. He would never take me with him.'

'He'll have to, Susannah. You're his ticket back. His general said with you or not at all.'

'Even so ...'

'Don't spring that on him now. Let him sit and let him stew. You might even let him think it's his idea.'

'He'll never ask.'

'Sit him down on the couch. Sit with him, stretch out. Let's both try to feel where his head is.'

'We'll see.'

'And Susannah ... if you go ... and you run into trouble ...'

'I can handle myself.'

'Yeah, you can. But you have friends who are better.'

Chapter Thirty-Three

Even Leatrice was startled by Emma's reaction to the mixture of strychnine and jam. Her body had seemed as if it might explode, so great were the straining and convulsions. The legs of her bed had lifted from the floor and were beating a tattoo on the tile. Duane had to put all his weight on the headpiece to keep the bed in one place. Her jam jar and butter knife had danced off the table. The jam jar had smashed on the floor.

Leatrice was certain that the room was quite soundproof but the vibration of the bed might be felt throughout the basement. She had asked Duane to go look in on Jennifer. He did so and reported that she hadn't stirred since the last time he checked her on the monitor.

'Have you locked her in?'

'I did that before.'

'And her dog? It's sleeping soundly?'

'Yeah, I guess. Nothing's moving. She sleeps with him under the covers.'

Well and good, thought Leatrice. There's no need to distress her. But Emma, now before her, skin flushed and bathed in sweat, was another matter entirely.

'Emma, dear,' she asked calmly, 'don't you think you're being stubborn? What could possibly be the use of such suffering?'

Emma did not respond. She only stared at the ceiling as her breath came in great heaving gasps.

'I have tried to be your friend. I've tried gentle persuasion.

You'll agree, I think, that my earlier efforts were a much more agreeable therapy.'

'Mmm-mm.'

'Was that in the affirmative?'

'Mmm-mm.'

'I'm delighted to hear it. This is hard on me as well. Are you ready to show me Teresa?'

'Mmm-mm.'

Leatrice reached a hand to Emma's throat in order to feel her arterial pulse. It was already beginning to slow. She watched Emma's eyes. They were starting to soften. Her jaw, her shoulders, were beginning to relax. Her fingers, once rigid, were quivering now as the pain from the strychnine abated.

Leatrice was pleased. It seemed to be working. She had never tried using strychnine before but was hopeful that Teresa wouldn't feel it. Alters seldom felt the pain that another had suffered, at least not to the same degree.

'Teresa? Is that you?'

She blinked her eyes slowly as one might upon waking.

'Teresa? Dear girl? Are you with us?'

Her eyes now were darting to her wrists, to her ankles, to Duane's face above her and to Leatrice at her side. Her expression was one of confusion, of surprise, but then it suddenly changed to one of revulsion. She puckered her cheeks. She was trying to spit through the holes in her mask. She was getting her first taste of the strychnine.

'I know, dear. It's bitter. That's the reason for the jam …'

She had twisted her head toward the bedpan at her side. She was straining to reach it. She was going to be sick. But she seemed very weak and the straining was feeble. She no longer had Emma's strength.

'Should I take off the mask? The kid was right about this.'

'The kid?'

'Next door. She was scared this one would choke.'

'She was in here?'

'She came in. I threw her out.'

247

'But she was never alone. She was never with Emma by herself, is that right?'

Leatrice wasn't sure why that should trouble her so, but it had caused an odd chill at the back of her neck.

'Like I told you. She came in; I threw her out.'

She grunted. 'Very well. You may unbuckle her mask. After that, you may leave while we talk.'

He removed the mask. He had to peel it from her face. Teresa gagged and tried to speak. Her tongue was too thick. Duane reached for the bedpan and brought it to her chin. She heaved, but nothing came up.

'Hey, you know?' said Duane, 'Don't get mad at me for this. But I never put this bedpan up here on the bed and I never put that blanket on her neither.'

'Then who did? The girl?'

'Wasn't no one else down here. Hey, watch it,' he shouted suddenly. 'She's loose.'

Too late, Leatrice saw an arm whipping toward her. A hand took an eagle claw's grip of her hair. It pulled her head forward; it shook it and wrenched it. She felt Emma's teeth as they tried to grip her ear. They found, instead, a clump of her hair. They bit down and held as Emma's hand, now free, groped for the strap that held the other. Leatrice tried to fight her; she scratched at the hand; she lost both her shoes in the struggle. But Duane had rounded to the side of the bed. He climbed on and pinned Emma's chest with his knee and began to pry at her fingers.

Leatrice was able to pull out from under. She backed away, one hand at her ear, blood trickling down the side of her face. She recovered her shoes and put one of them on. With the other, holding it by the heel, she proceeded to belabor Emma's head.

The face suddenly blanched. It looked shocked and surprised. It seemed only now to become aware that it was being hit with a shoe. She looked up at Leatrice and noticed the blood. The look of shock became one of horror.

'Oh, my gosh,' she managed, as she tried to wet her lips. 'Oh, Leatrice, what did she do to you?'

248

Leatrice lowered her shoe. 'You're Teresa once more?'

'Yes, I am. Oh, my gosh. I'm so sorry, Leatrice. She pushed through again while I was being sick.'

She seemed suddenly aware of the man astride her chest. She looked up at him. She asked, 'Who are you?'

Duane glanced at Leatrice. He said, 'Maybe it's her.'

Leatrice asked him, 'Why would you think so?'

'Because she don't know me. Teresa ain't ever seen me. Besides, she's not hurtin' from that jam stuff you gave her.'

'Duane, sit back just a little bit, will you?'

He obeyed and Leatrice stepped up to the bed. She raised a hand and slapped her face hard. Teresa cried out. She started to wail. The print of four fingers showed white on her cheek.

'Fool me once, shame on me,' said Leatrice quietly. 'Fool me twice, and I give you to Duane.'

Leatrice's ear was bleeding too badly for her to continue with this treatment. She would have to go upstairs and attend to it. Duane went with her as she left the room and walked down the basement hall to the elevator.

He asked, 'Missus Zales, what you said just now . . .'

'She's yours. You'll have until morning.'

'You mean for like screwing? I gotta be clear.'

'One more won't make a difference if that was Teresa. She already thinks she's been a prostitute. On the other hand, if that's Emma in there, no offense to you, Duane, but she deserves you.'

'Yeah, but see, here's the thing. I can't get it up.'

'Not at all?'

'Not no more. It was bad enough with what the Doc gives us here, but then I got more stuff down there in Virginia. Since then I can't even get started.'

'Then sleep.'

'You don't have a pill or a shot I can take? I haven't had good sex with a woman since the one that they sent me to jail for. And here you are saying, "Duane, help yourself." and I want to but I just can't.'

249

'No sex at all? Not even a rape? What about with Rachel's former therapist?'

'That one you sent me after? I couldn't then, either. I drowned her but that's all I could do.'

Leatrice dearly wished that she had not raised this subject. She had done so impulsively; her anger was speaking; she had wanted to punish whomever that was who had damaged her ear and her scalp. But perhaps, she decided, it might be just as well. Emma seemed in no mood to listen to reason. If the spasms of strychnine had failed to induce her, perhaps a few spasms of another sort might. At the least, it was no worse than she deserved.

'Very well,' she told him. 'I'll send Leroy down with something.'

'There's this new drug. From Russia. I heard the Doc talking.'

'Bromantan?'

'Yeah, that's it.'

'I'll get some from the lab.'

'That would be real nice. Thank you, Missus.'

'And a stimulant, perhaps, to help it along. You needn't be gentle with Emma.'

The truth was, thought Duane, that he didn't feel like screwing. He didn't feel like hurting Emma either. That was the thing. He didn't much care. They had fed him so much shit, this compound, that compound, that nothing seemed to matter anymore.

Time was, that doing bad would excite him. Taking chances, trying not to get caught, would excite him. People being afraid of him; that was good, too. It meant that he had respect. But it all got so different since he came to Belfair. Even that one time when Missus Zales asked him to go and take care of that therapist. That one, what's-her-name, who used to be Rachel's therapist and kept trying to get money from her father. Time was, when that would have been fun for him. Time was, when he would have made sure that she hurt, but that time all he did was make her dead.

Missus Zales asked him, after, what he did to that lady. He told her the truth, that he hardly remembered. It was as if all he'd done was pick up the dry cleaning. That was what it felt like, an errand. Missus Zales, he thought, seemed pleased with his answer. She wanted him to hardly remember.

The one thing he did do that made him feel good was stealing that puppy for Jennifer. He would have killed it. That wouldn't have bothered him. He would have snapped its neck; it would have been fast and clean. But he knew that Jennifer was lonely like him. Besides, Jennifer was the only one who would talk to him.

Not counting Missus Zales. And she was like him. She didn't feel much of anything either. But he used to feel things and she probably never did. So she didn't miss it. He did.

Duane turned and headed back to the monitor at his station. It showed Emma, or Teresa, whichever. She was quiet now and her eyes were closed. Her head was nodding up and down in little jerks like what happens when you're falling asleep. She was covered with a blanket up to her neck. He didn't remember covering her up. He thought that Missus Zales must have done it.

Something else about her looked a little bit funny. Her position was ... he didn't know ... different. She was tied back down; he'd strapped that one arm down himself. All it was, he decided, was that she didn't have her mask. He was used to her wearing her mask.

It struck him, however, that when he grabbed her right arm, she'd been trying for the strap on the left one. She couldn't have got it. She only had about three seconds. Even so, it would not hurt to check.

He went into her room. He asked how she was doing. All she did was twitch a little. Didn't open her eyes. He had reached to lift the blanket when he thought he smelled urine.

'Did you pee in your bed?'

'Mmm-hmm?'

He looked around the room. He did not see her bedpan. He knelt to look under the bed. He heard the bed squeak as she shifted her body. The sound did not alarm him, he had heard it many times. The last thing that he would remember clearly was starting to rise from the floor. After that there was a blur and his cheek felt all numb. It did not seem to hurt him very much, but he fell backward. From then on, it seemed like a dream.

There were bedpans, lots of them, stainless steel, shiny. They seemed to be flying through the air all around him and all of them were bouncing off his head. Making gong sounds. A woman, almost naked, was sitting on his chest. He knew who it was. It had to be Emma. And he knew, right then, that there was only one bedpan. It had looked like many bedpans flying around because she kept smashing him with it.

It still didn't hurt. It was like he was separate. He didn't even feel much like stopping her. Besides, it was Emma who seemed to be hurting. She kept arching her back; she was clenching her jaw. She was fighting off the pain from that jam she ate, the jam Missus Zales made her eat.

She got tired of hitting him. It was like there was no point. She seemed to know he didn't feel it anymore. But he could still see her through one of his eyes that he could still open a little. She dropped the bedpan. He heard one last gong. Then she sat up straight; he saw her looking around. He felt her reaching; she was groping for something. It was something she had seen on the floor. He saw it now, a silver thing in her hand. A butter knife. What did she want with a butter knife?

She was trying to cut him, but he wasn't afraid. Nothing much seemed to scare him since he'd gone to Virginia. He did wonder why anyone would bother to try to cut someone's throat with a butter knife. It could cut but it was so much more work.

It struck him, being separate, that Dr. Zales had been right.

Dr. Zales had said, when he took that last compound, that nothing would bother him, nothing would scare him.

Well, yeah, thought Duane. That part might be fine. But it also struck him that you should fight, not just watch, when there's someone trying to saw off your head.

Chapter Thirty-Four

Susannah had urged Grayson to sleep while he could. They would probably hear nothing before morning.

He didn't want to sleep because he didn't want to dream. There were too many worries and faces on his mind. He didn't need nightmares on top of them. She said she'd stay with him if he didn't mind. She led him to her couch, propped two cushions behind him, and placed a throw pillow on his lap.

'That one's mine,' she said. 'That's for me to stretch out.'

'On my lap?'

'It's so I don't wake up and find you gone.'

He wouldn't have argued; he was pleased that she was willing. She did stretch out with her head on his lap, her body turned on its side. He wasn't sure what to do with his hands. She said, 'It's all right to touch me. Relax.'

He laid his hand on her hip and looked down at her eyes. They were squinting as if she were listening for something. He heard nothing. He sat back. His own eyes soon closed.

He did drift off and the dreams soon began. The first of them seemed like no dream at all. He was there, in Susannah's house, feeling perfectly at home. He was in her guest bathroom. He'd been brushing his teeth. Susannah had already gone to bed. The tap was running; he was rinsing his mouth, when he suddenly realized that he wasn't alone.

A woman, arms folded, was standing there watching him. She hadn't walked in; she had simply appeared. It wasn't

Susannah, but someone much like her. It was the woman whom he'd seen performing at Cheryl's. Grayson reached for a towel.

'Hello, Sally.'

He didn't feel surprised in the least that she'd decided to make an appearance. This was, after all, Sally's house.

She said, *'I think we should talk.'*

Grayson dried his hands. He turned off the tap.

'Do you care for Susannah? I'm asking you straight.'

'Care for her? Sure. I think she's terrific.'

'Could you love her?'

'Who couldn't?'

'Don't give me "who couldn't." It sounds like a dodge. The who else in "who couldn't" ain't the issue.'

'Sally ... I just met her. A few hours ago.'

'I know that. I still need an answer.'

'Then, sure. I could love her. I almost do now.'

'Almost's not a bad start. It'll do for the moment. Let me tell you what's gonna happen next.'

Sally told him that Susannah, in about five minutes, was going to open her door.

'She'll be in a white nightgown; it's a lacy cotton gauze. It's long, it's flowing and whispery soft. It's romantically detailed with an embroidered sweetheart neckline and it's got a gently shirred bodice ...'

'Um ... Sally ...'

'Sounds pretty good, huh? Victoria's Secret. I got all those words from her catalog.'

'Sounds lovely.'

'Now, cowboy, we don't want to be dense about this. We know that ole' Sooz put it on for a reason.'

'Sooz?'

'Short for Susannah. Now, listen. She's gonna pretend like she's saying goodnight. She won't move to kiss you or nothing like that, but she's hoping that you'll take the bull by the horns.'

Sally then laid out in precise detail exactly how Susannah would respond at each step. What she likes, what she doesn't,

254

what she'll do and what she won't. And Sally kept reminding him that he had to go slow.

'Well, I wasn't going to rip off her nightgown.'

'You won't have to, cowboy. It slides off real easy. But don't let her boobs be the first thing you reach for. Her back is real nice; her back and her shoulders. That's where I'd start, I was you.'

Grayson felt himself blushing. 'Sally ... look, I appreciate the tips, but ...'

'I'm trying to tell you what Susannah's expecting. Don't wing it, Roger. You'll just screw it up. You want this first time to be special.'

'And ... where will you be?'

'It's just her and you.'

'Sally, why are you doing this?'

'Cause she won't. 'Cause it's what friends are for.'

He never did get to see Susannah's shirred bodice, 'so flowing and whispery soft.' He woke and Susannah was still with him, still dressed. She had turned from her side almost onto her stomach. He could touch her back now. He did so, very lightly. She did have a wonderful back.

He dozed again. An awful dream followed. He and Susannah were asleep on that couch when Nat Allen walked into the room.

Allen's face was terribly swollen and cut. His jaw hung crooked as if multiply fractured and most of his front teeth were missing. He was dressed in the uniform of a rural police-man, but he wore no identifying badges. He held a revolver in a badly gnarled hand. Grayson knew that his own boots must have done all that damage; they had also crushed both of Nat Allen's hands. All his injuries looked as fresh as they were on that day, but the Allen of his dream seemed neither crippled nor in pain. He wore a cruel smile made all the more ugly when formed with swollen eyes and thickened lips.

A second figure had come in behind him. Grayson, in his dream, was not greatly surprised to see that it was Janice Novak. She wore jeans and a sweater; her face was unmarked. She did not look as if she'd been dead all these months. She gave him a look of profound disappointment as she stepped to

255

Allen's side and spoke into his ear. She was pointing a finger at Susannah.

Grayson saw that Nat Allen had been ready to shoot him but Janice, apparently, had a better idea. Allen nodded agreement. He handed her his weapon. Janice took aim at Susannah.

Grayson, in his dream, leaped up from the couch. He tried to snatch the gun from her hand, but she dodged him and, again, she shot him in the knee. Then she fired at Susannah. He saw that she'd hit her. Susannah was clutching at her stomach.

At that moment, he seemed to divide in two. One part of him rushed to Susannah's side. Blood was spilling from her mouth. She was dying. The other part went after Janice. The shot that hit his knee didn't seem to affect him. This time he was able to snatch the gun easily because Janice, for some reason, had frozen. She didn't seem to realize that her weapon was gone. She seemed stunned. She was staring. She asked him, 'Who are you?'

That part of him reached out and seized her by the hair. He forced her to her knees and held her in place as he aimed the gun at Nat Allen's forehead. Allen's eyes went wide and he raised his hands. He was crying, 'No, don't. I quit. I give up,' as he had the last time they met. That part of Grayson had barely heard him then. He paid no attention to him now. He fired. Nat Allen's skull seemed to contract and then explode. When it did, the rest of him vanished.

That part of him felt a tug at his sleeve. He looked down at Janice. She was looking up at him. She asked him again, 'Who are you?'

He realized that he didn't know his name.

She was saying, 'You're not Roger. I made love to Roger. Roger and I had breakfast in bed. Who are you? You're not Roger. You're frightening me.'

He shot her.

His bullet tore through the right side of her skull. She showed no shock or pain. She showed only surprise. 'How

256

could you?' she asked. 'How could you have shot me? It was me who kept them from killing you that day. We only wanted to trade you.'

It surprised him, although mildly, that she could still speak after having been shot in the head. But Janice's voice was beginning to slur because her brains were spilling out on his shoe.

The other part of him, the part holding Susannah, called out and said, 'Come and help me.' He looked at Susannah and he knew that she was dying. He felt nothing for her, nothing at all. He merely wondered why his other half should be so upset over someone who would soon be of no consequence.

Her life was ebbing quickly. He could hear her heart. It was making the sound of those life-support machines that go beep and then end on a long sustained note that sounds like a last dying scream. But she wasn't dead yet. She was reaching for him. Like Janice, she began to pull on his sleeve. She was whispering his name, very softly.

'Roger?'

He answered, 'I'm not Roger. Why are you still alive?'

'Roger? It's okay. It's all right.'

He awoke with a jolt. It was as if he'd been slapped. But awake, he still saw her looking up at his face. She had reached a hand to touch his cheek. It took him a moment to clear his head and to realize that this wasn't part of the dream. His eyes darted toward the door and all corners of the room. His face relaxed only when his eyes returned to her and he saw no blood on her blouse.

'I woke you,' she told him. 'You were having a nightmare.'

He took several deep breaths. 'I was having a beaut.'

'You had more than one. You've been dreaming for hours.'

'Hours?' Surprised, Grayson looked at his wristwatch. It was almost four o'clock in the morning. He eased her away and rose to his feet. All the dreams, in a jumble, began to come back to him. He felt a rising sense of alarm.

Dreams are dreams. He knew that. Only random imaginings. They aren't omens, or warnings; they do not portend the

257

future. He knew, all the same, that dreams often tell the truth. They reach deep into the mind and they find what it fears. They find what the dreamer really thinks of himself when he doesn't have his conscious mind to lie for him.

But he hoped, in this case, that they did not tell the truth. He hoped that they hadn't given him a true glimpse into what had happened with Janice that day. The Grayson who shot her had felt nothing at all. He had barely remembered or cared who she was. Nor had that man, the part that split off, cared at all that Susannah had been murdered.

'Sooz, look … I'm going to leave. I have to get up there.'

'Up where. To Belfair?'

'But right now I need to use my computer.'

She followed him into her kitchen table. She'd assumed that he wanted to check in with Veronica. But he didn't go to E-mail, he brought up another web page. She watched as he typed in a series of numbers. A list of locations appeared on the screen. They seemed to be military bases. He high-lighted one of them. Susannah recognized it. It was Hunter Army Airfield in nearby Savannah. Grayson then hit a key. A new list scrolled down. It looked like base personnel. He read a phone number next to one of the entries and punched out that number on his cell phone.

'Who's that you're calling?'

'I'm getting a plane.' He took out his wallet. 'I'm requesting a military jet.'

Susannah watched and listened as he was put through to a Colonel-somebody at Hunter. He identified himself and read a series of numbers from a card he had taken from his wallet. She saw that the card had been signed by General Hoyt. From what she could read, it was an authorization to make use of any military aircraft. The colonel verified the numbers by reading them back, then he put the major on hold.

'Why so suddenly?' she asked him. 'Why the middle of the night?'

'I can't sit any longer. I have to.'

He didn't try to explain the real reason. So that Nat and Janice don't walk in that door. So that Nat ... Nat ... what was it about Nat? What was it that he felt but was just out of reach? He could not explain that to her either.

'I want Jennifer and Veronica out of that place. And the Carey girl, if I can manage it.'

'I'll come with you. I'll help.'

'Does this island have an airport?'

'Yes, it does. Did you hear me?'

'I'm not taking you, Susannah.'

'You'll need me, Roger. I heard General Hoyt. You were ordered not to show up without me.'

'I will not obey that order.'

'I'm coming all the same.'

She heard the colonel in Savannah come back on the phone. He had apparently cleared Grayson for transport. Grayson told him that he needed to be picked up, soonest, at the airport on Hilton Head Island. He'd be flown directly to Andrews in Washington, where he wanted a helicopter waiting. The colonel acknowledged. Grayson broke the connection. He closed his computer and stood it on end. He felt in his pocket for his car keys.

She told him, 'I need two minutes to change.'

'Susannah, look ... I appreciate that you care, but I said I'd keep you out of this and I will.'

'You've already blown that.'

'By mentioning this island?'

'By getting me involved with Veronica and Jennifer. I couldn't help Rachel's mother, but I'll try to help them. I won't walk away from this, Roger.'

'You won't have to. I'll get them out and I'll call you.'

'I'm coming.'

'If I should run into trouble, I'm trained for it; you're not. You're staying right here and that's final.'

She took a step toward him. She looked into his eyes. 'Were you dreaming about me, Roger? A little while ago?'

'About you? I ...'

'You were dreaming about me but you were talking to Sally. I have news for you, Roger. It wasn't a dream.'

He squinted his eyes. He did not understand.

'I can hear and see things that you can't, Roger Grayson. I might come in handy. Let's go.'

Chapter Thirty-Five

The two of them were airborne within ten minutes of arriving at Hilton Head Airport. The plane was a Gulfstream jet, Air Force markings, the same model used by corporate executives. He had hoped that the plane would be a two-seat jet trainer, room for him and the pilot, but no place for Susannah.

He had argued with her all the way to the airport. In the parking lot he had opened his trunk to get his pistol and speed rig. He had made a show of checking it and chambering a round. He knew that Susannah didn't seem to like guns. He supposed he hoped that seeing it would dissuade her.

She had asked, 'You think you'll need that?'

'I might need to wave it.' He told her that Zales's ex-convict guards might try to block him if ordered.

'Then you'll have your hands full. Don't be dumb about this.'

The jet was climbing. The horizon was still black. His ETA at Andrews was 5:52 A.M. His ETA at Belfair 6:28. It would still be dark when they arrived.

Susannah reached to touch him. 'We'll get there before sunrise?'

He nodded absently, then looked at her, frowning. 'How did you know I was thinking about that?'

'I didn't. I asked you a question.'

He was silent for a moment. He sat chewing his lip. When he spoke, he blurted a question of his own.

'And what did you mean back there at your house when you said you could hear things I can't?'

'All I meant were two extra eyes and ears. I was talking about these two, right here.'

'That's not what you meant. Those and how many others? What is it, do you people divide?'

Her eyes flashed with anger. 'You people? Us freaks?'

Grayson winced. 'I didn't mean it like that.'

She looked away. 'Fuck off, Roger.'

'Susannah, I'm sorry. That remark wasn't … me.'

'I know. It was your twin. Your murderous twin. I guess I should have known that was him in the parking lot, showing off with his dumb little gun.'

'Susannah …'

'Come to think of it, what happens when *you* two divide? How do I know that one of you isn't gay? You don't share needles, do you? I guess I'd better ask now on the *increasingly* remote chance that I ever let you touch me again.'

'Susannah, if you'll let me apologize …'

'You see this, Roger? You're looking for weird. I level with you, way against my better judgment. And now it's not enough that I admitted to Sally, now you're looking for me to turn into a crowd. It's good you got a big enough airplane.'

'Susannah, in fairness, you have to admit …'

'Tell me something. Is this how it's going to be? Are you going to be looking for bipolar symptoms every time I'm the least bit perceptive?'

'Well, no, it's not that, but …'

'Women have hunches. We have intuitions. I am not that different. It is not that big a deal.'

'Then how did you know I was dreaming about Sally?'

'Aside from the fact that you were talking in your sleep?'

'That's all there was to it?'

'That, and calling me Sooz.'

He nodded begrudgingly. That seemed to make sense. Not that he believed her, but at least it made sense. And he knew that she was right about how it would be. He would have to learn when to keep his mouth shut.

She was silent, ignoring him, for perhaps twenty minutes, before she finally spoke.

'Talk to me, Roger. But about something else.'

'Sure. Okay. Pick a subject.'

'This work that you do.'

'I was going to suggest that we talk about fishing. But you, of course, would have no way of knowing that because you're so normal and all.'

'Last chance, Roger.'

'Okay, I give up. But pick something less heavy.'

'No, I'd like to know more about those people you go after. Those militias, those hate groups of yours.'

'All militias aren't hate groups. Not all of them are danger-ous. In some, it's purely social. Just something to do.'

'Like stockpiling weapons? Blowing up federal buildings?'

'Susannah, most do nothing of the sort. '

A lot of them, he told her, are little more than gun clubs. Guns have always given people a sense of power that is absent elsewhere in their lives. A militia is a poor man's therapy group. Like most men, they're privately disappointed with their lives. They think there should have been more. The trouble only starts when they pick someone to blame and start dreaming of ways to get even. That someone might be a minority group, or the rich, or some branch of the govern-ment. Most times it's just talk, but it can get out of hand.

'Nat Allen's group, I take it, did get out of hand?'

'They had stolen some explosives. They were planning a bombing.'

'Bombing what? Do you know?'

'Yes.'

'You don't want to tell me?'

'The Holocaust Museum in Washington.'

She whistled.

'It wasn't going to happen. They'd been under surveillance. I'd been with them for almost two months.'

'As what?'

'As a Nazi fanatic. Like them, only more so.'

'But ... you knew who you really were all that time.'

'Susannah ... now *you're* doing it. Don't start.'

'Well, explain neo-Nazis. Why would anyone still join them?'

'They were already garbage. Now they're garbage with company. Very much like the Klan and other groups. Racial hatred certainly plays a part but it's secondary. The big thing is fear. You want people to fear you. Making people afraid gives you power over them. It's the only kind of power most of them could ever have, short of getting a job with ... a job with ... some police force.'

She heard his voice trail off. 'What just happened right then?'

'Right when?'

'Just now. Your eyes went sort of funny.'

'Oh, nothing. Now I've lost my train of thought. Where was I?'

'You went with the Nazis.'

'That's the long and the short if it.'

'You make it sound like a walk in the park.'

He shrugged. 'I stuck around long enough to see who was who and find out where they stashed their arms and explosives. When I did, most of them were arrested. End of story.'

'That's a pretty short story, Major Grayson. What else?'

'What more do you need? That's all that happened.'

'Did you hurt anyone?'

'Well, I didn't attack Poland.'

'But this group ... that was where you must have crossed Nat Allen. What happened between you and him?'

'Not much. Just a fight. A few bruises here and there.'

'After which you shook hands. No hard feelings, am I right?'

'There ... might be a little lingering grudge.'

She was silent for another minute or so.

He asked. 'Now what? Are you mad at me again?'

264

'I'm just sorting my feelings. Wondering whether to tell you. It's a thing that both of us know.'

'What's that?'

'And this is not ESP, so don't give me any crap.'

'I won't. I promise.'

'It's this guy, Nat Allen. The man who wants to kill you. I think he'll be showing up at Belfair.'

Grayson didn't know how she picked it up, or when. But he knew that she was right about Nat Allen. As for him, the thought had been floating out of reach ever since he woke up from that dream. The truth of it had only at last broken through when she asked him why people became Nazis.

What had triggered it was his mention of jobs on a police force. Nat Allen was believed to have worked as a cop but there was more to it than that. It was that E-mail that he sent to Veronica. It said that the *pervert* – whoever that was – in *Warrenton, Virginia*, wherever that is – had told him *one more place where soldier boy goes*.

Never mind, for the moment, that Hoyt had sucked in his breath at the mention of Warrenton, Virginia. Even if Hoyt had no knowledge of the man who was attacked there and Grayson had imagined his reaction, there was still Nat's mention of *one more place to look*. Grayson would have to assume that the *place* was real and not something the pervert made up. So where, he asked himself, does that leave us?

Those people already knew that he was quartered at Bolling, so it obviously couldn't mean the base. *Goes*, he assumed, means more than one visit so it couldn't have referred to Hilton Head or Duke. That left only Langley and Belfair. Langley was, if anything, more secure than Bolling, unless Nat could catch him en route. That would seem to leave Belfair. Only Belfair.

'Susannah?'

'Uh-huh?'

'We're going from Andrews to Belfair by chopper. It will land on Belfair's front lawn. I want you to stay with the pilot

265

in the chopper. I want you out of sight, not visible from the gate. No arguments this time, or I'll leave you at Andrews.'

'That gate is the only way in?'

'The wall's high and it's wired. You stay with the chopper; I'll bring the girls to you. I want you to give me your word.'

'You'll be out of my sight?'

'I'll be in constant touch. I'll have the chopper's transceiver. That's why I need you to be where you can hear me.'

It was not quite a lie. Not a big lie, at least. Doing it that way might even be better. And the chopper's crew would protect her.

She gave him an odd look but she nodded. 'Okay.'

Grayson settled back again. He closed his eyes. Little lie, big lie; it was probably not needed. Nat Allen might indeed want to scout out Belfair. He might indeed have left that house in Virginia and proceeded directly to Maryland. But he wouldn't be there, not at this hour. He'd need daylight to observe who comes and goes for a while.

Either way, thought Grayson, one thing was certain. That man was still hunting him and enough was enough. Grayson had had it with sitting on some base, barred from leaving the grounds without an escort.

He had some leave coming. He would take it and use it. He'd get word to Nat Allen where he'd be, where to find him. He'd be waiting for Allen. He would end this.

He'd wished that he'd finished it that last time they met. He might have if he hadn't been stopped. On that day, when he fought him and had put Nat down, they say he picked up a heavy rock. They say he used it to smash both of Nat Allen's hands so that he'd never have full use of them again. They say he was about to crush his knees as well. It was not a thing that Roger Grayson would have done. It was a thing that the man he was playing would have done. Even so, he should have remembered it.

No matter, he thought. Things were very different now. Susannah Card had entered his life and Nat Allen would kill her if he knew that he cared for her. Grayson would make sure that

Allen never got the chance. Nor would he need to become someone else. He would kill him as plain Roger Grayson.

'Roger?'

'Mmm?'

'It's okay. We'll fix this. It's going to be fine.'

He had reached for her hand but a beeping sound stopped him. He picked up his laptop and opened it. There was a new E-mail, this time from Veronica. He scrolled down to the message. It came in two parts:

Roger ... it's getting pretty weird around here. First we heard all these gong sounds. Like when you bang pots together. The noise was coming up from the basement. We could hear it through the dumbwaiter shaft. Jennifer says the only thing down there that makes that noise would be a bedpan. She was afraid that Duane was hitting Emma with it and she wanted to go down and take a look. I didn't let her. Then a little while later we could hear a man screaming. He was yelling for help. Jennifer says he didn't sound like Duane. She thought it sounded like Leroy. Anyway, it stopped soon and we both fell asleep.

If that's not weird enough, then listen to this.

You're not going to believe what just woke us up.

This place is being invaded.

Chapter Thirty-Six

It had seemed to Leatrice that she'd barely drifted off when she heard an urgent rapping at her door. She looked at her clock. It was only half past five in the morning.

She called out, 'What is it?' A night shift guard answered. He said a big Army truck was at the front gate. Mr. Teal was with it. He wanted the gate opened.

'An Army truck? What's he doing with a truck?'

'I dunno; he said his car had a flat. But I think he was being sarcastic.'

Leatrice, both confused and annoyed, dressed quickly in a white smock and lab coat. She hurried down one floor to the Security Office. She pounded on her husband's locked door as she passed it. She did not wait for him to answer.

The Security Office had a bank of monitors that showed all the main hallways and all entrances. She paused to note that the basement seemed quiet, but the basement was not her concern at the moment. Then she looked at the monitor that showed the main gate. She saw Prentice Teal. He was standing by the truck. He was facing the camera but not looking at it. He was checking the watch on his wrist. She reached to press the button of a speaker.

'Mr. Teal,' she asked, 'what is the meaning of this?'

He glanced up. 'Move it, Leatrice. I don't have all day.'

'You will kindly come back at a decent hour, at which time you'll state your business respectfully.'

Teal raised a hand to the first of the trucks. He made a circle

268

with his hand in a John Wayne-ish gesture and pointed his finger at the gate. The driver revved his motor. He slammed the truck in gear.

She gasped. 'What on earth ...?'

'Open up or lose the gate. You have three seconds.'

She spat a curse but she jabbed at the button. The gates swung open; the truck started through, but Teal made no move to climb aboard. She saw a second truck, smaller. The smaller one had been lurking behind and its headlights were only now on. Teal had been waiting for that one. An armed and helmeted soldier jumped out. He took a position inside the gate. She saw Teal climb onto the truck's running board and order the driver to proceed.

She pressed another button, a general alarm, that would summon all available guards. It usually meant that a patient had escaped or that several patients had rioted. They would come with their flashlights, their Mace and their Tasers. She tapped the first button. It should have closed the gates. But she saw that the soldier had jammed them. She stepped out of the room, saw her husband emerging. He was asking running guards what was happening. She ignored him except to say, 'Fix your hair, Norman, dear,' and marched out to confront Prentice Teal.

The larger truck had gone off to her left and had stopped at the laboratory's door. Two soldiers and a civilian climbed out. She knew the civilian, a Los Alamos technician; he worked with the laboratory computers. The two soldiers were dressed in fatigues and heavy boots, and wore helmets that seemed to have binoculars built in. Their helmets contained two-way radios, as well. She saw microphones on wire bands that curved around to their lips. Both soldiers were armed with automatic weapons that seemed of a *Star Wars* variety. More than that, they were carried in a no-nonsense manner. The technician used his card to enter the laboratory. He turned the lights on. One soldier went with him. The other stood guard at the entrance.

Prentice Teal had directed the smaller Army truck to pull

269

up at the front entrance. He hopped to the driveway; three more soldiers emerged; they were equipped like the others, one a sergeant. The sergeant had something draped over his shoulders. It looked like an empty duffel bag.

Leatrice faced them, her hands on her hips. Six guards and her husband had assembled behind her. Norman Zales was still tucking in his shirt; he was coatless. Other guards, holding flashlights, were coming around the building from their quarters in what once were the stables. She scanned the faces of the guards who stood with her.

She asked, 'Where is Duane?'

They didn't know.

'And where is Leroy? Why aren't they here?'

Zales asked her, 'What's happening?' She ignored him.

He called out to Teal. 'Why have you brought these trucks?'

'Think about it,' he answered, 'it will come to you, Doctor.'

Leatrice designated two guards who stood with her. She ordered them to gather some of those then arriving and secure the laboratory area. She told them that nothing must be taken from that room without her explicit permission.

Teal watched her for a moment in mild amusement.

He said, 'Sergeant Kristoff? Spell it out for her, please.'

The sergeant snapped to what was almost attention. He advised Leatrice that he and his men were on a classified military operation. They were authorized to meet resistance with force. Shoot to maim if feasible, for effect if need be.

Teal had watched the guards' faces, they seemed not to understand. 'What the sergeant is saying is we'll try not to kill you. We'll try to only put holes in your legs. Don't fuck with us, guys. You can't win this.'

Teal saw that they did not seem intimidated, especially, but they didn't seem truculent either. They didn't really seem to care either way. He knew that for some it was the drugs they'd had at Langley. For the rest it was whatever Zales put in their food. He was glad, on the one hand, for their lack of aggression, but he'd hoped to see a little more life in them.

He glanced up when he saw many lights going on in the windows of the third and fourth floors. Several faces were peering down from those windows. The alarm Leatrice sounded had woken them. He decided that he'd better get on with this.

He left two of Kristoff's men to flank the front entrance. He instructed them to keep all the guards outside and especially Leatrice Zales. He told the guards to disperse. Some obeyed. Some merely stared. He brushed past a sputtering Leatrice Zales and took Norman Zales by the arm.

'Inside, Dr. Zales. Move along.'

With the sergeant at his back, he took Zales to his office. Once there, Teal produced a notebook from his pocket. He flipped it open and showed a marked page to Zales.

'Here's a list of what I need. I want it now. Everything you have on Richard and Chameleon.'

Zales peered at the page. 'This includes patients' files.'

'It includes what we've paid you for. Let's get busy.'

'Well, you have no right. You can't take them.'

Prentice Teal shrugged. 'Watch me, Doc.'

Teal walked to the cabinet where Zales's notebooks were kept. Zales had shown them to him in the past. He snapped his fingers at Kristoff. Kristoff tossed him the duffel. Teal began sorting through the notebooks he found. He chose several of these; they would go in the duffel. The others, he left atop the cabinet.

Zales was white with fury. 'This is utterly outrageous. I'm going to call General Hoyt.'

'Ah, yes. That reminds me. Where are your cell phones?'

'Norman! Tell him nothing,' came Leatrice's voice. It came from outside the main entrance. Teal paid no attention; she couldn't get in, but he supposed that he should have closed the door.

'Did you hear me, Dr. Zales?'

'What, my cell phone? I won't tell you.'

271

'In your desk, your briefcase, your car? We'll find them. In any case, you're welcome to speak to General Hoyt, but you'll do it after we're finished.'

'Mr. Teal, sir,' said Kristoff. 'I have a report.' He tapped his radio to indicate its source. 'Your technician is saying our computers have been breached.'

'Could he tell by whom?'

'He thinks so, sir. He says he built in a tracer that's ...' The sergeant rolled his eyes. 'Now he's trying to tell me how it works, sir.'

'I don't care how it works. Bottom line, Sergeant Kristoff.'

Kristoff listened as the technician reported.

'Sir, he says it's internal. He says the hack had to come from this system.' He gestured toward Zales's office computer.

Teal looked at Zales. 'Naughty-naughty,' he whispered.

'Naughty who? You mean me? I did no such thing.'

Teal turned to the sergeant. 'We will take Dr. Zales's computer with us. Gather up any disks and tapes you can find. Be sure you check out his safe.'

Zales moved to block Kristoff. 'I won't let you have them. Those are confidential records. There is nothing of yours in my computer.'

'If there isn't, you'll get it all back.'

'You're not taking it.'

'I'll borrow it now or put a bullet in your hard drive. Your choice; I'm okay either way.'

The sergeant was listening to his earpiece again. He said, 'Sir, it's the lab. Another report. Someone's been into the drugs, last two days.'

Teal wasn't surprised. He threw a glance at the psychiatrist. 'Care to shed any light, Dr. Zales?'

'I haven't touched them.'

'Then Leatrice?'

'I don't ... I don't know.'

Sergeant Kristoff, still listening, relayed what was said. 'Sir, your man says what's missing is no big deal. Some strychnine, some ketamine, both in very small amounts. And he thinks someone needed a hard-on.'

'Say, what?'

'He says someone's been into that Russian aphrodisiac, but there's not enough gone to get excited about.'

Teal grunted. Someone surely, he thought, felt the need to get excited. Either Leatrice, in order to endure sex with Zales, or Zales so he could get it up for Leatrice.

He told Zales, 'I will also require three diaries. You know the three I want. You'll get those back as well.'

'What good are they to you?'

'They might keep our friends in line.'

'I refuse to give them up for such a purpose.'

Teal stared for a beat. He could scarcely believe it. An ethical protest from Zales.

'You won't have to, Doctor. I'll get them myself. Come to think of it, however, I believe I'll want four. I assume Camal's wife keeps one, too.'

Although the two soldiers had barred her from entering, Leatrice could hear much of what was said in the office. She could hear her husband the most clearly of all because he spoke with such outraged, though unfruitful, conviction. She had twice attempted to come to his aid by forcing her way past Teal's sentries. One had asked her to kindly not try it again and she answered by slapping his face. He responded by raising his palm to her face and pushing her into a hedge.

Most of her own guards had drifted away. Two of those who had stayed helped her up. She ordered those remaining to seize the two sentries. Only one reacted. He reached for his Taser but his movements were slow, almost mechanical. The nearest sentry swatted the Taser from his hand. The guard watched it bounce. He made no move to retrieve it.

Leatrice allowed herself a squeal of frustration. She turned and stalked off in the direction of the laboratory. The remaining guards, all oddly somnambulant, wandered off with no evident sense of purpose.

One of the sentries, watching everyone disperse, shook his head in considerable bemusement.

'Those are the keepers?' he said to his companion. 'Jesus, then who are the nuts?'

His companion grunted. 'But watch out for the wife. Teal says he thinks she's from Venus.'

'And the guards?'

'I don't know. They're all on something. And if it's that same shit that Teal wants to peddle, I got news; it's still got a few bugs.'

The first sentry nodded. 'You okay here alone?'

'Yeah, why?'

'I'll see where she goes. Then I'll walk around back.'

'Keep your headset open. Keep in touch.'

Grayson had scrolled up the rest of the message that followed. This place is being invaded. It read:

An alarm went off like someone was escaping so we went and looked out the window. Army trucks and soldiers came in through the gate. All the soldiers have guns and very tech-y looking helmets. Mr. Teal is with them. The guards all came out but the soldiers pointed guns at them and made most of them get back around the house. Mr. Teal and Leatrice had an argument down in front. He came in with Dr. Zales but he made Leatrice stay out.

One truck went around to the side of the house. We can see that side from Shan Li's room. Wait … wait a second. Jennifer's in there. She says something else is happening.

Okay. The big truck backed up against a door down there. They're starting to load stuff into it. Jennifer says Leatrice went around to that side and … wait …

Jennifer says tell you we'll get back to you. Stay on.

Susannah read it as he did. She asked, 'Who's this Teal?'

'Project director. The man who sent me off to find you. All he ever really wanted was to get me out of town. We are just now finding out why.'

'Whatever he's doing … is it something you'd stop?'

'I might try if I knew what it is.'

'But whatever it is, you know Zales doesn't like it. So, maybe it's not a bad thing.'

Grayson, in his mind, dismissed that as flippant. Armed invasions tend to be bad. What Grayson wanted was not speculation; he wanted to respond to the E-mail. He wanted to tell Veronica he was on his way, to stay in her room, stay safe. But Susannah's reaction, her words, now struck a chord. Prentice Teal had told him the very same thing. He'd said, '*I know you don't like me, so you might not believe this. But what's happening is not a bad thing.*'

He touched Susannah's hand. He said, 'Maybe. Let's hope so.' He looked at his watch and blew a frustrated breath. 'We're still more than an hour away.'

Chapter Thirty-Seven

Leatrice hadn't stopped at the lab. She kept going past it toward the side of the building where her husband's Mercedes was parked. The sentry who had followed her was watching. As she unlocked the door, he called, 'Ma'am?'

She stopped and looked back at him, questioningly.

'Ma'am, do not start that car. You will force me to stop you.'

'You will shoot? Young man, don't be ridiculous.'

'Not you, ma'am, your car. You will force me to shoot out your tires.'

As if to dare him, she entered the car. She made a show of digging into her pocket and producing a thick set of keys. She held one up for the sentry to see and then used it to start the car's engine. She flipped on the headlights and turned on the high beams. Teal's soldier had to cover his eyes.

But he wasn't doing that. He was dropping his visor. Calmly, he raised his weapon to his shoulder. He fired two shots, they made a sound like loud spitting. Her two front tires bulged out and collapsed. He fired twice more. Those shots put out her headlights. The soldier raised his scope. He saw her face clearly. He saw shock, then fear. He lowered his weapon. He then saw, without the need for his scope, that she had hunched forward over the wheel. She was sobbing in helpless frustration. He reported the incident to his sergeant by radio, then returned his attention to patrolling.

But Leatrice was neither in shock nor was she sobbing.

She'd had no intention of trying to drive off, although she had considered ramming that truck. What she wanted was her husband's car phone.

She took it from its cradle and punched out the first number. It was that of General Hoyt. She would try him first. She would then call Rachel's father; she'd call Winston and Camal. She would demand of Hoyt and Carey that they stop what Teal was doing. She'd tell Winston and Camal to get to Belfair at once. She would tell them that Teal was betraying them. They must fight him or they would face ruin.

The army gulfstream had started its final descent. Grayson stared at the lights of the Capitol in the distance. He was less than an hour from Belfair. Suddenly more words appeared on his screen. He was getting the rest of the message.

Roger? I'm back.

Jennifer says Leatrice got into a car and a soldier shot at her when she started it. She says the soldier shot out the headlights and tires. She says Leatrice is still in the car, slumped over. Wait ...

Jennifer says there are no holes in the windshield so she doesn't think Leatrice got shot. Crazy, huh? You're missing a wild party, Roger. Veronica had signed off. Grayson clicked on her address and typed a short message.

Am on my way. I'm bringing a friend. Her name is Susannah; she knows all about you; she's very much a woman you can trust. You and Jennifer will leave with her when I get there. Try to be ready. Keep me advised.

The Dodger.

Susannah was frowning. 'What does "leave with *her*" mean?'

'I expect to be with you. I wrote that just in case.'

'They kept Zales's wife from leaving. You don't think they'll stop us?'

'Not Teal. He won't care. He might even have gone. But if things get crazy and I signal you to go, don't hesitate, don't argue. Just go.'

Leatrice, calling from the crippled Mercedes, had failed to

get through to General Hoyt. His machine had answered. She left a short message. She described for him, briefly, what was happening at Belfair and the treachery of his man from Los Alamos.

The next number she called was that of Congressman Carey. The phone rang several times. He answered; he seemed wide awake. She had barely identified herself when he asked, 'Leatrice? What the hell's going on?'

'Then you've heard?'

'Heard what? It's not even daylight yet and Hoyt's car just picked up my wife. I asked where they were going; she told me to go to hell. Now ten minutes later, you're calling.'

My goodness, thought Leatrice. They are both coming here. General Hoyt has a hand in this after all. They are probably coming to get Rachel.

'Get up here, Andrew. You must get here quickly.'

'Up to Belfair? What for? What's going on?'

'Mr. Teal has brought men with guns in two trucks. He is trying to cheat you of the fortune you will make. You must get here at once and you must stop him.'

Leatrice had assumed that the mention of money always springs men like Carey into action. That assumption was, however, premature.

He replied, 'Who is Teal? I don't know any Teal.'

'You don't know any … Listen to me, my dear man …'

'And fortune? What fortune? I don't know what you're saying. If you have a problem, you deal with it.' He hung up.

Denial, thought Leatrice. The first principle of government. She realized that she should have expected that response. She would not make that mistake with Camal. She punched out Camal's number. The call woke him.

She told him essentially what she'd said to his partner. She added that Teal meant not only to cheat him but to expose him if he should complain. She said that she overheard Prentice Teal demanding the diaries of his wife and his daughter, both of which might be terribly embarrassing to him, should they be copied and sent to his family.

'Your father, dear Luis, has been under the impression that your wife has run off, has he not?'

'Fucking Teal.'

'That your wife, and your daughter, emptied all your accounts and ran off to open a brothel somewhere. Is that not how you explained their disappearance to him?'

'Fucking Teal.'

'Your father is, I believe, the sole source of your income. I think you'd best get here, dear Luis.'

'You can't stop him yourself? You got twenty fucking guards.'

'Tut-tut. Mind your language. It is most unbecoming.'

'Never mind my f...' He swallowed the word. 'Look, Leatrice, you stall him. Can you keep him from leaving?'

'There's a problem, you see. He has brought men with guns.'

'I'll show the fuck a gun. You just hold him.'

This time it was he who broke the connection. She allowed herself a smile. He'll be on his way promptly, fairly flying to Belfair on wings of fear and greed, with a tailwind of hatred for Teal. As for holding Teal, however, that was going to be a problem. She supposed that she could still start Norman's car and get it as far as the gate. She could block the gate, but what then? The larger of Teal's trucks would simply push it aside.

Something would come to her. It always does. For every problem, a solution exists. One need only be alert to inspiration.

She had almost decided not to call Charles Winston. His residence was at least two hours away and poor Charles was no man of action. She supposed, however, that she'd better alert him. He had no less at stake than the others.

She dialed his number. It rang a few times. A male voice answered, 'Winston residence.'

'Would you put Charles on, please. This is Leatrice Zales.'

'Mizz Zales, who are you? Are you family?'

She blinked. 'Sir, to whom am I speaking?'

'It's the Warrenton police. This is Chief Webster speaking. I see you're calling from Maryland.'

Leatrice realized that Charles must have Caller ID. This policeman was reading Belfair's number. She said, 'This is his therapist, Dr. Leatrice Zales. Mr. Winston and his daughter have been under my care. What has happened? I insist that you tell me.'

'Dr. Zales, he's been attacked. He's been beaten and ... um, cut.'

'Oh, my stars. He's not ...'

'No, he's not dead, but he's the nearest thing to it. His housekeeper found him, we hope not too late. The heaviest bleeding and most of the damage is related to the victim's ... ah, lower regions. Can you think who might have done that and why?'

'I'm ... sure I cannot. Oh, my goodness.'

'Could the daughter have done it? I been hearing certain stories. Seems they had an unusual relationship.'

'His daughter is with me ... at a mental hospital ... Belfair. She hasn't been off the grounds in three years.'

'Ever heard Winston mention a man named Nat Allen?'

'Nat Allen? No. I don't believe that I have.'

'Well, that name is on the wall. It was written in blood. Whoever wrote it used the victim's ... well, whatever.'

The policeman had stopped himself. She understood why. Some details at a crime scene are usually withheld. But Leatrice urged him to say all that he could. She reminded him, falsely, that she was a psychiatrist and an expert in aberrant behavior. The policeman hesitated, but he answered.

'Whoever wrote it in blood used Charles Winston's penis. Nat Allen and one other name were smeared on the wall. Some sick bastard left someone a message.'

'Saying what, sir?'

'Can't tell you that but let me try the other name. The name, "Grayson" mean anything to you?'

She felt a light-headedness. 'Just ... Grayson?'

'Plus some words. It ring a bell?'

'I ... do know a Grayson, but he doesn't know Charles. At least ... oh, my goodness.'

'We should talk to him anyway. Do you know where we'd find him?'

'I'm sorry. Very sorry. I'm afraid I must go.'

'Dr. Zales, don't hang up. We're not through yet.'

'You will have to excuse me. Good-bye.'

Her husband's words were abuzz in her head. Grayson ... a fixer ... an assassin. Now with Teal taking everything – no doubt on Hoyt's orders – General Hoyt must be covering his tracks. He would have had his man start with the farthest one away. After Winston, the assassin would work his way north. Perhaps Camal would be next and then after him would come the congressman. After those two, no doubt, he would be coming to Belfair.

'But calm yourself, Leatrice,' she said under her breath. 'It is not at all like you to panic.'

She realized that her fears were probably nonsense. After all, she'd just spoken to both Carey and Camal. And although she knew little of the minds of assassins, she imagined that they rarely signed their names to their work. In any event, Camal was unharmed. Or at least he had been a few minutes ago. She had spoken to him. She found herself dialing his number once more.

There was no answer. The phone rang and it rang. It had to mean he'd already left. But in her mind, she saw Camal opening his door to see Major Grayson standing before him, an assassin's sharp knife in his hand. Camal barely had time to let out a squawk before Grayson's knife severed his throat. Oh, my goodness.

'Leatrice ... be calm. Take several deep breaths.'

She redialed Carey's number. It rang. He didn't answer. His machine began to speak. She knew that Grayson could not possibly have reached him in the time since she made her first call. This worm of a man had gone to ground; he was letting his erasable machine take the call. She waited for the prompt and then spoke.

'This is Leatrice Zales again. Oh, please be alive. Don't be another victim. Charles Winston is already dying or dead. Call his home if you wish. It's filled with police. I can't reach Camal. He might also be dead. Their assassin, beyond doubt, is General Hoyt's Major Grayson. If the general has removed his sister from your house, it was certainly to make sure that you would be there alone.'

She paused.

'Major Grayson? You're there. You're hearing this aren't you? Are you castrating him as you did poor Mr. Winston? Are you writing your name in blood with his penis? Are you …'

She heard a welcome click. 'Major Grayson?' she asked.

'No, it's me, God damn it. What the hell is …'

'Thank Heavens. Get up here where we can protect you. If you stay in that house, you'll be murdered.'

'By Grayson?'

'Or perhaps by Rachel. She's escaped.'

'Escaped?'

'You mustn't lose a minute. Get up here.'

She broke the connection with a satisfied smile. The mention of Rachel had not been intended but the mention was no less inspired. It should make it doubly certain that her father would come running.

As for Rachel escaping, what a wonderful idea. Escaping, disappearing, being nowhere to be found. That would seem to solve a number of problems.

She would think how best to do it. She would discuss it with Duane. But first things being first, there was the matter of Teal. Camal had indicated that he'd take care of Teal, but Camal wanted Teal to be held until he got here. She couldn't think how, but she would surely think of something. It seemed to be a day for good ideas.

Chapter Thirty-Eight

Teal had escorted Norman Zales from his office. He'd told
Kristoff to wait for him, to watch the office, and not to let
anyone near those files.

Zales had tried to resist being led down the hall. Teal had
pulled him, not roughly, toward the elevator doors. Once
there, Zales stood firm. He had told Teal that the elevator
couldn't be used unless he entered a code.

'So punch it in.'

'I will not.'

'Behave yourself, Norman.' Teal reached for the panel and
punched in the code. He had memorized it the first time he
saw that Zales was concealing it. He had no doubt that
Grayson had done the same thing.

The elevator started. Zales folded his arms. He said, 'I will
cooperate no further.'

'Sure you will.'

Zales saw that Teal carried only a transceiver. 'You …
don't seem to be armed. How will you coerce me?'

'Well, I could slam your face into the wall a few times, but
I'd really much rather keep this nice. Be good, Dr. Zales, and
we'll be gone before you know it.'

The elevator opened on the fourth floor. He had Zales
walk ahead of him down the long, narrow hallway. All
the doors were closed but many rooms had their lights
on. Their occupants, no doubt, were all at their windows,
watching the activities below. Teal came to the room that

bore Rachel Carey's name. He looked in. It was empty.

'She's still down in the basement?'

Zales was pouting. He gave a vague shrug in response.

'I don't see her diary. Is that down there with her?'

Zales still didn't answer. No matter.

Teal scanned the room; its decor was a strange one. There were feminine touches here and there as if someone had done her best to soften it. Teal's guess was that the someone was the gentle one, Teresa. The rest of the room was a cross between the bedroom of your normal pain-in-the-ass-teen-sloven and the crash pad of a butch outlaw biker.

He gave Zales a little push and they walked farther down, almost to the end of the hallway. Teal stopped at a room with no nameplate on the door. There were others without nameplates in that section.

He asked Zales, 'This bunch, they're not multiples, correct?'

'They are ... each quite ill in other ways.'

'Oh, I'm sure they are now. What about before they got here?'

'There are ... many types of illness, Mr. Teal.'

Teal almost smiled. He had to shake his head. He had often marveled at the way these psychiatrists kept finding new things to treat. A psychiatrist could take any simple human problem, give it a name, call it a pathology, and announce that he was the leading authority. That, however, was not the case in this section. This was where you went if your biggest problem is that someone has decided you're a pain in the ass. This section is Stashville. This is Roach Motel.

Teal opened the door. He saw Camal's wife. She sat in a chair slowly rocking and humming. A small-boned woman, midforties, olive skin, she was swathed in a bathrobe several sizes too large. She had not looked up. She gave no sign that she saw him. Teal could only guess what drugs she'd been given. It looked like a permanent heroin nod. He heard himself asking, 'Does she ever see her daughter?'

'It is ... better this way. She might recognize Shan Li, but Shan Li would not recognize her.'

'Where's her binder?'

'Her diary? She has none. Those are only for multiples. As you see,' he said, pointing, 'she has no pens or pencils either. We can't let her have anything sharp.'

Teal looked where Zales had gestured. He saw a well-worn pad and a jumble of used crayons. Teal stepped into the room and picked up the pad. It was filled with writing, some decipherable, some not. He asked the woman, 'May I borrow this, please?'

She said nothing but he thought he saw a smile.

As Teal turned to leave, his transceiver crackled. He brought it to his ear. He said, 'Problem?'

Kristoff answered. *'Sir, we have a report from the gate. A police car has made two slow passes outside. It's possible that Mrs. Zales called them.'*

Teal doubted that greatly. If she had reached a phone, she wouldn't have called the police. A passing patrol car had probably just wondered why so many lights were on at this hour. 'I wouldn't worry, sergeant. He can't do much. We're federal.'

Kristoff asked him to hold. He was getting further word.

'Sir, now the lookout says that car isn't local. It has West Virginia markings and plates, two men in it. An older model Chevy, looks a little beat up. No Mars light on top, just a single blue bubble. Says Police on the fender but it doesn't say a town.'

'Did they see your man?'

'No, sir. He's up on the roof of that guardhouse; it gives him good cover and a view of the road. The most they could have seen are the two trucks out front and maybe one man at the door.'

Teal gave a shrug. He was more curious than troubled. 'Just keep an eye on him,' he said.

'And, sir, we had to shoot up Dr. Zales's car. His wife tried to start it. No harm to her, though.'

Teal grunted. 'Okay, sergeant. We'll be finished here shortly.'

Teal was watching Zales's face throughout this exchange. He seemed relieved to hear that the police car hadn't stopped. He seemed all the more relieved that it had West Virginia markings as opposed to, for example, those of Baltimore. But the only time his heart seemed to truly sink was on hearing that his car now had holes in it.

Perhaps. Or, perhaps it was on hearing that there were no holes in Leatrice.

Teal proceeded down the hall until he reached a large dayroom. To one side was a door that led to the fire stairs, or rather the old servants' stairway. Teal looked at the door. It had no push bar, no keyhole. He asked Zales, 'How does this open?'

'It's electric.'

'Really? How does anyone get out if there's a fire?'

'The doors are keyed to the alarm. They'll unlock automatically.'

Teal raised a foot. He kicked through the door. It splintered at the lock and nearly tore off one hinge.

Zales gasped at the sight. 'Are you out of your mind?'

'What, just now? Not at all. That was rational behavior.'

'Rational behavior? What was rational about it?'

Teal pretended to be nonplussed by his reaction. 'Well, you see, we're only going down one floor and the elevator's way down the hall.'

Zales sputtered. 'But the *patients*. They'll be wandering all over.'

'Silly me. Didn't think. Well, spilt milk. Let's go down.'

Chapter Thirty-Nine

Nat Allen had turned up a darkened side road. His deputy had asked him, 'Well, what do you think?'

'I believe that fat pervert was tellin' the truth.'

'About what? All he said was that Grayson comes here now and then. That don't mean he'll be here today.'

'And he said it's an asylum but you saw them Army trucks. That place is no ordinary nuthouse.'

'Could it be the Army has its own loony bin?'

'Could be. I never saw an officer, lieutenant on up, who I thought was right in the head.'

'Got that right.'

'It's that mind control that the government puts them through. A lot of them can't take it, their brains turn to soup. Others go rabid like trash-dump raccoons.'

'Or else, you know what? That place is where they do it.'

'Do what? Mind control?'

'Well, why not? Them Jew scientists who do it, they gotta do it somewheres. What's a better place for that than a nuthouse?'

'Makes sense to me, friend. Damned if it don't.'

'Jew scientist named Zales, he's in charge of this place. It gets me thinking. You know what I bet? I bet they did mind control on Grayson. When he said he was that Nazi, maybe he wasn't faking. He was one mean son of a bitch.'

'He was faking. Damned spy. Janice said it was an act.'

'Yeah, well, Janice also said he had a real gentle side.'

287

Nat Allen spat. 'She learnt better.'

'But you see, here's my point. Not to rub it in or nothin', but the way he stomped you … I ain't never seen the like.'

'That's because there ain't no one ever whupped me.'

'I seen his eyes that day. He'd have messed you up bad. He didn't want to whup you. He wanted to squish you. It was like he was taking his own sweet time deciding what part to bust first. If we hadn't jumped in when he was mashin' your hands …'

'I was there, remember? Would you … mind shuttin' up?'

'I was makin' a point.'

'Make some other point.'

'But don't you see? That was no man who whupped you. You were fightin' against a damned robot.'

'A robot?'

'A lot of this mind control … they do it with electrodes. They plant these little radio things in their brains and that's how they make them act different ways. Wasn't no man who whupped you. That was a machine.'

'Maybe so.'

'Stands to reason. Ought to make you feel better.'

'I'll feel better when I pull his damn plug.'

'So, what now? We just sit here, see if Grayson turns up?'

Nat Allen wasn't sure. He didn't want to just sit. He could think of two other choices. One was to get their rifles out of the trunk, go over that wall and wait in the bushes. Good scopes on the rifles. Good thick hedges inside. If they were going to do that without being seen, they'd best climb that wall before daylight.

But they still had time to sit a while longer. See who went in and out. See who drove by. Maybe use his police light to stop one of them, get some answers on what was inside.

'We'll sit tight for a spell,' he decided.

Chapter Forty

Teal had Zales walk before him down the narrow stairs that led to the third-floor landing. He could hear, behind him, patients entering the stairwell. Some were tentatively making their way down.

He reached the third floor and led Zales down the hallway, reaching the large foyer at its end. The rooms of the Camal and Winston girls were the last two rooms on his left. Shan Li's room was first. They found her playing with a puppy.

'Shan Li?' Zales knew that dog. 'How did you get it?'

She smiled and jabbered a few words in Chinese.

'Is Jennifer here? Is she on this floor?'

Shan Li nodded. She gestured toward the room next door.

'If you don't mind,' said Teal, 'we're not here about a dog.' He pushed in past Zales. He saw Shan Li's diary among her text books and tapes. He pointed to it. 'May I borrow that, please?'

She shrugged. She didn't care. Teal took it. He slipped her mother's notebook into Shan Li's blue binder and put them both under his arm. He turned and went out toward the Winston girl's room. He paused for a moment.

'Just out of curiosity,' he asked the psychiatrist, 'does Shan Li understand that Camal is her father?'

'She ... knows that he's Carita's father, yes.'

'Don't start that shit. Does she know it or not?'

'We try not to discuss it. It brings on a fit of rage. While she might not see Luis Camal as her father, she seems nonetheless sympathetic to Carita. Carita, you'll recall, is an hysterical mute, resulting from being forced by her father to …'

Teal stopped him, shaking his head. 'Never mind.' Try to get a short answer from a shrink.

The two of them stood at Veronica's door. The young woman, sitting in her chair by her computer, seemed to have been waiting for them to appear after hearing them in Shan Li's room. She nodded a greeting that was tentative, watchful. Once again, Zales entered first. He was looking for Jennifer. Once again, Teal pushed past him as he spotted the binder. It was on the floor, open, as if someone had been reading it.

'Veronica, I need to borrow your binder.'

She seemed visibly relieved. 'Sure. Take it.'

Zales asked her, 'Where is Jennifer? How did she get here?' He scanned the room; he glanced under her bed; he walked to the bathroom and checked it as well. Teal didn't interrupt him; he was curious to see her. He had never seen the twelve-year-old multiple. Jennifer, however, was clearly in hiding and Veronica seemed unwilling to say where.

Teal nudged Zales. He gestured toward the computer. 'I thought I told you to find her another toy.'

'You told me that yesterday.'

'That meant do it yesterday.'

'And I told you that it would destroy her. Take it away and there's no more Veronica. Don't do that to her, Mr. Teal.'

Teal took a step closer. The monitor was dark. But he thought that he was able to see a dim pattern. He realized that the brightness control had been turned down to conceal what Veronica was doing. He reached past her and felt for the row of little wheels that were under the base of the screen. He restored the brightness. An E-mail page appeared. She had written:

Hi, Dodger:

It's quiet now but everyone's awake. Someone's gone upstairs, then we heard a loud noise and … oops. Hold on. Someone's coming.

Teal asked, 'Veronica, who is this Dodger?'

'She's ... just a friend. That's her Internet name.'

'She's a woman? Which woman? A patient?'

'She's a ... cyber pal. That's like a pen pal.'

Teal squinted to read the E-mail address. 'That address ... isn't that a satellite feed?'

'You heard the doctor, shithead. Get away from that computer.'

The voice, youthful, raspy, had come from behind him. He turned to see a little girl in a bathrobe. She stood, hands on hips, glaring up at his face. Her eyes had a shine that he'd seen in those of other patients, most recently in those of Camal's wife.

Zales spoke first. He said, 'Jennifer, how did you ...'

She cut him off. 'I'm not Jennifer, you asshole. My name is Bruno. And I'm telling you two creeps to take a walk.'

Teal emitted a sigh. He stepped away from the computer. He leaned over and picked up the blue binder.

Zales asked Jennifer, 'Your name is ... Bruno, did you say?'

She ignored him. She seemed about to attack Prentice Teal, but she stopped and cocked her head as if she heard an inner voice. She said to the voice, 'I don't care who he is. He messes with me and I'll kick his skinny ass the same way I'm going to kick Duane's.'

'Duane?' Zales straightened. 'Why? What's Duane done?'

'I was down in my room. The prick threw me out. He dumped me up here with the nerd and the chink just so he could have his jollies with Emma.'

'Emma? What exactly is he doing with Emma?'

Teal held up a hand. He said, 'We'll see for ourselves.' He asked Veronica, 'Why a satellite feed?'

Bruno answered, 'Australia, you stupid shit.' She stepped up to him, her hands balled into fists. 'You need a satellite feed for Australia.'

Teal tried to ignore her but she moved even closer and reached up to seize his lapels. 'I'm warning you, Teal. Don't say nothing to the Dodger. If you blow this for Veronica, if you say one damned word, you'll get more of me than you can handle.'

'Um ... don't tell her what?'

'Don't tell her that the nerd is a mental patient here. Dodger thinks she's a nurse, not some nut.'

'Then what's Dodger?'

'She's a cripple. Fucking useless. This is all she does all day. She sits on the Net and finds people in hospitals and gets them to listen to her whining.'

She cocked her head again as if she heard another voice. And again she made a swipe with her arm as if to keep someone away from her. Now she turned toward it. She shoved with both hands. She was fighting it off but she seemed to be losing. She was muttering, 'Uh-uh. Not now, you pussy. Stay in.' But Teal could see that she was weakening visibly.

The hands that were pushing came slowly together. They clasped as if they were at prayer. Teal watched as the shine in her eyes became a glow. She turned those eyes upward as if to the heavens. She began singing softly, then with burgeoning gusto until she was finally bellowing. The song was a hymn: 'What a Friend We Have In Jesus.' Teal watched, transfixed, as she went through two verses. He couldn't believe that he was listening to this.

She had finished that song and had begun 'Amazing Grace' when Teal, without a word, took Zales by the arm. Zales resisted; he did not want to leave. This alter was the first that she'd allowed him to see; he told Teal that he wanted to take notes. But Teal pulled him away, steered him out of the room and escorted him back down the hall to the stairs.

Zales said to him, 'I knew it. Didn't I tell you? I knew that this one would be special.'

Teal answered, 'I don't want to hear it.'

'But don't you see ...'

Teal turned and raised a finger in the face of Norman Zales. 'What we're going to do now, is go pick up Rachel's diary. You remember Rachel, don't you? She used to be a person.'

'If you're ... saying I'm responsible ...'

'Not another fucking word about how special they are. Not another fucking word about that child.'

292

'Jennifer? ... Bruno?' Veronica called softly.

The girl raised a hand to her lips as she sang. She was waiting to be sure that the two men had gone. She listened as their footsteps faded away. One pair of those footsteps seemed to do a little dance and she heard a loud crash from down the hall. It was like the one she'd heard before they came. She realized that Teal must be kicking through doors. She could hear them walking down stairs.

Jennifer stopped singing. She grinned. 'It's just me.'

'You're sure?'

'I think Mr. Teal was going to take your computer. I saw them loading computers on their trucks. That was all I could think of to try.'

Veronica blew a breath of relief. She said, 'Man, that alter of yours, Bruno. I never saw one like him.'

'He isn't an alter. I just made him up.'

Veronica was doubtful. 'Are you ... sure about that?'

'Who would want someone like that for a friend? You'll meet my friends later. They're all nice.'

'But your language. It was awful. Where'd you learn stuff like that?'

'In your diary. That's Amanda. That's the way Amanda talks. She wrote words like those even in the parts you let me see.'

Veronica glanced at the floor where her diary had been. It was true that she remembered seeing most of those words. 'But Amanda never called me a pussy, I don't think.'

'What, "Stay in, you pussy?" No, that was from Emma. Emma's always saying that to Teresa.'

Veronica nodded slowly but she still was uncertain. 'Where'd you get the little angel who sings hymns?'

'That's just sweet little me. Want to hear one again?'

'And your eyes got all funny. That even scared me.'

'Veronica, don't you ever act crazy? Any time you want someone to go away fast, all you ever have to do is act needy or crazy.'

'I suppose.'

293

'Except for psychiatrists. They don't want to go away. I haven't figured out what that takes yet.'

'Being sane might do it.'

'You've got to be kidding.'

'Why is that wrong?'

'Because psychiatrists don't ever think anyone's sane. They don't even think other psychiatrists are sane.'

Veronica considered that. It was probably true. Dr. Zales often looked at his wife like she was crazy. And she looked at him the same way.

'Jennifer? A question.'

'Hey, I hear people moving. They're coming down the stairs.'

'Dr. Zales and Teal?'

'They had shoes. These don't.' She listened, then shrugged. 'I guess everyone's loose. What were you just going to ask me?'

'You said you heard Emma call Teresa a pussy.'

'Stay in, you pussy.' I must have heard that five times.'

'But you said she was gagged. She had that bit in her mouth.'

'Veronica ... quit it.'

'Did you hear it or not?'

'A friend of mine heard it. Now stop.'

Grayson's plane was on the ground. It was taxiing, according to the tower's directions, toward the designated helicopter pad. Another message from Belfair came in.

Dodger, it's Jennifer. Mr. Teal and Dr. Zales were just here. He was up on four, then he came down to three. He collected the diaries of Shan Li and Veronica. He said he was only borrowing them. Dr. Zales didn't want him to take them but he did. He was also going to take Veronica's computer but we stopped him. He saw one of our E-mails, but only one line and it was addressed to 'the Dodger' like this one. He doesn't know it's you or that you're coming.

He went downstairs with Dr. Zales. I heard him say they're going to go get Rachel's diary. We can't figure out why he'd want them. He also broke the fire doors on both three and four. The patients from four are starting to come down. I've been down those fire stairs. They lead to the kitchen. From there, they can all get loose if they want.

Hurry, Dodger. We're here. We'll be waiting.

Susannah had read it. She was shaking her head. 'This man Teal is freeing inmates? Is he out of control?'

Grayson shook his head. 'Not Teal. He'd have a reason. I don't know why he's taking those particular diaries but I'm sure he has a reason for that, too.'

'How soon do we get there?'

'Another thirty minutes, tops.' He pointed out the window. 'There's our chopper.'

Chapter Forty-One

Emma had been listening, her ear to the shaft. She had heard the elevator when it first went up. She was waiting for it to come down. She hoped, she prayed, that she would find Leatrice on it. She would be ready for Leatrice when she came.

She'd been hearing other sounds, unusual sounds, especially for this time of day. She'd heard engine sounds that must have been trucks and then sounds of movement through the partition that walled off this part of the basement. Then much later she heard a dim slamming upstairs. She'd heard that sound twice. In between, she heard singing. There seemed to be a lot going on for this hour of the morning, but she'd been far too busy to dwell on it.

She had wasted time and effort on Duane and Leroy. She had tried to prop them up against the elevator door. But their bodies were too limp and her body was too slippery. She had not taken time to find clothing to put on. Her nakedness was another disadvantage.

She had tried to find the clothing that Teresa had bought, then remembered that Leatrice had taken it. But she did find a stack of fresh whites in a cabinet; no shoes but she found shower slippers. Even dressed, however, and with traction on her feet, Duane's body kept flopping back onto the floor every time she almost had it in position.

Too bad. When the elevator came and the door slid open, it would have made a nice surprise for Leatrice.

Failing that, her new plan was to put them in her Quiet Room. It turned out to be just as much work. Leroy was smaller than Duane; he was closer to her size, but she still had to strain to lift him onto her bed. She tied her canvas mask over his face and covered his body with the blanket. He would do. She need only fool Leatrice for a minute or so until she could get her hands on her throat.

With Leroy in place, she had dragged Duane back in and propped him in a chair by the bed. Duane would appear to be sitting with her. She had used wet towels to clean both of them of blood and she'd dressed Duane in clean whites. All that remained to do was to mop up the floors. She wished that Leroy had brought his mop and bucket, but all he came down with were those drugs for Duane that Duane hoped would give him an erection.

Emma shivered at the thought of it. A man's thing inside of her. She knew that both Rachel and Teresa had often had a man's thing inside them. Rachel because she was always a tramp and Teresa because ... well, perhaps not Teresa. If Teresa really did have all the sex her diary spoke of, it was only because she was a doormat. That infuriated Emma but she put it aside. There was still more work to be done.

All that dragging and lifting had left her exhausted, but she'd been reluctant to ask Jennifer to help. Jennifer had helped her in a number of ways, not least in loosening her straps just enough. It would not have been enough except for Leatrice's visit and the pain that Leatrice had inflicted on her. What the pain brought was sweat that had made her skin slippery. It brought writhing and pulling on her bonds. It was really Leatrice, therefore, who had helped her get free. She would definitely remember to thank Leatrice.

Leatrice Zales was still out on the grounds. She had gone to the rear of the building. She had hoped to enter through the door to the kitchen, but that sentry, the one who had humiliated her, was standing at the far corner, watching.

All at once, however, the kitchen door opened. A patient appeared, and then another behind her. She could now see

297

others through the windows. They were wandering through the kitchen and through several other rooms. One by one, they were discovering the exit.

Leatrice, at first, did not know what to think. The only way that they could have come down was if the fire-stair doors had been opened somehow. But those doors were electric. She did not understand. Was it possible that Teal had released them?

A third and a fourth stepped out of the door; all were dressed in their bathrobes and slippers. Her impulse was to stop them, to round them all up, and at least to contain them in the house. But she reminded herself that this was not her first duty. Her first duty was to delay Prentice Teal until the partners she had called could arrive. She still didn't know how she would manage to do that; she knew only that she must get inside.

In that instant, a means presented itself. She saw that the sentry had become alarmed at the sight of the patients being loose. She could see him speaking into that radio in his helmet. He was clearly reporting, or requesting assistance. All the while he was gesturing to this patient or that, trying to keep them from wandering past his post. The first two ignored him. They paid him no mind. They seemed interested only in smelling the air and admiring the moon and the stars.

He turned and went after them. He took one by the arm. But the others were strolling in different directions. He tried running from one to the other. His confusion gave Leatrice the chance that she'd been hoping for. She moved quickly toward the door where she eased herself through a knot of patients who were still coming out.

None made way. Some barely noticed her. But others paused and stared. Some seemed completely indifferent to her presence while others began to seem less than affectionate as they realized that she had no guards with her. One, an older patient, one of those fourth-floor wives, was staring intently at Leatrice's hands. She seemed to note that they held nothing. They held no syringe, no strap, no canvas mask; no means of coercion or discipline. That one patient reached out to try to claw at her face. Leatrice easily pushed past her.

Leatrice didn't even remember the patient's name, let alone what her complaint might have been. But that patient, regardless, had made her aware that she carried no means of defending herself or of inducing other people to obey her.

Once inside, she moved quickly into the kitchen where she found a drawer that contained carving knives. She realized that this wasn't unnoticed by the patients but she couldn't concern herself with that now. Her eye fell on a butcher knife. It was big, wide, and gleaming. It was also, she realized, rather hard to conceal. She could not very well start skulking about with some horror-film weapon in her hand. She chose a fillet knife. Much better.

She made her way from the kitchen to the fire stairs. She was about to open another door that led to the main hall and offices. But suddenly she heard shod feet on the stairs. Heavy feet coming down. Two pairs. Teal and Norman.

All at once, she had a plan. She would hide and wait in ambush. She would leap out and hold her knife to Teal's throat. She would hold him hostage. She would reason with him. She backed up and hid behind a door.

The steps grew nearer. She could hear Teal speaking. He was on his little radio to the soldiers outside. She held her breath and waited.

Teal, coming down with the binders in one arm, was listening to reports with his free hand. The first was from the sentry out back, describing the wandering patients, now a dozen, and asking what he should do.

'Are they bothering anyone?'

'They're just milling around. One is rolling in the grass. Another's on her knees picking flowers.'

'No Belfair guards back there?'

'A few. They're just watching. Listen, sir, we were talking. Whatever it is that these guys here are taking, if it's anything like . . .'

'It won't be. Don't worry.' He heard a clicking in his ear. He said, 'I have to take another call.' He touched a button, and said, 'This is Teal.'

'Mr. Teal? Main gate. We have two more drive-bys. A Lincoln

Town Car, government plates, and a red Porsche convertible, Washington plates. Whoever they are, the two drivers know each other.'

'What'd you see?'

'The convertible stopped, man got out, pushed the buzzer. No one answered; he tried to force the gate, couldn't do it. Tried the little side door, tried to kick it, couldn't open it. The Lincoln came by; this was the Lincoln's second pass. He said something to the first guy. First guy seemed glad to see him. Then they both drove up the road and parked. I can see them from here. It looks like they're talking it over.'

Teal turned to Zales. 'The Lincoln would be Carey. Who drives a red Porsche?'

'That would be … Luis Camal.'

Teal muttered a curse. Damned cellular phones. 'Your dear wife has been busy, it seems.'

Zales blanched. 'I'm not to blame. She is … beyond my control. She's caused all of this, you know. It wasn't me.'

'Norman … you're a weasel. Shut up.'

Teal knew that he should have had the sense to lock her up downstairs with Rachel. As for Zales, he was no problem – he was thoroughly spent. Not even his patients paid him much attention as they squeezed past him on the stairs. Teal brought his transceiver back to his lips.

'We're almost through here. Just one stop down in the Quiet Rooms. Any sign of that police car you saw?'

'No sir.'

'Okay. Ten minutes. Be ready.'

Leatrice had been listening. She was ready to lunge. They were passing within mere feet of her. She heard them go by and stepped out, her knife ready. But Norman, the fool, was between her and Teal. Teal had already reached the paneled door to the hall. She had half a mind to stick that knife in her husband for daring to put all this on her. She restrained herself. It would not be productive. It would put Prentice Teal on his guard.

They were going through the door. Her moment had been

lost. But a voice within her said, *Not a bit of it, Leatrice. You heard where they're going next. Think.*

The elevator, surely. They were going to the basement. The elevator, like the fire-stairs doors, needed electrical power to function.

Of course.

And the main power switch was in the fuse box near the kitchen. She would wait until she heard the elevator descend, and she heard the doors open below. One touch of that switch and the house would be in darkness.

And Teal would be trapped in the basement.

Emma had decided to wake Jennifer after all. She was tired and could use a little help. She would first close the door on Duane and Leroy. There was no need for Jennifer to see them.

She would say that Duane had cut himself on a glass and was now up in the infirmary getting stitched. He'd bled quite a bit and it had to be cleaned up, but none of the other orderlies had come down. She would clean it up herself but she was much too weak and the sight of it was making her ill. Would Jennifer mind please wiping it up? There were plenty of towels in the cabinet.

But Jennifer, she discovered, was not in her room. Not her, nor that puppy Duane brought her. Emma tried to think where she might have gone. She was sure that Leatrice had not taken her upstairs. Jennifer could not have worked the elevator herself because only the staff knew the code.

Nor was Jennifer hiding. There was nowhere to hide. Emma looked in each cabinet and under each bed.

It was only when Emma checked Duane's room again that she realized how Jennifer must have escaped. There, high on Duane's wall was a single small window. She would not have expected a window down here. It had probably once been a coal chute. Jennifer could easily have stood on the dresser and squeezed herself through it with her dog. She must have gone after Leatrice left, but before Emma settled with Duane.

Emma couldn't imagine where Jennifer might have gone.

All that mattered was that she'd gone through that window. Emma studied it, estimated its width. It was possible that she could fit through it as well. She would have to smear Vaseline over her hips. The Vaseline ought to help her squirt through, but that meant that she'd have to be naked. No matter. She would throw her clean whites through it first.

At that moment she heard the sound of the elevator. Someone had entered it on the floor just above her. She realized that it was descending.

Oh, let it be Leatrice, she said to herself. The window, the Vaseline, the escape … they could wait. First some quality time with dear Leatrice.

After that, she would leave. She would visit old friends. She would begin by dropping in on those who had put her here. After Leatrice, she would visit Rachel's father.

Teal had guided Zales through the elevator doors. He was about to step in when he heard Kristoff call him. Kristoff beckoned him from the Security Office. Teal stepped out again. He kept Zales with him.

'Can it wait?' he asked the sergeant.

'You might want to take a look.'

Sergeant Kristoff hadn't known that he'd planned to free the patients. He wanted to show Teal the result. Teal paused to look at several monitor screens. He saw that some patients were still exiting through the kitchen. They were moving slowly and with much hesitation as if entering a world that was new to them.

'No problem,' said Teal. 'Good for them.'

But it did suggest a problem. Even Kristoff's men saw it. He had planned to release them to keep the guards busy. But the guards, to his surprise, had offered little of resistance, not even when ordered by Leatrice to act. They were compliant to the point of being useless.

One of the monitors caught Teal's eye. He saw that little girl on it, standing in the hallway with Shan Li and the dog. He wasn't sure whether he believed her little act. If it were real, he felt sorry for her. If an act, she wasn't bad. Not bad at all.

There were other fourth-floor patients milling about. They had reached the third floor and were exploring it. He saw the kid take Shan Li by the hand. She seemed to be pointing to a patient who'd come down. Teal recognized the patient. It was Luis Camal's wife. It almost seemed that the child was introducing them.

Teal lowered his eyes. That's exactly what it was. He asked Kristoff, 'Are there cameras in the basement?'

'These four.' He clicked them on. Teal scanned them.

He saw the guard, Duane, his back to one camera. He was sitting by a bed. 'Is that Rachel?' he asked Zales.

Zales muttered something. It had the sound of a whimper. Teal didn't know why he bothered asking.

Teal saw the little girl's room, more comfortable than the others. He saw that she seemed to be in her bed. She had rigged it that way. Damned kid. A lot of trouble. But he found himself smiling, admiring her.

He said to Zales, 'Okay, let's go down there.'

He turned to Kristoff, 'Then we're out of here, Sergeant.'

'Yes, sir. Can't be too soon for me.'

Chapter Forty-Two

The route to Belfair had taken Martha Carey and Hoyt up Maryland's Arundel Parkway. They would exit the parkway where the sign said Glen Burnie. Hoyt's driver would follow that road to the shore.

Hoyt had told his sister that they would talk in the car, promising to explain the full reason for this visit. But Hoyt had said little. His excuse was the driver; he had whispered that they probably shouldn't talk in his presence.

Martha wouldn't have cared – there was nothing to hide. It was well known that Rachel was a patient at Belfair.

'Let's just wait,' said her brother.

'No, talk to me, Harlan.'

'Martha ... please trust me. Let's wait.'

'Harlan, if you say those words one more time, I am going to bust you in the mouth.'

'Let's just ... see.'

She saw him flinch as he said that. It was hardly an improvement. But Martha did not make good on her threat because something else had caught her attention.

'Did you see that car?'

'Which?'

'The one that just passed us like we were standing still. That's our car. The Lincoln. That was Andrew.'

'Couldn't be.'

'Harlan ... it was Andrew. I know my own car. How could he have known where we're going?'

'If you didn't tell him? He couldn't.'

'Then why is he rushing toward Belfair at this hour? I'd assume that's where he's going, wouldn't you?'

'Unless it's a hell of a coincidence.'

Hoyt had to assume that Carey had been told that his daughter might be in dire trouble. He had probably been summoned to help quash it. Hoyt told his driver to continue on, but to approach Belfair's gate with his lights off.

'But why?' Martha asked. 'Why not catch him and ask him? Let's find out what he knows and why he's up here.'

'Let's just wait.'

Nat allen had seen the one man kicking the gate, heard him yelling to be let inside. He saw him climb into his little red Porsche and drive another block or so past. The man parked and got out and stood looking at the wall. He seemed to be thinking about scaling it.

Then a black car pulled up, and another man got out. The smaller man ran to him; they knew each other, sure. The small man pointed back toward the gate; he was waving his arms all excited or mad. The second man was trying to get him to listen. He seemed to be saying, 'Never mind all that now. I think I got worse news than you do.'

Of course he couldn't hear that from where he was. But judging from their motions, that seemed to be the sense of their discussion. The only thing sure was that they both knew this place. They both knew more about it than he did.

He told his deputy. 'Let's flip on our blue. Let's see what those two have to tell us.'

Hoyt's car had arrived within sight of Belfair some ten minutes later than Carey's. His driver had turned off the headlights. Belfair's gate was still a quarter mile ahead but he could see the upper floors from that distance. It seemed strange to see that the lights were all on – he would have thought that all the inmates would be sleeping.

Up ahead, well beyond Belfair's gate, a blue police light began strobing. He could see two cars pulled up at the curb.

Martha squinted. 'That's the Lincoln,' she said. 'The police pulled Andrew over.'

Hoyt wasn't surprised, given how fast her husband had been driving. Except Carey should have slowed on approaching the gate. That was where the policeman would have caught him. Why would he have been stopped way up there?

'Harlan, look. Are they scuffling? Andrew's down on one knee.'

Hoyt looked. He didn't think so. The policeman, by then, had knelt at Carey's side and was shining his flashlight on the ground.

'He just dropped something, Martha. Cop's helping him find it.'

All the same, thought the general, there was too much going on here so early in the morning. He touched his driver's shoulder and asked him to pull over. Where they stopped, his own car was nearly invisible from either the gatehouse or the cars up ahead.

'No hurry,' he said. 'Let's watch for a while.'

Nat allen hadn't got more than two questions out before deciding that he didn't much like these two men. They didn't want to answer questions; they wanted him to go away. Like the city nigras say, they were dissing him.

The little one in the Porsche said, 'That's none of your business,' when asked why he was banging on that gate. The one in the Lincoln turned his nose up at the cruiser. He sniffed when he saw that it had West Virginia plates, and made lawyer-type talk about jurisdiction. When Nat told them, 'Let's see some ID,' and the one with the Lincoln said he didn't have that right, Nat whacked him in the face with his flashlight. He dropped to his knee with one hand to his mouth. Nat knelt with him, shined his light on something white.

'You see that right there?' he asked. 'That's a tooth.'

'You ... bastard.'

Then the other one chimed in. 'Do you know who that is? You just hit a congressman, you hayseed.'

306

'Well, now, why don't you two just climb in my car? We need to get who's who sorted out.'

Martha was watching. 'They're being arrested.'

Hoyt saw them being led to the police car. 'More likely, that cop just wants them to sit while he verifies Andrew's ID. He won't arrest a congressman without calling his superiors.'

'Should we tell him? You can vouch for him.'

'I … do not think I'd care to,' Hoyt answered.

'Then for God's sake, Harlan, let's do what we came for. I want to go in and see Rachel.'

'Yes, let's.' He told his driver to go forward.

The driver asked, 'Can I turn on my headlights?'

Hoyt realized, as he asked that, that the road had become darker. It took him a moment to realize why. All the lights inside Belfair had gone out.

The elevator door had no sooner slid open than the basement went entirely dark. Zales let out a gasp; he seized Prentice Teal's sleeve. With his free hand he groped for the LED panel and tried to enter the start code by feel.

'Hey, Norman. Get a grip. That's not going to work either.' He pulled his arm free and spoke into his transceiver. 'Sergeant Kristoff? What happened to the lights?'

'Sir, someone threw a switch. It could have been a patient. I'm looking for the fuse box right now.'

'And it could have been Leatrice. If you see her, put her down. Don't fool with her, Sergeant – knock her out.'

'Yes, sir. And sir? That police car is back. Cops are questioning those two from the Lincoln and the Porsche. They made them get into the police car.'

Teal frowned. 'That same car? The one from out of state?'

'Yes, sir. And now there's another car. This one stopped short of those two. Driver turned off his headlights and he's staying back. That's all our lookout could see.'

'Thank you, sergeant. Get to work on that fuse box.'

That third car, Teal would bet, would turn out to be

Winston's. But he still didn't know what to make of that police car. He was not, however, going to stand here in the dark, trying to make sense of all the traffic.

He felt for Zales's shoulder. 'No emergency lights? No backup down here?'

'Yes, there is. In all the hallways. They ... they should go on soon.'

Teal could feel him shaking. 'You still carry that penlight?'

'Oh, of course. Oh, yes. I'd forgotten.'

Zales patted his pockets; he fished out the light, and shone it out the elevator door. Its effect was not great but it was better than the blackness. He swallowed and called out, 'Duane?'

No reply.

He lowered the beam to the floor before him so that he could see where he was walking. He squealed.

'What's the matter?'

'That's blood on the floor. Look. A great deal of blood.'

Teal bent to touch it. It was certainly blood. Some had clotted; some was wet. It was not very old. The monitors upstairs had shown hallways, but not this one. The monitors for the basement showed only the inside of the rooms.

'Duane?' Zales whispered the guard's name once more. He swallowed hard. He called, 'Emma?'

There was no response. He called her name again, his voice now higher in pitch. This time he heard a soft moan.

'That's a woman,' said Teal. 'Could you tell where that came from?'

'I ... don't know. Her room? I couldn't tell.'

Teal guessed that it had come from that one open door. The monitor had shown Duane in his chair by the bed where Carey's daughter lay bound. 'Let's go look,' he said.

'Not me,' Zales shook his head.

'She's strapped down. We saw it.'

'We also see blood and Duane doesn't answer. I'm not taking a single step out of here.'

Teal decided that Zales might have a good point. 'What weapon could she have? What would make this much blood?'

'No weapon. No knives. They eat only with plastic. Duane had no Taser, no spray.'

Teal was not reassured. There were cameras, wires, pencils, and pens. Almost anything could serve as a weapon, including a metal chair that he saw. But that chair could also serve as a shield.

He seized Zales by the neck and pushed him out into the hallway. Zales tried to recover but he slipped on the blood. He was down, and vulnerable, but no attack came. Teal quickly stepped over him; he picked up the chair. He gripped it with one arm, its legs pointed forward. He prodded Zales with his foot. 'Let's go see.'

But Zales wouldn't move. He had scurried away, crablike, and pressed his back against the wall, shining his penlight this way and that. Teal jammed his transceiver into his belt, and snatched the penlight from Zales. Zales squealed again. He tried to snatch it back. Teal ignored him and eased toward the door.

The door was fully open. Its hinges opened out. Teal swung wide so that he could see behind it. There was no one hiding, no Emma in a crouch. He approached the doorway, sweeping with his light. He saw Duane's back and the figure in the bed. He saw a toilet, one small cabinet, but no place to hide. He saw Rachel's diary on the cabinet. Near the diary he saw a mound of what looked like jam and a part of the glass jar it came in. Near it was a vial that held some kind of powder. On the floor beneath the cabinet was a bedpan, badly dented.

He moved in past Duane and now saw that he was dead. His cheeks and his temples were grotesquely swollen. His throat had been chopped at with something ... some weapon ... that appeared to have been poorly suited for the job. There were stab wounds, or attempts, that were rounded and shallow. There were slash wounds that didn't seem to cut very deep. Nor was there any blood. Duane had been washed. Even Duane's whites were fresh and clean. Someone had dressed him, well after he was dead.

Teal made these observations while remaining alert to a

likely attack by Emma. He expected that attack from the person in the bed. He had assumed that the blanket-covered shape was Emma and that she was no longer strapped down.

He said, 'Emma. Emma? Let's give it a rest. You come off that bed and I'll clock you.'

Teal had his light on her. No movement. No response. He took one step nearer and snatched at a towel that was covering the upper part of her face.

It wasn't Emma. It was a man in his forties, thinning hair, slight of build. Teal turned to face the door before looking closer. The man had something jammed in his ear. Teal saw that it was a pencil, broken off. Teal didn't bother to slip the mask off him. He knew who it was; it had to be Leroy. He remembered that Leatrice had asked where these two were when she'd gathered her guards on the steps.

In the hall, lights were sputtering. The emergency lights. There would be one, two at most, mounted high on the wall. Their timers were trying to kick in.

He was about to call to Zales when he heard a choked squeal. He heard the sound of slaps and scrapes on the tile, and knew that Zales was doing his crab dance again.

He also knew that Emma had gotten him.

Chapter Forty-Three

Nat Allen had the two men who seemed to know Belfair. He had sat them in the back and waved his gun in their faces. He had taken their wallets and examined them.

'A congressman, huh? Well, I'm not real impressed. Bunch of lyin' bottom-feeders, every one of you.'

He opened Camal's wallet as his deputy kept them covered. 'Now this little one's a greaser. I don't much like greasers. I …'

His deputy nudged him. 'All them lights just went out.'

Nat glanced out the window. 'Sure enough. Every one.'

'Other houses are lit. Must be that one blew a fuse. Oh, look out. There's another big car comin' towards us.'

Carey turned. He was holding a handkerchief to his swollen mouth. He blurted, 'That's Hoyt. That son of a …' His handkerchief came up. It must have looked like he was waving, because the deputy pistol-whipped down against his wrist. Carey yelped. Nat Allen reached out and seized Carey by the hair. He jerked him down so he could get a better view.

He asked, 'Who's this Hoyt?' He twisted Carey's head.

Carey answered through his pain. 'He's … a general.'

'Friend of yours? No. Didn't sound like a friend.'

'Believe it. He's no friend of mine.'

Nat saw that the car was turning in toward the gate. 'I suppose they'll let him in, him being a general.'

'We're … expected. He'll look for us.'

'This general you're not fond of?'

'We're ... still supposed to be there. He'll be sending people out.'

'If you're so expected, why'd they turn this Mex away? I think you told a fib, Mr. Congressman.'

The deputy squinted. 'Car's not goin' through. Guess it can't if that front gate's electric.'

'Power's out. That's right. But if that man's a general, they'll send down some privates. The privates will rip the thing open.'

'Or they'll crank it. Hear that? Hear that grinding sound? Sounds like they're doin' that now.'

Nat listened. 'Sure enough.'

'There he goes. He's goin' in.'

'That's good. We'll have this street to ourselves.'

Grayson's pilot had asked Grayson, 'Are you *that* Major Grayson?'

'I'm sure there are several Major Graysons, Lieutenant.'

'I get you, sir. Shut up and fly.'

Susannah leaned toward the pilot. 'What have you heard?'

'Miss, I think you would have to ask the major.'

She turned to him. 'Well?'

'I've pretty much told you.'

'Yes, but what would he tell me? Are you famous?'

'Not really.'

'Notorious, then.'

'Susannah, I don't know how stories about me get started. But I've yet to hear one that I've recognized.'

He was afraid that she would ask him to share a few with her. She didn't. She said, 'Then we both know how that feels.'

Grayson's chopper, a Blackhawk, had followed the shore of the Chesapeake until the lights of Glen Burnie were in sight. He was no more than five minutes from Belfair. On an impulse, he typed a short message to Jennifer.

'We're almost there. You two stay together. Watch for us from your window.' He wanted to be able to see where they were.

312

He tapped SEND and sat back to await a reply. He had watched the screen for only a few seconds when a band across the bottom winked on. It told him that his message did not go through. It read:

'Address not valid or unable to receive.' Susannah saw it. 'What does that mean?'

'I'm not sure. Her modem's down. Maybe someone ripped it out. Maybe someone realized that she's been our source. Or maybe all those patients are trashing the place.'

'Not the way they're kept drugged. I think Jennifer can handle them.'

'She's a child, Susannah. She's only a child.'

'I'm not sure the word "only" applies to her.'

The sounds of Zales's crab dance had slowed to a spasm. He wasn't dead yet. Teal could still hear him squeaking.

With his chair held up and ready, Teal slipped into the hallway. What he saw there caused him to relax.

'Hello, Emma,' he said quietly. 'I'm assuming that you're Emma.'

She glanced up but only barely. She was busy, for the moment, securing the grip that her legs had around Zales's waist from the rear. She, too, wore fresh whites. They were too big for her. She had her right arm under his chin and was squeezing it into a choke hold. Her left arm was tucked underneath it. Zales couldn't speak. He was turning purple. The veins at his temples seemed ready to burst. His glasses, on crooked, were steamed.

Teal supposed that he could jump her, or kick her, or club her. He still held the metal chair in his hand. He did neither because Emma was holding a knife pressed just under Norman Zales's jawline. It was only a butter knife but it wasn't made of plastic. He could see that its cutting edge had been honed, probably by scraping it on cement. She could slice through his carotid in one swipe.

He was watching her eyes. They seemed businesslike,

313

detached. The rest of her face was a mess. Swollen lips, one black eye, one big mouse on her cheek, and one earlobe ripped down the middle.

He said, 'Emma, it's polite to acknowledge a greeting.'

She looked up. She wet her lips, but said nothing.

Teal sighed. He put his chair down. He sat. 'So, what now?'

She wasn't going to answer, but she saw the blue binders. He was holding three on his lap.

'You a shrink?'

'Shit, no.'

'Who are you?'

'The bad guy.'

Her voice was strained from the effort of holding Zales, but otherwise it seemed perfectly calm. 'You're collecting binders?'

'Uh-huh. You mind?'

'What good are they to you?'

'I don't know. I'm not sure. Things are not working out as I'd hoped.'

That remark brought a smile. A satisfied smile. She thought he meant because she had Zales.

'Are you … under the impression that I care about him? If you'd like to cut him up, be my guest.'

Zales tried to buck. She sank her teeth in his ear. She kept them there until he stopped struggling. When she looked up again she had blood on her chin. She was looking at Teal with interest.

'You're not going to try for me?'

'Nope. I'm just waiting.'

'What for? For help? It won't come in time.'

'No, I'm just going to sit until the power comes on. When it does, I'll ride up and go away.'

'Me, too.

'How will you manage that?'

'I can turn into smoke. I can go anywhere.'

'Oh. Sorry. I forgot. You're fucking crazy.'

She smiled.

But the smile didn't seem in the least bit abnormal. No glassy-eyed mania, no lunatic giggle. The smile seemed to say, 'Wait and see.'

There was light in the third-floor hallway now, but it was only the emergency lights. There was no light, no power in the rooms. Veronica's computer was dark.

Veronica had not been troubled at first when all the power went out. She was not greatly bothered that her screen had gone blank. She had, after all, turned it off many times just before climbing into her bed. But she always could have it at the press of a button. She knew that it was almost a living thing. It could speak to her, hold memories; it could take her on trips; it could show her the whole of the universe. But now it was gone. She could not get it back. She could feel herself starting to panic.

Jennifer could see it. The panic was growing. Veronica was frantically checking wiring and plugs, uselessly trying all the buttons and keys. Now and then she would mutter a foul word, a curse. Jennifer realized at once what was happening.

'Veronica, listen. You are still Veronica. Your computer is still here. You're still alive.'

'I ... I can't ... I can't feel ... '

Jennifer sat with her. She took her hand. She promised that Amanda wouldn't come. They wouldn't let her.

Veronica was trembling. 'She was close. She was here.'

'I know that. I heard her. She said some bad words. But we're going to keep her away.'

'If we could only ... turn my ... computer back on ...'

Jennifer raised her hands to Veronica's cheeks. 'Veronica, listen, I lied to you before. I told you that I made up Bruno. Remember?'

'You what? Oh, Bruno. I remember.'

'I didn't make him up. He's real. He's going to help you.'

'Help me? ... Oh, shit. Shit fuck shit.'

'Now you see? That's Amanda. She's already scared because

315

she knows how tough my Bruno is. He's not always nice but he's my very good friend. You can trust him, Veronica. Would you like him for a friend?'

'Well ... yes, but ... he's your friend. How can he be mine?'

'I'm lending him to you. He wants to come over. He can come to you right through my hands.'

'You can do that?'

'You already feel it. You see? There he is. He's inside you now but he's not going to say much. All he'll do is sort of stand there like a big bodyguard in case Amanda tries that again.'

Veronica closed her eyes. She drew a breath. 'I can see him.'

'See how big he is? Hey ... he's much bigger with you.'

'He's ... growing. You're right. He's really big.'

'And look at Amanda. No one gets past Bruno. Now it's her who's afraid because she has no place to go. Oh, look. She can't even go back into her binder because Mr. Teal took it with him. Oh, wow, look at that. She's breaking up in pieces. She's vanishing, Veronica. She's gone.'

'Oh, wow.'

'That was great, Veronica. And you did it yourself. All Bruno had to do was just stand there.'

'I know.' A shy grin. She was feeling much better.

'Listen, Veronica, I have to go. I won't be gone long. But Bruno is going to stay, so don't worry.'

'But ... how do I tell him what I need him to do?'

'You won't have to. He'll know. You just take care of Chewey.'

'Okay, but where will you be?'

'Back here. Before you know it. Sit tight.'

Jennifer knew that she should probably stay. That had been a close call with Veronica. But she should be all right as long as she thinks that Bruno is with her standing guard.

And Veronica would have been doubly upset if Jennifer had said where she was going. She was going to the basement for a quick look. She wished she'd gone down there to check it out when she'd first heard all that banging and screaming.

316

She would just make sure that Emma was okay. And that Duane, or Leroy, hadn't hurt her too badly.

Camal had said nothing to these yokel police.

He was sitting on his hands in the back of their car. He was staring straight ahead, not moving. Camal had come here to settle with Teal. Fucking Teal, who had decided to cheat him. Fucking Teal, who had threatened to blackmail him if he didn't roll over and accept it. But Carey had told him it was much worse than that. That Hoyt had suckered them all, even Teal, and had his own plans for Project Richard. That Hoyt must have decided to kill them all, even Teal, in order to cover his tracks.

He had not believed it. Hoyt just didn't seem the type. But then Carey told him what Leatrice had found out. She told him what Grayson had done to poor Winston. And she told him that Grayson would have done it to Carey and to him if Leatrice had not called to warn him. Grayson would have done it to all of them. Even Leatrice.

Grayson. Hoyt's snoop. But he wasn't a snoop. He wasn't some aide who went around taking notes. He was Hoyt's cleanup man. His fucking butcher.

Camal remembered Teal saying, 'Who, Grayson? He's nothing. I'll handle him. Leave him to me.' And Camal had told him, 'Handle him or I will.' He wished now that he'd followed his instincts.

Goddamned Teal.

'Hey, Mex?'

Teal thought he was so smart. And Hoyt had suckered him.

'Hey, Mex. You still with us?' The policeman reached to poke him.

Camal snapped himself out of it. 'What?'

'This General Hoyt of yours ... who's with him, you think?'

'In his car? How do I know? A driver.'

'Yeah, but I saw three heads in that car. There wouldn't be a major in that car with him, would there?'

317

Camal was about to say, no, just Carey's wife. But he caught himself. He narrowed his eyes. He asked, 'Could you mean ... Major Grayson?'

Nat smiled. 'Now you see?' he told his deputy. 'I just knew I'd like this one. That's why I never hit him. You saw that.'

'God's truth.'

'Now, Luis ... now we're friends ... you tell me and don't fib. Will I find Major Grayson here this morning?'

Camal's eyes became slits. 'You are looking for Grayson?'

'You could say that. Now, Luis ...'

'To kill him or to try to arrest him? Which is it?'

'I will ask the questions. Now, Luis ...'

'It's to kill him. I can see it. You are here for Major Grayson.'

Now Nat saw something in Camal's eyes as well. An eagerness. An approval. 'What would that be to you?'

'That fuck killed our partner. Now he's coming for us. If you're up here looking to blow him away, you stopped the wrong people; we'd do it ourselves.'

Nat's face went slack. He wasn't sure he could believe this. But the Mexican said, 'You want proof? I'll give you proof. Point your guns someplace else for a second.'

Nat glanced at his deputy. Their eyes met and they shrugged. Both men turned their weapons to one side. As they did so, Camal leaned forward in his seat until his face was six inches from Nat's.

'Here's your proof.'

Nat went rigid. He looked down his nose. He could clearly see the distinctive flat shape of a Glock automatic pistol. He could feel its square muzzle pressing into his throat. His ears heard a buzzing as if from a distance. He knew he'd made a bad mistake.

Camal's voice was a whisper. 'You see this gun? I have been sitting on this gun. I could have blasted you any time I wanted.'

The buzzing was louder. It was more of a hammering.

Camal said, 'Real easy, put both of yours down. You don't need guns for us. Put them down.'

318

Nat reached to touch his deputy. He blinked and he nodded.

The deputy, reluctantly, lowered his weapon. Carey took it from his fingers. He hefted it. Turned it. He drew back his arm to smash Nathan's face with it. Camal blocked him.

'No, no. Don't you get it? These two are our friends.'

'Have you lost your mind? Let's get out of here *now*.'

'The enemy of my enemy is my friend. You never heard that?'

'Not these two. What can they do for us?'

Camal looked at Nat whose head was still pinioned. 'You want Grayson? What for? He did something to you?'

Nat managed to say, 'He sure did.'

'You want Grayson, you got him. That's probably him with Hoyt. But Grayson doesn't do shit on his own. He only does what Hoyt tells him.'

'Hoyt's his boss?'

Carey sucked in a breath. 'Hey, Luis, hold on.'

Camal ignored him. He asked Nat, 'Why not go for them both?'

Nat's brain was awhirl. He did not understand this. The buzzing, the hammering, had turned into a flapping. Camal's Glock still held him; he could not turn his head, but the thing that was flapping was not in his mind. It was a helicopter landing. It had turned on bright lights. It was lighting up Belfair and the whole street outside.

Camal pinched Nat's cheek. He said, 'Easy. Relax.'

Carey muttered, 'A chopper? Who'd be coming by chopper?'

'I don't know. I don't care. Let's be quiet and think. We need to work out a deal with our friends here.'

'Not me.'

'Those guns you two have. Are they all you have with you?'

Nat Allen hesitated, but answered. 'Deer rifles.'

'Where? In your trunk?'

'Two Brownings with four-by-forty scopes. Couple of bulletproof vests.'

'Luis …' Carey hissed. 'I'm a congressman, God damn it.'

'Then wait in the car. You guys hear what I'm saying?'

Nat blinked. 'What, an ambush? We get them coming out?'

'No, we don't wait because we don't have all day. We go over the wall. I spot them for you. Two shots, they're dead, we go home.'

Carey rolled his eyes. 'I'm getting out of this car.'

Camal swung his Glock. 'You stay put.'

'The hell I will. I'm …'

Camal jammed his gun against Carey's ribs, but he was looking at Nat. 'What do you say?'

'Could I ask … why you want this … what you got against Grayson?'

'He cut up a friend of mine. He cut off his dick.'

Nat stared. 'This friend … is he … local?'

'What's the difference?'

'Just wondered.'

'He cut off his dick and wrote things on the walls. You know what he wrote with?'

'Um … no.'

'Winston's dick.'

Chapter Forty-Four

Prentice Teal was actually enjoying his conversation with Emma. She would not have been his first choice to take to the prom, but she did have a degree of composure for a homicidal maniac. But of course, those first two, the men she slashed in their cars, must have seen her put her best foot forward as well, or else they would have kept right on cruising.

'I have to say, you sound better than you look.'

'Thanks a lot, smooth talker. Like you care.'

Some marks on her face seemed fresher than others. 'Was most of that done since they got you back here?'

'A lot of it was. Are you hungry, by the way?'

The question surprised him, but he went along. 'I could handle a Danish if you have one.'

She shook her head. 'Got some nice jam inside. You have to sweeten it, though, with the sugar you'll find in there next to it.'

'Sugar, my ass. What's really in that vial?'

She smiled. 'It's a Leatrice Zales special. It's strychnine. It's for punishing naughty little girls.'

Zales stiffened. She squeezed. He wilted again. Teal wondered if he'd known about the strychnine.

'Emma, now that I think of it, why did you come back?'

'Come back to Belfair? Zales drugged me and brought me. He tricked me, didn't you, Zalesy?' She jabbed him.

Zales barely reacted. Just a hint of a moan. Teal wondered if his mind had gone elsewhere.

'I mean, according to him, you were free and had new clothes. You even had his wife's credit card.'

'And a knife.'

'There you go. What more could a girl need?'

'It wasn't a good knife. It was better than this but it was only a shank. One of the guards must have made it, I guess. They used to make them in prison.'

'How'd you get it?'

A sneer. 'My good buddy, Leatrice. She lent me a purse. She put the shank in there where I'd find it.'

A gasp rose from Zales. He was still with us after all. Teal paid no attention, nor did Emma.

'So why did you come back?'

'I wouldn't have.' She stifled a yawn. 'I called Zales so I could show him what I did to those numb-nuts, especially the rich one who looked just like him. After that, I don't know, I must have been tired. I started to drift in and out.'

Teal tapped her blue binder. 'Is all that in here?'

A smile. No answer. 'Why'd you say you wanted those?'

'I was going to keep them. I'm not sure I will now. I was going to use yours to put the screws to your father.'

'You mean Rachel's father. He's nothing to me.'

'Whatever.'

'He's a scumbag.'

'So I'm told.'

'But those diaries won't help you. All the real good stuff in them wasn't written by us. It was written by Leatrice Zales. That's her thing.'

Prentice Teal was about to open her binder when he noticed the expression on Norman Zales's face. The fear, the choked terror, were more apparent than ever. But adding to them – overwhelming them – was a look of ... not shock, not even disbelief. It was a look of profound crushing sadness.

'Is that true?' Teal asked Emma.

'You'll see for yourself.'

'Um ... not that I'd want to stick up for Dr. Zales here, but I think what you just said is news to him.'

322

He held up a hand; his transceiver had crackled. 'I'm sorry. One second. Do you mind?'

'I'm not busy.'

Teal listened as Kristoff gave him a report, every word of it unwelcome information.

'Sir, no sign of Leatrice and she took all the fuses. We're looking all over for spares. There's an Army chopper right over our heads. Landing lights are on. It's coming in.'

'Who could that be?'

'Well, it's not General Hoyt because he just drove up. Our lookout didn't spot him until it was too late. He was watching those cops cross the street with Camal. It looked like ...'

'Wait. Is the general inside?'

'He might be by now. They had to crank the gate back. Our guys couldn't ... you know ... tell a general to get lost.'

'I understand. Is that truck loaded up?'

'We have everything you listed. And we took Zales's computers. We can roll as soon as you get up here.'

'Don't wait for me. If Hoyt says stop, you didn't hear him, okay?'

'Truck are noisy. We won't.'

'What was that about Camal?'

'The two cops and Camal ... there was no sign of Carey ... they took two shoulder weapons out of their trunk. They looked like they were planning to go over the wall.'

'The wall? The wall's wired.'

'Um, sir ... the power.'

'Oh yeah. Shit.'

Teal realized that he must have been wrong about those cops. Now it appeared that they must work for Camal. Camal must have told them to meet him here. But what, he wondered, could Camal hope to do? Try to make us put everything back?

'Sergeant Kristoff, go. Get out of here now.'

'Sir, what about you?'

'I'm okay where I am. I'll see you back at Langley.'

'Sir, we should disarm those two cops before we go.'

323

'I'm more worried about Hoyt disarming you. Get out of here, Sergeant. I want those trucks gone.'

'*You don't want the lookout? I could leave him for cover.*'

'I want everyone out … and Sergeant …'

'*Yes, sir.*'

'I want everyone very hard to find.'

Grayson's pilot was hovering, unable to land. Several patients were wandering on the lawn beneath them. Some seemed oblivious to the beat of the rotors and the glare of the bright landing lights. Others spread their arms and turned up their faces as if refreshed by this powerful wind from the sky.

Grayson saw that the grounds and the buildings were in darkness except for a dim glow from deep within. It had the look of an auxiliary-lighting system.

'Now we know why the E-mail wouldn't go through,' said Susannah. 'Which window is Veronica's?'

Grayson pointed. 'Third floor. The one that's wide open.'

'Can you see her in there?'

He peered. He shook his head slowly. He could see figures moving in other rooms, at other windows, but he couldn't see anyone who looked like Veronica, or who might be Jennifer's age.

He saw the trucks that Veronica had described. As he looked, he saw a belch of exhaust come from one truck and, quickly, from the other. Their engines had started; they were readying to leave. He recognized Sergeant Kristoff at the truck parked in front. He was using hand signals to gather his men, and was directing them to the trucks. All the while he was speaking into a headset. Grayson assumed that the sergeant was talking to Teal, but he wasn't able to spot him.

He saw a black staff car squeezing through the front gate, which was only partially open. He could make out two stars on the staff car's front bumper. He knew that it had to be the general.

Grayson saw no Belfair guards nor did he see Zales. Susannah touched his arm. 'Is that Leatrice?'

Grayson looked where Susannah was pointing and saw that

it was definitely Leatrice. She was moving at a crouch, trying not to be seen. She seemed headed toward her husband's Mercedes. But Grayson saw that its front tires were flat. He saw jagged metal where the headlights should have been. He saw Leatrice, regardless, slip in and start the engine. It flapped on its rims toward the larger of the trucks. Her intent seemed to be to block it in.

She did. She stopped it and quickly climbed out. He saw her draw her arm back as if throwing a rock. He saw shiny metal fly through the air toward a place beyond Grayson's field of vision.

'Her car keys,' he said. 'Did she throw them to someone?'

Susannah stretched to peer out the far side of the chopper. She said, 'Just into some pine trees and bushes ... um ... wait.'

'What is it? Do you see something else?'

'I saw men in those trees. I don't see them now.'

'Zales's guards? They're probably rounding up patients.'

'Sooz ... I don't think so.'

'Sally, not now.'

'That could have been the people who are hunting this guy.'

'No, not likely. They wouldn't be inside.'

'I just got a glimpse, but my impression was cops. Ask Grayson if the guards here dress like cops.'

'Roger,' she asked, 'do the guards here wear uniforms?'

'Uniforms? Sort of. They wear ... wait a minute.'

The subject of guard uniforms had fled from his mind because the trucks had now started to move. The larger one that Leatrice had hoped to block was easily pushing the Mercedes aside. Grayson saw its hood spring loose and fly up. The windshield became a web of stress fractures and the car slowly heeled onto its side. Grayson could see Leatrice. She was furious, frantic. Several patients near Leatrice were watching this episode. One was laughing and applauding. That enraged her even more. Leatrice turned on her and maced her, then ran on behind the house. Grayson could no longer see her.

The truck turned the corner and started down the driveway. The smaller truck fell in behind it. Hoyt's car was coming up. It stopped short of the circle. Grayson saw General Hoyt get out of his car and try to wave down the oncoming trucks. They sped by him. They continued to the exit where they slowed long enough to exert steady pressure on the partly opened gate. It yielded, then collapsed. Strips of iron flew off. The trucks went through and sped off.

'Major, we can touch down.' It was the voice of the pilot.

'When we do, keep this rotor turning and ready.'

'Do you mind if I ask ... what the hell we're flying into?'

'A bad dream, Lieutenant. And two very bad ideas.'

'You know I'll be asked to write a report.'

'I'll tell you what I can when we're on our way out.'

The pilot gestured toward the staff car on the driveway. 'Just a guess, but I see two stars on that staff car. Would they belong to Gen. Harlan Hoyt?'

'They would.' The aircraft was almost on the ground.

'And were they Special Forces, those troopers with the trucks?'

'Something like that. Special unit.'

'Special enough to blow past two stars when they're being ordered to stop?'

'It would seem.'

'You on good terms with the general?'

'Maybe not at the moment.'

'You must lead an interesting life, sir.'

Nat allen was still bewildered as he crept through the pine trees, his deputy behind him, the Mexican in front. He and the deputy wore their Kevlar vests and were carrying their Browning deer rifles. He'd have liked M16s for work like this. It would also be easier on his busted-up fingers. But he'd been handed a gift; he'd make do with what they had. He could scarcely believe his good luck.

He saw himself as a man who understood control. He knew how to intimidate, turn other men to mush. Stand close, real close, look them hard in the eye. Dare them to sass you the least little bit and then pound them into dog meat if they do.

He had done just that with the other man – Carey, the man

who turned out to be a congressman. When the Mexican told him, 'You just hit a congressman,' he could hardly help showing how pleased he was to learn it. He had decked a real congressman – he could brag on that for years.

That might have been why he had not been on his guard when the Mexican shoved that gun under his chin. That aside, he'd been distracted when the Mexican announced that he wanted Grayson dead just as much as he did. Not just Grayson, but even the general who commanded him. The Mexican would help him to kill them.

It was too much, too sudden, too much of a surprise. Nat Allen's instincts were telling him to go slow, back off, take some time to think this over, let it settle. But what dimmed those instincts was the wondrous development that came when the Mexican gave his reasons. According to the Mexican, it was Grayson, not himself, who had castrated that kiddie-porn man down in Warrenton.

He did not understand how the Mexican could think it, but he dared not ask any questions. All he could do was throw his deputy a look that said, *Don't say a word. Go along with this. Don't give him any reason to think different.*

Before he knew it, they were over the wall. It was wired, would have zapped them, but the wires were dead. They had left the congressman handcuffed in the back with a wide strip of duct tape slapped over his mouth. The Mex had called the congressman a coward.

But once over the wall and halfway through the trees, the Mexican was a little less sure of himself. He had seen the helicopter; that was not a surprise. What he hadn't expected were these heavily armed troops, most equipped with night-vision goggles. He had not expected the dozen or so inmates who were walking around in their bathrobes. He had not expected that hovering chopper to light up the front of the house and the lawn.

But those armed troops were leaving, getting into their trucks. The helicopter was trying to land, so they would soon have the cover of darkness again. A woman in white tried to

327

stop the bigger truck. She blocked it with a car and then threw away the keys. For an instant, she seemed to be throwing them right at him. He saw the keys glimmer as they sailed through the air and realized that other eyes might be following them as well. Just in time, he dragged the others into shadow.

Her effort went for nothing. The truck slapped her car aside. The trucks turned down the hill and raced to the gate. The general tried to stop them. He couldn't.

The Mexican was muttering. 'Too much going on.'

Nat Allen said, 'Sure is. But it's thinning out some.'

'And I haven't seen Teal. He didn't leave with those trucks.'

'Who's Teal?'

'Another prick. Never mind.'

'I just want Grayson.' Nat raised his scope to sight in on Hoyt's car.

'Not now. Not yet.' Camal hissed in his ear.

'Rest easy. Just lookin' ' He answered. He put his crosshairs on the general's head as the general turned to get back in his car. He moved the scope to take in the driver and the third head he'd seen in the back.

He said, 'Damn. That's not Grayson. That's some woman.'

'Hoyt's sister,' said Camal.

'You can see that from here?'

'Carey told me she was coming. Look, this isn't smart. Let's back off here.'

'What's wrong?'

'That chopper's been hovering too long without landing. Maybe Hoyt called it in just to light up the place.'

'Lights been out fifteen minutes. He wouldn't have had time.'

'And look up in those windows; must be ten patients watching. I just saw one of them pointing at us.'

'Crazy people see things that ain't there. It won't matter.'

'Hey, you notice?' said the deputy. 'All we seen here is women. I thought we'd see all generals and such.'

'You seen one. A big one. He'll do for today.'

The Mexican shook his head. 'This is bad. Let's back off.'

328

'We'll just see if that thing lands. We'll see who gets out.'

'Then you stay. I'm going.' He pushed to his feet.

Nat scowled. 'You turnin' out to be a Mexican pansy?'

'Well, I'm not a fucking rube. You two stay if you want.'

'Oh, I think I get it now. There are too many grown-ups. Your speed's little girls. Would that be about right?'

Camal's hand went to his Glock. 'Say that again?'

'You know. Little girls. Like your fat partner, Winston. Do you do little girls like your partner?'

'What … wait a minute. How'd you know about …'

'Too long a story. Goodnight, sir.'

'What?'

'Deputy?'

'I hear you.'

Nat didn't have to look. He heard the movement, he heard the sound, of a rifle butt hitting the Mexican's temple. He saw the Mexican topple forward on his face.

'You got him good and clean?'

'He'll be out for a time.'

'Take his pistol.'

'What then?'

'What's then is we're going to be famous, you and me. Grayson or no, I'm going to take out his general. Same time, you take out the general's sister.'

'Kill a woman?'

'Not just kill her. Put a hole in her head. Same place as the hole they put in Janice.'

The deputy watched as the staff car climbed the driveway and stopped at the building's main entrance. Hoyt climbed out first; he lent a hand to his sister. Hoyt paused for a moment to look up at the chopper. He spread his hands in a questioning manner. The deputy didn't know what the question was. It was either, 'Who are you?' or 'Why aren't you landing?' Then the general turned away. They were going inside.

'Good chance right here,' said the deputy. 'Shoot them now?'

'No, we wait 'till they come out. Grayson could be inside

or he could be in that chopper. Either way, we can catch them all together.'

'You're the boss.'

'Two things, though,' said Nat Allen. 'Grayson's mine. He's all mine.'

'You got the right.'

'Other thing is, I don't do him with no scope. I do him so he's looking right into my eyes. I want him to see who puts his lights out.'

'Chopper's landing.'

Chapter Forty-Five

Teal was thoroughly disgusted, not least with himself, for not having chained Leatrice to a hot radiator back when they had her within reach. But at least Sergeant Kristoff had gotten away with almost everything they had come for. He shoved the transceiver back into his belt. He saw that Emma had been listening with interest.

'Bad start to your day?' she asked.

'Couldn't be a lot worse.'

'You know something? I like you. You're an interesting man.'

'Thank you. We'll have to do lunch.'

'Does that mean you like me?'

'You're a piece of work yourself. By the way, what's next? Do you have some kind of plan?'

'Did I hear that Rachel's father is outside on the road?'

'He was. If he's smart, he took off.'

'Oh, I hope not. I hope he's still there.'

'Why is that?'

'He's nothing to me, but he did dump me in here. I'd like to see his face when I tap him on the shoulder. When he turns and I say "Hello, Daddy."'

'So would I.'

'But I can't go yet. I'll hang out for a while.'

'Yeah, I guess I will, too. Unless you know a way out.'

'I told you. I can turn into smoke.'

'That's a trick I could use. Care to teach me the secret?'

331

She smiled. 'I'm fucking crazy, remember?'

There is crazy and there is crazy, thought Teal. He was fairly sure that she knew a way out, but she wasn't about to share it.

'Norman?' He snapped his fingers at Zales. 'Those fire stairs don't reach down here, do they? Hidden panel, maybe? Could there be a secret passage?'

Zales was deep within himself. He didn't answer.

'Norman, snap out of it. She doesn't want to kill you, or she would have done it already.'

Zales tried to wet his lips, but he had no saliva left. He managed to say, 'You can't leave me.'

'How about a window?'

No answer from Zales. But he saw that Emma's smile had departed. She sighed. She shrugged. 'It won't do *you* any good.'

Teal got up from his chair and took the chair with him. He knew that the Quiet Rooms had no windows. They faced the interior of the house. He went to the side that faced the exterior. The only room there, behind the glass-enclosed station, was Duane's room. It did have a window, high up, very small. He did not think that Emma could possibly squeeze through it. For himself it was out of the question.

He reassured Emma. 'It will be our little secret.'

He scanned the hallway. He saw the dumbwaiter door. It was set in the wall about two feet off the floor. The door was another three feet high. He realized at once how the kid had gotten out, but neither Emma nor he could fit in it. Besides, he thought, it was probably electric. It wouldn't use an old-fashioned pulley.

That thought had barely processed in his mind when he heard the dumbwaiter moving. It was not electric after all. As it bumped against the sides of the shaft coming down, he had a feeling that Jennifer was about to come calling.

He still wasn't sure whether she had been putting him on when she'd done her 'Bruno' act upstairs. But maybe Bruno, if she brought him down with her, could kick down a wall and get him out of this dungeon.

332

Teal watched as the girl climbed out of the shaft. She seemed mildly surprised to find him in the basement but she barely acknowledged his presence. He saw something in her fist. It looked like a roll of dimes. He hoped that she hadn't come down here to slug him.

'Um ... Bruno?'

'I'm Jennifer. Bruno's busy.'

She said it distractedly, merely saying the words as if the answer was neither here nor there. She turned her back to him and pulled on the rope. The dumbwaiter rose back up two or three feet. She leaned in. She seemed to be looking for something. Whatever it was, she didn't reach in. She took another look at the thing in her hand and dropped it in the pocket of her robe.

She walked past him; her eyes were on Emma and Zales. Zales looked like a corpse, but he was breathing.

'Emma, what are you doing?' asked Jennifer.

'Go look.' Emma tossed her head toward the Quiet Room she'd occupied.

'I don't think you want to go in there,' said Teal.

Emma shook her head. 'No, let her see.'

Jennifer moved closer. She stepped over Zales's legs. She stopped at the entrance to the room but didn't enter. There was no light except that from the hall.

'That's Duane in the chair?'

Emma smiled. 'Scratch one caregiver, kid.'

'Who's that in your bed?'

'That was Leroy. Scratch two.'

'Oh, Emma, why? They weren't so bad.'

'Jennifer, don't give me any grief about this. You saw what Duane was doing to me. You don't know what he was going to do later.'

'Like what?'

'Like rape me.'

'He wouldn't. I heard him. He doesn't like lesbians.'

'I have a flash for you, Jennifer. We still have all the parts.'

333

'Then I don't think he could have. None of them can. They all take a special medicine so they can't.'

'Want another flash? Come here. Reach into my pocket.'

Emma twisted her body to allow access to it. Jennifer knelt beside her. She patted the pocket, then reached in and removed two medicine vials. One contained a green liquid, the other held pills.

'Ever heard of Spanish fly?'

'No.'

'Well, that green stuff's like an antidote for the other drugs they take.'

'All the guards have these vials?'

'Those two in there did. Leatrice told Duane, go ahead, have your fun. Duane said he couldn't unless she got him these. She sent them down with Leroy.'

Prentice Teal had chosen not to enter this exchange, preferring to witness how these two interacted. But he realized what the vials must have contained; those dosages that seemed to be missing from the lab. His eyes went to Zales, who was looking up at him. He could see that Zales had known nothing of this. It was one more blow. Teal felt sorry for the man.

Emma tossed the vial with the liquid aside and handed the other to Jennifer. She said, 'This one's just an upper. I could use these myself. Shake out a couple for me, okay?'

Jennifer took the vial. She made no move to open it. She put it in her pocket and looked up at Teal.

'Would you leave us alone a few minutes, Mr. Teal?'

'Where is it that you think I can go? There's no power.'

'I'll fix that soon if you'll give me some time.' She reached into her pocket and took out the small cylinder that he thought could be a roll of dimes. She held it up so that he could examine it. He saw that it was a fuse.

'Where … did you get this?'

'It was rolling around on the top of the dumbwaiter. The rest bounced down to the bottom of the shaft. Whoever pulled them from the fuse box threw them down there.'

'And you'll go up and put them back in the box?'

'Go wait in Duane's room. Please close the door. I just need a few minutes with Emma.'

Teal did walk around the glass-enclosed nursing station. He shut Duane's door but not behind him. He stood, out of sight, very quietly, and listened. He heard her say, 'Emma, may I hold your hand?'

'What's going on?'

'Duane and Leroy ... I feel bad that you did that.'

'You don't have to. They didn't even mind.'

'Mind what? Being killed? How could anyone not mind being killed?'

'Well, they didn't.'

'You could tell?'

'They weren't scared. They didn't fight much. I was kind of surprised. Hey, where are those pills?'

Teal took a slow breath; what he heard did not surprise him. He remembered how those guards had acted like sheep.

'Emma ... those two ... they weren't the first. Whose blood was that I saw on your new skirt and jacket?'

'Just some men I bumped into. Give me those pills.'

'Hold my hand. Hold tight. Will you let me touch your face?'

'No, Jennifer, it's sore. It's been touched too damned much.'

'I'll be gentle. Did those other men do this?'

'One did some. He fought me. They were men who would have used me.'

'How many?'

'Just two.'

'So that's ... four men you killed?'

'No, I think it's a lot more than that. There were men before I came here. I killed lots of men.'

'You did? Or Rachel did? Or maybe Teresa.'

'Rachel would have, but she didn't. And Teresa ... she couldn't.'

'I'm glad.'

335

'How come?'

'Because if they didn't, neither did you. You didn't exist before you came here.'

'Sure, I did.'

'No, you didn't, because Leatrice invented you. She wrote things in your diary and she wrote the name, Emma. She kept doing that until you came out. I don't think you were even a lesbian at first until she wrote down that you were.'

'That can't be true.'

'I'm not lying, Emma.'

'Well, anyway, so what? I'm real now. I'm here.'

Jennifer ran her fingers over both of Emma's cheeks. 'Where's Rachel? Can you feel her? I can't.'

'I can't either.'

'Can you feel Teresa?'

'I'm not letting her out.'

'But you feel her. So do I.'

'Wait a minute here, kid. What the hell are you doing? If I'm not real, neither is she.'

'No, she's different.'

'How?'

'She was always part of Rachel. But you, you never were. You're kind of ... well, part of Leatrice.'

'Oh, bullshit.'

'I know that it sounds all mixed up, but it's true. You can't hate Teresa just because she's not mean. When she comes, you can sleep. You're so tired and hurt.'

'I'm ... not sleeping. Not until ...'

'Listen, I have to go. I'll be back very soon. Will you let me take Dr. Zales?'

'No, I won't. Not ... just now.'

'That's okay, Emma. I'll come back for him later. I know you won't hurt him because he wouldn't have hurt you. Ease up, though, all right? He's tired and he's hurt, just like you.'

'Wait ... Where are you going?'

'I have to turn on the lights. We have company.'

Prentice Teal quickly opened and closed Duane's door so

that Jennifer would think he hadn't heard. He watched Jennifer walk past him toward the open dumbwaiter. He watched as she gathered the rest of the fuses and climbed up on the dumbwaiter shelf.

He said, 'Jennifer ...'

She paused, only half turning her head. 'I know that you listened, Mr. Teal.'

'Well, yeah, but to what? What just happened back there?'

'Do you ever keep your word?'

'Now and then. What is it that you just did to Emma?'

'I can't talk now.'

'Yeah, I heard. You have company. Could you mean General Hoyt?'

'I mean Major Grayson and Susannah.'

'Major Grayson and Sus ... you mean that girl from Zales's book?'

'From a book? No, she's real. She's here with Roger.'

'Yes, but ... how could ...' Teal threw up his hands. 'How the hell could you know who's here and who isn't? How the hell could you know Grayson, let alone this Susannah?'

'They're here. I have to go. Pull me up.'

'Jennifer ... hold it. What kind of kid are you?'

'Mr. Teal, I have to go. I'll pull myself up.'

Teal would have helped, but by the time he could move, she had already reached the first floor. He turned back toward Emma. She had let go of Zales. She was sitting on the tile, her back against the wall, the butter knife dangling loosely from her fingers.

Zales had barely stirred – he seemed afraid to chance it. But his eyes were wide open and desperately afraid. Teal thought he saw more. Perhaps betrayal. Perhaps rage. Teal hoped so. He hoped that something, anything, was left in him.

'Norman? Get up now.' Teal reached down to take his arm. 'Get up and go wait by the elevator.'

Zales moved a little. Emma moved not at all. Teal half-lifted, half-dragged Zales out of her reach. Zales got to his knees. He was trying to rise. Teal left him and knelt in front of Emma.

'Emma?'

No reaction.

'Emma. It's me. Are you still here, Emma?'

She nodded, only barely. She asked softly, 'Was she right?'

Teal couldn't answer. He did not understand this. He found himself wanting to comfort this girl who had murdered four men. And he found himself wanting to murder all the therapists who had ever worked their theories on young Rachel. He found himself wondering if a twelve-year-old child was able to do things that they hadn't been able to do.

A burst of light made him blink. The power was back. The elevator doors kicked closed and then open. He saw that Zales was staggering toward them. He heard sounds of air being pushed through the ducts and he heard popping noises as circuits connected – or perhaps as cold light bulbs exploded.

'I have to go now. But I'm going to come back. I'll try to take care of you, Emma.'

A wan little smile. 'You're the bad guy, remember? Don't switch around like me. It's too confusing.'

Teal wanted to touch her as Jennifer had. He did begin to reach for her hand. What made him stop was another pop he heard. This one wasn't a light bulb.

That one sounded like a shot ... a rifle shot.

Chapter Forty-Six

When the power burst on, the effect was blinding, especially on the people outside. Nat needed a minute for his eyes to adjust to the front entrance lights that lit the whole lawn like spotlights. He cursed them, but realized that he should have known. A nuthouse – even a military one – would be lit like a prison.

The only good thing was that the chopper touched down directly between him and the entrance. It blocked his view but it kept him in shadow. The other good thing was that it kept its motor running. The big fan on top kept going 'Whap, whap, whap.' That noise was good cover as well.

'Damn thing,' said the deputy. 'It's in our line of fire.'

'Shift up the slope a little. See who's gettin' out. There's a hedge up there. You get behind it.'

'Pilot's staying. I can see him. The pilot ain't Grayson.'

'See any passengers?'

'I see a woman inside. Someone else is with the woman but I can't see past her.'

'Well, they won't stay in there. Shift over, I said. I'll move down so we see from two angles.'

The deputy moved twenty yards to his right. He called back, 'I see him. Man gettin' out. Damn, can't see his face, but no uniform on him. Wouldn't Grayson come here in his uniform?'

'Don't mean nothin'.'

'Hold on. He's turning. Goin' back toward the chopper.

Goin' back because the woman got out. He's sayin' 'don't.' '

'See his face? Is it Grayson?'

'He's back lit. Can't tell.'

'Keep watchin'. He'll be front lit soon enough.'

'Roger, listen, I can't shake this feeling. I think that man who hates you is close.'

'Have you seen anything? Heard anything?'

'It's ... Sally. She thinks she might have seen them.'

'Susannah ...'

'I think I saw them myself. Grayson, don't blow me off. There are two of them near, maybe three.'

He glanced down toward the gate that was no longer in place. 'That's where they'd be. We're not going that way. I'll take care of them later. I promise.'

He asked the pilot, 'Lieutenant, are you armed?'

'Survival pistol.'

'Keep it handy, okay? And keep this woman here.'

'Sir ...' The pilot gestured toward the front of the building. 'There's General Hoyt. He's staring daggers at you. Would you mind getting me his stamp on all this before I start looking who to shoot.'

Grayson turned. He saw Hoyt. He had exited the building and a woman was with him. Susannah had to squint, but she said, 'That's Martha Carey.'

Grayson had guessed as much. But no Zales, no Teal. They must have found no one inside.

'Stay here, Susannah.'

'Grayson, I know her.' Her eyes flashed at being told. 'I can help you explain why we're here.'

'I'm not going to take the time to explain.'

At first, Camal didn't know where he was. He knew only that his head felt as if it were bursting. He remembered guns – there were men with guns. His first thought was that he must have been shot.

He had staggered to his feet as he felt for a wound. There

340

was blood and a welt behind his left ear, but his fingers could find nothing worse. He heard the whap, whap, whap. He thought the sound was in his head until he saw, through the pines, the machine that was making it. He saw the lights of a big house beyond it. He remembered now. This was Belfair, but what happened? He felt for his Glock, but it was gone.

He stumbled forward, falling once. He heard a low voice that seemed to come from a hedge. The voice was whispering, 'Get down. Get down.'

He saw the man now. He remembered him. The deputy. One of those two hayseed cops. He lurched toward him. 'What happened? What happened to me?'

'Damn fool, shut up, or I'll whack you again.'

Camal saw him clearly. He was lying on the ground with a rifle. As the deputy raised an arm to wave him down, Camal saw his Glock; it was in the man's belt. He wanted his gun back. He reached for it.

The deputy tried to hit him but his leverage was poor. He hit Camal's arm with the butt of his rifle. Camal's fingers found the scope. He gripped it and held it. With his other hand, he groped for his Glock. The deputy, struggling, turned his head to call for help. He dared no more than the loudest he could whisper. He called, 'Nat. Nat!! It's the Mex.'

Nat heard him and he heard the sounds of their thrashing. He cursed. He was torn. He could either help his deputy or finish this now. He had seen the man turn and walk to the chopper, turn again and start off toward the entrance. He'd been back lit all the way, but no doubt it was Grayson. He had heard the woman with him say his name.

Grayson gave no sign that he had heard those two struggling. He was marching, thought Nat, like a good little soldier, straight up to where his general was waiting. Nat had him in his cross hairs. He could take half his head off. But first he would get his attention.

He swung his sights to that puffed-up general, all pretty and medaled in his uniform. First him, then the woman; he

341

wouldn't wait for the deputy. The deputy should be able to handle the Mex. After them, then Grayson. But he had to see it coming.

He squeezed the trigger on the general's strip of medals, but just as he fired there were shots to his right. The sound made him flinch and caused his shot to miss the heart. But it hit him. It spun him. It got part of his chest.

Those shots from up the slope, they were pistol shots. Four of them. Had to be by the deputy, blasting the Mex. Nat couldn't take the time to look and see just yet. The general was down and the woman was down with him. It struck him that maybe she'd been hit as well. Maybe the deputy got done with the Mex and started spraying the front steps with that Glock.

And there was Grayson. Praise the Lord, there was Grayson. He had whipped around and dropped down to a crouch. He had his weapon in one hand and was waving everybody down with the other. He was looking and peering, trying to see where those shots came from. He was looking every place but the right place.

Nat Allen had time. He even had choices. One thought was to catch him looking over toward the deputy and shoot off the lower part of his face. That would leave him alive, it would leave him conscious, not to mention it would leave him real ugly. But that shot would be tricky, too easy to miss, and Grayson would see where it had come from. A better choice, maybe, was to cripple that gun arm. Nat aimed above the elbow. He fired.

Prentice Teal, with the binders under one arm, had dragged Zales to the elevator with the other. He anxiously punched out the code. His only thought about the source of that shot was that Leatrice might have had some firearms stashed, and had managed to rally some guards.

Except those guards were useless. He'd seen that. He was sure of it. Even so, there was shooting. Who was it they'd shoot at? The only target he could think of that might tempt her was Hoyt, but even Leatrice could not be that crazy.

342

The door closed, and the elevator began grinding upward. It was only one floor but he cursed its slow speed. Zales was standing; he seemed to be recovering, but he still wore that thousand-yard stare. Zales moved toward the door as the elevator stopped, but Teal used his elbow to ease Zales aside. The door slid open. Teal was startled to find himself looking straight into the eyes of Leatrice Zales.

The cool and calm Leatrice of other days was gone. This Leatrice was in a black rage. She raised one hand; his first thought was a pistol, but a cloud of mist was suddenly burning his eyes. He saw her turn it on her husband as well. He heard Zales bellow, try to cover his face. She tried to spray them again but the Mace can was spitting. It had lost its pressure, nearly empty.

As the stack of diaries fell from Teal's right hand, he reached out to seize Leatrice with his left. His left hand found her hair and he drew the other back, ready to smash her with his fist. But he felt a shock of pain in the arm that had seized her. He saw what had caused it. She had slashed him with a knife.

His attention had been on the hand that held the Mace. Her other hand, he saw, held a thin-bladed knife, the kind that was used to gut fish. He tried to keep his grip on her hair but his fingers were losing their strength and felt numb. He knew that she must have cut deep into muscle and had probably severed a nerve. She slashed at him again; she tried for his neck, but he turned and his shoulder took the cut. He leaned back to kick her but couldn't get a firm footing. His shoe merely brushed her. He fell.

Teal was crippled, half-blinded, and he knew that she had him. All he could think of was protecting his throat but his arm wouldn't even do that. He would try to keep her off with his feet, or else hope that she'd go after her husband. He readied himself but the attack didn't come. Squinting through tears, he could see a moving blur and he heard the stamping of feet. The blur and its sound were too large to be Leatrice. He heard a great thump and he felt the floor shake. He could not see Leatrice. He could only see Zales.

343

It took Teal a moment to realize what had happened. Norman Zales had physically thrown himself at her – he had smashed her to the floor with his body.

She no longer had the knife. It had been knocked from her hand. Teal could see her squirming, trying to locate it. Teal struggled to his feet. He kicked it farther away. Leatrice saw him do it and looked up into his eyes. She was on her back, her husband's weight pinning her, his hands now seizing and holding both her arms. Even so, her expression seemed to show no awareness that her purpose had in any way been thwarted. Her eyes seemed to say, 'Very well. A new strategy.' She proceeded to try to bite her husband.

Then Teal heard more gunfire. Four small bore, one larger. He had to get out there and see who was shooting. He snatched a handkerchief from his pocket and he tried to wipe his eyes. He pulled up his sleeve to look at his arm. The cut was a bad one. Blood pumped out in spurts. He snaked the handkerchief around his upper arm. He managed to loop it, to try to fashion a tourniquet, but he couldn't draw it tight without two hands. He saw someone else coming toward him down the hall. He squinted, tried to focus. He recognized Jennifer.

She said, 'I'd better help you with that.'

Just behind, walking with her, was the other girl, Veronica. Veronica was in shorts and a Rolling Stones T-shirt. She was lugging a computer and keyboard. She was wide-eyed at the sight of Zales and his wife in a death grip on the carpeted floor. Jennifer's puppy was following at their heels. They were hugging the far wall as they came.

Jennifer had a pillowcase slung over her shoulder. Its contents looked heavy; she needed both hands. She set her load down on the nearest hall table, asked Veronica to stay with the dog, and came forward. Teal saw that the pillowcase fell partway over and some of its contents spilled out. All it held were Veronica's manuals and disks.

Jennifer, with one eye on the struggling Zales, gripped an end of the wet and bloody handkerchief and handed the other to Teal.

344

'Pull tight. Real tight. That's good.' She knotted it.

Teal saw that Zales was grunting to his feet. He had his wife in a headlock and was lifting her with him. She was scratching him, she was pinching him, but he didn't react. That dull, distant stare was all that showed on his face as he dragged her back into the elevator. He gave her neck one powerful squeeze. It stunned or surprised her just long enough to enable him to punch in the code.

'Where's he taking her?' Teal asked.

'I don't know. Is that better?'

'And you. Where are you going? What's with the . . .'

'She needs it. I explained that. And we're going with Roger.'

'Yeah, well, stay here. There's trouble outside.'

'Was that shooting we heard?'

'You stay here. Let me look.'

As Teal turned away, he heard the voice of a woman. An angry, shouting voice. It came from outside. But it wasn't the voice of a traumatized woman – it sounded neither fearful nor anguished. It seemed to be berating somebody named Nat. It was telling this Nat who she was.

Jennifer said to Veronica, 'That's Susannah, I think.'

Teal didn't think so. That voice spoke a name. The name he thought he heard was Janice Novak.

Chapter Forty-Seven

Grayson had ducked at the sound of the shot. He had seen its impact on the general's tunic. He had seen General Hoyt start to fall. Grayson clawed at his Beretta and spun into a crouch, then dodged side to side in an attempt to draw fire. His brain had told him who the sniper must be. He was sure that the bullet was intended for him. He was open, exposed, but at least he was moving. His one chance, his only chance, was to see a muzzle flash and to empty his clip at that spot.

More shots had come quickly, but from the wrong place and their muzzle blasts seeming to go the wrong way. They came from uphill of the waiting helicopter. The first one had come from the downhill side. He hoped that someone, perhaps one of Teal's men, had spotted the sniper and engaged him. In between, he saw Susannah. She was moving toward him. He heard himself shout, 'Get back, Get down.' He saw the pilot scrambling for his pistol.

Now he saw a man, a small man, stumbling out of the trees on the uphill side of the chopper. He wore a dark suit, he had a gun in one hand and what looked like a telescopic sight in the other. The suit was covered with dirt and pine needles. He seemed injured, wounded – blood glistened on his scalp. The sight gave Grayson hope that the shooting was over. That thought had barely formed in his mind when a white tongue of flame licked out to his right and a bullet smashed into his gun arm.

The impact turned him; it knocked him to his knees. He

felt little pain, just a curious calm. His mind told him that he needed to detach himself from the body that had taken the bullet. He reached for the Beretta that was loose in the fingers of an arm that seemed no longer his. He gripped it with his right hand. It felt part of him again. The gun was ready to kill whoever had done this but first it would need some help finding him. He held the weapon low and out of sight. He would wait.

'Hey, Mex?' A voice called. The name it called confused him. He'd expected the voice to call Grayson's name. In that instant, the gun that had shot him boomed again.

But no bullet struck him, no muzzle blast reached him, even though the shot was fired from much nearer this time. He turned. He looked up. He saw a tall man who was dressed as a policeman. The man stood near a helicopter that must have just landed. He was back by the chopper's tail rotor. The Blackhawk's pilot was at the side hatch. He was trying with one hand to hold a young woman. His other hand held a pistol. The pilot, although frightened, was looking for a shot. But the man who held the rifle was beyond his line of sight. The pilot could do nothing but wait for his chance.

It was in Grayson's mind that he knew that young woman, but he had no time now to try to place her. His eyes went back to the man with the rifle. He could see livid scars, a once-broken nose. Grayson knew that face. It seemed to him that he'd caused those scars himself but he could not quite remember this man either. The man was looking at him, nodding, as if to say, 'Yes, it's me.' The man was smiling at him.

The man turned his head slightly and pointed with his chin. He was pointing up the slope where that other man had been. Grayson looked. He saw that the small man was down. He was rolling, writhing, clutching his belly.

'Shot my deputy, that one,' said the man with a sneer. 'No loss to you, though. That Mex didn't like you.'

He's talking, thought Grayson. He has things he wants to say. That's good. Say them all. Lose your focus for one instant; give me time for one shot.

347

'Got your general. He's down. And maybe his sister. I'll look in on them in just a minute.'

He was grinning.

'Wanted you to know that. And you heard about Winston. He's dead – or he wishes he was.'

Winston? thought Grayson. Who is this Winston? The name meant nothing to him.

'Love to stay and visit longer but we'll catch up in hell. Say good-bye, Major Grayson. Oh, and this is for Janice.'

'Nat!!' An angry shout. An accusing shout. It came from that woman who the pilot was holding. Nat, thought Grayson. That must be the man's name. The man threw a glance toward the source of the shout, but the most he could see were her legs and feet showing under the helicopter's fuselage.

'Nat, damn you, it's me. It's Janice. Janice Novak.'

Nat Allen stiffened. He froze in place. His reaction gave Grayson the chance that he needed but her words had caused him to freeze as well. It seemed to Grayson that he knew a Janice Novak. That Janice, like this one, often wore jeans and she had a similar voice. Even so, this one seemed very different. He saw the pilot try to hold her by grabbing at her sweater but this woman pushed him away. Now she was stepping out into the open so that the man called Nat could see her.

Nat only glanced. He blinked, 'Who are you?'

'I'm Janice, you imbecile. You're ruining this. Who the fuck asked you to butt in?'

'What the hell ... you're not Janice! Get up there with him.'

She walked straight at Allen, she was baring her teeth. She said, 'Look at me, damn it. Look in these eyes. Look deep and try to tell me I'm not Janice Novak.'

He blinked again. He wavered. Grayson knew that he should shoot, but the woman was almost between them.

She said, 'Look at me. Are you looking at me? Now look at the man who fucked me and killed me. He's mine, God damn you. No one kills him but me.'

She turned from him. She didn't wait for an answer. She took several long steps to where Grayson was crouched and

348

she aimed a kick at his face. Surprised, he fell backward. The kick glanced off his chest. She jumped on him, clawed at him. She was going for his gun. She seized it and twisted it; she brought it to her mouth. She put her teeth on the padding of his thumb, but didn't bite him.

Nat Allen was yelling. 'Get out of the way.'

She snarled, 'Back off, Nat. You cover that bunch.'

Allen lifted his eyes to the several new faces that had appeared at the entrance to Belfair. A uniformed sergeant who was General Hoyt's driver was dragging the general toward cover. The woman, Hoyt's sister, was helping. A tall man, bleeding, a white bandage on his arm, was staring, just watching, through eyes that were swollen. He only moved when two patients pushed past him. He grabbed them both, tried to push them inside, but the little one, a child, slipped his grasp and kept coming. She came walking down the lawn with a sack over her shoulder and a little dog following behind her.

'It's true. She's Janice,' the little girl was saying. 'They do that here. It's what Belfair is for.'

Allen shook his head rapidly. 'Oh, no. She ain't Janice. No way in hell.' But his voice had a quiver, a break.

'And look. See that girl?' She was pointing toward that other one now coming down. The other one wore shorts. She was carrying a computer. 'You know her, don't you? Don't you know Veronica?'

'I don't ... I don't know no Veronica.'

'Sure, you do. That's Molly Pitcher. She sent you that E-mail. She was just as dead as Janice, and now look at her.'

Grayson heard all this. He did not understand it. And this woman who was biting him ... still she wasn't biting hard. She had her hands on his gun but wasn't trying to take it. She was guiding it ... toward herself ... she was turning the muzzle ... she was raising it up so that it pointed at her face. It almost seemed that she wanted him to shoot her.

'Look at me, Cowboy.' Her voice was a whisper. 'Look at me. Who am I? Say my name.'

'You're … Janice?'

'No, God damn it. Snap out of it, Grayson.'

'I … I don't …'

'What you're gonna do now is raise this gun to my shoulder. When you lay it there, blow that sucker away. I'll brace you and shield you, you shoot him.'

'He doesn't have to shoot,' came the little girl's voice. 'This man with the rifle doesn't want to shoot either. Look at him. He's lowering his rifle.'

Grayson tilted his head in order to see. It was true; the man had lowered his weapon. Not much, but enough, and he was backing away. He looked as if he wanted to run.

The little girl went to him. She reached up and touched him. 'Wait. You don't want to go just yet. First you want to give your rifle to that man from the helicopter.'

Grayson saw that she had cocked her head toward the pilot. The pilot had come up from Nat Allen's blind side. He was holding his pistol in two trembling hands and was aiming it at Allen's chest. Allen saw him. He shifted. He seemed to be weighing his chances.

The little girl said, 'No, you'd better not move. That man's very nervous. He'd rather not shoot you, but he will if you move.'

Another voice, a calm one, spoke to the young pilot. 'Son, aim at his head. He's wearing a vest. Aim higher.' This was the man who had come down behind these girls, the man with the bandaged bloody arm and swollen eyes. He said to the pilot, 'I'd better take the gun.' He eased the pistol from the pilot's hands and while keeping its line on Allen's skull. He said, 'This little girl … she did her best to save your life. You can live a little longer. Up to you.'

Nat Allen looked at the pistol. And he saw Grayson's pistol. He knew that he was dead if he moved, but he knew that he'd be put on death row if he didn't. He looked at the woman who had wanted to kill Grayson. He asked her, 'Janice … can you help me?'

'She'll be busy.' said the other man as he reached and took

the rifle. 'Right now, get on your belly. Get down on the ground.'

Nat Allen hesitated. He had tears in his eyes. 'Would you tell me … sir … is that really Janice? Did you people really bring her back to life?'

'Sure we did. Now get down.'

Nat Allen looked into the eyes of Prentice Teal. He saw that tears were streaming down this man's cheeks as well. He knew nothing of the mace that had caused those tears. He thought only that this man must be telling the truth if he, too, was crying over Janice.

Nat Allen sank to his knees.

Chapter Forty-Eight

Grayson awoke. He thought he'd been napping. He'd had another terrible dream. He heard the Blackhawk's engine at its full cruising pitch. He saw Susannah sitting beside him. He tried to raise his arm to look at his watch. He thought they should be getting to Belfair very soon. But he couldn't lift his arm. It was numb.

'My arm,' he whispered. His mouth was dry.

'Lie still. We're taking you to a hospital.'

She said this while looking off to one side. She did not seem to want to meet his eyes.

'A doctor? What happened?'

'We did it, Roger. You got them out. See who's here? It's Veronica and Jennifer.'

He remembered his dream. Bits and pieces.

'Hi, handsome,' grinned Veronica. She sat hugging her computer. 'Do you see where we are? It's my first helicopter ride. It's so cool.'

'Hi, Dodger,' said Jennifer. 'And this is Chewey.' She held her dog up for him to see.

Grayson tried to smile, but he couldn't help staring. It struck him that Jennifer looked just as he'd imagined her, but he knew that this was the first time he'd seen her.

He asked her, 'Wait a minute. We've already been to Belfair? How ... how did we get you all on this chopper?'

'Mr. Teal said go – he said he'll clean up. He said to tell you that the general isn't hurt too badly, the bullet only busted some ribs.'

'The ... general?'

'I saw him,' said Jennifer. 'He was talking and cursing. He's not mad at you, though – just everyone else.'

Grayson looked at Susannah. 'How did he get shot?'

'You ... don't remember anything that happened?'

'It's the morphine,' said Jennifer. 'Rick gave you a whopper.'

'Rick?'

'Our pilot. He had some in his kit. And Susannah wrapped your arm. She's real good at first aid.'

She's real good at a lot of things, thought Grayson. 'But what happened to my arm? Did I get shot, too?'

'Same as the general. The same man shot you both, but then he gave up. Mr. Teal took him up to the ...'

'Jennifer,' said Susannah. 'We ought to let him rest.'

'No, wait.' Grayson tried to rise. 'Someone tell me what happened.'

Susannah, once again, averted her eyes. Her manner seemed ... he wasn't sure ... almost ashamed. Oh, God, he thought.

'Susannah, what have I done?'

'You? You did fine. You were very brave, Roger.'

'Well, can someone fill me in? And where are we going?'

'Sir, we're stopping first at Andrews,' the pilot called back. 'An ambulance will be waiting to take you off. After that, I'm taking these young ladies to Roanoke.'

'Roanoke, Virginia? What's in Roanoke?'

'It's where I asked him to take us,' said Susannah.

'But what for? How will I find you?'

'You'll know where to find us. But don't for a while. We need some time, Roger. Don't come.'

He tried to clear his head. 'I don't understand.'

'You will. When things settle. It's better this way.'

'But when will I see you? And Veronica. And Jennifer.'

'When it's time. And if you want to.'

'Well, of course, I'm going to want to. How could I not want to?'

'It'll come to you, Roger. Give it time.'

Chapter Forty-Nine

It did come to him, much of it, by that afternoon. Some of it came as they prepped him for surgery to repair the damage to his arm.

A shot of Demerol began to open a door that his mind had apparently closed. Even then, he had trouble trusting his memory. What he seemed to remember could not have been possible. Susannah Card had become Janice Novak. She had stood, side by side, with Nat Allen. She had attacked him. She said she wanted to kill him.

But then she changed. She had her hands on his gun. She was no longer Janice, nor was she Susannah. She was another woman whom he'd seen once in a dream. She had called him 'cowboy.' She was Susannah's friend, Sally.

Sally had said to him, 'Snap out of it. Shoot him. Blow that sucker away.' He knew that she meant Nat Allen. But then the little girl, Jennifer, appeared on the scene and told her that he needn't bother. Jennifer then managed to convince Nat Allen that he ought to put down his rifle.

Grayson thought he remembered each of these things. But he knew that they might not have happened.

Other pieces floated back when he woke from the surgery. But each answer brought with it a great many questions.

The surgeon came in later to check on his status. The surgeon, a captain, asked if he had family or anyone else who might need to be notified. Grayson asked the surgeon to contact Prentice Teal and say that he wanted to see him. The surgeon tried. He called all the right numbers. He said that he could find no such person.

Grayson then asked him to call General Hoyt. Again the doctor tried. He reported that the general was in stable condition after a serious automobile accident. He would be in seclusion for some time.

'Automobile accident?'

'That's what I'm told.'

'Then what happened to me?'

'Firing-range mishap. It says so right there.' The surgeon gestured toward his chart.

'And you endorsed that? You damned well know better.'

'Go easy, Major Grayson. You'll have a visitor soon. Your visitor will tell you what he can.

The visitor was the shadowy Pentagon shrink, the one who'd got him into this in the first place. He appeared at Grayson's door three days later. Grayson's arm was in a cast. It rested on a sideboard that kept the arm raised.

The shrink sat. A rueful smile. 'Well, I did warn you. I did offer to help. I told you that Teal would run rings around all of you.'

Grayson remembered. 'Have you seen him?'

He shook his head. 'But I've been up to Belfair. Me, and about twenty others; we've restaffed it. We're trying to sort out who everyone is, try to get them detoxed, interview them. But we don't have any files on any of those women – no records of any kind. Nothing.'

'Teal cleaned them out?'

'From what we can gather. Can you shed any light?'

'I've only seen a few of them. Can't Zales reconstruct them?'

'Dr. Zales can't even reconstruct Dr. Zales. His mind is gone. He's nearly catatonic.'

Grayson cleared his throat, 'I guess I'm sorry to hear that. Then, what about his wife? Can she help?'

A snort. 'Not bloody likely. Teal saw Dr. Zales drag her into the elevator. It was after she'd slashed him with a knife.'

'Slashed Zales?'

'Slashed Teal. Cut his arm to the bone. Are you telling me you didn't know that?'

'No, I didn't.'

But he vaguely remembered that Teal's arm had been bloody. He saw that when Teal held a gun on Nat Allen. He was about to ask what became of Nat Allen, but the Pentagon shrink was still talking about Leatrice.

'Teal was also the last one to see her alive, not counting, of course, Dr. Zales. It seems that Zales had taken her down to the Quiet Rooms where he strapped her down on a bed. He put a mask on her face and sat at her side. He fed her a mixture of strychnine and jam. He fed her just a little bit at a time. A few of the patients say they heard muffled screams for the better part of the morning.'

He paused. The Pentagon shrink closed his eyes partway as if he were revisiting the basement. 'I found her myself. It was that afternoon. The mask Zales put on her had a thick leather bit. She had chewed it in two. She had also dislocated both her shoulders and one ankle in her struggles against those straps. I don't know if you're aware of what strychnine can do ...'

'I know about strychnine. What about Zales?'

'What was left of him? Still sitting there. Smiling and drooling. He did look up at me when I walked in. He said, "She murdered her parents, you know." Those were pretty much the last words he's ...'

'Wait a minute. Rachel Carey. She was down in that basement.'

'Not when I got there. She was out in the street, along with six or seven other patients. She was sitting on the curb by a police car.'

'She's okay?'

The eyes of the Pentagon shrink clouded over. 'Roger, nobody in that place is okay. Not even the ones who don't belong there.'

Andrew Carey, the shrink told him, was found in the back

of a police car up the street. He'd had a heart attack. He was dead.'

'That's the story?'

'What ... like you had a mishap on the firing range? No, this one was real. I was at the post-mortem. Your friend, Nat Allen, cuffed him, put duct tape over his mouth and stuffed him in the well of his locked backseat. Suffocation was deemed to be a causative factor. His daughter was just sitting there. I don't think she even knew him. Nor did she seem to know how she got there.'

'How did she?'

'I know she smeared herself with Vaseline and squeezed through a basement window. But she claimed the first thing she could remember was standing by that car, looking in.'

'Um ... what did she tell you her name was?'

'Teresa.'

'Did she mention the name Emma?'

'Who's Emma?'

'Never mind.'

'Damn, I'd love to find those files.' The shrink scratched his chin. 'The other patients tell me Carey's kid was a horror. Ask me, she's as nice as she can be. Ask me, I'd say she's perfectly sane if you discount the fact that her name's not Teresa. I'd like to ask her mother but they've both vanished.'

'You can't find Martha Carey?'

'Or the daughter.'

'Could Martha Carey have taken her home?'

'She went home, all right. Packed a bag, got some cash and drove off. We know she called from that phone to the general. Reamed him out pretty good. Call was taped. We know she called her son to tell him about his father. He phoned to claim the body, didn't seem all that bereaved. Neither did the wife, for that matter.'

Grayson had an idea where Martha Carey might be. He chose to say nothing to the shrink.

'What about Shan Li? She's the one who speaks Chinese.'

'Odd you should ask. She didn't kill her father either.'

357

Grayson narrowed his eyes. 'What are you talking about?'

He listened as the shrink recounted the story that he'd heard from several patients who had witnessed the events. 'They said they saw the shooting. Some saw it from their windows. A man, later found to be Luis Camal, had struggled with a man who was dressed as a policeman. Camal broke away. He shot the policeman with a handgun. Didn't kill him, only hurt him; those cops both had vests. But I'm getting ahead of the story,' he said.

'The other policeman ... we're talking Nat Allen ... had been seen to shoot two other men. For the record, we never found those two men, but the victims were you and General Hoyt. That same policeman then spotted Camal and shot him in the groin with a rifle. Camal wasn't dead either; he was squirming on the ground. Later on, right after the helicopter had gone, another man – it was Teal – came out of the building with both Shan Li and Shan Li's mother.'

'Wait,' said Grayson. 'Who is this Camal?'

'I just said. He's Carita's ... well ... he's Shan Li's father.'

'Yes, but, what was he doing there? Was he trying to help me?'

'Are you kidding? He was in league with those cops. He brought them in specifically to kill you.'

'Wait. I know why the cops would, but why would Camal?'

'We don't know. Teal must. But we can't find Teal.'

'This Camal came to kill me and he brought his wife with him?'

'No, the mother ... Camal's wife ... was another of Zales's inmates. Anyway, let me finish the story.'

Teal, said the shrink, got the wife and the daughter. He brought them over to Luis Camal and told them they were free to help themselves. Someone heard him suggest that Shan Li use her nails to pop out his eyes one by one. The daughter wouldn't. Apparently they just watched him suffer for a while. Then the mother put an arm around the daughter's shoulder and walked her back into the house. Teal waited for a minute. Then he knelt down beside Camal, and grabbed him by the hair. He slid one arm underneath Camal's chin and snapped his neck with the other.

'He did that with one useless arm?' Grayson asked.

'Well, it's what I was told. Nor have we found the body.'

'It was gone when you got there?'

'Lots of bodies were gone. There are patients who say they saw a man with a bad arm drag the wounded cop into the shrubbery. They heard a shot. Then they saw him walk Nat Allen back there. They heard another shot. That's all they saw.'

'You looked in the shrubbery?'

'Found blood. Bits of bone. The bone's probably cranial. No bodies. Another place where we found a good deal of blood was down in another of those Quiet Rooms. Again, no bodies, but two guards are unaccounted for.'

Grayson couldn't imagine why two guards would be killed. But he remembered what Jennifer had told him. She said that Mr. Teal had promised to clean up. He had never imagined that Teal's notion of cleaning was to execute at least two men in cold blood. A part of Grayson was glad that Nat Allen was gone. But another part of him felt ... regret ... even shame, that it was Teal, not himself, who had finished Nat Allen.

'Roger, how are you doing? And I don't mean your arm.'

'I'm okay, I think. Just a little bewildered.'

'It happened again, didn't it?'

'What happened again?'

'You got hit. You blacked out. You became someone else.'

'Doc, that's horseshit. Don't start that again.'

'You had your gun out. It was in your right hand.'

'Who says so?'

'I heard. It did happen again.'

An exasperated groan. 'Do you see my left arm? Notice anything about it? Ask yourself why I might have had to use my right hand.'

The shrink allowed the sarcasm to pass. 'Your gun was not only in your right hand,' he said, 'but you were about to shoot the woman who you'd brought with you to Belfair.'

Grayson seemed to remember that. But he said, 'That's not true.'

'Who was she, Roger?'

'She's none of your business.'

'Was that Susannah? You did find Susannah?'

'I don't know anyone by that name.'

He folded his arms. 'Well then, let's see. If that wasn't Susannah, who could she have been? As it happens, I know. Shall I tell you? That was Janice Novak, come back from the dead. How, you might ask, could I know that she was Novak? At least a dozen patients heard her say it.'

'Mental patients … get confused. They make very poor witnesses.'

'Uh-huh. You're not the only one counting on that. Teal all but took a bow with them watching him.'

Grayson said nothing. He was chewing on his lip.

'Be straight with me, Roger. What happened back there?'

'I'm not sure. I'm honestly not sure.'

The pentagon shrink came back two days later.

He told Grayson that the general seemed out of danger but was now being treated for depression.

'He's a good man, Roger.'

'I know he is.'

'He's a good man who tried to do a good thing. But he tried it in a not so good way, and he knows it.'

Grayson nodded. Sadly. He thought of his report. The fact that Hoyt had brought him in as a watchdog might help, should there be an inquiry.

'Still no sign of Teal but we know he's been busy. Oh, and we have a real name for Nat Allen. Are you ready for this? It's Willis Lilly.'

Grayson blinked.

'You've heard the expression, 'What's in a name?' He must have grown up being called Willy Lilly. He'd have made up his mind to try to build a new image. Understandable, I guess, but I'd say he overreached. He was, in fact, a small-town cop at one time. Got fired for brutality. He maimed a few people. I suppose, thanks to Teal, we're well rid of him.'

'We could never learn his name,' said Grayson. 'How did you?'

'Found his fingerprints somewhere. I'll get to that in a minute. I haven't asked you about two young patients, the two you flew out of Belfast.'

'Just as well. I have nothing to tell you.'

'One is twelve years old. Could that be correct? She's known as Jennifer. That's the only name we have.'

'Same with me. That's the only one I've heard.'

'The older one is nineteen. She's Amanda Winston. I assume you know about her father.'

'I know her as Veronica. I know nothing of her father.'

'Well, that's strange,' said the shrink, 'all things considered. For openers, he was in business with Teal, along with Carey and Camal and our friend, Norman Zales. They were going to market the new compound you call Richard. Does any of this ring a bell?'

Grayson shook his head, no. But he wasn't surprised.

'What he also has in common with Carey and Camal is that Winston is as dead as his partners.'

That did surprise Grayson. 'Teal killed him?'

'Guess again.'

'Doc … I'm in no mood for …'

'Nat Allen … Willis Lilly … amputated Winston's penis. He was looking for you. He had reason to think that Winston knew you and even that you might be in residence there. Yet you tell me you knew nothing of Winston.'

Grayson closed his eyes. 'Where did Charles Winston live?'

'An estate called Oakmont down in Warrenton, Virginia.'

Grayson let out a breath but said nothing.

'Nat left his prints. That's how they ID'd him. He also wrote your name, and his, on the wall. He added a message. Care to know what it was? He added, THIS IS FOR JANICE.'

Grayson was silent. He felt sure that this was true. It did

361

look as if Veronica had set up her father, and yet he could not, he would not, believe it of her.

'Roger, I have to ask you again. Do you know where those girls are?'

'I do not.'

'Do you care about them?'

'Very much.'

'Then you damned well better find them before Prentice Teal does. It seems that Mr. Teal has had a brainstorm.'

The Pentagon shrink handed him what looked like a memo. 'Don't ask where I got it. I'll say only this – I got it last night from a friend who was shown it, and has since been unable to sleep well.'

It was a photocopy, three pages in length. The addressee, and the distribution list, had both been inked over. But the stamp, TOP SECRET – EYES ONLY was visible. The last page was signed with the initials P.T.

The first part of the memo was all about Jennifer. It began with what little Teal knew of her background and how she came into Zales's hands. It said he'd seen no value in a twelve-year-old multiple, nor in any of the others who partook in Chameleon. But then, quite by chance, he personally witnessed what this one subject, Jennifer, could do.

The first example he cited was in the Winston girl's room. He'd been about to confiscate the Winston girl's computer when Jennifer came into the room to prevent it. She claimed that she was an alter named 'Bruno' and threatened the writer with physical violence if he didn't leave the Winston girl alone. Teal wrote of that incident:

This seemed laughable at the time, but we did leave the room. Time was short, we had more urgent business. Not long afterward, however, I was trapped in the basement with a homicidal patient called Emma. Emma had managed to capture Dr. Zales. She held a blade to his throat. She could have killed him at will. Grayson paused to rub his chin. He did a quick scan; the next two paragraphs dealt with Emma's activities of the preceding thirty-six hours. It said that Emma had murdered four men.

362

It was not more specific than that.

'Four men?' Grayson asked. 'What four would they be?'

'We're still missing two guards. Beyond that, I don't know. But this Emma, I take it, must be Rachel Carey.'

'Let's, um, give her the benefit of the doubt.'

'Read on, Roger.'

Teal's report, to whomever, said that Jennifer soon came down to the basement. She had learned that she could travel through the dumbwaiter shaft. Jennifer approached Emma and, quite unafraid, began to mold Emma's mind. Emma, within minutes, was no longer dangerous. She no longer cared to harm Zales. Jennifer told Emma that she must go away and allow a gentle alter to replace her.

The writer, Teal, was astonished to see this, but was soon to be even more impressed.

Jennifer then announced that she had to leave because Grayson (see below) and Susannah (see below) had come for her. Those two had arrived. This indeed was the fact. But Jennifer could have had no way of knowing that they had just landed in a helicopter. She had no way of knowing that they were even en route. She had no way of knowing that Grayson had been sent to find this Susannah, or even that Susannah existed. Grayson smiled.

'What's funny?'

'Teal has never liked computers.'

'Um ... how is that significant?'

'Doesn't matter. Never mind.'

'I assume, incidentally, that I'll hear no more denials that you found and enlisted this Susannah.'

Teal's report cited the next example of the power that this child seemed born with. He saw her control the mind of a man who had come to assassinate Major Grayson. He saw that man – a vicious brute and a bigot – fall so totally under the spell of this child that his capture was effected without effort.

He later learned, on interviewing other patients, that she'd had an equally amazing effect on the Winston girl, It seems that when she needed to leave the Winston girl (in order to go down to the basement) the Winston girl became agitated. Jennifer then 'lent' her this 'Bruno' persona and told her that 'Bruno' would protect her. She transferred this 'Bruno' to the Winston girl's mind. She did so, apparently, through a laying on of hands. This laying on of hands was also the means by which she had exorcised Emma. *We have learned subsequently that Emma is no more. Indeed, a docile alter has replaced her.* Grayson felt the shrink's eyes on him. He put down the document.

'You're not smiling,' said the shrink.

'Why would I be smiling?'

'You're supposed to guffaw at what you've just read. You're supposed to tell me it's the biggest crock of shit you've ever seen in your life.'

'Some of it is.'

'But then you're supposed to be very concerned that Teal has an interest in what she can do. The least that it means is that he'll find her and snatch her. The ... *addressee* will put her in one of its facilities. She will never have a life that a child should have. They will study her, test her, look for ways to make use of her. They will try to turn her into a weapon.'

'Doc ...'

'You doubt it?'

'That shit doesn't happen.'

Don't be dense, thought the psychiatrist. It happened to you.

Grayson read the rest. It was all about Susannah. Teal had seen her become different people at will. He had seen her take, or appear to take, the spirit of a woman, several months deceased, and convincingly become that woman. Her voice, her accent, her use of language had changed. He had seen her demand of the aforementioned assassin that she, not he, must execute Major Grayson. She attacked Major Grayson; she was wresting his weapon, when Teal saw yet another transformation. She was suddenly a person, not Susannah, not the dead one, but a woman who spoke with a Texas accent and who now wanted him to kill the assassin.

The next-to-last paragraph was fully blacked out. The last line of the memo was not. The last line offered to deliver these subjects in return for 'the consideration that we have discussed.'

Grayson's face had darkened. 'He'll deliver them for money?'

'Oh, no. Not Teal. He wouldn't care about money.'

'Then for what?'

'Some favor. The man deals in leverage.'

'May I keep this memo?'

'No, you can't. I had to promise.'

'Can you get me out of here? Can you get me released?'

'I don't have that authority. But I can help you dress.'

'I'll need a car.'

'What you'll need is a driver.' The shrink jangled his keys. 'Can you think of one you can trust?'

Chapter Fifty

The Pentagon shrink owned a white BMW. Grayson's laptop was already on its front seat. Grayson hoped that this man was genuinely interested in trying to protect Jennifer from Teal. He had, after all, moved quickly into Belfair to care for all the others left behind. He was kind in his assessment of what Hoyt had tried to do. Either way, Grayson realized that he needed him.

'I don't suppose you picked up my Beretta.'

'Glove compartment, but try not to need it.'

Grayson opened the glove box, checked his pistol, but left it.

'Do you have a screwdriver?'

'Tool kit in the trunk.'

'Let's get this car off the base first.'

They were able to exit the base with no problem. Their departure, however, was noted at the gate and their license plate taken down. Grayson pointed to a large shopping center outside. He asked the shrink to pull in.

They were back on their way some five minutes later. Grayson had found a similar BMW, not white, but close enough, a light tan. He persuaded the shrink to steal that car's plate. The shrink was nervous; he lost one of the screws. No matter. 'We'll put it on later,' Grayson told him.

'We did this ... why?'

'We'll be harder to find.'

'And we're going, I take it, to where your friends are in hiding?'

'We'll see.'

'Will I meet them?'

'I doubt it. But we'll see.'

Grayson had no intention of going to Roanoke. Susannah's request to be flown to that city was probably an attempt at misdirection. Once there, she would likely have rented a car and driven to one of two places.

Grayson and the shrink had been driving six hours when Grayson pointed to an upcoming exit.

'Let's get off,' he said.

'At Durham?'

'Yes, Durham.'

'Your Susannah is a graduate of Duke, as I recall. Might she still be living in this area?'

'She might.'

'Well, Roger, I happen to have some good friends at Duke. I'm sure that if we should require some help, my friends will be very discreet.'

Grayson looked at the shrink. 'It's time you told me your name.'

'That is not the way we work. You know that.'

'Then who are your friends? I mean down here at Duke.'

The shrink rattled off a number of names, all in the Psychology Department. One of those names was Dr. Daniel E. Cohen.

'How well do you know Cohen?'

'I've served on a couple of committees he's chaired. I've known him for at least twenty years.'

'Why don't we look him up?'

'Why him in particular?'

'Don't play games with me, Doctor. I think you know.'

The shrink only grunted. He said nothing.

'When we see him he's going to address you by name. Don't you think that I might overhear it?'

The Pentagon shrink sighed. 'My name is William. William Thorne.'

'Nice to meet you, Bill.'

'No, it's William.'

Grayson knew that Thorne had tried to find Susannah well before Grayson had first read about her. All Thorne wanted, he'd said, was to interview her. Thorne's search would surely have started at Duke. And at Duke, just as surely with Cohen.

The shrink drove directly to the same campus building where Grayson had first met the professor. He stopped to ask the same student receptionist where Cohen might be at the moment. The student said he should be in the faculty lounge. The shrink said he knew where it was.

Dr. Cohen was there. He rose to greet them as they entered the lounge, eyeing the cast on Grayson's arm. Grayson could see that he'd expected the cast. He knew that Cohen had spoken to Susannah. Grayson thought he seemed surprised, perhaps even annoyed, to see him in the company of Thorne. He cleared his throat as he offered Thorne a hand. The gesture was perfunctory at best.

'What brings you here, William? As if I didn't know.'

'My purpose, in this instance, is entirely unselfish. I am merely trying to help our young friend here.'

'Unselfish, you say? You're not still with the Pentagon?'

'Perhaps not for much longer. I might well have over-stepped.'

'Then it isn't too late to leave well enough alone. You might both consider having some lunch and then turning around and going home.'

Thorne said, 'Lunch would be nice. We do need to talk.'

Grayson nodded. 'While we're eating, he'll give you a memo to read.'

They had lunch brought in to Professor Cohen's study. Thorne was reluctant to show the document to Cohen, but Grayson had left him no choice. Cohen read Teal's memo with growing distaste.

'Please tell me that this man isn't serious.'

'Prentice Teal? Oh, I assure you, he's serious,' Thorne answered.

'But you. You've read this. You can't believe this drivel.'

'There are witnesses, Daniel. It can't all be drivel.'

Cohen turned to Grayson. 'You told me you'd stop this.'

'I told you I'd try.'

'He did more than try,' Dr. Thorne insisted. 'Belfair's finished; Zales is finished. Army doctors are seeing to the rest of Zales's patients. Major Grayson, I assure you, was as good as his word.'

'So I'm told,' said Cohen dryly. He straightened the letter. 'I'll start with what this says about Jennifer.'

'She's safe?'

'She's safe.'

'Martha Carey and her daughter?'

'They are in good hands. That's all I will say. Let's begin with these mind-control powers of Jennifer's.'

Utter nonsense, said Cohen. The so-called observations of the man who wrote that memo were easily explained and dismissed.

'Both Veronica and Emma had been on psychotropics for a period of three years or more. Among them was Haldol, a hypnotic drug. Young Jennifer knew this perfectly well. She knew, therefore, that Veronica was highly suggestible. All Jennifer had to do, in order to help Veronica, was to tell her what Veronica needed to believe. She needed to believe that "Bruno" would guard her. As far as she was concerned, Bruno did.'

William Thorne asked, 'Is there a Bruno?'

'There could be. And any number of others. Jennifer's much like Susannah. Unlike Susannah, she takes it in stride. But, of course, she's still only a child.'

'So she never actually ... *transferred* this Bruno.'

'*Actually?* Shame on you. You can't use that word. Jennifer knew that she *actually* didn't. Veronica thought that she *actually* did. Jennifer, I assure you, cannot walk down the street tossing *Brunos* at everyone she passes.'

'What about the effect she had on Emma?' asked Thorne.

'Several factors were at work. Emma was fading. Hadn't

slept in two days. Jennifer had already befriended her, it seems. And then even before Jennifer went back down to that basement, Emma had been calmed by her chat with this Teal.'

'Teal was down there?' asked Grayson. He had not been aware of that. 'And Teal managed to control her by *chatting?*'

'If that surprises you, Major, it shouldn't. Almost no one ever *chats* with these patients. We observe, we evaluate, and then we put them away. We listen, we talk, but one can't say we chat. Our chatting is reserved for *normal* people who don't tire us by needing our attention.'

'And yet chatting,' added William, 'is exactly what they need. More than empathy. Real listening. Real contact.'

'That,' added Cohen, 'plus Jennifer's touching. This man saw her touch them and his first thought was witchcraft.'

'You see,' explained William, 'no one really ever touches them either. No one holds them. No one loves them. But Jennifer did.'

'As you did, Major Grayson. With Veronica. With Susannah. You have done more for them than you know.'

'If that's so, why doesn't she want me to see her?'

'She ... has her hands full at the moment,' answered Cohen.

'Jennifer's with her?'

Cohen nodded.

'Have you told anyone where?'

'No one. And I won't.'

'Then the answer is yes. Veronica is with her as well.'

'How is she doing?'

'She is dangerously fragile, thanks to Norman Zales. She's convinced that she and her computer are one. She's afraid of becoming Amanda again.'

'You don't mind her being ... someone who's not real?'

'What's to mind? You know her. How else would you want her?'

That, thought Grayson, was what Norman Zales had said. But Professor Daniel Cohen was not Norman Zales. 'I guess I'm asking you whether you'll try to undo her.'

370

'Not a chance. Nor will Amanda. Don't worry about that. Not while ...'

'Not while what?'

A mischievous smile. 'Not while Bruno's around to prevent it.'

Grayson thought that Cohen was pretending to be joking, perhaps to ease his concern. But Grayson had watched the older man's eyes. Grayson didn't think he was joking.

Dr. Cohen asked Grayson if he'd mind stepping out so that he and Dr. Thorne could speak privately.

'To talk about this? I think I should hear it.'

'No, Major Grayson. It's to talk about you. It's rude of me, I know, but I still feel the need.'

'No offense taken, but in that case, I'll leave. I think you can guess where I'm going.'

'Um ... how will you travel?' asked William Thorne.

'I won't need your car. I'll get there on my own.'

'No, please.' Cohen stood. 'You and I need to speak. I will tell you why Susannah is ... wary of you. Please give us ten minutes. No more.'

Cohen saw that Grayson would prefer to hear that now, but Grayson did not refuse him.

Cohen listened as his footsteps receded in the hall. He watched through his window as Grayson appeared in the quadrangle where the two of them had first spoken. Cohen offered more coffee to Thorne.

'Add that arm to his limp, he's not all that he was. Any thoughts of retiring the young major?'

'That thought has been his own before this.'

'Is he a Chameleon?'

Thorne showed his surprise. 'Since when does Dr. Daniel E. Cohen use that term?'

'Dr. Cohen does not, but he knows that you do. Is he, or is he not, a Chameleon?'

'He has always had the gift. We've developed it.'

'He can play any role? Become someone else?'

'He isn't a multiple if that's what you're asking. He still has to study and train.'

'Is he, in your judgment, a dangerous man?'

'Ordinarily, no. He's quite gentle.'

'But he doesn't, I take it, react well to being shot. Did he murder that Novak woman or not?'

'*He* didn't. Not the man that you see.'

'Then who did?'

'He'd been … conditioned to react if his life should be in danger. No one thought it would work quite that well, me least of all.'

'It wasn't rage? It wasn't amnesia?'

'Amnesia of a sort. He lost all sense of self. He didn't know who he was, or who he was shooting. To him, I suspect, they didn't even have faces. To him, they were attackers; he was coldly efficient. Much the same thing almost happened at Belfair.'

'You know why I'm asking.'

'You're concerned about the one you call Susannah.'

'My … Susannah said he didn't know her either.'

'Um … when? When she shrieked, "It's me, Janice Novak"? When she screamed, "This guy fucked me, then he killed me", You mean then? I would think that there was room for confusion in that instance.'

Cohen smiled. He nodded. 'I imagine there would be. Does Grayson understand what was happening at that moment?'

'Not really.'

'Susannah … you're aware that she's a natural, I think.'

'So I hear. I'd like to see for myself.'

'I'm sure you would. But Susannah's quite genuine, one of the few. Susannah, unlike Grayson, doesn't need to be conditioned. She's whatever she needs to be, within reason. At that moment she needed to be Janice Novak.'

'And Grayson, I take it, had told her about Novak?'

'He had not told her much. She inferred certain things. But when this man who shot Grayson said, 'This is for Janice Novak,' she saw a chance to confuse him and she took it. The

372

trouble was, she also confused Grayson. She was lucky that he didn't execute her again.'

'That was – all the same – some very quick thinking.'

'I'd say so. Yes.'

'Resourceful. Courageous.'

'Yes, but stop where you are. You can't have her either. Do a paper on Grayson, if you must, but not her.'

Cohen glanced out his window. He no longer saw Grayson. But, ah, there he was. He was walking toward the library. Cohen wondered why. A man that impatient does not stop to browse.

'Do you use the term "Mosaic"?' asked the Pentagon psychiatrist.

'I don't. But it does fit Susannah.'

'It fits Jennifer as well?'

'That and more. She's a marvel.'

'Teal's memo. You dismissed it. Was that for Grayson's benefit?'

'Well, she isn't a witch, but I'm sure she did those things. She's quick, she's confident, and she's utterly composed. God knows what else she can do.'

'Will you test her?'

'I will not. I'll will try to protect her. But I'm here and they're there. I'm also not a young man.'

Thorne nodded. 'This … is leading back to Grayson, I assume.'

'Tell me this. What has he said about Susannah?'

'Not much. But he loves her.'

'After one day? Ridiculous.'

'He's fixated then, if you like that word better. Either way, let us not expect judicious behavior. He'll kill anyone who tries to harm her.'

'You said he's not dangerous.'

'I said ordinarily. It depends on the trigger.'

'And that trigger might be this memo from Teal?'

'I think he'd kill Teal in a heartbeat.'

Cohen fell silent, frowning deeply. Thorne thought he'd

best change the subject. 'What about Susannah?' he asked.

'What about her?'

'What are her feelings toward Grayson?'

Cohen almost didn't answer. The frown had remained. But he seemed to shrug off what had been troubling him.

He said, 'I think, for good or ill, she might feel the same way. I think she's always dreamed of finding a man who is able to love her as she is. Grayson might be that man, but not for long and she knows it. There are certain ... anomalies ... he'll find hard to accept.'

'Such as?'

'They're none of your business. Here he comes, by the way. I wonder what's upset him. He's running.'

Grayson hadn't intended to go into the library. He was anxious to get to the Raleigh-Durham Airport and grab the first flight into Hilton Head. He thought he had enough cash; he wouldn't have to use plastic. He thought he could get there without leaving a trail, but he would have to be sure that Thorne didn't follow and note the flight that he'd taken.

On an impulse, however, he'd decided to go in and take another look at that yearbook. Not least, he wanted to see Susannah's face. The one that was grinning, watching soft-ball with her teammates. Of the three, that was Grayson's favorite. He would also discreetly remove all the pages that gave Susannah's full name. Doing so wouldn't frustrate Prentice Teal very long, but it would make him take the time to find another.

He found the volume, same rack, same position. He opened it to the section on women's team sports. But even as his eye began searching, he felt the hairs on his neck start to rise. The page was gone. All those pages were gone.

They'd been neatly sliced out at the seam.

Chapter Fifty-One

Susannah rarely answered her phone. She preferred to let her machine take all calls. Each time that it had recorded a message these past days, she hoped, or she feared, that she would hear Grayson's voice. A part of her wanted him to walk in the door. A part of her hoped that he wouldn't.

But she had, every night, gone to sit on the beach where the two of them had sat and watched the stars. It was where he said he dreamed of being with her each evening. They'd sip a glass of wine and watch the sunset, he'd said. Nothing else would matter. Only being there together. It was a nice dream, but just a dream.

Instead, she had gone there with all of her house guests, but only when the sun had gone down. She would sit on a blanket with Veronica and Jennifer. She would bring along Sally's guitar.

Martha Carey and Teresa would come with them to the beach but they preferred to take long walks by themselves. They were slowly becoming acquainted. They would share little stories and tell little jokes. It had been the first time Susannah ever saw Martha smile. Now both of them were smiling all the time.

Teresa would delight in almost everything she saw. Seashells, sand dollars, the blowholes of clams. Even the foam lines left by the surf. All of these small things were new to her.

When they had first begun taking these walks, Jennifer had gone with them. She would walk between them holding both of their hands. She would steer them into subjects that were pleasant to discuss and away from those that were better postponed. Some would never be mentioned again.

Veronica still had to be near her computer, but Susannah had suggested that a laptop might do. So Susannah rented an IBM Thinkpad that Veronica could carry around with her. It worked. The Thinkpad linked her to her own computer that was set up in a corner of the studio.

Susannah had borrowed a monitor from Cheryl to replace the one they'd had to leave at Belfair. Cheryl kept two machines at the cabaret's office but one only served as a spare. Cheryl sent over food and extra clothing as well. She and Martha wore about the same size.

Susannah had asked Jennifer, 'Will Emma be back?'

'I don't think so, but I've been watching.'

'And no Rachel either? All that's left is Teresa?'

'We'll have to wait and see. I hope so.'

'I've seen you sitting, holding hands with Teresa. Do you mind if I ask what you were doing?'

'Just helping her forget things. There are things that she remembers people doing to her but they're things that never actually happened.'

'Those two uncles who abused her?'

'Uh-huh. They weren't real.'

'And she knows that?'

'Bit by bit. She wants to believe it. And that's easy down here. It all seems far away.'

'Does Martha ... does her mother mind calling her Teresa?'

'Uh-uh. Why should she?'

'Well ... her daughter's name is Rachel.'

'But that *is* her daughter. Who cares what she's called?'

Susannah smiled, and shook her head. Jennifer had asked her, 'Why does that make you smile?'

She answered, 'I just wondered what Dr. Cohen would say if he knew that you were doing all these things.'

'What would he say?'

'Well, he sure as heck wouldn't call it psychiatry.'

'It isn't. What it is, is just living.'

'Susannah?'

'Yes?'

'I think you're wrong about Roger.'

'Wrong about what? I haven't said a word.'

'After what you both did, after coming to get us, not saying a word is a lot.'

'Well ... I'll work it out. And you're too damned smart.'

'I could talk to him for you. I could take him for a walk.'

'Don't you dare. Don't you even think of it.'

'Then let Sally talk to him.'

'That's all he needs. I think he heard from Sally once too often up at Belfair.'

'Susannah, this is dumb. He's my friend, too. And I want to know why you're behaving this way. It can't be you're afraid that he'd hurt you.'

'You mean physically? No. I'm not afraid of him that way.'

'Then what way?'

'I think that he'd find me ... tiring, eventually. He thinks I'm so talented, so smart.'

'Well, you are.'

'No, *they* are. I have friends he's read about, but he's only met Sally. And Sally is a much better ...'

'What?'

'Never mind.'

'I don't think you were going to say "singer".'

'I wasn't.'

'And you've got the same body so you couldn't mean at sex.'

'You've ... got a lot to learn. Now shut up about that.'

'Did you already do it? Or you didn't know how.'

'Know how? Well, of course I know how.'

'So did you?'

'Doggone it, Jennifer, he was here for one night. The subject never even came up, except ...'

'You thought about what it would be like?'

'Mind your business.'

'Susannah, take my hand.'

'Don't try that with me.'

'Then help me understand what the problem is here. You're scared he'll get tired of boring old Susannah? Is that all you think of yourself?'

'No, I think I'm okay. I like who I am.'

'You are very okay. And you do have all those talents. All you've done is divide them up a little.'

A shrug.

'Why don't you say what the real problem is? Sometimes problems go away when you talk about them.'

Susannah closed her eyes. She gritted her teeth. 'I can't believe I'm saying this to a twelve-year-old.'

'I'm almost thirteen. Just say it.'

'I ... adore having sex. I'm not uptight about that. But if he ever said, "Susannah, just for a change ..."'

'He'd want sex with Sally?'

'Or maybe ... I don't know ... he might even ask for Janice. I think ... I hope ... that he knows I was acting. But what if he asks to see her again? What if he wants to make love to her again?'

'So ... you do like yourself. But you don't think much of Roger.'

'Oh, no. I think he's wonderful. But looking down the road ...'

'Susannah ...'

'It happens. You'll see when you're older.'

'When I'm older I'll look for someone like Roger. And I won't look down your dumb road.'

It was midafternoon when the telephone rang. Susannah, in her studio, was sketching out a mural that Cheryl had wanted for her dance floor. She let it ring. She waited for the voice. It was only Dr. Cohen asking her to pick up. She put the phone to her ear.

'Susannah,' he asked, 'are your friends all there with you?'

'They're around. Is anything wrong?'

'Major Grayson is here.'

She felt that thump in her stomach.

'Do you remember Mr. Teal? You saw him at Belfair. Major Grayson thinks that Mr. Teal may have found you. He wants you all to get out of that house. Is there a place you can go?'

She took a deep breath. She was silent for a moment.

'Susannah?'

'Why doesn't he tell me himself?'

'He's afraid you won't listen. You've been willful in the past.'

'That's not what he's afraid of. He thinks I'm … never mind. But tell him not to worry. We're okay right here.'

'Susannah, you might not be.'

'Thank the major for me. We'll be fine.'

Chapter Fifty-Two

Grayson's flight to Hilton Head landed two hours later. He had checked the small bag containing his pistol. He had to hope that checked baggage was not being scanned. If it were, he would have had to show his ID. His ID would then have been on a computer and he could have been traced to this island. But the bag came through unchallenged. He was glad, but he feared that he might be too late.

His car was still in the lot where he'd parked it. His cast and sling were clumsy but he was able to drive. He threw his bag and laptop in the passenger seat. He stuck the Beretta in his sling.

It was just after six when he reached Sea Pines Circle and turned north on Pope Avenue toward Susannah's house. He passed the complex of shops where Cheryl's was located and the Holiday Inn where he'd yet to spend a night. Susannah's street, Mallard Lane, was just ahead. Grayson was barely into his turn when he realized that something was wrong. He saw a police car outside Susannah's house. He could see that a crowd had gathered there. The sight of the police car nearly caused his heart to stop.

As Grayson approached, all the faces turned toward him. They seemed to close ranks. A few moved to intercept him. But then a woman whose face seemed familiar called out to them and motioned them back. She waved at him. She was telling him to come on.

Grayson realized where he'd seen her before. It was Cheryl,

the singer, the cabaret owner. Next to her, holding a bat in his hand, was one of the bartenders she'd wanted to send out to protect Susannah on the night when he first met her. He recognized Eddie, the Holiday Inn manager, who had not been pleased to see him with Susannah. All of the others were strangers to him, but he realized that they were no strangers to Susannah. They had all gathered there to protect her.

Susannah's door opened as he reached her driveway. Jennifer appeared. She came running to him. She was dressed in white shorts and a Hilton Head T-shirt. Her skin had been reddened by the unaccustomed sun. He hoped she'd burned her robe and pajamas as well.

Susannah herself stepped through the front door. A police-man in uniform followed and stayed with her. Susannah tried to show Grayson a smile, but she wasn't able to maintain it. She looked well, but she seemed very nervous.

Jennifer kept at least a part of her smile when she saw the cast on his arm. She asked him, 'How is it? Does it hurt?'

'Not much. It mostly itches. How is everyone else?'

'They're okay. You'll see later. Susannah needs to take a walk with you first. Will you tell her to let me come with you?'

'Um … Jennifer, no. I think we need to speak privately.'

'This walk won't be private. It's to meet with Mr. Teal. The walk after that might be private.'

'Jen … wait a minute. Teal's here? You've seen him?'

'He called a little while ago. And he knew you were coming. Does that mean Susannah's phone is tapped?'

'Let me park. Try not to be frightened.'

'I'm not afraid of him. That's why I should go with you. I know what he was doing up at Belfair.'

'So do I.'

'Yes, but I bet I know what he wants.'

'Jennifer … I know very well what he wants.'

It's you, thought Grayson, and he's not going to get you. Not while I have a breath in my body.

Grayson waited for Susannah to come down the walk. He

saw Veronica waving at him through a window and he thought he caught a glimpse of Martha Carey. Susannah came forward. She was glaring at Jennifer.

She said, while pointing, 'Into the house.'

'But, Susannah, I can help.'

'Not this time, you can't. You get in the house. Stay inside until we get back.'

Jennifer made a face but she was going to obey. She said, 'When you come back, I'll show you some stuff. Come in and see Veronica's ...'

'Jennifer!!'

'I'm going.'

Susannah met his eyes, then she dropped hers at once. 'He's waiting farther up on the beach.'

'Did he tell you why he's here?'

'All he said was that he hopes you'll listen to reason. You know him, Major Grayson. Is he someone you can deal with?'

He grimaced. 'I'm back to Major Grayson?'

'I'm sorry. I'm ... just on edge. Does this Teal keep his word?'

'I don't know. It depends. He's a complicated man.'

'Aren't we all. Let's go see him.'

Teal was standing in the open, perhaps six houses down, in front of a beach house that was shuttered. He stood with his jacket slung over his shoulder. One arm, as with Grayson, was supported by a sling. At first look, Grayson saw no one with him. But on the deck of the beach house, to the right of Teal, he saw two other men who were watching him. He saw that one was Kristoff. Both were in civilian clothes. Their jackets hung open; they stood with arms folded. Their right hands were concealed, likely resting on weapons.

Teal greeted them with a wink, but his eyes were on Susannah. He bowed. He said, 'I'm impressed by your posse.'

'Just say what's on your mind, Mr. Teal,' she answered.

'I mean, it's touching that they care, but why do you need them? From what I've read ... and seen, you're all the posse you need.'

Susannah held his gaze. She said nothing.

He said to Grayson, 'She's really quite lovely. The last time I saw her, the lighting was poor. But then, of course, she wasn't herself.'

'You heard her. What do you want?'

Teal said to Susannah, 'Could I see that one again? Could I see how you switch or ... are you that one already?'

Grayson saw her stiffen. He saw her glance at him sheepishly. For an instant it seemed that she was deeply embarrassed by Teal's reference to her talent for switching.

Grayson leaned forward. 'Teal, just so we're clear, keep in mind that I'm not very happy with you. Keep in mind that I could kill you before those two can move.'

Teal pursed his lips. 'You're no killer, so stop that. Or you are, but you aren't, at least not today.' Teal leaned forward himself. He peered into Grayson's sling. 'Gun in there, huh? We're not doing guns. I'm here to tell you what I want and what I'm offering.'

'You have nothing I want.'

'You need to think about that. There's a lot you can lose. You should both hear me out, then talk it over.'

Teal had asked them to walk with him. He waved off his two men. He stepped out of his shoes and stripped off his socks. Susannah pressed him again to say why he had come, but Teal pretended that he didn't hear her. He had noticed the people who were strolling the beach. Some hand in hand. Some riding bikes in tandem. Some were tossing balls for the dogs they were walking.

'All wisecracks aside,' he said, 'I envy you this. I don't have a home. I don't even have a neighbor. Please believe that I don't want to take this away.'

They waited.

'Here's what you have that you don't want to lose. This lady has her home here, her life here; she can keep it. I can fix it so that any attempt to locate her would have to come through me in the future.'

'Why you?'

'Because I want you to owe me. I'll get to that in a minute. There are other things you don't want to lose, especially those escaped mental patients you're sheltering. Rachel Carey, I gather, is now someone named Teresa, but the law isn't going to care about that. The Rachel who was Emma is a murderess, big time. Her body count is at least four that I know of. If I drop a dime, they will put her away. She can be this Teresa – she can be the Virgin Mary – but she'll still spend the rest of her life locked away.'

Four bodies again. 'Which four bodies were they?'

'Make that two. The second two, the guards, won't ever be found, but the first two are up in a Baltimore morgue. It wasn't her fault if that makes you feel better. Leatrice set it up – she really caused all four. I assume you've heard that she's dead.'

Grayson nodded.

'She did die smiling. I know. I saw the body. But you can't say that Leatrice had the last laugh. She wasn't having a nice time at all.'

Grayson understood. The frozen grin. Strychnine rictus. 'And Zales, I'm told, has had a total mental breakdown?'

'Not much more than usual. Who told you that?'

Grayson waved off the question. 'It isn't important.'

'Then where was I?'

'You were saying you might drop a dime.'

'Oh, yeah. I was threatening you. What I said was that I could. Another dime could be dropped on your young friend Veronica who used to be Amanda Winston. She is an accessory to the murder of her father. She might not realize it; she might not even know him, but she definitely set him up.'

'How could you know that?'

'Young Jennifer blew that one when she called her Molly Pitcher. Your friend, Nat, eventually filled in the blanks.'

Grayson stared. 'He's not dead? I was told that you killed him.'

'Who said that? Who's telling you these things?'

'You were seen.'

384

'By who?' Teal frowned but the frown relaxed instantly. 'Oh,' he said, 'you mean by Zales's patients. No, the fact is, all they heard was a shot. I'll admit, just to you, that I might have capped his knee. I might have done that because I was highly pissed off that a piece of shit like him could try to kill a man like Hoyt. I didn't want him dead. I had some questions to ask him. I am told, however, that he later succumbed.'

'Mr. Teal … is he dead … or is he not?' Grayson asked him.

Teal looked him in the eye. 'I could stand here and shrug. I could make you always wonder. But I'm not quite the bastard you think, Major Grayson. Sergeant Kristoff delivered him to some town in West Virginia. He dumped Nat Allen's body, and that of his deputy, in front of the building where those Aryan clowns meet. That was my gift to Hoyt. And to you.'

Grayson remained doubtful. 'I haven't heard that. I would have heard about that if it's true.'

'Checked the Internet lately? Tuned into their web site?'

Grayson blinked. He hadn't.

'I don't think they'll try for you again, Major Grayson. They think it was you who dropped them off.'

Teal asked Susannah to give them five minutes. 'Major Grayson,' he told her, 'can tell you what I've said. You'll know, but you won't have been a witness.'

She looked at Grayson. He nodded and said, 'Please give us five minutes.' She stayed behind. They walked on.

'Project Richard,' Teal told him, 'needs considerably more work. I know you're aware that it had a few bugs. I read your report, the one you left in your machine. It's no longer there, by the way.'

'I didn't think so.'

'You said that the fear part works like a charm but it vitiates critical judgment. It vitiates a lot more than that. You never got to see what it did to Zales's guards. They had no fear – but neither does a radish. That bunch might as well have been lobotomized.'

'Yet you're going to pursue it.'

'Sure, I am.'

'Why?'

'Because one of these days, we'll get the thing right. Done right, as Hoyt told you, the stuff will work miracles. Done right, it will be worth all the trial and error.'

'And that's how you'll still do it. By trial and error.'

Teal shrugged. 'How else does anything get done?'

'It gets done in real clinics. It gets tested on mice. If it's safe, it gets tested on real volunteers who understand what you're doing to them.'

'You're kidding, right? Would you volunteer?'

'And you do it with every safeguard you can think of. You do it according to the book.'

'What book?'

'Whatever rules of clinical practice apply. Whatever laws and regulations require.'

'Hey, Grayson, you're federal. You can't still believe that. Do you think we have a book at Los Alamos? What we have are black budgets. Nothing happens without them. Do you know how many approvals it takes to order a fucking new lawnmower these days?'

'Well, I'm still putting in my report. I kept the disk.'

'No, you're not. That's my price for going away. You're going to keep your mouth shut about it.'

'I won't do that.'

'Why not? It won't matter. You'll have zero to support it. There aren't any records anyone will ever find.'

'Then why do you care?'

'All you'll do is force me to spend time up in Washington swearing that your report is incompetent. Carey's committee ... sans Carey ... might very well believe you but they won't have any basis for action. The most they can do is hold up some funding.'

'That at least would be something. I hope so.'

'It won't matter. Los Alamos has billions of bucks stashed away in case some committee gets religion. We make a ton of money by selling our technology. We'll make more, down the road, selling new, improved Richard. Some day it might even be legal.'

'My report goes to Hoyt. Hoyt will back me.'

'Yeah, he will if you submit it. He's that kind of man. He'll say, 'Tell the truth.' He'll say, `Answer their questions.' But you can't do that without hurting his sister and seeing her daughter put away. Do you want to put Hoyt in that position?'

Grayson turned away. He looked back at Susannah. Prentice Teal followed his gaze.

'Above all, there's Susannah. You don't want to hurt her. That's a hell of a woman you have there.'

'Mr. Teal ...'

'You ever notice how she stands? Chin high. Proud and straight. Her way of looking you in the eye. Those eyes can melt your heart or they can spit out darts. I wish I'd had the chance to know her better.'

'But you mean to, don't you?'

'Um ... what are you saying?'

'Let's have the rest of it. What do you want?'

'There isn't any rest of it. I told you. No report.'

'You're a liar, Mr. Teal.'

He seemed startled. 'Well ... yeah, but on what?'

'You want Susannah. You want Jennifer. And I *will* kill you first.'

'I ... want them for what? Fill me in.'

'I saw your memo.'

'What memo is that?'

'The one you wrote, you son of a bitch. The one in which you offered to sell them.'

Teal had asked him to recite what the memo had said. He wanted to hear it as close to verbatim as Grayson was able to recall it. Teal listened intently, his face showing little. Grayson finished; Teal nodded; he had turned his head. Teal was looking not at him, but at Susannah.

Teal said to him, 'You heard my proposal. Decide what you'll do about your report.'

'That's all you have to say?'

'You can think what you want.'

'You wrote it, Teal. Because no one else could have.'

'I'll call you for your answer in two hours.'

Chapter Fifty-Three

Grayson had wanted to smash Teal's lying mouth, stand over him and tell him he'd shoot him on sight the next time he saw him here or anywhere. He couldn't do that and Teal knew it. He walked back with Susannah, telling her what Teal had said. He told her that there was no trusting Teal. They would have to decide what to do.

She was silent until they were almost at the house. Her friends, her neighbors, were still gathered outside. Jennifer, looking worried, was waiting in the driveway.

'If you did what Teal wants, what would that do to you?' she asked.

'Susannah, I'm the least of your worries.'

'Could you stay in the Army?'

'That's not an issue. I'm going to resign.'

'Because you'd feel … that you've failed in your duty?'

'That's not it,' he told her. 'There's honor and there's honor. But I'd been leaning toward leaving the service before I got involved in all this. I'll stay in long enough to help you relocate. I'll try to fix you up with good paper.'

'New identities? You can do that for all of us?'

'There's a DOD section that does nothing else. I've worked with them before. I think they'll do me a favor.'

'We have friends here, Roger. You've seen. They'll protect us.'

'Susannah, you heard Teal. He thought they were cute. All the friends you have here won't add up to a speed

389

bump. He'll hit you the same way he hit Belfair.'

Jennifer came toward them. She reached out to touch Grayson. 'How'd it go? Was it bad?'

'Jennifer ...' said Susannah. 'Don't do that with your hand.'

'Susannah, my hand touches. That's all my hand does.'

'All the same ...'

'It's all right,' Grayson told her, 'let's just go inside.'

'You should have let me help you. I know Mr. Teal. I know what he wants and we have it.'

'Um ... Jennifer, what is it that you think he wants?'

'We saw him take everything. He took the computers. He took drugs and machines and diaries and files. But mostly he wanted the computers.'

In his mind, Grayson said, *But now you're what he wants. He wants you and he definitely wants Susannah.* But aloud, he asked, 'What is it that you have?'

'We have everything,' she answered. 'We have all of it.'

'All of what?'

'All the Belfair files. All the records from the laboratory. We have something called Project Chameleon and I'm in it. There's a Project Richard. Duane was in that. We have ...'

Grayson couldn't believe it. 'Wait ... how did you get them?'

'Veronica hacked them. She can hack anything. Except she said it was using up all her memory so she copied nearly all of those files onto disks. You remember that sack of stuff I took out? That was all of her manuals and all of her disks.'

'And it's here? Right now?'

'I tried to tell you.'

'Show me, Jennifer. Let me see what you have.'

It was no exaggeration. Veronica pulled it all up. She had everything in there but the diaries.

Grayson spent thirty minutes on Chameleon and Richard. Every drug combination, every dosage was detailed. He found an action plan and budget for broader testing of Richard. Winston's factory would make it, Los Alamos would mix it, Camal's Mexican firm would distribute it. Carey would provide the political grease. They would have been very rich men.

Every part of the plan was totally illegal. Teal had his stamp, if not his name, on enough of it to guarantee a criminal indictment. Hoyt's interest was peripheral but it was there. He wanted the drug for the reasons he'd given. Combat troops, combat veterans, the mentally ill, and especially for his sister's sick daughter. It showed that Hoyt had no part whatever in any financial relationship. But he had to have known about the action plan and that would be enough to disgrace him.

That would not happen if Grayson could help it. He could now tell Teal that he had all these files and give him a few disks as proof. But Grayson didn't know how much that would accomplish. Teal would still be fairly sure that he would never bring Hoyt down. But the files did, no question, seem to strengthen his hand. Teal might agree to call it a draw, and at least give up on any design that involved either Jennifer or Susannah. Or he might, just might, decide to hit this house tonight. If he didn't find the files he might burn it to the ground. He might take Jennifer, Susannah, Veronica as hostages. It was hard to know what Prentice Teal was capable of – he would probably do almost anything.

But he might have no interest in the files on Zales's patients. All of those, with selective deletions, needed to be given to the Pentagon shrink so he could know who and what his people were treating. Dr. Thorne was probably still up with Dr. Cohen. Dr. Cohen's office was equipped with a computer. Perhaps he could download those files to Cohen's machine. He asked Veronica whether she could do that.

'I guess.' She seemed hesitant.

'I'll call him right now and set it up,' said Susannah.

'Veronica? Is there a problem?'

'There's … stuff about me. It was in Amanda's file. I don't like people reading it. I don't think it's true.'

'I'm sure much of it isn't. Don't worry.'

'Do you mind if I erase that part?'

'Not at all.'

391

She hit a few keys, and her past disappeared.

'Roger ... there's something else. Can we talk?'

Grayson hoped that this was not about what had happened to her father. 'Sure, Veronica. What's on your mind?'

'I met a boy. He lives down the street. I like him. I think he likes me.'

Grayson was relieved. 'I think that's ... very nice.'

'You're not upset?'

Grayson thought he knew what her concern was. 'This begins to sound like you're dumping me. Are you?'

'No. I still love you. But he's ... you know ... young.'

'And I'm Roger the Codger. I get it.'

'Did that hurt your feelings? I do love you, Roger.'

'And I love you, too. But you're right.'

'He asked me where I'm from and where I go to school. I didn't know what to tell him.'

'I can fix that, Veronica. I've discussed it with Susannah.'

Jennifer said, 'Let's just make up new files. We can make them say anything we want.'

Grayson was about to explain that they'd need more of a fictional history than that, but Jennifer had pulled up a chair next to him. She sorted through some disks. She put one in the A Drive and opened it.

'Oh, wait. That's not us. That's just letters and stuff.' She hit the SCROLL button. 'Those are Doctor Zales's letters. They're mostly to parents. They mostly tell them bad things that their daughters say about them, then he asks them for another donation. But one of these ... it's somewhere in here ... is a letter that's all about me. There was someone who wanted to buy me from him.'

'That was Teal.'

'No, this was before.' She tried a few keys. 'Veronica, how do you do a scan?'

'For your name? Here, I'll do it.' She reached in between them. Her fingers danced on the keyboard. The screen began scrolling. 'There it is.'

'Oh, yeah. That's it. Here's the guy who tried to buy me.'

392

Grayson's lips parted as he stared at the screen. The letter was signed by William Thorne.

Finally the phone rang. The machine took Teal's voice. 'I need your answer, Grayson. Pick up.'

Grayson did. 'Where are you?'

'In a bar. What's your answer?'

'Tell me first, do you know a shrink named William Thorne?'

'You figured that out? So did I, sitting here. I'm ready to hear your apology.'

'My apology? You want an apology from me?'

'Or am I wrong? You still haven't figured it.'

'There's nothing to figure. I know that you and Thorne …'

'Grayson, get your ass down here. I'll spell it out. I'll speak slow.'

'Where are you? I'll be there.'

'Down the road. Bar called Cheryl's.'

Susannah asked, 'why would he pick Cheryl's?'

'I don't know, but I'll find out. You wait here.'

She shook her head. 'I'm coming. This is too close to home.'

Jennifer insisted on coming as well. Susannah said, 'No. Not a chance.'

She answered, 'Hey, it's me who they wanted to buy. I'll walk down by myself if I have to.'

Grayson, on second thought, agreed with them both. This could be a ruse to lure him away and then grab them while he was gone. He said, 'We'd best all go together.'

Susannah drove the car; they were there in three minutes. They saw Prentice Teal standing at the door waiting. Grayson asked Susannah to keep the engine running while he scanned the other cars in the lot. Teal seemed to be alone, as far as he could tell. Grayson waited until a carload of patrons arrived before stepping out of his car.

Teal seemed surprised, but not at all displeased to see that Jennifer and Susannah had come with him. His manner on the phone had been brusque. Now it was cordial. It seemed to be written all over his face that he had plans for both of these ... subjects. He greeted them both and opened Cheryl's door for them. He gestured toward the poster in the window. 'Nice picture of you. I didn't know you could sing. I'd love to hear you some time.'

Grayson had forgotten about that poster.

They went inside. Grayson scanned the interior. He didn't see either of Teal's men. The restaurant was quiet. A dinner crowd only. The cabaret show wouldn't start for some time. Prentice Teal recovered his drink from the bar and moved toward an isolated table in the rear.

He said to Grayson, 'You look a little tense. Could it be you're afraid of a snatch?'

'It did cross my mind. Where is Kristoff and your shooter?'

'They sent their regrets. They had to run and catch a flight. Is anyone in the mood for a steak?'

Susannah asked him, 'Why did you pick this place?'

He answered, 'See that? I get that a lot. People always seem to think that everything I do is planned. I'm here, Susannah, because I wanted a bourbon and this was the first bar I saw.'

Teal looked at Jennifer. 'Am I telling the truth?'

'He is,' Jennifer told Susannah.

'Want to touch me?'

'I don't have to. It's the truth.'

Teal asked Grayson, 'What about you? Are you ready to apologize yet?'

'You said you'd spell it out. We'll listen.'

Teal opened his good hand and extended it to Jennifer. She looked into his eyes. She took it.

'For openers, Major, I never write memos. Memos get copied. They get passed around. I do the odd report when it can't be avoided but I almost never sign those reports.'

'Not even with initials?'

'Not even that. When I deal, I like to deal face to face.'

'You still wrote that memo. It had to have been you.'

Teal glanced at Jennifer. She was watching him intently.

'Secondly,' he said, 'I do not sell children. I do not use

children; I don't let them be used. I am not fond of people who do.'

Jennifer wet her lips. She nodded to Grayson.

'Thirdly, I happen to like this little kid. She scares me, but I like her. I like you both, too. I don't run into many honest people.'

Grayson brushed that aside. 'Are you going to try to tell me that Thorne wrote that memo? It wasn't in his voice. It was your voice, your descriptions. It described events only you could have seen.'

'Or that someone had heard me describe, Major Grayson.'

'You're saying Thorne?'

'I made a few calls. I've now heard the whole memo. I did speak to Thorne when his team got to Belfair. You think he rushed over on a mission of mercy? He wanted Zales' files. They're an extortionist's gold mine. He also went up there to grab a few multiples. He was hoping that Jennifer, here, was still there. He knew all about her from Zales.'

At least that last part was true, thought Grayson. 'You told Thorne what you saw?'

'What these two did, yes. Especially Jennifer. I wouldn't normally have shared it, but I couldn't get over it. I might also have wanted to bust Thorne's chops a little because I was there to see it and he wasn't. He got all excited and went to Zales to confirm it. Zales might have been able to fill in a few blanks. Your friends from the third floor filled in a few others, notably the transfer of Bruno to Veronica.'

'You'd seen that yourself.'

'Don't be thick. I could not have.'

Jennifer nodded. 'He'd already left.'

'But ... you're saying that Zales told Thorne some of what happened?'

'The parts in the basement. What's your problem with that?'

'Zales couldn't have told you. Thorne said Zales was cata-tonic.'

'I'm sure he did but I'm telling you he wasn't. Zales never

stopped babbling the two days I was there, but he did have his moments of lucidity. If he's now catatonic, Thorne made him that way. I don't think we'll see much more of Zales.'

'You were there for two days?'

'Yup.'

'Thorne said he never saw you.'

'Jennifer?'

'I don't think he's lying.'

'Jennifer,' said Susannah, 'don't let people see this. Don't let people think you can do things like this.'

'I wouldn't, but he already knows.'

'Thank you, Jennifer,' said Teal. 'Are you sure you're not hungry? How about a burger and fries?'

Grayson asked, 'Who is Thorne? What is he, exactly?'

'Thorne? You might call him the Pentagon's Leatrice. He's not nearly as crazy, but he does the same thing.'

'Which is?'

'He makes monsters, Major Grayson. Don't you know he made you? You were one of Thorne's first experiments.'

'That's ridiculous.'

'Jennifer?'

'I don't think it's ridiculous.'

Teal declined to expand on what he had said about Thorne. But if even a fraction of all this was true, thought Grayson, it seemed to explain many things. He already knew that Thorne had lied when he said that he knew nothing of this latest assignment except that he'd be working with Teal. When Thorne later gave his reasons, Grayson thought he understood them. Thorne had hoped that he'd help him find the famous Susannah. At the least, Thorne had hoped that he'd spy on Teal for him.

'You and Thorne are ... competitors?' Grayson asked Prentice Teal.

'He had his turf. But he's coveted mine. I would have handed him the Chameleon project, and welcome, if he'd had the good manners to ask.'

'This was why he was so eager to help me find Jennifer?'

'I would not have let him have Jennifer. Or Susannah.'

Grayson was afraid to ask his next question. 'Is Cohen in this? How is Cohen involved?'

A shrug. 'I'd never even heard of the man. I tracked Susannah the same way you did. Yearbook picture; I didn't need Cohen. Thorne, however, hoped to sucker you into thinking she needed protection from me. I'd say he did a pretty good job.'

Susannah asked Teal, 'Is Dr. Cohen in danger?'

Teal made a show of checking the time. 'No, but he's probably gone to the police. Last I heard – and this was just before you drove up – he went out to have dinner with Thorne. He's probably wondering why two men grabbed Thorne and threw him into a car.'

'Those two men would be …?'

'I think you can guess.'

'What will happen to Thorne?'

'I think you can guess. I said I'd protect you and I'm proving it, Grayson. Are you ready to give me that disk?'

A waitress had brought the burger to the table, along with a steak for Prentice Teal. Grayson waited until she had left them, before saying, 'Things have changed a little. I have all the files.'

Grayson told him what he had; that it was all on disks. He had everything except the diaries Teal had taken and those that were still in patients' rooms. Teal, at first, said he didn't believe it. Grayson told him how the files came to be in his possession.

Teal's first reaction wasn't shock, not anger. It was more an amused disbelief. He sat back in his chair. He turned his head to Jennifer. She was removing the onions from her burger.

He asked, 'Is Grayson telling me the truth?'

'Uh-huh.' Jennifer looked at his sling. 'Would you like me to cut up your meat for you?'

'Let me get this straight. You walked out of there with them? You had that sack … a pillow case, was it? You walked right past me, and you had *everything?*'

'Uh-huh.' She took his plate and started slicing his steak.

'And Veronica had hacked Zales's computers and mine? She'd been doing this right along?'

'Just for practice. She wasn't trying to hurt anybody.'

'But she hacked them on a computer that I would have taken if you hadn't gone into your Bruno routine.'

'Dr. Zales tried to tell you not to take it.'

'And your ... Bruno is now elsewhere. You lent him to Veronica. I assume he's now guarding all those records.'

'I guess.'

'Those diaries, by the way, have already been shredded. I did have a use for them; I don't anymore.'

'It's good that you did that,' said Jennifer.

'Do I get to hear how you pulled all this off? How you knew that Grayson would show up in a Blackhawk? How you knew that Susannah would be with him?'

'Computers.'

'Computers?'

'You remember that E-mail? The one to the Dodger? Roger's the Dodger. Bruno lied.'

Teal smiled wanly. 'Have I mentioned that I really hate computers?'

He took a bite of his steak. He was silent as he chewed. He swallowed, then asked Grayson, 'Will you give me those files?'

'I'll give you these,' Grayson told him. He drew several disks from his pocket. He put them on the table. 'That's a sample.'

'And what do you want for the rest of them?' Teal asked. 'Please give careful thought to your answer.'

'The same deal you offered. This will help you keep your word.'

'Jennifer? Will I keep it?'

'You'll ... keep most of it. I think.'

'What part won't I keep?'

'I don't know. Nothing bad. I'm not sure that you're such a bad man.'

'Well, I am.'

'Not to us.'

'Then I'll tell you the part of the promise I won't keep ... I might not stay away. I might want to come and see you some day.'

Chapter Fifty-Four

Susannah had said little at the table at Cheryl's. She said nothing at all in the car going home. Grayson was almost equally silent. It was slowly sinking in that he had been an experiment since the day he first reported to Bolling.

The things he had done, the more violent things, had always seemed to him the mere playing of a part. Like an actor absorbed in a role. But he wasn't an actor. He was a freak. He was somebody else's invention.

'You're muttering,' said Jennifer. 'You're talking to yourself.'

'Hmm? Oh. I'm just thinking.'

'You said you're a freak.'

Grayson looked at her, squinting. 'Can you really read minds? I know that I didn't say that out loud.'

'Yes, you did.'

'Yeah, you did,' said Susannah. 'I heard it, too. Except I think you meant us when you said it.'

Jennifer poked her. 'Susannah, stop the car.'

She tried to wave it off. 'I apologize. I'm sorry.'

'He doesn't think we're freaks, Susannah. He's the one man who doesn't. Why do I have to keep telling you that?'

'The ... two of you have been talking about me?'

'Roger, she's afraid you'll get sick of her.'

'Jennifer!' Susannah slammed on the brakes. It was dark in the car, but Grayson saw her color rising.

'Well, it's true,' said Jennifer. She tapped Grayson's shoulder.

400

'And she goes to a spot where you two sat on the beach and she thinks it will never happen again because she thinks you'll never be able to accept … '

'Jennifer, I adore you. But if you don't shut up …'

'Okay, I'll change the subject.'

'I, um … think I like this one,' said Grayson.

'Susannah will give me a bop on the head. But I'm glad I said it. Now it's out in the open.'

Susannah pressed the gas. The car moved forward. 'And another thing, big mouth.' She glared at Jennifer through her mirror. 'You told Mr. Teal he was welcome to visit. Why would you say such a thing?'

'Because he'd come anyway. This way he won't sneak.'

'Jennifer, don't ever go near him alone.'

'But he likes us. He said so. And he wants to hear you sing. Besides, I don't think he has many friends and he's sad that you still don't like him.'

'He's a psychopath. Textbook. He doesn't get sad.'

'Susannah, everybody gets sad.'

The car turned onto Mallard Road.

'I'll tell you,' said Grayson, 'what I think about Teal.' He thought he'd try to lighten this discussion. 'I think our young Jennifer has him under a spell. And he thinks that she can actually read minds.'

'Is that good?' asked Susannah. 'Or might that be bad?'

'Not now,' he said quietly. 'But we'll talk about that.'

She pulled the car into her driveway.

Jennifer leaned forward. 'It's not hard to read minds.'

'Now you're telling me, what? That you can?'

'Sure, I can. Sort of. It's not some weird thing.'

'Then explain it. What do you do?'

'You just watch peoples' faces. You can pretty much tell. It's not so hard to know what people are thinking. Unless …'

'Unless what?'

'Unless what they're thinking is some real dorky thing like what's going to happen down some road.'

Susannah sucked in a breath. 'Someone's going to get strangled.' She threw the shift into Park.

'Well, she's ... right,' said Grayson. 'You'll need to make plans. I'll still get new paper for Veronica and for Jennifer, but there's a lot more than that you'll have to think about. Do you intend to have them both live with you?'

'Clueless,' muttered Jennifer. 'Totally clueless.'

Susannah ignored her. 'We've discussed it. They want to.'

'What about Martha Carey? Will she stay here with Teresa?'

'She'd like a few more days. Then she wants to go home.'

'And I guess you'll have to find a good therapist for Veronica. Maybe Dr. Cohen will come down here and work with her.'

'She doesn't need him,' said Jennifer. 'We can do it.'

'You and Susannah?'

'And you,' said Jennifer. 'Veronica needs you. It might take a while, but we can do it.'

'Well ... Jennifer, nobody's asked me to stay.'

'*Someone* will. Unless *someone* is real stupid,' she said.

Susannah seemed to melt. Finally she raised her hands in surrender. 'Jennifer's right. I saw you with Veronica. I thought ... maybe if you'd care to stay for a short visit ...'

'I can't stand this,' said Jennifer. 'We're getting out of this car. But I'm not letting you in the house.'

'You're not what?'

'I'm going to run in and get some wine and two glasses. You two are going to take a walk on the beach. You're going to go to your spot and sit down.'

'Um ... Jennifer ...'

'And Susannah, you're going to leave Sally with me. You can do that. All you have to do is think it.'

'That's impossible.'

'No, it isn't. I do it all the time.'

Chapter Fifty-Five

Jennifer watched them go. Then she followed part-way. She found a place behind a dune where she could watch. It was too far to hear them but she would not have listened anyway. All she wanted to see was how they acted.

Susannah, as she'd feared, was talking too much. Her head was bobbing, she was flitting her hands, she had trouble looking into Roger's eyes. Jennifer whispered Sally's name in her mind.

No answer. She called again. 'Sally?'

'I'm here.'

'Oh, my gosh.' Her eyes widened. 'Are you really?'

'Why is that a surprise? You asked her to leave me and she did.'

'Yeah, but I didn't think it would actually work. It just seemed a good thing to try. You're really here?'

'Not really. You're imagining me. But that doesn't mean we can't talk.'

'Okay. What's Susannah telling Roger right now?'

'Same things she told you. And a couple of things more. Did you know that one of her friends is a man?'

'One of mine is, too. Is hers a problem?'

'Shouldn't be, I don't think. He's her handyman friend. He comes when she needs to do plumbing and the like. He does it and goes. Doesn't say much.'

'Well … he might take some getting used to for Roger.'

'All Grayson has to learn is to just let him work. It's really

403

the same as when Susannah is painting. Just leave her alone. Let her work.'

'Like when you're singing?'

'Same thing, I'm mostly only out when I'm up at the mike. Then, and when I think she could use a little help.'

'Don't you think she does now? With Roger, I mean?'

'Not now. She only needs to shut up.'

Jennifer stood on her toes. Susannah was still trying to say things to Roger, but Roger was putting his fingers to her lips. He was reaching to put his good arm around her. Now he was just holding her. Rocking her.

'Sally?'

'Uh-huh?'

'Are you sure you're not here?'

'I don't know. I'm not there. So I might be.'

'She's afraid that you might have sex with Roger. You wouldn't ever have sex with him, would you?'

'Are you kidding? In a minute, if she didn't want him. But she does, so it won't ever happen.'

'Would you go out by yourself and have sex with other men?'

'I don't know. I don't think so.'

'She worries about that.'

'That happens when an alter doesn't feel the same connection. But I do. I like Roger just fine.'

'Well, if you're ever tempted, will you talk to me first?'

'You're a pistol, you know that?'

'Will you?'

'You bet.'

'Sally … were you there when we met Mr. Teal tonight?'

'I was there. She wanted me to hear it.'

'What did you think? He won't bother us, will he?'

'He doesn't intend to. You were right, he does like you. And he's real short on people he respects.'

'Yeah, but when you say he doesn't intend to … what do you think could change his mind?'

'You might be too good to pass up.'

'I don't get you.'

'Grayson knows. He thought about it in the car. It was when he told Susannah, "Not now. We'll talk later." You, him, and Susannah, each all by yourselves, are not what I'd call short on talent. Added up, you're one hell of a trifecta.'

'What's a trifecta?'

'Figure of speech. And if you throw in Veronica, the queen of the hackers, I expect it's only a matter of time before Teal thinks how he might use you.'

'Well, if it's for something good …'

'He'll make it sound that way. But let's only cross that bridge when we have to.'

Jennifer brightened. 'Hey, look. They're kissing.'

'That's Susannah kissing him. That's what I like to see. That's better than him kissing her.'

'They're picking up their wine. I think they're going back home. I was hoping they'd stay and drink their wine.'

'I think they might have something else in mind.'

'Like what?'

'Well, it ain't a back rub.'

'Oh, yeah. Well … cool.'

'Let's go home ourselves. But let's make ourselves scarce.'

'Let's put on some music. And turn down her bed.'

'To be sure she gets the hint, turn it down on both sides.'

This is great, thought Jennifer. It's going to be fine. She'd pick out some good music. Maybe something classical. Frank Sinatra or the Beatles.

Just as long as it isn't country western.

Haven
John Maxim

The Black Angel...
She was the Israeli's greatest secret weapon in the Middle East. Driven by vengeance, she struck her enemies brutally and without warning.

The Fox...
Martin Kessler, a top East German spy, vulnerable to no one...except the Black Angel.

The Haven
An island off the coast of South Carolina, where the Black Angel, on the run from a team of crack cold-blooded killers, has gone to ground. But what should be her haven could turn out to be the most dangerous place of her entire career...

Praise for HAVEN

"Intriguing tale...with a good plot"   *The Bookseller*

"[a] high-octane thriller"   *Publishers Weekly*

"This is one thriller that hits you right between the eyes"
Northern Echo

Shadow Box
John Maxim

Michael Fallon has it all. Devoted friends and family, a beautiful fiancée and a great career. Then a random spasm of New York violence robs him first of the man who raised him, then his lover. Tragic coincidence, Michael is told. But inexplicably fired and blacklisted by Wall Street, suddenly he finds people are trying to kill him.

Michael must search for the reason his world has been shattered. It won't be easy. For his entire life has been built on lies – and a vast conspiracy of corruption that someone will go to any lengths to keep concealed...

"[a] crackerjack thriller" *Publishers Weekly*

"A great fast-paced page-turner. Highly recommended"
Publishing News

"A page turner ... readers may need blood pressure pills"
People

"Scary ... Maxim pulls his readers in" *Chicago Tribune*

"A great read – fast-paced, original, and very frightening"
Michael Palmer, author of *Extreme Measures*

The very best of Piatkus fiction is now available in paperback as well as hardcover. Piatkus paperbacks, where *every* book is special.

The prices shown above were correct at the time of going to press. However, Piatkus Books reserve the right to show new retail prices on covers which may differ from those previously advertised in the text or elsewhere.

Piatkus Books will be available from your bookshop or newsagent, or can be ordered from the following address:
Piatkus Paperbacks, PO Box 11, Falmouth, TR10 9EN
Alternatively you can fax your order to this address on 01326 374 888 or e-mail us at books@barni.avel.co.uk

Payments can be made as follows: Sterling cheque, Eurocheque, postal order (payable to Piatkus Books) or by credit card, Visa/Mastercard. Do not send cash or currency. UK and B.F.P.O. customers should allow £1.00 postage and packing for the first book, 50p for the second and 30p for each additional book ordered to a maximum of £3.00 (7 books plus).

Overseas customers, including Eire, allow £2.00 for postage and packing for the first book, plus £1.00 for the second and 50p for each subsequent title ordered.

NAME (block letters) _____

ADDRESS_____

_____

I enclose my remittance for £ _____

I wish to pay by Visa/Mastercard   Expiry Date:_____
